This is a fantasy.
Of a shifting city
hidden in the weeds.
Of princesses turned to
metal and rust.
Of knights eternal
and
a queen of dreams.
And a deep
underground.

JUD

by

Michael Breen

2

For Denise.

PART

1

1

In another life, the girl had spent her summer days in the city playing games, or watching boats sail the river, or reading books in Alex's study. Now, she barely remembered that world.

In those instances, when such memories entered her mind, they would last only a few seconds, fading away as quickly as they had arrived. It was hard to make sense of things in the underground, and although it had been weeks since she'd left the city, it may as well have been years. Time was different down here.

Dagny had been marking the days in her journal so she wouldn't lose track, ticking each one away with a crisp, straight line. It was all just guesswork, though. She had no idea if it was morning or evening anymore. At first, she tried to estimate the hour based on the hunger in her stomach, but by now, the days had all morphed into a single, never-ending night.

Dagny didn't expect to be down here for so long, but it took a while to find the boy and took a good deal longer to convince him to come out of his hiding place. He'd seen the drowned twins, Tewdred and Galwed. They had walked right past his hole, close enough to grab. The girl with the scarred face had even stopped to have a look at him. Dagny knew that gaze, and she knew it would have terrified anyone, let alone a child. The boy thought the twins would take him then, but they kept on marching into the darkness. Disappearing along the Under Road.

Who knew how long the boy had been hiding in the wall? Dagny would've crawled over to him, as slight as she was; the hole was just so narrow she couldn't make her way through. So instead, she sat on the ground outside for what felt like days, trying to reassure him.

"They're not after you," she said. "They're looking for something else." *Someone* to be more precise. The twins were after her sister, Gretchen. Dagny couldn't say *why* she thought this, exactly. It was more of a feeling she had. A horrible, gut-wrenching feeling.

Eventually, the boy emerged—although it was probably more from hunger than anything else. His name was Melwes, and Dagny had met him the autumn before, near the old palace kitchens, during her first excursion into the underground.

"I knew you'd run out of food at some point," Dagny said, offering a gentle smile as Melwes dusted off his clothes. "I'm glad you did. I'm almost out myself."

She'd been nervous until then, even after the spirit lights discovered her wandering blindly along the ancient passages. It had been the fear of getting lost and starving down here that had set her heart into a near-constant panic. Of course, such fears had been obvious going in, and she'd taken as many provisions as would fit in her sack. Forgoing an extra shirt or a favorite book, to make room for a tin of crackers, more candles, or another canteen.

Water, at least, had been surprisingly easy to come by. There were plenty of small pools and puddles, and the day before finding Melwes, she stumbled upon a deep pond, filled up over the years by dripping stalactites that hovered above like the jagged mouth of some monstrous beast. Still, even with the spirit lights as her guide, even with plenty of water to drink, she didn't relax until that very moment when Melwes crawled out from his hole and gazed at her with those soft blue eyes of his. There was a confidence about the boy. This was his domain, and Dagny knew she could trust him.

Dagny tried to talk to Melwes, asking if he was alright—if he was hurt or hungry—but the boy simply took her hand, led her down a crumbling staircase and into an enormous cavern. The floor there was smooth, like black steel, and if there was a ceiling, Dagny couldn't see it. She had so many questions, she didn't know where to start. Everything was so strange; it was a struggle just to keep up.

They walked a good distance that first day together, surrounded by dozens of the blue glowing lights. *Spirits of the Under Road,* Melwes had told her. When Dagny had first seen them, they reminded her of snowflakes or glowflies. None of that was really accurate, though. Snowflakes weren't alive, and glowflies couldn't communicate with children or take you safely through the underground.

Dagny came here seeking her sister. Had it been almost a year since she disappeared? Grete ran off with a group of misfit musicians led by the singer Marfisi, chasing after dreams of a shifting city. Dagny believed it was the same city Marfisi was from, and she had a strong hunch that Melwes knew the way to get there.

After some time, their journey through the cavernous chamber ended. Melwes took her to a rough canvas tent, tacked against a small curve in the wall, and said, "We shouldn't talk much in the caves. Sometimes things hear you, and follow you back."

"Oh, okay," Dagny said, as Melwes held the tent-flap open. She peeked inside, observing an old mattress on the floor covered by a heap of blankets. "What kind of things?"

"Hungry things."

"Like me. I'm starved."

Melwes scratched his head and wandered over to a trunk on the floor. After a moment of digging through various items, he pulled out a jar, smelled its contents and shrugged. "Here. You can eat this."

Dagny almost asked what it was but didn't really want to know. Her stomach was tight and empty.

It was an awkward reunion. Dagny hadn't known what to expect when—or even *if*—she found the boy. She thought maybe he would've shouted her name and given her the tightest hug of her life. Watching him scrounge through the trunk, she didn't know why she had thought that. He was all but oblivious to her presence. Still, he was only a child. Dagny was the adult here. She should've been the one to say something. It was just... well, she had a hard enough time navigating certain relationships in the world above. Down here, she didn't know what to do.

"I didn't think I'd see you again, ever," Melwes said, as Dagny scooped the jar food into her mouth. She wasn't sure if pickled pudding was a thing, but that's what it tasted like.

"Me neither. I'm happy to see you. Are you happy to see me?" she asked.

"Yes," Melwes said, his face buried in the trunk. "You shouldn't've come, though. People like you aren't supposed to be here."

She was taken aback by his comment. "People like me, huh? Well, I didn't have much of a choice."

"I figured that." The boy popped out of the trunk with a ratty toy animal, then stepped onto the bed next to her and plopped down. "All the same, you should probably leave."

"You want me to go so bad?"

"No. It's not me. It's for your own good. *Gorveil sithe...* the stranger gets eaten in the dark."

That phrase was a new one. "Eaten by what? Those hungry things?"

Melwes shrugged again.

"I see..." Dagny said, nodding her head. "I can't leave. Not yet, anyway."

Melwes squeezed the toy animal and moved its arms around, staring blankly at the floor. "Why did you come back?"

The boy knew Grete. He was the first one to find her, all those months ago, hiding in the palace gardens. Dagny told him about what had happened since then—about how Grete had run off, and about the men from Limer's Town. And she told him about Jud.

Melwes continued playing with his toy, more as a distraction than out of any sense of joy. "If she left you," he started, "maybe she doesn't want to be found."

"Grete was trying to protect me. *That's* why she left," Dagny said, speaking as much to herself as to the boy. "She knew something was after her. I can't let her go. I need to find her."

"You think she came down here?" he asked.

"I don't know. Maybe she passed through on her way."

"To Jud?"

"Yeah," Dagny said, watching the boy scratch at his backside. "Do you know it? Could you take me there?"

"You shouldn't go."

"I have to... One way or the other. I have to find out where she went. Can you help me?"

Melwes considered her question before responding. "I suppose. But you need to wait until the door opens."

The "door," it turned out, wouldn't open again until summer's end. "It's hard to explain," Melwes said. "You can only get in when the city wants you to."

Summer's end? That was months away. "I need to get there sooner than that," Dagny said. Too much time had passed already. Grete disappeared last autumn, and Dagny spent the entire winter and part of the spring sitting around the Benzara house doing nothing. The guilt over her inaction ate a hole in her belly, but it had taken so much time to figure everything out. And now, with the Gort twins breaking free and entering the Under Road... "I have to find another way."

Melwes replied with a nonchalant shrug and a terse, "You have to wait."

"Aren't there other doors?" she asked.

"Yes, but this is the only one I can show you."

"Why?"

"Some doors have faded away. And some are far underwater. And *some,* you can only pass if you have an invitation—and I don't have one," the boy said emphatically.

And that was it. As Melwes said, Dagny would just have to wait, sitting for months in the underground with the boy and his spirit lights, and just *wait* for summer's end.

∽

"How do you know so much?" Dagny asked one day as they scrounged for salt bugs in the Upper Reach.

"What do you mean?" Melwes replied.

"Well, you're only a child."

Melwes twisted his mouth and scrunched his face. "I don't know how to answer your strange questions," he said.

Maybe she did ask strange questions, but that's just how she was. At eighteen, there would be no changing it now. At least she got along well with children. Usually.

The salt bugs weren't bad, and food in the underground wasn't too hard to find if you knew where to look for it. They caught black fish in a place called the Murgdens and gathered bluish roots in a series of caverns littered with ancient bones. The mushrooms were common and surprisingly delicious, and one time they found a sludge that seemed to pulsate—Dagny passed on that one.

The smell took some getting used to. Portions of the underground were incredibly musty, and the only opportunity to wash their bodies was at a trickling, ice-cold stream nearby. It was already chilly enough without getting wet, so Dagny would only make use of the stream to wash those parts of herself that were absolutely essential to keep clean.

In the beginning, the boy's stink was awful. Dagny tried her best to be nice about it. Melwes would curl up next to her on the mattress when he went to sleep, and she had to spend those first nights breathing through her mouth. Luckily, after a couple of weeks, she barely noticed. Besides, Dagny knew she must've reeked like something special, too (honestly, she was fascinated by the smell her own body could produce now). Sometimes, back home, she'd go days on end without bathing. This, however, was unfamiliar territory.

One of her biggest mistakes was only bringing two pairs of socks. She'd worn her first pair for a week straight, and by the time she finally got around to washing her feet, the socks had turned so rancid there was no saving them. After that, she spent most of her time barefoot, unless they went somewhere far, and then she'd take her socks off and wash them as soon as possible.

Socks were just socks, though. There was only one thing that held any real importance to Dagny: her sister's bracelet. A tin circle, engraved with simple flower petals. She'd found it in Grete's hiding place, under the wigmaker's shop in Limer's Town, shortly after losing Morgan's coat. The stars had offered her a trade, in a weird kind of way—a memory of her brother for a piece of her sister. Although the bracelet was tight on Dagny's small wrist, she hadn't taken it off since coming down here. She didn't think she ever would.

The lights were always around. Sometimes only a few would appear, dimly illuminating their path, while on other occasions, they would be surrounded by hundreds. When they went to sleep, the lights went out, but Dagny knew they were still there. Invisible; watching over them.

"How come you're alone?" Melwes asked one day. "Did you lose all of your friends?"

"I still have friends," Dagny responded, somewhat defensively. "I didn't want to endanger them... thought it best I should do this myself."

Melwes nodded. "In case you died, you mean? In case you fell into the Gorge, or the twins got you. You didn't want the same thing to happen to them."

"Right."

"Do you miss them?"

"Of course," Dagny said, but the underground was so enthralling that her friends, Max, Alex's family... it all felt like a vague dream.

Dagny tried to ask Melwes questions, too. There were some topics that were clearly off limits—like anything concerning the boy's past. Dagny made that mistake early on, asking Melwes if he had a family. The boy didn't talk to her for a whole day after that. Dagny was afraid he might never talk to her again until finally he poked her in the back after breakfast the next day and asked if she wanted to see the Fire Gorge.

She thought it would be lonely in the Great Below—she had a hard time imagining anyone besides Melwes down here. But on their way to the Gorge, they had lunch with a mute traveler who communicated with Melwes using hand signals. He had stooped shoulders and a hunched back (probably from years spent ducking in the tunnels), and wore a dinged-up bucket helmet. Not for battle, but to protect his head from those same low ceilings.

She wanted to meet more travelers of the Under Road, but Melwes warned her, "Not everyone is friendly here."

Melwes spent their waking hours showing off his favorite places in the underground. In addition to the flame-spewing Fire Gorge, there was an abandoned temple for miners from some forgotten age, and an empty way station that Melwes said used to house sailors of the Silent Sea.

In the quiet hours, when Melwes would count his buttons, or go off and talk to himself, Dagny would sit and try to think about the life she had left behind. She wondered if any of those people really missed her. She wondered if she really missed them. She knew she cared about Max and the others, only now, she questioned how strong those feelings had actually been. She was keenly aware of her ability to detach from things.

To open the boxes in her mind, fill them with her thoughts, and then seal them away forever. She didn't know if it was a skill or a curse.

The days turned into weeks, and the weeks into months, until finally the time had arrived for Melwes to take her to the door. He'd barely spoken of Jud since their first conversation. Every time Dagny tried to bring it up, Melwes would just change the subject. She tried to be delicate about the whole thing. She could tell something about it upset him. Maybe it was the thought of her leaving again, or maybe it was something about the shifting city itself. But Dagny had wasted so much time already, she needed to know what she was getting herself into. So the night before their journey to the door, Dagny intended to be more forceful about it. She'd barely gotten the word "Jud" out of her mouth when Melwes cut her off.

"Do you know about the Cat Prince of Veil?" he asked with sudden excitement.

Dagny shook her head.

"He was an abandoned house cat who lived in the city a long time ago, and his family just left him behind one day. He had no idea where they went or why... and he was sad and alone and got picked on by all the other cats. He was blind in one eye and his ear was chewed almost clean off. He was also really nice and would climb as high as he could, away from all the other mean cats, and would sing his songs, hoping his family would hear him and come back."

"One day, the cat was climbing higher than he ever went before and came across the tallest tower in the entire city. He entered a window into a young girl's bedroom, but someone had bricked the door up from the other side. A small bird had also made its home there, and it told the cat that the little girl's family had angered the king, so they bricked her up inside..."

"That's horrible," Dagny said.

"The cat and bird stayed there for a while, and one day, while bathing himself in front of the mirror, the cat accidentally kicked it with his paw, and..." Melwes paused for dramatic effect, "it went straight through! Like water. It was a magic passage to a hidden castle. There weren't many people there, but cats protected the place. And they were all nice. The Queen of the castle was the little girl who had been bricked up all those years before. She'd escaped through the mirror. The cat had many adventures, made a lot of friends, and was taken in by the Queen to live with her, becoming the Cat Prince of Veil."

"That's nice. I'm glad it had a happy ending," Dagny said. Although she thought it was an odd thing to talk about right now. She opened her mouth to speak again, when Melwes started back up.

"Did you know that the entire city of Jud used to be a single enormous tower back in the first days? Did you know that?"

"No." Dagny said.

"It stretched across time and up to the stars. And it was ruled by someone called the Thorned Prince, who had stickers and thorns that pierced his skin. There was no entrance to the tower-city, and if one wanted to see the Prince and to see the stars, they had to make a sacrifice. It's called a *tribute*. Do you know what that is?"

"Yes," Dagny said.

"Okay... because I didn't. I had to figure it out... it's when you have to cut off your own ear and scrape out your own eye... or cut off a finger, or sometimes your whole hand, and who wants to do that? But the entire land was sinking, actually all the lands were, and all the people were desperate to escape. So they came to the Tower and begged the Prince to allow them inside, to open the gates so they could be safe with their children. But the Prince refused—he refused them! Only those who would pay the tribute were allowed inside. Most tried to run away and tried to find a hill or something, only there was nowhere to go and they sunk under dark waves. Some did make the tribute... only a few though because it's really hard to do something like that to your own eye and ear... the Prince drenched their faces with silver milk and they became his companions."

Dagny took a moment before speaking, making sure the boy was done. "Why are you telling me all this?"

"Sometimes the same story has different versions. It's important to remember that." Then Melwes rolled away from her on the bed, pulling his stuffed animal close to his chest.

She tried to ask about Jud one more time, speaking gently. But Melwes didn't respond, and eventually they drifted off to sleep.

∞

They started the long walk after a breakfast of sweet porridge that Melwes had acquired shortly before Dagny's arrival. He'd found it in the world above and was saving it for a special occasion. The meal brought back memories of sitting in the Benzara kitchen with Lucas and Abrielle before Dagny would have to rush out for school. It was another memory that wouldn't stay, and by the time Dagny had tied her boots and grabbed her pack, it was gone.

They would travel over the Fire Gorge and toward the Lower Reach. "That's where the main pathway is. The one that goes closest to Jud," Melwes said.

"You've been there before, haven't you?" Dagny asked, as they walked.

"Mm-hmm."

"Maybe you can help me figure some things out."

"Alright," Melwes said under his breath. The spirit lights swirled around them, reflecting off of the smooth dark floor. "There's plenty of time for your questions now. I know you've been *dying* to ask them."

Dagny stifled a laugh. She'd grown used to the boy's coarseness, but every so often it still caught her off guard. "I guess the first question I have is about Odestinas. She was the first queen of Jud."

"I know that."

"Right... This is going to sound weird. I think Grete is looking for her. Do you know where she's buried?"

"Somewhere hidden. Probably somewhere very deep. That's not really important. It's not what you should be asking about." Melwes turned his head and whispered something to several of the spirit lights.

"Okay. What should I be asking?"

"Don't you want to know how Jud stays hidden? Why all you people are so dumb about it?"

"I do. I *do* want to know," Dagny said. "Every time I try to bring it up, though, you change the subject. Last night you told me those stories, and I still don't have any idea what they're supposed to mean."

"Jud is the shifting city, because it doesn't really exist here. Part of it does. But part of it doesn't. It exists in dreams."

"Dreams? Like we can dream about it?"

"Not people's dreams. The *land's* dreams. You can get lost if you don't know your way—which you don't. If you go in the wrong building, or go down the wrong street, and the shift happens, you could get trapped for a very long time."

"I don't understand," Dagny said. "How can that happen?"

"And that's not the worst part. There's old things still around, guardians watching the gates—like the one we're going to now. Hopefully, this one's sleeping, but who knows for sure? The guardians have been there for so long, they've lost all their sense. They just sit around watching the gates, even though Jud fell apart after the Withering and no one goes there anymore."

"Is that why people are searching for Odestinas? To try and save the city?" Dagny caught herself. "Wait, do people think Odestinas is still alive? Are they trying to save her?"

Melwes shook his head in frustration. "You don't understand anything. There's nothing to save."

2

They rested by an enormous vine wall stretching up into the misty, underground sky. There was a faint light here. Natural, murky, distorted light, coming from somewhere high above. The last remnant of sunlight perhaps, making its way into the Lower Reaches… breaking off of cavern walls, bouncing through ancient tunnels, funneling across the deep until the last rays of a distant sun finally died on the cloud-like mist overhead. It should have felt gloomy, but Dagny thought it was one of the most beautiful things she'd ever seen. It had been months since she last saw sunlight. She was not meant for the underground.

Would she see the sky in Jud? Dagny still didn't know what to expect. Everything out of the boy's mouth had been so cryptic. Even though he'd been answering all of her questions since they started their walk today, she felt clueless.

Melwes was watching the light as well. He almost always wore a serious expression, but Dagny thought she saw hints of a smile there.

"When's the last time you've been outside?" she asked.

The boy broke his gaze from the light, responding solemnly. "Yunis. Guardian of the Hidden Door. First among many. She was one of those great cats of the Under Road. The Drey Garders. She is now the *last* of many."

"The Drey Garders are all gone?"

"Except for Yunis."

Dagny nodded. "She's sleeping, you said?"

"I hope she's sleeping."

"Right."

She didn't want to leave Melwes once they found the gate. She wanted him to come with her. Past the hidden door and into Jud, all the way until she found Grete. Even longer, if possible. He stank just as bad as when they first met, and strangely enough, she knew she would miss it.

Melwes brought his copper crown for this journey—two sharp triangles popped up from the sides of it, like the ears of some metal fox, framing his sweet, innocent face. But his eyes held the wisdom of someone much older. She was afraid to ask him to stay with her. She didn't want to upset him. The first time she asked that question back at Lomenthal Station, he had run away, disappearing into the underground. Dagny thought she had lost him forever then.

"I've never seen her," Melwes said. "You should know that. I've only heard stories of Yunis."

That relaxed Dagny somewhat. "So you don't really know if she's alive, do you?"

Melwes stood and stretched his arms wide. "I just want to be honest. I don't know what will happen."

"I understand. But you've been to Jud, right? Or was all of that just based on things you heard, too?"

It took a moment before the boy responded. "That was a long time ago, before I was re-born into the light."

Dagny let out a nervous laugh. "How long could that have possibly been? You're like ten years old."

Melwes glared at her and scrunched his face.

Dagny smiled. "I didn't mean anything by it. You're probably the smartest ten-year-old I've ever met. And you've helped me more than you could ever know." She reached over and touched his arm. "I'd never have gotten this far without you."

"I know."

Her thoughts shifted to Grete. What odd world had her sister stepped into? Dagny vividly remembered the way Grete looked the night she left: her cropped hair, dyed blue like their brother's; her pretty, dark face and worried eyes. They had played one last game of Talvarind while hiding in Tash's house outside of the city. Grete had acted calm, but Dagny sensed something was off. If she'd only known what Grete's intentions were...

In some ways, Dagny felt like a failure. She had tried so hard to find Grete the first time. Traveling across the lagoon and into Limer's Town. Traversing the old palace with Jauson Tasher. Running from the twins. Almost dying in the forest. She thought she had done it—secured a life for them both, but the world had different plans. Some people slipped away, no matter how hard you tried to hold on, like sand from a fist. It changed nothing, though. It was just the way things were. Dagny was on the path now, and she'd follow it to the end.

There were other people she allowed to slip away. Like Max. She couldn't understand why she felt so distant now. She cared about him a great deal. That was true. And it was true she didn't want to put him in danger. That *was* the reason she had snuck out before dawn that day... Or at least, it was *a* reason. Still, she couldn't help thinking there was something else going on with her. If she loved a person so much, shouldn't she be missing them more? And why were these thoughts coming to her now at the edge of the underworld, at the gateway to Jud? It was a lot to unravel.

"How much further is the gate?" she asked.

Melwes stepped away and whispered into a cluster of spirit lights, asking for guidance, most likely. Dagny stood as well, dusted herself off, and examined the wall. Underneath the moss and vine was heavy, stacked stone. Evidence that someone had constructed it in the distant past.

She almost called out to Melwes, then stopped herself. The boy seemed to be engaged in a deep discussion. Dagny never strayed too far from the lights, as the darkness of the underground could be all-consuming, but there was enough natural light here to see her way around. She reached under a weave of vines and touched the stone, then gazed down the chamber. The wall stretched on for some distance before curving away and vanishing in the misty black.

What are you hiding? she thought, wondering why someone had built such a thing so far from the world above. Could this be related to the gate they were searching for? There were so many mysteries down here, who really knew? Before she realized what she was doing, Dagny had wandered away from Melwes and was halfway to the bend.

She continued to poke at the wall as she walked, scooping out loose bits of crumbled stone and sand; rubbing it over her fingers and between her nails. Dagny liked the feeling; something about the grit of dirt on her body in places where it shouldn't be.

What would the city people say if they could see her now? She hadn't encountered a mirror since leaving home, and knew she must look quite ghoulish. Her hair—messy and wild on a normal day, was no doubt fantastically deranged. And the smell. What would they make of that? The thought made Dagny chuckle.

The light ended where the wall curved. Dagny was hesitant to wander any further from the boy. She had no way of knowing if any dangers lurked in the shadows ahead. She thought they were alone, but she'd been wrong before.

Instead, she stood there, listening for a moment, taking in her surroundings. There was a dripping sound coming from somewhere beyond, and she caught a whiff of staleness in the air—faint and unsettling—that made her nose twitch. Dagny turned to head back, but the next time she inhaled, the smell was overpowering. Dagny covered her mouth and stepped away, trying not to retch. As accustomed as she'd become to the scents of the underground, this one was different. Sourly sweet. Rotting. Almost putrid. Like someone had opened a grave.

Dagny ran to Melwes, gagging as tears flowed from her eyes. "There's something *wrong* back there," she spit out. The spirit lights swirled around them both, then darted away, toward the smell. The boy seemed unconcerned.

"When the amber kings came to Jud, they sealed it off from everywhere else," he began. "Most people believed the kings wanted to trap the city, keeping it all for themselves. Others said the kings could predict the future, and saw that a new kind of man was coming... and that enchantments of Lazim were needed to protect the city."

"Lazim? That's the forest, right?" Dagny asked. Marfisi had mentioned it that day in the woods with Grete, in the shadow of the Nedgling Tower. *What did she call it? The Eternal Forest?*

"Lazim used to stretch across the world," Melwes said, then walked away, following the lights.

"Wait," Dagny said, reaching toward him. "Is it safe? The air smelled toxic. It could be poisonous."

"We can stay here if you want," Melwes said but didn't stop.

Dagny bit her lip and pulled her shirt up over her face, walking cautiously behind the boy.

"Sometimes people and things get trapped inside," Melwes said over his shoulder. "Then they can't get out until it opens again, and like I told you, that only happens once a year... sometimes longer."

"You're talking about the *door*? Is it here?"

The boy stopped and faced the wall. A narrow opening had appeared, like a small window into the stone, barely big enough for Dagny's head and shoulders to fit.

"That wasn't there before," she said. "I would've seen it."

"Come," Melwes replied, clambering up the wall.

"Hold on." Dagny walked up to the hole, still covering her nose and mouth, as Melwes dropped inside. Disappearing into the darkness stretched a long tunnel. The lights fluttered ahead, illuminating the frames of old paintings hanging on the interior walls and a high-arched ceiling. "That smell... is it from something dead?"

Melwes turned and faced her. "You don't have a lot of time to be asking so many questions," he said.

"How long do we have? I don't want to get trapped in there."

"Usually, about a day. The shift *usually* happens at twilight. When the dreams of the land begin again. But it's hard to say for sure."

Dagny placed her free hand on the stone. "How far away is the exit?"

Melwes sighed and waved her forward impatiently. "*Come.*"

Dagny dared to take another sniff. The air seemed a little better than before but was still quite putrid. "Alright, just a second," she said, then climbed over the edge and plopped into the hallway.

In the pale, blue glow of spirit lights, Dagny could make out shapes on the ground. A body, maybe? Or bodies? *How many things had been trapped in here over the years?*

"Hey, once we make it to the other side, how do I come back?" she asked, as they made their way along the passage.

"From Jud?"

"Yeah. What if I need to return?" There was a large object in the shadows ahead, blocking most of the hallway.

"You have to wait until summer's end *next* year, or find another path," Melwes replied. "Like I said, there are other ways."

Dagny shook her head. *Thanks... That's very helpful,* she thought. "What is this place exactly?"

"Nowhere. We're inside the outer wall. It's not really a place."

The shape of the object became more defined as they moved closer. Dagny saw an axle and a wheel on the ground. Smooth, ornate wood twinkled in the light, and a crest was emblazoned on its side.

"A carriage," Dagny muttered. "This is an interesting place for it, huh?"

"Things get lost here." Melwes stopped near the broken axle, looked down an intersecting passageway, and scratched his head.

Dagny glanced inside the carriage as she walked by, half-expecting to see the skeletal remains of the former coachman. There were plush, velvet seats, and what appeared to be a rumpled wedding gown on the floor. "I wonder what happened to the bride," she said.

"Let's keep going straight," Melwes said. "This other tunnel doesn't feel right."

"Okay..." She didn't like his lack of confidence in what direction they should be heading.

They were in a no-man's-land. The outside of the wall seemed quite real, but here, on the inside, there was a strangeness that was hard to define, like they were passing through a waking dream. The hallways reminded Dagny of palaces she'd imagined as a young child: elegant and grand. Then, the passage abruptly ended, and they crawled through a small door, sized for an infant, finding themselves standing in a flooded wine cellar, with water up to their ankles.

The lights never dimmed. Never left them alone. Even now, dozens of them floated in the air. Some twinkled, while others held a steady glow, bathing everything in gentle blue. If she'd been traveling alone, Dagny doubted she would've had the courage to enter this weird, hypnotic tomb. There was something so special about the spirit lights; they made her feel safe and hopeful. Protectors of the Under Road, indeed.

"When did you first see them?" Dagny asked, as they sloshed through the cellar. "The lights."

"During the Second Rupture. They found me near the breach at the gates to the old sanctuary."

"I don't know what that means."

"You don't need to. The old sanctuary is lost now, anyway." The boy stepped onto a large wine rack that had toppled over and gazed around the chamber. "Look for stairs."

"Where are we now? What *is* this?" Dagny felt like she was losing her grip on reality. Only moments before, they had been walking through grand hallways—desolate, but at least they were dry. "This is my last pair of socks," she muttered to herself.

"It's all part of the same place," Melwes said, hands on his hips like the stalwart first mate of some slow-sinking vessel. "We're still inside the wall.

The castle just got jumbled around. Probably during all the shifting. It's hard to hold things together for such a long time."

"The castle, huh?"

"Yeah." Melwes pointed into the darkness across the room. "Check over there. I'll explore this corner." Then he splashed into the shallow water and wandered off. A cluster of lights joined Dagny, illuminating the space.

"Don't go too far," she called, but didn't get a response.

Stairs should have been easy enough to find. Dagny kept her gaze focused on the ceiling while trying to avoid the mess of broken wood and glass bottles hidden by the water. The ceiling, like everything else, seemed strangely out of place. It appeared to be made of packed earth, and there were no rafters. "*Stairs...* see any stairs?" she asked the lights. A pair of them fluttered around her head briefly, then darted away. She didn't really expect them to answer. "You'll speak to him, but not to me?" she asked, half-jokingly. "Even after all the times we've shared? That's okay, I get it."

Dagny made it to the opposite wall. "You see anything yet?" she called to Melwes.

"No!" he shouted from across the room. "You probably won't see 'em unless you're real close. Just watch your step!"

My step? Dagny thought. He couldn't mean... She called back into the darkness, "Wait! Are you telling me they're under the water?"

"Watch your step!"

Dagny sighed. The boy's style of communicating could be so frustrating, like talking to one of those legendary hyena-men who only spoke in riddles. She scanned the water but couldn't see anything beyond a couple of feet.

"Can't *you* look and tell me if you find anything?" she asked the lights. This time, a single orb floated up in front of her eyes and rested on her nose.

"I'll take that as a no…"

Suddenly, the boy shouted gleefully, "Over here! I found 'em before you did!"

Dagny had to laugh at that one. "Hold on, I'm coming."

She sloshed across the room, and the lights joined together, brightening the water even more. Sure enough, several feet below the surface, a gaping pit angled awkwardly into the floor. *Or was it the ceiling upside down?*

"So, look—" Dagny began.

"You don't want to go. That's alright, I guess," Melwes replied, somewhat disappointed.

Dagny took a deep breath, then slowly exhaled. It wasn't the first time she'd been confronted with dark water. It seemed to be a recurring theme in her life.

"I don't like getting wet either," Melwes continued.

"It's not that. My whole family drowned when I was your age, caught up in a flood. I barely got out… I had nightmares for years. I hate the water."

"Your whole family except your sister, right?"

"Right." Dagny only found that out later, though… For most of her life, she believed Grete had drowned with the rest of them. She could still recall waking up screaming in the night, with thoughts of her sister gasping for air while floodwaters pulled her down.

As if they were sensing her hesitation, a large group of lights swirled around Dagny's head and torso.

"They like you," Melwes whispered. "You don't have to be afraid."

"I'm not as afraid as I should be." In her prior life, the one spent aboveground, Dagny had been terrified of the thought of going underwater. But now, for some reason, she felt... calm. "Is that because of the lights?" she asked.

"I don't know. It could be." Melwes shrugged. "Maybe it's just you."

Several orbs flew into the underwater pit, lighting up the stone.

"I guess I've stayed dry for long enough," Dagny said. "It's about time I had a proper bath, huh?"

Melwes stared at her, his expression dead serious. "I didn't wanna hurt your feelings, but you smell bad."

"Yeah..." Dagny said. "I suppose I do. Okay, let's go. I don't want to think too much." She grasped her pack close to her chest, took a deep breath, and dropped into the pit.

She wasn't a strong swimmer. Despite her fears, Alex and Cate had forced her into swimming lessons back in Rork. Dagny had thrown an enormous fit, threatening to run away forever, but Cate was unrelenting. It was simply too dangerous for a girl living on the lagoon not to know how. So Dagny spent the better part of that summer, angry and terrified, neck deep in neighborhood pools, trying her best to learn the basics so she would never again be forced to swim.

The cold water rushed over her head, and Dagny felt her feet hit the stone underneath. She spun her body around and kicked off the wall, deeper into the oddly shaped stairwell, focusing on the lights ahead.

A second later, she heard a muffled splash from behind, as Melwes jumped into the flooded staircase. Otherwise, there was only a stillness. The passage twisted and dropped, and Dagny couldn't tell if she was going up or down, but she had no sense of fear. She just knew everything would be alright. Shortly after releasing a small bubble of air, Dagny saw the lights break out of the water and illuminate another room.

She gasped for breath as soon as she popped up, her lungs burning hard. She hadn't realized how close she'd been to the limit of what her body could handle. Dagny pulled herself onto an old flagstone floor; a quick glance revealed a meeting room of sorts with an enormous fireplace and several heavy, wooden tables. The stuffed heads of strange animals gazed down at her from the walls, but she had no time to study them further. Spinning around, Dagny watched the water for Melwes, readying herself to jump back in, when the boy splashed out with a gasp of his own.

She reached down and pulled the boy out, letting him catch his breath before speaking.

"Are you alright?" she asked after a moment.

"I'm fine," he said, while trying to slap the water from his ears.

As much as Dagny wanted to ask where they were, she was aware she'd been repeating that same question since they entered the wall. It was embarrassing how little she knew.

Melwes looked up at the animal heads and frowned.

"Kinda sad, huh?" Dagny said.

"It's the knights. When they were bored, they slaughtered things."

Dagny nodded her head, like she knew. Melwes glanced at her like she didn't. "The Knights Perilous," he continued. "After the Queen vanished, they were made to try and find her."

Dagny nodded again. This time she knew which queen he meant. *Odestinas.*

"Who was she, exactly? I know she was the first queen, but not much else. Why was she so important?"

Melwes sat down at the table and pulled off his small boots, dumping water onto the floor. "Everything was connected to her. And when she left, it all fell apart. The Kings... the Imposter... the Giant... they wanted what she had, but it wasn't meant for them. In the end, none of them could control it."

"They all ruled Jud?"

"They tried to."

"Right. Who rules it now?"

"No one. It can't be ruled," Melwes said. "You'll see."

Dagny took her own boots off, then tried ringing the water out of her socks. "And what became of the knights? This place looks like it hasn't been used in quite a while."

"Oh, they're still around. Maybe you'll meet them, or maybe you won't... If you're lucky," Melwes said, laughing at his own joke.

"The knights I heard about were always helping people, defeating wicked men... Those kinda things. That was all from old stories, though."

"These knights are different."

"Oh yeah? Are they bad?" Dagny asked.

"Depends who you ask." A small group of lights swirled around Melwes, lighting up his face.

"You," she said. "I'm asking *you*."

As if he was listening to the lights, and not her, Melwes stood up and stared across the room. "They found the path."

"Okay, is it much further?"

"A bit," he said, putting his boots back on.

Dagny gave her best smile, but she was worried about the boy getting back home after taking her through the castle. She didn't want him getting trapped in here. Although without him, she'd be lost.

"We need to go," Melwes said, then suddenly marched off into the shadows.

Dagny quickly stuffed her bare feet into her boots, shoved her socks into a pocket, and chased after him. "You sure you'll be alright?" she asked. "After you take me to the other side—you'll be able to get back, right?"

The boy reached the far wall and opened a door, ushering her through. "One thing at a time."

3

They entered the castle's windowless library. Large chandeliers loomed overhead, and books covered the floor. Piles of them. In fact, there wasn't a single book on any of the shelves. Bone-white statues and suits of armor lay strewn about as well. Nothing was in its right place. Pastoral paintings hung crooked on the wall. Vases and other antiques, smashed to bits on the ground.

"What happened to this place?" Dagny asked.

"Not sure," Melwes said. "I've never been here."

"Could it be the shift you've been talking about? Walls changing... buildings getting shook around?"

The boy scratched his head. "Yes?"

They skirted the piles, carefully stepping over broken things.

"There's something else I should mention," Melwes said. "Time is sneaky here. Sometimes you forget how long you've been walking or sitting around for, and before you know it, everything changes."

That comment concerned her. "Are you saying we might not have as much time as we think?"

"Only that we don't wanna take a nap or anything."

"I wasn't planning on it."

At the end of the library, a single, enormous painting remained undisturbed. It took up almost the entire wall and featured an angelic-faced woman gazing across a mist-covered field. As old as it was, the details were crisp. She wore a crown of leaves; thorny vines weaved around her face and throat; and she flashed a faint, sweet smile.

"That's her, isn't it?" Dagny said. "She looks rather... normal. I mean, for a fairy-tale queen of a mythical city."

Melwes gazed up at the face. "Yes. I suppose she does. Not like I imagined."

"You've never seen a painting of her before?"

"Uh-uh."

Dagny studied the image again, taking it in like they were standing in some posh gallery back home.

"Odestinas brought the animals, you know," Melwes said softly. "The guardians. She came from the forest and was birthed from the mist of the Sillweed. The animals and her were the same." The boy looked at Dagny. "That's why people think she's still alive, because the guardians are still here."

"Is she? Still alive?"

"No." Melwes pointed at the painting. "Not like that anyway."

"How can you know for sure?"

Melwes nodded at the lights. "They know."

"My sister, Grete... I think she's connected to Odestinas, in a way." Dagny glanced at Melwes before continuing, but he didn't react. "And it's not just me; other people think it, too. Like that Marfisi I told you about, her and that band, *The Mirage*. That's why they took Grete away."

"I remember."

"It sounds weird, but Grete told me of this dream she had. She was trapped in a palace made of wood, and she found this *woman* torn open. In the dream, Grete reached into the woman's chest, pulled out her heart, and ate it."

"Gross…"

"I wonder if that was Odestinas in her dream. Grete had this puzzle box, some ancient artifact found near the lagoon. She thinks she solved it while dreaming and really ate what was inside."

Melwes yawned. "All this dreaming talk is making me tired. We need to keep moving. You don't wanna fall asleep here."

"Yeah, you said that already."

"Just making sure you heard me. That's how Mia went," Melwes said, pointing at one of the lights. "She dozed off and didn't get out again for a year. By then she was… well… kinda dead." The orb, presumably Mia, grew bright for a moment, then darted forward.

"I guess she wants us to move now," Dagny said.

They left the library and entered the castle's main hall. Everything was disheveled here, too. The rugs were torn, and it looked as though something had busted large holes in the wall. They walked over the debris-covered ground, making their way toward the front of the chamber and a set of enormous wooden doors.

They had to be getting close, Dagny thought. It seemed like hours had passed since they entered the wall. She watched the boy in front of her and felt a sudden weight of sadness, knowing she would lose him soon, but that it had to be done. "I think you should head back now," she said, more forcefully than she intended. "Tell me what I need to look for, and I'll find the exit from here."

"No," he said.

"No?" Dagny stopped and gently grabbed the boy's sleeve. "Look, I don't want you getting trapped here. It's too dangerous and I've asked you for too much already. I couldn't live with myself if something bad happened to you."

"Bad things have already happened."

Dagny softened her tone. "What are you talking about?"

"There's nothing to be done about it. Anyway, I've made my decision."

"Huh?" Dagny suddenly felt very nervous. "And what decision is that?"

Melwes stared at the ground, his voice becoming so quiet that Dagny could barely hear him. "Through the underground and into the briar wild. With the twilight hour, bringing the untamed mist. It won't be long now."

"Can you stop that, please? What are you saying?"

"I'm taking your path now. Into Jud. It's been decided."

"Really?" Dagny knelt down so she could see his face. "Are you sure?"

"Yes."

"Melwes... I don't know what to say..." Her sadness evaporated. She felt like she could cry. Dagny reached out and grabbed the boy, pulling him into a tight embrace.

"*Stop that.*"

Dagny released him. "Sorry. You really don't like hugs, do you?"

"You were wrinkling my clothes."

Dagny couldn't help herself. She burst out laughing, much louder than she should have. It might've been the loudest Dagny had ever laughed in her life. She knew she sounded ridiculous, but she couldn't stop. Tears welled in her eyes.

She expected Melwes to scold her for being so loud in the castle, but when she glanced down, he was smiling, on the verge of laughing himself.

"Stop... it," he said, struggling with the words. "Seriously. We need to go. You can laugh when we get out."

Dagny covered her mouth and tried to take a deep breath, finally calming herself enough to speak again. "Okay. Where to?"

Melwes motioned toward the set of double doors in front of them. "Beyond there should be the atrium, then the courtyard and *then* the gatehouse."

"And then Jud?"

"Mm-hmm." The boy kicked a half-busted vase across the floor. "The castle road leads right to the Sanctuary. Most everyone lives around it. Your sister is probably there."

Grete. Dagny couldn't believe they were so close now. She reached down and grabbed Melwes' hand. "C'mon! We can go faster."

Melwes smiled at her, and the two of them went sprinting toward the exit. The spirit lights zipped playfully around them, and a small cluster blazed ahead, twinkling brilliant blue over the sea of broken glass.

"This is beautiful! Isn't it beautiful?" Dagny exclaimed.

They reached the doors, both of them placing their hands on the solid wood at the same time.

"On the count of three," Dagny said. "One... two..."

The darkness overtook them immediately. Everything went black, the spirit lights extinguished in an instant. Dagny could still feel the cold wood under her palms, could smell the musty breath of the chamber; otherwise she was blind.

"Melwes... are you there?" she asked. "What's happened..."

There was a slight whimper to her left. "I'm so sorry..." Melwes said, his voice trembling. "I forgot about her... I just forgot..."

"Forgot—"

"*Yunis...*"

A surge of adrenaline hit her, and she threw all of her weight into the door. "Push!" Dagny commanded. "Just push!"

"I'm *trying*!" Melwes cried. But despite their efforts, the doors wouldn't budge. It was like they were trying to force open a wall.

Dagny turned and stared into the darkness, straining her eyes. "Where are they? Where are the lights?"

A heavy thud landed on the other side of the hall, sending shockwaves across the floor. Dagny could hear rattling from all around and smelled the dust of old stone in the air. They couldn't stay here. That thing—Yunis—whatever it was, had sensed their presence, and there was no doubt in her mind that it was coming for them now.

She tried to remember what the chamber looked like; the other exits. They had entered from the back corner, near a fallen candelabra, but that was too far away. They'd have to cross the entire room to reach it.

Dagny thought she had seen another, smaller hallway nearby. She'd only glimpsed it from the corner of her eye, though, as they ran toward the double doors. Simple and nondescript, like a side-entry for the castle's servants. But she wasn't *certain* it was there... it was possible the passage didn't exist at all.

"Melwes," she whispered, reaching for him in the dark. "Take my hand."

The boy didn't respond, but she found the wet sleeve of his shirt and traced it down to his wrist.

Dagny said nothing else. She quietly slipped away from the double doors, tip-toeing across the floor of broken glass, dragging Melwes along with her.

She could feel his thin body shaking, like the cold shivers one gets after a heavy rain. She needed to get them to safety, more for his sake than her own. As much as she wanted to sprint away from here, there were too many objects littering the room, and if she tumbled and fell...

Something dragged on the far side of the chamber. Something enormous and long. Dagny could hear the heavy sliding and a deep, guttural breathing—deeper and more powerful than anything she'd ever heard. There was something unrelentingly raw there. She could feel it in her chest. The thing... *Yunis*... was coming.

Despite her better judgment, Dagny's mind took over, and she started to imagine what the creature looked like. She'd seen pictures of the Drey Garders before. First in Grete's sketchbook, and later in a painting near the old palace kitchens. They had tusks and long, floppy ears. Their build was muscular and their fur was covered in spots. And there was a coldness in the eyes—the stare of a killer.

She imagined this one meaner than the rest, and larger... it had to be larger. Melwes said it was the first and last of the Drey Garders. But shouldn't the cat be agile? What was the *dragging*?

Dagny saw it sooner than she would've liked. Even in the horrifying darkness, with her thoughts running wild, the beast Dagny dreamt up was nothing compared to the monster pulling itself toward them now.

It was lit by a single fluttering orb. Dagny glimpsed it only for a moment, before the light went out again. And in that flash Dagny saw its giant face, hanging low, fur and flesh dripping like candle wax. One eye drooped lower than the other, and its tongue lapped at the air.

She stifled a scream and clutched Melwes, pulling him along in the blackness toward the opposite wall.

"I can't see anything!" Melwes shouted, his voice high and shrill. "I need you! *Now!*"

A flurry of spirit lights suddenly appeared, blazing brightly over the ruined chamber. The shock of the light almost sent Dagny reeling. It was like she'd stepped into the afternoon sun.

Forcing her eyes open, she saw it. The side-passage. It hadn't been her imagination. The tunnel was probably no wider than a few feet. Just enough space for the two of them to slip through and escape. If they could only make it, there was no way the beast could fit.

Her boots crunched on glass, and they hopped over the remnants of a shattered pillar. Dagny feared, at any moment, the monstrous cat would be on her. How could they outrun such a thing? It felt like they were moving so slowly. Each step was laborious and disjointed. She couldn't run here, on this broken ground. She tried to stay focused on the hallway. *Just focus on that, nothing else,* she told herself. The lights swirled around, but they were not the playful lights she'd grown accustomed to. They whipped and whirled ferociously, embers caught in a storm.

Dagny reached the passage and pushed Melwes ahead, taking a quick look over her shoulder. Yunis was halfway across the chamber, dragging itself by its front limbs in a lurching, jerky motion. It was still coming... only slowly.

The beast *was* enormous. Long and sleek, its back stretched into the shadows and disappeared. At one time, it must've been truly glorious. Only now, centuries had toiled away at the creature, morphing it into a deranged, slobbering mess. Watching it struggle, Dagny couldn't help feeling pity for the cat, then Melwes grabbed her shirt and yanked her away.

The hallway was even more narrow than she expected. Dagny could have reached out and touched both sides at once, although she avoided doing so. The walls, cracked with sickly yellow paint, looked like they could crumble at the slightest disturbance. *Where to now?* she thought. The passage was taking her further and further away from Grete.

The lights continued to blaze, illuminating everything.

"They're nervous," Melwes said. "I've never seen 'em like this."

"Who can blame them?" Dagny replied. "I'm nervous myself."

"They're not like you. They're protectors of the Under Road. They don't get frightened."

Dagny ignored the harshness of the boy's comment, focusing on the passage ahead.

"We're gonna get lost now," Melwes said. "The exit was back there."

"I realize that. But this hallway has to go somewhere."

"No, you *don't* realize it. The *only* exit was back there." Melwes stopped and shook his head. "We have to go back."

"And do what? Get gobbled up by that thing?"

The boy faced her down, planting his hands on his hips. "Of course not."

"So what's the plan? You need to tell me first."

Melwes chewed his lip. "... Yunis will get bored, and then we'll sneak back in."

Dagny had to be careful here. Melwes was clearly rattled and not thinking straight. He'd lost control of the situation and didn't know how to handle it. If she let him lead now, they'd probably get killed. Yunis may have slowed in the centuries—or millennia—since it'd been brought here, but it was still deadly and horrifying. There was a hungry derangement in the creature's drooping eyes. Dagny had seen it. If the "guardian" caught them, it wouldn't let go.

"Do you know how that animal is still alive?" Dagny asked, trying to steer the conversation to one she could manage. "It's kind of sad, don't you think?"

"They probably live forever," Melwes said. "Yunis has been here since the beginning. When you spend all your time alone and in the dark, it warps your mind and spirit."

"I suppose it does," Dagny said with some consideration.

"Entire cultures have collapsed and been reborn since Yunis was created."

She watched him for a moment. "You don't sound like a ten-year-old, you know? I've always thought that. How come you're so special?"

"I'm just telling you what I heard. I didn't come up with these things."

"Alright." Dagny smiled. "You're still special, though."

"Maybe we can see where this hallway leads," Melwes said. He seemed to relax slightly. "It'll give Yunis time to go away."

Dagny smiled even wider. "Sounds like a good idea."

They had taken two steps when the rumbling began.

It started slowly. In the ground. A faint tremor, like the earth was breathing. At first, Dagny's brain wouldn't allow her to realize what was happening—there was only so much she could handle. Then the rumble rose into the walls, cracking the paint and plaster. Turning from a breathing to a painful groan, clattering the wooden floorboards and rippling across the ceiling, until the whole passage shook violently, like it was being pulled apart.

"The shift!" Dagny cried, almost losing her balance. "Is this it? Is it happening?!"

The spirit lights had whipped themselves into a frenzied blur. She'd never heard them make a sound before. Now she thought she heard a high-pitched whine.

Melwes tried to steady himself against the wall. His eyes were wide with panic. And then, as he glanced behind her, he screamed.

The creature, Yunis, was in the hall. Dagny couldn't understand how that was possible, but there it was—its head taking up the entire space, from floor to ceiling. It was the only part of the beast that Dagny could see. A giant, drooping, maniacal face. The creature was squeezing itself through the narrow doorway. The walls pulled at its loose skin and fur, peeling back the cat's eyes and lips; changing its pitiful expression of madness into a deformed portrait of hatred and rage.

Its teeth clattered like the loose floorboards underneath... clattered into Dagny's bones. And its tongue, that awful tongue, stretched toward them... reaching... as the creature continued to *push*.

Melwes stood spellbound; rooted in place by the sheer horror of what was taking place. Dagny tried to say something, but nothing came out. She grabbed him around the waist, lifted, and stumbled down the hall.

Go. Go. Keep going, Dagny told herself. She passed openings in the hallway leading to small, empty rooms. The walls buckled, constricting the passage even more. She bumped the sick-yellow stone as she lumbered forward, scraping her shoulder. Just then, the lights flashed past her, rounding the corner, as the passage took a sharp right turn.

Panting hard, Dagny dropped Melwes onto the floor, took his hand, and pressed on. At the end of the hallway was a single door. Nothing else.

She looked back before approaching it, wondering if the creature could turn the corner.

"Come," Melwes said, much calmer than Dagny would've expected. He walked ahead and opened the door.

Dagny stepped closer. She hoped the passage would offer an escape, but the room beyond was nothing more than a long closet.

"We're trapped..." Dagny muttered. Her mind raced, trying to come up with another solution. There had to be a way out, something she had missed. She turned around, ready to head back into the hallway.

Melwes gently took her wrist. "Inside," he said.

The lights cast their glow over the closet. After Melwes closed the door behind them, he motioned to the back wall.

"Is there another passage here? A secret one?" Dagny asked hopefully, scanning the room.

Melwes took a deep breath. "I don't think so."

The rumbling never stopped, and if it got louder, Dagny couldn't tell. She stood by the far wall for several minutes, inspecting the area for hidden handles or latches. Or, at least, that's what she pretended she was doing. The truth was Dagny was trying to calm her mind. None of this could be real, could it? She had to be trapped inside of some weird dream. Like the kind Grete had when she ate the heart.

Dagny glanced at her shoulder, the one she scraped against the wall. It was bleeding, and without thinking, Dagny pressed her fingers into the wound, causing a sharp pain to radiate down her arm. This was real enough alright.

Melwes stood nearby, staring at the door. Preparing himself for what was coming. The lights had slowed too. No longer swirling, they simply hovered nearby, clustering around the boy.

Maybe Yunis would get stuck in the hallway. Maybe that had already occurred. Then what? They surely wouldn't be able to get around the creature. Dagny examined the stone wall, wondering if there was a way to dig themselves out. She kneeled down and tried to pry off one of the wooden floorboards. It was hopeless. She sat there for a long while, listening to the castle rattle and groan.

"How long do we have?" she finally asked.

"Until Yunis comes?" Melwes responded. He didn't look back at her.

"Until the shift happens."

He said something, but Dagny didn't fully hear it. She thought he said *sorry*. A moment later, the boy coughed, clearing his throat, speaking louder this time. "I should've known better than to bring you here. This is a place of death."

Dagny stood and walked over to him. "You were trying to help me. I don't want you to feel bad about that. If anyone should feel bad, it's me. I dragged you here... I took you away from your home." She could feel her throat constricting, on the verge of sobbing. "I endanger everyone around me. It happens more than you'd think. I deserve what's coming."

Melwes turned, facing her. There was a strange emotion behind his eyes. A mix of anger and fear. "We were so close. Beyond this wall is the castle's end... and the path to Jud. I didn't do it just for you, if you wanna know the truth. I wanted to see the city again, too." Melwes looked back at the door. "The castle will vanish soon."

A calm melancholy washed over Dagny. "Where do you think it goes?" she asked. "How does something just vanish, anyway?"

She never got an answer to her question.

A monstrous howl erupted from outside their room, followed by the creaking of wood. Something snapped and the resulting boom sent shockwaves across the floor, tossing Dagny onto her back. Dust spilled into the closet from underneath the door, casting a haze over everything.

Dagny turned over and pressed her hands into the ground, but instead of wooden floorboards, she felt dirt.

"Melwes..." she coughed, the dust from crushed stone caking her throat.

The boy rushed over and tried to help her stand. "Are you okay?"

She stumbled to her feet, trying to regain her senses.

Melwes spoke again; his voice changing from concern to excitement. "Dagny, look... *the wall.*"

She spun around. The back of the closet was no longer blocks of gray stone. In an instant, it had turned to black earth with snake-like roots poking out.

"The shift! It's happening now!" Melwes shouted over the thundering roar. "We're at the edge of it... Hurry! We need to push through!" He rushed over and dug frantically at the earthen wall.

Dagny was right behind him. The spirit lights zipped past her face and swirled around the roots, as if they were trying to help pull them free. Dagny stuck her hands into the dirt, straight to her elbows, yanking out fistfuls of rich soil with every pull.

Glancing to the side, she noticed that the shelves lining the closet were gone, and the contours of the space no longer held the squared shape of something built by man. It was rounded, almost amorphous. A changing, *shifting* tunnel.

She dared to look back. To see if the door on the far wall was still there. Although, they were further away now, deep into the passage, Dagny could still make out the simple wood frame encased in black. It appeared to be floating in a void, shimmering in the glow of spirit lights.

The object no longer held any meaning to her. It was as if she'd entered a trance, hypnotized as the door began to shake.

Shaking... why was it shaking? She knew she should be digging, not looking at doors. *Dig. Turn around and dig,* she ordered herself. But... there was something there. Something on the other side. Something she felt compelled to see....

Yunis.

The first and the last.

It burst through, shattering wood and stone. Spitting soil onto her face and clothes. One of its eyes was gone now. Torn off, perhaps in the hallway. But its teeth were there, still attached to that drooping, slobbering mouth... It eclipsed her entire world, as if it were the only thing that existed. That had ever existed. Its terrible head lunged forward, snapping the air. Dagny could feel the dampness of its tongue.

The terror she felt was primal; deep within her core.

"*Dagny!* Hurry!" the boy screamed. "I can see the exit!"

She spun her head around, gazing back into the shifting tunnel. At the far end of her vision was a small opening and sunlight.

"*Hurry!*" Melwes screamed again.

A puff of hot, sour breath swarmed over her body, clinging to her skin. She could taste it in the air. There wasn't enough time. She sensed the beast lurch forward; felt the floor collapsing underneath her.

"Go!" she shouted at Melwes. "Just go!"

The boy looked at her now. She could see the horror in his eyes. Illuminated by a single twinkling orb. *The lights... Where were the other lights?* Had they been abandoned again?

"No!" Melwes yelled.

Dagny turned and saw a massive group of lights clustered around the monster's head. Swirling between whiskers, circling its snout, blinding its single eye in a furious eruption of blue.

Melwes rushed past her; she sensed it happening and reached out to grab him. Just then, the great cat dislodged its jaw, as if readying an enormous yawn, and inhaled.

It was like stepping into a storm. Dagny's clothes pulled away from her body, and her hair flapped violently across her face. She felt the soft cloth of Melwes' shirt and grasped it with everything she had, fearing the boy would be sucked into the creature's mouth.

Melwes stood strong, feet planted on the ground. Other things flew through the air, zipping past their bodies: bits of crumbled stone, roots, splintered floorboards, and dirt. So much dirt. She could feel it in her nose and taste it on her tongue. Dagny tried to step backward into the tunnel, toward the small window of sunlight at the other end. Her satchel tore loose and flung away. And the boy screamed. For a moment, she almost lost her grip on him. It was the most horrible, gut-wrenching sound. She forced her eyes open, half-expecting to see Melwes torn in two, but when she looked, the boy remained firmly in place.

It was the other sight that almost jolted out a scream of her own. The spirit lights. Dozens of them, struggling helplessly against the force of the monster's pull, were being sucked into the blackness of the great cat's maw.

One by one, they flickered out, disappearing behind a wall of mangled teeth. The handful that remained were desperately trying to fly away, trying to reach the tunnel. Melwes yanked at Dagny's hand to pry it from his shirt, and when she didn't let go, he punched her in the ribs. She wrapped her arm around the boy's chest, lifted him off the ground, and pressed toward the sunlight with all the strength she had left.

Thick chunks of earth fell from the ceiling, and the soft ground under her feet began to thicken and change. She was ascending now, struggling with the weight of the boy as she stepped up onto hard stone. The earth was morphing into *stairs*. But the window of light still seemed so far away. Her legs burned, and with every breath, she inhaled more dirt than the last.

Still, she pressed on. Focused on that promise of light. Dagny could picture it warming her face. She imagined lying in the Benzara garden back home, soaking in the sun's embrace. She imagined Lucas and Abrielle smiling and laughing, chasing each other along the bank of the pebbled pond.

Melwes went limp, and Dagny pulled him even tighter, fearing he would slip away. She would take him out of here, into the world of sunlight and laughter. Into a place of safety and love. There was nothing she could do about the spirit lights, but she could protect the boy. She would make sure of that.

The sunlight was closer now. So close she could almost feel it... could almost *reach* it if she stretched. Just a step away. A single step to freedom from the underground, from Yunis and the castle. To Jud and Grete. Dagny took that last step, readying herself for the sunlight. But she found a pit of blackness instead, and tumbled down, losing the boy in the fall.

4

Dagny didn't know how long she'd been falling. At times, it seemed like she was dropping into an endless abyss, only to feel the sensation of wet ground underneath, funneling her down and away from the sunlight. She had lost her grip on Melwes almost immediately and tried calling out for him, but couldn't catch enough breath to make a sound. When she finally stopped falling, Dagny found herself sprawled on the ground of some darkened room.

Not pitch black, but close. She couldn't remember landing exactly, nor could she remember how long she'd been lying there before regaining her senses. Maybe she had passed out and not realized it. Everything had been such a blur.

Dagny knew she was in a room because she could see a stool in the shadows, and then shelving on the walls. The boy, however, was nowhere in sight. As soon as she was able, Dagny pushed herself onto her knees and screamed for him. Howling until her throat hurt. Even after she knew he was gone, she kept shouting his name anyway. It was the only thing she could think of to do.

Dagny stumbled to her feet, her mind turning, trying to come to terms with what had happened. Was she hurt? It was possible. Her blood was pumping and adrenaline could conceal quite a lot. All her parts seemed like they were in the right place. She shouted one last time for Melwes before wiping tears from her face. She hadn't even realized she'd been crying.

Where was she now? Her eyes darted wildly around the room. She was still underground, that much was certain—the space had that kind of *feel* to it—there were also steps here... and a *door*. She half-expected Yunis to come bursting out of this one as well. *If you're coming, then come already,* she thought. But nothing happened. Still, it took a while before Dagny was comfortable walking forward. She studied the ceiling, trying to figure out how she got here, scanning the surface for an opening. If there had been one, it had sealed itself back up already.

And there was light—a soft, natural light seeping in through dirt-filled cracks above. *Floorboards.* The sudden realization spurred Dagny up the stairs. She paused momentarily before throwing the door open and stepping into...

A kitchen. An old, cobweb-covered kitchen.

In the back of her mind, she hoped the boy was nearby, but it quickly became apparent that no one had come this way for a long, long time. The kitchen was a cozy space, with a black kettle tucked between cupboards and a washbasin beneath a small glass window. It was from that window that Dagny caught her first pure glimpse of the outside world since early spring. She rushed over and put her hand on the glass, feeling the warmth from the setting sun. It would be dark soon enough, but for the moment, the sky was burnt and golden. The twilight hour. Melwes had told her that was when the shift came.

Oh, it had come alright.

It had come and taken him away. It had also saved her life.

If she could have, Dagny would've crawled outside right then. She desperately wanted to reach the sun before it disappeared; the window was simply too small for her to fit.

She stepped out of the kitchen and into a hallway from which several other rooms branched off, and a narrow, rickety staircase connected the ground floor to the upper level. Everything here was pleasant enough but also had the look of something from another time. More like a house the Rork scholars would have used hundreds of years ago. And while the place was a bit strange, at least it seemed real. Not the dreamlike weirdness of the castle. Dagny's mind was finally slowing down enough for her to get a handle on things.

It was possible Melwes could be somewhere nearby. Maybe the shift had spit him out here, too. Dagny didn't want to think of the alternative—that he was still trapped inside that awful castle, sealed between worlds.

The front door stood only feet away. Dagny rushed over and reached for its handle just as a shape passed a murky window nearby.

"Melwes!" she shouted, instinctively. The shape stopped and faced the glass, cocking its head. Dagny suddenly realized it was much too tall to be the boy.

She threw her hand over her mouth and dropped to the floor with her heart thundering.

The shape said something she couldn't understand. Glass and thick wood muffled the sound. It could've been speaking her language, or something entirely different. She could only hope it was human.

Whatever it was, it had seen her. The shape moved away from the window and disappeared behind the front door. She hoped it would turn around and leave. There was only so much she could take. Just then the handle rattled.

Glancing up, Dagny saw a heavy iron latch, likely rusted shut, sealing the door to its frame. She crept away, to the rickety staircase, as the door banged against the latch. Something smacked into the wood, sending a jolt down her spine.

Like the door itself, Dagny's hands shook, and by the time she reached the top of the stairs, a cold sweat had formed under her arms, making her body feel slick and ill. Dagny knew her nerves had been shattered. From the castle to Yunis, the shift and now this... she might've laughed at the absurdity of it all, if she wasn't so frightened.

She raced into a small study near the end of the staircase and spotted another window there. The sunlight was all but gone. Still, she could see the outline of a roof nearby and an alley below. Wherever she was, the buildings were close together; a neighborhood of sorts. Straining her eyes, Dagny could make out more rooftops against the bruised-purple sky. Was this it? Had she made it to Jud?

Dagny moved closer to the window and quickly inspected the glass. She could've fit through this one, but like the latch downstairs, its hinges were rusted shut. If she wanted to get out, she'd have to break it.

The front door stopped rattling, allowing Dagny a moment of relief before another wave of panic took hold. In one way, the silence was even worse. She no longer knew where the shape was or what it was doing. Maybe the thing was circling the house now. Maybe it was even staring up at her from the ground below. Dagny sucked in air and took a step back, slipping into the darkness. She could just wait here til morning. Her throat was dry and sore, but she could still go without water for a while. The shift *shouldn't* happen again until next twilight. Maybe if she spent the night here, the shape would move on and leave her alone. *Maybe.*

After backing herself into the darkest corner of the room, Dagny crouched on the ground, ready to spring away if she had to. There'd be no sleeping tonight, she was sure of that. Dagny touched the tin bracelet on her wrist, brought here all the way from Limer's Town. Grete would have to wait a little longer. Dagny needed to find Melwes first. She couldn't stand the thought of him alone and afraid. The boy was resourceful, but how long could he last in that castle? Dagny thought of his friends, those poor spirit lights being sucked into oblivion by that horrible creature, and began to tremble with rage. She'd been so helpless in the castle; she hated that feeling.

Outside, the sun completed its descent, and an evening wind gusted against the glass. Her boots and clothes were still damp from the swim earlier, but at least she had stopped sweating. The coolness of the room was good for something.

No sooner had Dagny repositioned herself on the floor when she heard a thud on the roof outside her window. It was too dark to see, but she knew it was there. The shape.

Racking her brain, Dagny tried to think of an escape before coming to the awful conclusion that she was trapped in the house. Even if she ran downstairs, the front door was rusted shut, as were all the windows. Dagny was better off trying to hide than giving away her position. Slowly, she crawled over to the study's crude desk.

Something tapped the glass, causing her to freeze. It was followed by another sound. A voice. "You in there?" it said. She couldn't tell if it was *menacing*, but it didn't sound friendly.

"Let me in," the shape demanded. The voice was clearer now, and Dagny gasped as a pale face pressed against the window. Its eyes were two black voids in the night.

This time, an object smacked the glass hard, causing Dagny to flinch and shut her eyes. When she opened them again, fractured spider webbing had spread across the windowpane. The next blow shattered it onto the floor.

Dagny choked down a scream and crawled further underneath the desk. She could hear the shape knocking out what glass remained on the frame, and then hopping into the room, crunching across the floor as it approached her hiding spot.

"Come out now," a male voice said.

She peeked between the floor and the desk and saw the glow of lamplight, cascading over heavy boots and a club. That same club then rose and tapped the wood above her head.

"I said, come out," he repeated.

Dagny didn't know what to do. "Who are you?" she asked, still balled up defensively, wondering if the person planned to hurt her.

"Pren. Who are you?" When she didn't answer, he continued, sounding more relaxed. "I heard screaming. Thought the Grouchers got someone."

"I was calling for my friend. I thought maybe you were him," Dagny responded through the wood.

"Oh... Do I know you? Are we friends?"

"No."

Pren shuffled his feet. "I didn't scare you then, did I?"

What do you think? she almost shouted, before regaining control of herself. Her heart felt like it was going to pound out of her chest.

Sensing her hesitancy, Pren repeated the question, his voice gentle this time. "Did I scare you?"

"Yes. A little."

"Sorry. Who are you?"

"Dagny."

He muttered something, like he was disappointed in her name. "Do you need help?"

It took another moment for Dagny to answer. "I might." *I might? That was a stupid response*, she thought. Despite the circumstances, she felt embarrassed to admit such a thing.

"Do you want me to help you?"

Dagny looked again at the boots, now inches from her face. "Yeah... okay."

She carefully crawled out from under the desk, stood, and studied the person. Dagny couldn't put an age on him, but he seemed young. Her age, maybe? Maybe older? There were dark circles around his eyes, like a raccoon, and facial marks stretched further down his face, almost to his chin. She couldn't tell if the markings were permanent or something he applied, like paint. His hair was chopped short; messy and uneven.

"What's with the club?" she asked.

Pren slapped it against his hand. "Just a tool. Useful for breaking things and keeping Grouchers away."

"Grouchers? That's the second time you said that. What are those?"

He eyed her skeptically. "Where are you from?"

"The umm..." she tried to come up with a lie, before finally giving up and saying, "The lagoon. Rork, if you know it."

"The outside?" Pren gazed at her. "You're an uninvited, are you?"

"I guess... Where am I? Is this Jud?"

Pren nodded. "Mm-hmm. The outskirts anyway."

"Really? Are we near the castle?" she asked quickly.

"The castle?"

"Yeah, with Yunis, inside the wall—the *castle*! I need to get back there."

Pren furrowed his brow, like he was thinking hard. "The guardian? You're talking about the mythical cat?"

"Yes!" Dagny said, then paused. "Wait. What do you mean, *mythical*?"

Pren shrugged. "What do you think I mean?"

"It's not mythical. I just came from there. It's as real as you and me."

Pren narrowed his eyes skeptically. "The castle in the wall..." He was considering her story. "I'm puzzled, because *that* gate has been sealed since before I was born, and it's *not* nearby."

"How far?" she asked, feeling a sense of dread drip down her back.

"The other side of the city."

Dagny was stunned. "How did I get over here?" she said, but she wasn't really asking.

"I don't know," he responded anyway.

"Is it big?"

"The city? Big enough."

She took a deep breath before walking over to the window. "I better get moving then. Can you point me in the direction?"

Pren moved next to her and pointed into the night. "That way."

"Thanks," Dagny said, although his vague direction was meaningless. "I guess I'll climb down..."

"Alright."

Dagny glanced over the window ledge, then turned back to face him. "Oh. You never told me what the Grouchers are."

"Creatures. They kind of look like us, although they can take on many disguises. They're *not* to be trusted. No one lives out here except them."

"You're here."

"True. But I'm not a Groucher. I'm looking for something..." He scratched his head. "Although, now I'm thinking I won't find it."

"What kind of thing?"

"A building. *The Majestica*. It only appears every ten or twelve years. It's been ten, so I'll probably need to come back in two."

"Okay. I didn't know what to expect when I came here... glad we speak the same language, at least."

"We're descended from the same folk. People in Jud know much more about your world. We're both the watchers and the keepers of secrets."

"Oh."

Pren gently prodded her with his club. "Hey. You should know that outsiders aren't supposed to be here. You might not be allowed to leave."

Dagny took a step away from him. "You're gonna keep me here?"

"No. Not me." Pren said, lowering the club. "I'm just telling you. Although, if you are able to get out, you have to keep the secret. You understand? Does this make sense? *Itha pey, shakko thane.*"

Those words. He sounded like... "Do you know a boy named Melwes?"

"Hmm. I don't think so. He's your friend?"

"Yeah." Dagny rubbed the back of her neck. "I need to find him."

Pren put his hand firmly on her shoulder. "Do you understand what I said? You have to keep the secret."

Dagny nodded slowly, trying to give her most solemn expression. "I understand. I will."

"Good."

Gazing into the night, Dagny considered her next move. "I should get started. I just wish it wasn't so far. How long do you think it'll take me to get there?"

"A day, maybe three. It's possible you'll never get there."

Dagny stared at him. "What?"

"You don't know your way around," Pren said. "You can only get so far before things change. If you're not used to it, you'll get lost."

Dagny's fear had been replaced with frustration. She let out a loud, drawn-out sigh. "I don't suppose you'd show me."

"All the way to the castle gate? No. I've got things I need to do."

"Okay," she said. *Couldn't hurt to ask.*

"If you're hungry, you can have some of the stew I was cooking. You don't want to stay in these buildings—"

"Because of the shift?"

"Right. If you're caught in the wrong one..."

"I'll disappear with it."

Pren nodded. "The people in Jud know what to look for. We can sort of sense it coming. But you?" Pren shook his head. "I wouldn't recommend it."

"Thanks for the advice, but I don't want to be inside, anyway." Dagny felt a twinge in her stomach. "I will take some of that food, though."

∞

Pren's campfire was a short distance from the house, hidden in the alleyway between tall, moss-covered buildings. Everything out here was covered in some kind of foliage. Wild trees sprung up from the roadways, and a courtyard nearby had a massive rose bush growing out of an old well.

"What's for dinner?" Dagny asked playfully, sitting on the ground.

"A bit of everything," Pren answered, stirring a small pot. "I wasn't expecting company, obviously, but there's enough left." He filled up a wooden bowl and passed it over. Dagny could see carrots, potatoes, and some kind of shredded cabbage suspended in thick broth.

"Thanks," she said. "It's been a long time since I've eaten anything other than mushrooms or black fish."

Pren prodded the dying fire with a stick. "Oh, why's that?"

"I was living in the underground for a time."

"You're quite adventurous."

"I guess." Dagny started into the bowl of stew, expecting it to be bland. It didn't really matter, as hungry as she was, but the food was surprisingly tasty, with delicate hints of garlic and pepper. "I came up the Under Road. Do you know it?"

"Oh, sure." Pren continued working the dying fire, his attention focused on bringing new life into it. "That road used to be easy to find. Used to run all the way into the inner city."

"What happened?"

"Things fell apart. The entrance at Sanctuary disappeared or collapsed or something. Now you have to take the long way 'round."

"I entered the road at the old palace, near Deep Lake."

Pren gave her an odd look. Clearly, he didn't know what she was talking about.

"Have you ever been outside of Jud?" she asked.

Pren went back to the flame. "Oh, sure. I've been all over the place. The Mist Hills, and Giant's Tear. I've even been to the Brothmuck… before it was the Brothmuck, of course," he said with a laugh.

Dagny had never heard of those places, even in stories. "Ever been to Vahnes or Satchels, or the lagoon?"

"Hmm. I don't think so."

A long, awkward pause followed before Pren spoke again. "Why did you come here?"

"I'm looking for my sister."

He nodded. "You're looking for a lot of people."

"Only two." She could handle that, couldn't she? Dagny finished the stew and chased it down with water from a clay jug, feeling somewhat relaxed for the first time in a long while. "Thanks for the food," she said.

Fumbling in his pack, Pren produced an ornate smoking pipe, lit it with a piece of tinder, then offered it to her. "Happy to share."

Dagny waved him off. "No. I'm fine."

"Suit yourself." Kicking his feet back, Pren proceeded to puff out thick, gray circles of smoke. Dagny watched them drift upward and fade into the cloudless black.

The stars lit up the sky brilliantly out here, far away from her own city. There were so many that Dagny had difficulty picking out the star lines she knew. Craning her neck, she scanned the sky for the Endahl and the Adventurer's Compass. If she could locate it, she could orient herself and maybe figure out which direction the castle was.

"Looking for something?" Pren asked.

"The great bull, but I can't seem to find it."

Pren threw his head back as well. "Which one is that?"

"It's got three horns," Dagny said. It was absurd how many stars were out tonight. "Maybe, if I find Gylathrik first..."

Pren pointed sharply at the sky. "Gylathrik is right there. See?"

Dagny crawled over to him, trying to see where he was pointing, but still couldn't find the constellation. In a weird way, it made her think of nights at Stardust, and one in particular, that she had spent lying on her back with Max, studying the evening sky.

"Do you know his eye was torn out and tossed across the heavens?" Dagny asked.

"Never heard that one," Pren said.

"Yep. Kinda gruesome, but it happened."

"Who told you that?"

She paused before responding. "A friend."

"You have a lot of those?"

"I do." Or at least she did. Dagny wondered what it would be like when she returned to the City. She had a hard time imagining Sarna ever talking to her again. Their friendship had ended as quickly as it began. And Rodolph? She hadn't even seen him since that day in the forest. That one was clearly her own fault. She'd just felt so guilty about what happened to him, she couldn't bring herself to visit, but she should've put those feelings aside. She should've been a better person. Then there was Max. Dagny couldn't fault him if he never wanted to see her. She knew she'd hurt him by making promises she couldn't keep and running off. Tash would probably be the most forgiving. Dagny hadn't really wronged him at all. In a lot of ways, she felt the most connected to that boy. But it didn't really matter... all those people, the ones she'd grown so close to last year... They all seemed like ghosts to her now.

Pren was watching her, and Dagny spoke before he could question her anymore. "My sister ran off with a girl named Marfisi. I think she was from here."

Pren nodded. "Oh, Marfisi is from here, alright."

Dagny's heart raced. "Why'd you say it like that?"

"She's got a decent following," Pren said. "Not enough to match one of the great houses, but big enough to go noticed. Some charm on that one. People are drawn to her."

That wasn't surprising. Dagny herself had been drawn to the singer before she stole Grete away. "Where's she live?" Dagny asked, then leaned closer. "I *really* need to find her."

"That's three now."

"Huh?"

"Three people you need to find. Your list is getting longer by the hour."

"Right."

"Marfisi and her group live around Bright Quarter."

"I'm guessing that's in the inner city? By Sanctuary?" Dagny asked.

He gave her a broad smile. "You're a quick learner."

"The inner city..." Dagny said, thoughtfully. "Is it in the middle of Jud?"

Pren nodded. "Mm-hmm. You'll pass through it on your way to the castle."

"Okay, great." Dagny stood and looked down the alleyway at the main road. "This way?"

"Wait," Pren said. "You're leaving now?"

She didn't really want to leave. Her body was on the verge of exhaustion. She just felt like she *had* to leave.

"I wish I could stay," Dagny mumbled. "For a little longer, at least."

"You'll get lost, I'm telling you. Also, there's good reason no one else is out here." There was a seriousness in his voice.

"And what's that?"

"The Silent Keep. All roads from the 'skirts pass through it. That's why most stay away."

"Sounds scary," Dagny said with a hollow laugh.

"Oh," Pren said, grimly. "It is."

5

Dagny had agreed to stay until morning. Pren said it'd be safer that way, but she awoke in the night with an overwhelming sense of alarm, picturing Melwes trapped in the castle, alone in the dark, hiding from Yunis.

Before falling asleep, Pren had spent the evening educating her about the path to Sanctuary and the castle beyond. "Jud is a labyrinth," he said. "You need to read the signs. Always take the winding path and avoid sharp turns."

The "winding path" was the *old road*—a natural pathway through Jud, formed during its creation; back when Jud was birthed from the Eternal Forest. Everything that came after was built on that foundation.

"The sharp turns, the straight roads, anything angular—that's all from *other* places," Pren continued. "They'll lead you astray and into the shift."

"Got it," Dagny replied. "Seems easy enough."

Pren puffed his pipe. "It's not, though. Not really."

She listened to him snore now. Watching his chest rise and fall in the dim glow of the dying firelight.

Dagny was lucky to meet such a person here. If she had more time, she could see them becoming friends. At this point, she'd take all the friends she could get. Even though she'd lost so many, she seemed to be replacing the people from her old life rather quickly. *Replaced. That's an interesting way to put it*, she thought. Dagny felt guilty that the word had even entered her mind. She didn't want to be someone who *replaced* people. In fact, the only reason she was alone was because she didn't want to put anyone in danger. Max and Tash definitely would've been here, had she asked. Maybe even Rodolph. But she couldn't have asked such a thing. And after Yunis, Dagny was glad she hadn't. She thought of what Hanette had said to her, all those months ago in Stardust: that Dagny was nothing but a manipulative, selfish liar. Maybe Hanette was just trying to be hurtful, but the comment had stuck. That was not the kind of person Dagny wanted to be—or thought she was.

A snort and cough caused Pren to roll over and tuck his hands under his chin. His face seemed so peaceful now, almost innocent. Dagny could still make out the raccoon circles around his eyes, but the other markings had been smeared away.

Would she be able to live with herself if another person got hurt because of her? What if something worse happened? What if someone ended up dying? *What if Melwes...* she couldn't think of that. Moving as slowly as possible, Dagny got onto her knees and crawled into the darkness. She thought about taking one of Pren's canteens and maybe a couple of those potatoes, then decided against it. The inner city was only a day or so away, and she didn't feel good about stealing from someone who'd been so helpful... So instead, Dagny gulped down as much water as she could and snuck off.

On the open road, Dagny could see much better. The sky was cloudless and the moon bright. Between that and the stars, she easily navigated the path in front of her. But the night erased the color of things, and the buildings were draped in that leafy gray cloak of foliage and moss. It seemed more like walking through a weird forest than a city.

Even the road was mostly earth. She tried to follow Pren's advice, steering clear of any angular crossroads, and staying on the long, winding path. Occasionally, Dagny's foot caught a broken stone, or she stepped over something metal and unnatural, but for the most part, the route was easy. All of that changed when she reached the bridge.

Sanctuary was to the northwest and would've been a simple walk, Pren had told her, if not for all the *city* around it. Dagny thought she knew what he meant. She had grown up in one of the largest cities outside of the Vahnland and accumulated a good deal of experience navigating busy streets and crooked alleys. But the scene that stretched in front of her now was so jarring, Dagny considered walking all the way back to Pren and begging him for an escort.

It wasn't an unusually long bridge—probably half the length of City Centre's—and this one didn't seem to cross anything. Maybe at one time there had been a stream or creek underneath; now it was nothing but scarred ground. The sun began to rise shortly before Dagny stepped on the bridge, and by the time she reached the middle, the first rays of light illuminated a cityscape so dense with jumbled buildings that Dagny couldn't see a single pathway through.

It was a massive wall of interconnected windows and boarded-up doors; chimneys and gutters; plaster and brick. The color was inconsistent and splotchy. Some buildings were the plain brown of sand, while others were rich shades of yellow and green. It all blended together in a single, impenetrable block of city that seemed to shout at her, *You'll never get through!*

The road ended at a crescent-shaped plaza in front of the wall. Dagny sat on a stone bench near the embankment and rested, studying the scene. She wondered why Pren failed to mention this last night; wouldn't this *wall* have been something important for her to know?

There was no light inside any of the buildings and there were no people here (none that Dagny could see, anyway). It gave the whole place a sense of eerie abandonment, making her wonder if anyone had ever lived here. A few of the doorways had old signs hanging above them with writing so faded they were indecipherable—except for one. On a giant hunk of white plaster, spelled out in crude form, was the word *GrOucherS*.

Dagny stayed calm, staring at the word. Who knew how long ago it had been written? She listened to the wind, and slowly glanced up the face of the buildings, scanning the windows. She didn't feel like she was being watched, but it was possible.

As she considered her options, Dagny suddenly spotted an open window, a short way off from the plaza, facing the bridge. It was on the ground level and there appeared to be something flapping inside. Intrigued by this new development, Dagny cautiously walked over, keeping her eyes focused on the wall for any other movement. She heard the singing before she saw it. A songbird, gold and red, chirped from the middle of an iron cage.

The room inside had the look of a parlor, full of treasures found in a junk heap, and just beyond the cage was an open door leading to a dark hallway. Dagny turned her attention back to the bird. The animal was beautiful, while the cage was rusted and worn; fastened with a polished silver lock.

Whoever was taking care of the bird could be lurking in the building beyond, but this also appeared to be the only way through the city-wall. Resting her hands on the windowsill, Dagny considered climbing into the room and seeing where the hallway led. She had hours before the shift happened—an entire day, in fact—but that's exactly what she thought when she entered the castle with Melwes, and time had slipped away so quickly.

Something clanged in the distance behind her. Instinctively, Dagny ducked down and pressed her back against the stone. Across the bridge, coming from the same direction she'd come only minutes before, were several figures shambling forward. One was much taller than the rest, even though its back was bent, and they all moved in a jerky, awkward manner. She heard more clanging as they walked, metal on metal, like a dull bell. They did not look like people Dagny wanted to meet. *Grouchers*, she thought, scanning the area for a place to hide. If they hadn't seen her yet, they would soon enough.

Dagny peeked into the room with the bird. *Someone has to be inside taking care of you, right?* Or maybe this was the home of the things that approached her now. She wished she had time to explore, but she needed to move quickly. Dagny placed her hands on the windowsill and climbed over.

The bird stopped singing as soon as she landed. Dagny smiled at it and pressed a finger to her lips. *Just act natural friend; don't tell them I'm here.* No sooner had she stepped into the room, however, than the bird let out an ear-splitting screech. The noise jolted Dagny back toward the window, ready to jump out, but she stopped herself. The screaming bird was so loud, Dagny knew its voice had reached the bridge. She poked her head around the window frame and saw the figures rushing over, their limbs dangling wildly as they ran, like marionettes cut loose.

She sprinted across the parlor, almost slipping on the grimy marble floor, and stumbled into the adjacent hallway. Something else jangled nearby; Dagny didn't dare slow down to inspect it. She passed a dining room where two women-like beings sat. Their faces were old and leathery, and one of them pointed at her as she ran.

Dagny hit the front door hard. In her panic, she tried to reach for the handle, missed it and smashed through rotten wood, landing on the street outside.

The sun had risen quickly; its glare almost blinding now. Dagny shielded her eyes and tried to look around. Buildings surrounded her, separated by shadowy pathways that branched out like a spiderweb. She searched for the winding path, but every route looked sharp and angular. Someone crunched on the ground behind her. Without looking back, Dagny sprinted off into the alleys.

Almost immediately, Dagny knew she'd made a mistake. This was probably the most jagged alleyway she had ever been down—like a staircase turned on its side—and with every angle she cut across, Pren's warning pounded in her head, *Avoid sharp turns.*

For a while, it felt as though she was going in a circle. She feared she'd emerge at the beginning: face-to-face with the women and their dangly marionettes, and that stupid bird. But when Dagny finally reached the other end, she rushed out to an open road.

No one else was here. Old metal street lamps loomed overhead, and a row of decrepit buildings stretched off in both directions.

Dagny stopped for a moment, gathering her breath, not sure of which way to go. She marked the position of the sun. The road seemed to head northeast and southwest... neither direction would take her to the inner city. How did she get lost so quickly? She cursed Pren. How could she stay on the winding path when everything out here was straight? Why did everything have to be such a riddle?

Her throat was already getting dry, and Dagny wished she hadn't left the canteen behind. She sighed in frustration before deciding on the route to the southwest. Maybe she could find another path along the way, one that cut north, and preferably something with a curve to it.

Other passages split the tall buildings here, but Dagny hesitated to explore them. They were dark and narrow, and the quietness of the place made her uneasy. It wouldn't do her any good to get lost in a labyrinth of more crooked alleys.

Eventually she did reach a crossroads where the street forked out in two directions. The path to the south looked peaceful, with roses and other flowering plants sprouting up along its sides. The path to the north looked hard and cold, with stone pavers and two large metal statues of mounted riders. She didn't even notice the people until they spoke.

"You lost there, squinter?" one of them called. They were crouched by a rusted old gate near the southern path. Beyond was an overgrown yard and a series of fountains and benches. A park of sorts.

It took a moment before Dagny could put a face on the voice. There were four figures that she could see, all dressed in black: black hats, black boots, and long black cloaks that seemed to be made of bird feathers. It hid the shapes of their bodies, making the figures appear like formless, feathered sacks.

"No. I'm fine," Dagny shouted back.

Two of the figures rose and sauntered over. The smaller of the pair had a young face and delicate lips. Her cloak moved as she walked, exposing a thin body and tight dark clothes.

"Don't-chie lie. You're a lost one," she said. "We know all woozies around here. We can help you. We're really nice."

The taller one moved to Dagny's side, blocking her from retreating down the road. "What do they call you?" This one's voice was deeper, with lips just as delicate as the girl's, and his nose protruded like a beak.

"My name's Corlie," Dagny lied, spitting out the first name that came to mind. "Just passing through on my way to Sanctuary."

"An *inner city* squinter girl?" the smaller one said, then clicked her tongue. "We don't find many around. Why is that? You don't like us?" The girl stepped closer. Dagny thought about backing away but didn't want to appear afraid. This girl was smaller than her, and there was still enough space to run. If she needed to.

"I don't even know who you are. Why wouldn't I like you?" Dagny asked.

"Aww. That's a nice one to hear... I didn't think they grew 'em up so pretty in the inner city. We like pretty girls with pretty things." The girl smiled and softened her voice. "Do you have any pretty things?"

"No. Not really."

"That's too sad, too bad."

Dagny could see half-a-dozen rings on the girl's fingers, a pair of necklaces, and several bracelets on her thin wrists. It looked like she'd robbed a jeweler, or a grave.

"Anyway, I should probably get going," Dagny said, discreetly hiding Grete's bracelet under her sleeve.

"Oh no, why? You've only just arrived."

Dagny sensed the beak-nosed man eyeing her intently.

"I just need to," Dagny responded, somewhat forcefully.

"Don't drop a tear, and give a smile first?" the girl said. "You're a scared squinty. I'd be lost to think we scared you."

The request made her nervous. "I'm not scared," she said, offering a nervous smile.

"No. One with teeth, a *real* smile." Before Dagny could react, the girl's fingers were on her chin, pulling her lip down. "Now, was that hard, blood-brain?" the girl asked, studying her mouth. It was such a strange intrusion, Dagny didn't know what to do. "Your teeth bottoms are real crooked. Did you know that? Your teeth are crooked."

Dagny pulled her face away. "I'm aware."

"I made you all mad," the girl said with a laugh.

"I'm not mad."

"Yes, you are. I can tell. It's not our fault your teeth bottoms are crooked and gross."

"What?" Dagny felt a sudden wave of self-consciousness. "No, they're not."

The girl stifled another laugh. "Yes, they are. I thought you were pretty from far away."

"Yeah. You're not pretty," the man said from over her shoulder. "You're *gross.*"

Dagny covered her mouth but then snapped back, "Well... *good.* I'm glad I'm gross. I'm not trying to attract creepy girls or awful men."

The man's eyes were daggers. "You shouldn't say things like that," he whispered.

The girl shook her head. "Don't-chie know, ugly *and* nasty."

"Me?" Dagny said. "You're the ones who are nasty."

"Hey!" the girl shouted suddenly, pointing at Dagny's wrist. "What's that?"

Dagny covered Grete's bracelet with her other hand. "Nothing. Don't you worry about it."

"Give it here," the girl demanded, then snapped her fingers. "Give it!"

"No," Dagny stepped back. She didn't know if the man was reaching for her or not, but she clinched her fist anyway and swung wildly, punching him straight in the armpit. The man grimaced and before he could do anything else, Dagny sprinted away from them, running down the northern pathway.

"Hey! Hey!" the girl shouted. "We'll remember that! Don't-chie *ever* come back here!"

Don't worry, Dagny thought, as the road dipped and the figures disappeared from sight. She never wanted to come back here again.

There were no buildings on this street, just a long iron fence bordering both sides. The brush that crept up to it was so thick, Dagny couldn't see what lay beyond. She wanted to put the encounter with the feathered people out of her mind as soon as possible, but she knew it would gnaw at her for a while. Touching the tin bracelet, Dagny thought of Morgan's coat and how she'd lost that to the Limer's Town men. No one was going to take Grete's bracelet from her.

She walked along for an hour or so before stopping to rest at a bench. Weeds and vines threatened to smother it, and Dagny looked carefully for insects before sitting down. She'd spent enough time itching in the underground.

The first thing she was going to do once she found Melwes and Grete was take a hot bath. A really hot bath. Pulling back her sleeves, Dagny examined her arms; they were covered in red scratches and bite marks, illuminated for the first time in the bright sun. She was surprised at how white she looked. Dagny had always been pale, but now she was *pale* pale. She touched her face and felt her crooked teeth. Maybe she did look gross.

But so what? Anything could be considered gross, depending on who was doing the looking, right? Dagny ran her hands over the weeds growing around the bench before shaking her head and standing up again. She could rest once she found Melwes.

The road continued to descend until the earth on both sides was so high it blocked out her view of the sun. Although she could no longer tell what direction she was heading, the path twisted and curved, bringing Dagny some comfort.

Gradually, the day turned hot. Even in the shade, it felt like the sun was sucking every bit of liquid from her body, and she found herself once again wishing for Pren's canteen.

It must've been lunchtime when Dagny had to stop again. Her stomach was starting to ache and her head had been throbbing for hours. It was a cruel joke the city played on her just then—putting a fountain in the middle of the street. Dagny rushed forward, hoping for water, but everything inside was green and black.

Perfect, she thought. *That's how I've always wanted to go... dying of thirst, face down in sludge.* All this walking was taking a toll as well, compelling Dagny to remove her boots, intent on rubbing the soreness from her feet.

She'd just pulled the second one off when a voice called out, "There you are! I had a feeling I'd find you here." Dagny spun around, almost falling into the fountain. Pren stomped down the path toward her, looking agitated.

Dagny smiled, trying to ease the tension. "Did you change your mind and decide to help me?"

"*Help you?* Stop playing games." He crossed his arms. "Where is it?"

"Where's what?"

"Don't play dumb. Come now. The compass! Where's my compass?"

Dagny studied him, trying to figure out if this was a joke. It wasn't. "I don't have your compass," she replied. "I didn't even know you had one."

"Look, I shouldn't've come here. This place is dangerous, but that compass is important. Give it up already, alright?"

Dagny opened her arms. "Do you see a compass? Do I even have a bag? Where would I hide it?"

Pren poked his head over her shoulder, looking into the fountain, then gazed around the area, looking for a hiding place. "You left, and the compass was gone. You sure you don't have it?"

"*Yes.* I'm not a liar or a thief."

Pren sat on the fountain next to her and sighed. "Must've been the Grouchers. That compass was important. They probably sniffed it out."

"I ran into some strange people-things on my way here. Would those have been the Grouchers?"

Pren shrugged. "Probably."

Dagny stared at the canteens slung around his body. "Don't want to be rude, but can I have some of that, please?"

"Fine," he said, pulling one off and handing it to her.

Dagny gulped down as much water as she could in a single breath, stopped, then drank some more. When she was finished, she wiped her mouth and said, "You know, I'm a bit mad at you."

"Why?"

"I tried following the winding path—it took me straight into Groucher Town, where all the roads were straight with sharp turns."

"You crossed the bridge?" he asked.

"Yeah."

"That was stupid. The bridge went *over* the old road. That's the one you were supposed to follow. And now—"

Dagny shook her head in frustration. "This place is so confusing. I don't understand anything."

"I told you. I knew you'd end up here, but I was hoping you hadn't walked so far. You need to listen—"

"Can you just explain it to me? How is this place even real? What causes the shift? How come no one on the outside knows about it? I mean, they know about Jud as a legend. People don't think it's real."

Pren closed his eyes and rubbed his forehead, like she'd caused it to ache. "What do you want me to say?"

Dagny sighed. "Can you tell me what causes the shift? Start there."

"I don't know. It's always happened."

"Okay..."

"Look, I'm trying to tell you something and you keep interrupting."

"Sorry," Dagny said. "What is it?"

"Listen good, alright? You're on the road to the Silent Keep."

"I thought all roads went there."

"Yeah, but you're on the wrong one. This particular road cuts straight down the middle of it. You stumbled onto the Path of Thorns and you dragged me here, too."

"I didn't drag you here," Dagny said. "I didn't take your compass, remember?"

Pren cocked his head. "How was I supposed to know that?"

Dagny almost laughed at him. "You *belong* here. You're just as confusing as this city."

"You keep changing the subject," Pren said. "You're not taking this seriously."

"Let's go back to the bridge and start over," she said, then thought of the beak-faced man and smiled. "We may have to run from some Grouchers, though. You have your stick?"

Pren frowned at her. "This is what I'm trying to tell you. You can't go back... Not anymore. We're on the Path of Thorns now, and there's only one place it goes."

6

Dagny glanced down the road, back the way she came, not sure how much she believed him. "So you're telling me that if I retrace my steps..."

"You'll still end up at the Keep. No avoiding it."

"Interesting," Dagny said, before biting her thumbnail. "Why is it so dangerous? Or is that impossible to explain, too?"

"No. That much, I can tell you," Pren replied. "We call it the Silent Keep, but long ago it was known as Dretgaol. Its ruled by the Prince. People call him that 'cause no one can remember his actual name. Some of 'em say the Prince and his tower were here before Jud itself."

"A tower?" Dagny thought of Melwes' story of the tower stretching to the stars.

"The Keep was built around it. The tower came first, and the only way to reach Jud Proper from here is to pass through it. Some roads are safer, like the winding path—that one weaves between old parts of the Keep that the Prince no longer watches."

"But the road we're on now..."

"...Runs straight through the center. Right to the tower."

Dagny nodded. "Great. And why is this Prince so bad? What will he do?"

"I don't know. You may get your chance to ask him."

Dagny considered this. "Okay."

Pren narrowed his eyes. "You're being too calm."

"What do you want me to say?" Dagny asked. "You're just telling me I should be concerned without telling me why?" She stared up at the canopy blocking out the sun. "Any idea what time it is?"

"No. And I can't tell you what he'll do, because no one has ever returned after meeting him."

"Oh... Well, if you want to make someone afraid, start with that," Dagny said. She thought she saw Pren smile.

"And *others* say the Prince will destroy your face and turn you into one of his knights, but only if he likes you." Pren studied her closely for a reaction.

"I get the point."

Pren scratched his chin. He seemed to be thinking hard. "*Actually,* they did find someone who went to the tower, but only part of him. His head and feet were missing."

"Stop it."

"No, really, that happened."

"You can still stop. I get it." Dagny stood and wiped the back of her pants. "What if we wait until the shift? Could that change things? Maybe put us in a different part of the city?"

"Little luck on that one," Pren said sarcastically. "We need to go to the tower and get it over with. Better to do so in the daytime. After twilight, the Prince's knights come out to hunt."

"Great. This keeps getting better and better."

Pren frowned. "I tried to tell you."

"If we have to travel to the tower, I want to go back the way I came. It's not that I don't believe you... I just need to see for myself, alright?"

Pren stood and started walking down the path. "Alright. But what I'm telling you is the truth."

On they went in silence. For a time, everything looked the same. The road ascended and the earthen wall on either side became shorter and shorter until Dagny could finally see the sun again. It sat high in the sky now, almost directly overhead.

She still couldn't believe that any of this was real. Morgan had told her so many grand stories of fabulous places; she had wanted to believe him, but as she got older, part of her wasn't sure if the stories were completely true. Not that they were *lies* necessarily, more like strong embellishments. Only now, walking through Jud, having fled from Yunis, on her way to this *Silent Keep*, she thought maybe Morgan had underplayed such things.

Surprisingly, he had never mentioned Jud. And, later, when Dagny came to live with Alex, she devoured any adventurer handbook she could get her hands on, although none had ever discussed the city in detail. The closest she'd gotten was a brief mention in the Talvarind Compendium, and even that glossed over the city and its queen, like they were fairytales written only to give context to the board game.

Dagny huffed in frustration, drawing Pren's eye. She felt entirely unprepared for this place. If she had crossed the Shallow Sea to Solevay or wandered into Ostrotha, she'd feel much more confident about what to expect. Dagny knew those histories like they were her own. But a shifting city? An actual *shifting* city hidden inside a mythical forest?

They passed the bench where Dagny had sat after running from the beak-faced man, but when they reached the horse statues (which should have marked the crossroads) everything had changed. There was no fork in the road; no gang of youths dressed in black-feathered cloaks. Instead, Dagny was greeted by an enormous stone wall with a gaping hole in the middle where the road pushed through.

Pren adjusted his pack and pulled out his club. Beyond the wall, Dagny could make out ash-colored buildings, scorched and scarred by fire.

"What happened here?" she asked.

"Told you."

"Is this the Keep?"

"This is the border," Pren said. "Dretgaol is a little further down. You ready?"

"No."

Pren ignored her and stepped through the hole. She thought he might reach back to help her over the rubble, but he didn't.

The road ran straight ahead. Dagny could see the buildings a little better now. Each one appeared to be a smith or foundry. A faint mist clung to the ground, and even though the fire that had blazed here likely took place long ago, the place still felt hot.

"What were they making?" she asked, glancing into the structures.

"Expanding the Keep—making the tower bigger and bigger. The pieces from this age are all metal."

"So you've been here before? To the main tower?"

"I've seen it from a distance."

They traveled past broken wagons and large metal husks twice the size of a man. A crow watched her from its perch on a stack of rusted iron gears caked with dirt and surrounded by weeds.

The creature made her think of the crow that had saved her life at the Nedgling Tower. Dagny hoped it was somehow watching her now; ready to come swooping down if she needed it.

"Hey Pren, I'm glad you thought I stole your compass. I wouldn't want to be walking through here alone."

"It's my own fault. I should've kept a better eye on it."

"Does anyone else live at the Keep, or is it just the Prince?" she asked.

"There's also the knights... there might be others. I don't know."

"Are those knights looking for Odestinas, too?"

Pren stopped and stared at her. "What now?"

"When I was in the castle with Melwes, we came across a meeting hall for the questing knights."

"The Prince's knights are different."

"Are they looking for Odestinas? It seems like everyone else is."

Pren shook his head. "I'm not. People worship her as if she's a goddess or something. It goes beyond curiosity. It's dangerous. A lot of people have died in that quest." He studied her before speaking again. "You're not, are you? Looking for her? Is that why you came here?"

"No," Dagny said, a bit defensively. "I could not care less about her, honestly."

"Good."

The road turned a corner, then stretched into a long bridge.

"Here we are," Pren began, pointing forward. "Just beyond is the Keep."

The bridge was grated metal, and Dagny could see a moat of jagged stones underneath. "Is it safe?"

"Oh, the bridge is not what you have to worry about," Pren said as he stepped onto it, then lowered his voice. "I never been this close before."

"You don't seem nervous," Dagny said. "You don't work for the Prince, do you? You're not leading me into some trap?"

"Is that a joke?" Pren asked, without turning around. "I don't seem nervous because I don't get nervous. I'm a wonder like that."

Dagny cautiously stepped onto the bridge behind him. "I wish I had that talent."

"You don't seem nervous, either," he said.

"Trust me. I am." Dagny watched as chunks of rusted metal fell onto the jagged stone below with each step they took.

They were about halfway across the bridge when Dagny got her first look at the tower. It peeked over a set of ramparts in the distance, growing in size as they walked. Twisted and multi-pronged, the thing looked like an upside-down claw. The central shaft, massive and dark, ended in a sharp point—the tip of a spear.

"I was expecting it to be more intimidating," Dagny said, chuckling to herself in a vain attempt to ease the tension.

"You don't think that's intimidating?" Pren asked, not realizing her joke. "Wait until we get closer." In a weird way, it felt like he was disappointed in her reaction.

"I also expected it to be taller," she said teasingly.

"Most of it has sunk into the ground. You should probably stop talking now."

The bridge led into a gatehouse; the details of which slowly came into view. The structure had a red hue and appeared to be made of iron, but she had already figured that out from the smell. They were stepping into a world of rust and decay.

Beyond the gate itself stretched a narrow tunnel. Pren stopped before walking under the portcullis. He seemed to be looking for something;

watching for any sign of knights, perhaps? Dagny wanted to ask what his plan was, but kept her mouth shut. After a minute, he stepped to the side and gestured for her to take the lead. *Are you serious?* Dagny thought. *I'm not going first.* She shook her head and Pren shrugged before walking forward.

Anyone could've been watching them here. Either from thin slits that lined the tunnel walls or from small openings in the ceiling. Dagny knew what those were: kill holes where defenders could dump burning oil or poke you with spears. It harkened back to a more brutal age, when people would butcher each other up close.

This was such a bad idea, Dagny thought, as she followed Pren, unsure of her options. The tunnel groaned as they went—a deep aching sound. Like the metal itself was alive. It echoed off the walls; Dagny felt it in her chest.

So much for keeping quiet, she thought, gritting her teeth. You could probably hear the noise across the entire complex. Suddenly, Pren covered his ears and ran ahead without looking back.

Dagny rushed after him, and as soon as she stepped from the metal onto earth, the groaning stopped. She glanced around quickly, almost expecting an entire horde of the Prince's knights to descend upon them. But they seemed to be alone.

In front of her was a courtyard framed by several buildings with glass domes. At the opposite end was a pathway leading to the tower itself. Dagny walked over to Pren and whispered in his ear, "Where to now?"

Once again, he ignored her and began to walk toward the pathway. Dagny reached out and grabbed his shirt, but he shrugged her off and kept going.

What was he *doing?* Dagny thought. This was foolish. She would not be marching up to the tower. There had to be another way. At the very least, shouldn't they make sure they weren't walking into an ambush?

She scanned the courtyard carefully and looked at the glass buildings, trying to see if there were people inside watching them. The buildings reminded her of giant solariums. *Is that what you are? Built to study the sky?* The glass was surprisingly clear, and Dagny could see straight into the structures. They appeared to be elegantly furnished with tall bookshelves and large desks. She didn't see anyone hiding inside.

Pren was halfway across the courtyard by the time she looked over. *Are you really going to leave me?* She didn't want to travel alone, but she would if she had to.

Dagny racked her brain, trying to remember if there had been other paths by the foundries. What if she crawled down to the moat? Maybe she could circle the Keep and climb back out on the other side. It would probably take a lot longer, but might be safer than this. As Pren neared the end of the yard, Dagny wondered if this could be the same Prince from Melwes' story. The one who demanded a tribute. She didn't like the idea of losing her eyes or fingers or anything else that was presently attached to her body.

Her course was decided. Dagny would leave the courtyard, follow the moat of jagged stones, and if the stars allowed it, she'd see Pren on the other side.

As soon as she turned around, the knight grabbed her neck. Panic whipped through her body. The grip was so tight, Dagny thought he might crush her right then, but the knight seemed content just holding her in place. Dagny's mind raced, trying to process what was happening. She couldn't see anything beyond the knight's mask: a blank sheet of silvery metal, cruelly reflecting her own terrified expression. She pulled at the hand, trying to pry it open with all her strength. There was no relief. The grip held firm. A vice of tarnished steel.

Other figures appeared at the edge of her vision. They moved in silence, like wraiths. Dagny tried to get a better look at them but couldn't turn her head to see. It was becoming a challenge just to breathe.

She was afraid of what could happen now if she resisted too much. There was no way she'd be able to fight them off or try to escape. A moment later, another knight came into view, carrying a large chain-linked net. Dread swelled in Dagny's chest as she realized the metal-man intended to toss her inside. Lifting a single leg, she feebly attempted to kick the net away, but the knight simply took her ankle and raised her up awkwardly. As she tilted backward, Dagny's world was consumed by sky, cloudless and blue, and then darkness as the iron net dropped down, enveloping her. The links pulled painfully at her hair and pinched her skin, and Dagny did her best to shield her face. No one said a word. Then, one of the knights yanked the net into the air and moved, leaving no doubt in Dagny's mind where they were taking her.

7

The journey to the Keep was longer than she thought it would be. The knights seemed to walk forever, jostling her around like a meaningless sack of junk. Dagny tried to stay quiet and limp; the men—or what she presumed were men—felt so cold that Dagny knew there'd be no reasoning with them. And Melwes' story of the Prince and the Tower kept playing through her mind. She didn't want these knights to take her tongue by drawing attention to it.

Eventually, the knights stopped. Dagny heard a slight creaking sound, and when they moved again, it was the jerky descending motion of traveling down stairs. She wondered about Pren and whether the knights had him as well. There was no way to know it, though. The metal links kept out almost all light. She hoped he had gotten away and was planning a rescue, but the more she considered this, the more depressing the prospect became. Pren didn't know her, and he certainly didn't owe her anything. The only reason he was even here was because he thought she was a thief. Pren was probably long gone by now.

Dagny felt a coolness wash over her, and a few steps later, the knights dropped her on the ground. The heavy links weighed heavy on her body. Still, Dagny didn't dare to move. She just lay there waiting, certain that at any moment, the knights would yank her up again. And when nothing happened, Dagny started counting the seconds in her head. Finally, after reaching one hundred, she slowly reached out and opened the net, poking her head through.

The space she found herself in was much different from the one she expected. Dagny feared the knights would have dumped her in some dank prison with ancient corpses tacked to the wall, where she'd wait until it was time to have her eyes plucked out. Instead, they had left her near the entrance of an enormous, circular chamber. Small flames glowed in clear lamps throughout the area, and thin translucent curtains covered alcoves in the wall. Dagny could see figures standing on the other side. She hoped they were statues.

Behind her was the staircase she'd come down; there was no sign of the knights. Dagny briefly considered running back up, although something told her that getting out wouldn't be so easy. She scanned the area. Like Pren had said, everything was metal here. The ceiling was domed and emblazoned with star lines; thousands of them. From what she could tell, it appeared someone had painstakingly carved out every single star in the sky and the faint lines connecting them.

Dagny carefully moved across the grated floor, similar to the bridge from earlier. She could see multiple levels down below, each with their own set of pale lights, giving the appearance of even more stars—as if she were surrounded by them; walking through the night sky, only one made of twisted iron.

The curtained figures watched her as she crept forward. They stood erect and still; some appeared to be men with swords and open-faced helmets, but there were beasts and children here, too. Dagny passed a creature resembling a goat with one horn, standing upright on its hind legs; the next alcove contained a boy and girl holding hands. Their features were soft and deformed, almost like they were melting. It was possible that some artisans could have crafted sculptures this realistic, but Dagny was still afraid to pull back the curtains to check.

She reached the center of the chamber. It reminded her of an auditorium in one of those academies back in the City. Several other passages led off from this room, and Dagny studied them, trying to decide on a course of action, when she heard the sound. It stood out as the first thing she'd heard since passing through the gatehouse. Even the metal net—she couldn't recall if that had actually made a noise.

It sounded like... a sigh; a deep releasing of breath, coming from somewhere above. It cleared the fog that had clouded her mind, and Dagny could suddenly feel the weight of the chamber. There was an energy around her of something powerful, like a storm approaching.

The iron grate quivered. Dagny nervously watched the area, her eyes darting between the various passages, trying to figure out where to go; expecting a monstrous beast like Yunis to appear in one of the darkened hallways. She wanted to hide and stay quiet, but that seemed impossible. Dagny could hear her own heart pounding away, threatening to burst from her chest. It was probably echoing across the entire room. And whatever was coming must have already known she was here.

The Thorned Prince. The nameless ruler of Dretgaol. It had to be. Dagny could feel eyes on her body. She knew he was watching.

The chamber itself seemed to be breathing—the dome above slowly contracting and releasing. She stood there, waiting and vulnerable, unsure of what to do. Whether from nerves or the lack of water, her mouth felt so dry, Dagny didn't know if she'd even be able to scream when the time came.

Would the Prince really take her eyes or chew off her hands? She hadn't ever considered something so terrible before. Almost a year ago, men from Limer's Town meant to beat her to death on the roof of the Nedgling Tower; and yesterday the great cat tried to devour her, but Dagny hadn't had time to contemplate either of those things in the moment. Standing here now, waiting for the Prince, none of that seemed as horrific to her as what was coming... The idea of losing her sight... of having some thorned finger reach out to pluck—

The breathing became very distinct. No longer a suggestion of breath, it turned raspy and drawn out. Lingering in the air. Dagny thought she heard a whisper.

Hello? Dagny tried to say, although she wasn't convinced she'd actually said anything out loud.

Something responded, but she couldn't comprehend the words. Mumbled and foreign, it sounded like someone speaking on their deathbed.

"I'm sorry, I don't understand," Dagny said.

The voice strained. A haunting murmur from somewhere beyond. *Was it really a voice?* And, as odd as it seemed, Dagny sensed a sadness in its tone. But if the Prince was speaking to her, it wasn't in a language she'd heard before.

"I'm sorry," Dagny repeated. Her own voice sounding meek and pleading in the great star chamber. "Please don't take my eyes."

There was one last sigh and then silence. A moment later, metal from above creaked as something heavy moved across. It was enough to break the fear rooting her in place. Without another thought, Dagny took off running down a random passage, leaving the great chamber behind.

She *hated* everything about this place. She hated the smell and taste of its rust. She hated the brutality of the knights; the feeling of their hands on her neck. Mirrors lined the walls of the passage, and just like the grated floor, they were seemingly on the verge of falling apart. Dagny glimpsed her reflection in the black-spotted glass as she thundered down the hallway. She could hear the sound of her soft boots on hard metal, echoing loudly.

Dagny stumbled into another chamber. A large and rectangular one, with flakes of rust spread across the floor like the fallen leaves of some weird, corroded autumn. Flames from a ruined chandelier high in the ceiling cast an eerie, orange glow across the space. Dagny stopped to catch her breath. Listening to hear if she was being pursued, and just as before, there was only silence. That mattered little, though. The knights had been silent when they descended on her near the gatehouse. They could be silently pursuing her now.

Glancing down, Dagny noticed her boots and pants were covered in bits of rust. *This whole place is rotting away and taking me with it,* she thought. The Keep may have been the oldest thing in all of Jud, but Dagny wondered how much longer it would last. Someday, soon perhaps, the Silent Keep would collapse in on itself, becoming nothing more than an awful memory. That was fine with her. So long as it waited until she found a way out.

There were more mirrors here; encased in elegantly curved frames. They seemed like strange decorations in a place of such hardness, where legends were born of an eye-stealing Prince. Everything else in the Keep felt savage. Maybe this was part of some cruel joke by the Prince. He'd fill the Keep with fancy mirrors but take your eyes so you'd never be able to see yourself again.

Dagny slowly crossed the room, carefully stepping over the rusted flakes. Even though she'd been racing down the hall only moments before, she was once again concerned about making too much noise. There was something about the place that made you want to stay quiet.

She hoped the chamber would give way to a staircase or passage that could lead to an escape, but as the far side of the room came into view, her heart collapsed. A solid wall of iron greeted her there. No doors... no other hallways... nothing but hard metal. Dagny panicked again, realizing that she would have to return to the star chamber. That's probably why no one chased her now. The Prince knew she'd have to come back. He was probably waiting for her. Allowing Dagny one last chance to view her reflection in his rotting mirrors.

He'd still have to catch her, though. Dagny would not be a willing participant in his game. She was regaining herself. Allowing her frustration to push against the fear she'd felt since being taken by the knights. She turned, readying herself to head back to the star chamber, when she heard another noise. It was not the raspy breath of the Prince; this was a soft humming. A muffled sound, with the tone and rhythm of a voice. An actual voice. As if someone was trying to speak through glass...

Dagny moved between the mirrors, quickly examining each one; trying to figure out where the sound was coming from and which of the mirrors could be false.

She found it on the fourth try. Its surface was speckled with black rot like the others, but there was no reflection there. Instead, Dagny saw a hallway beyond the glass, tapering off into darkness. This wasn't a mirror. It was more of a *window*. She traced the edge of the frame, searching for a hidden latch, and when one didn't reveal itself, Dagny took off her boot, ready to punch it through.

"*Wait*," the voice said, still muffled. Then, suddenly, an image appeared on the other side of the glass: a pale, thin girl with brilliant green hair that flowed down to her waist. The girl approached and pressed her face close to the window. "You mustn't shatter the threshold," she said.

Dagny leaned forward until her own nose and lips were inches from the surface. "Can you help me get out of here?" she whispered.

"You must be *calm*," the girl said. "Take my hand and move very slowly or you'll be caught in the glass. Do you understand?"

Dagny nodded, but she couldn't have been more confused.

The girl placed her hand on the window. "Now you, but be *gentle*," she stressed.

Dagny copied the girl's movements, carefully placing her hand on the glass. A moment later, the girl reached through and grabbed her. Dagny tensed, ready to pull away, when the girl shook her head. "Be gentle."

Moving slowly, like she was trying to enter water without making a ripple, the girl pulled Dagny toward her. It was the strangest sensation. The glass felt cold and soft, like clay, and Dagny watched as the transparent surface stretched and slid around her wrist, then her elbow and shoulder. Instinctively, Dagny pulled her head back as the glass reached her face, then shut her eyes and grimaced, allowing herself to be guided through.

When she emerged, she was standing in a hallway of stone. Dagny could no longer smell the blood-like scent of rust in the air. In fact, she didn't see any metal at all.

She was about to ask where they were when the girl whispered, "Follow me," and turned around.

Dagny hesitated briefly, but obeyed. "Who are you?" she asked softly.

"I'm Lieta. I was brought here a long time ago." The girl was barefoot and wearing a beautifully tailored green dress.

"Brought here? By who? The Prince?"

"No. Not the Prince," Lieta said. "It doesn't matter."

There was sunlight in this new passage, streaming in from stained-glass windows set high in the ceiling above. Dagny looked down at her hands and shirt. Everything was covered in brown flakes of metal, just like her boots.

"Did you see anyone else? I was with a boy when the knights grabbed me," Dagny said, then tried her best to describe Pren.

"If the knights capture someone, they're brought to the Prince's chamber," Lieta replied. "It's only you."

Even though Pren had basically abandoned her, Dagny felt relieved.

She stepped along behind Lieta, following her down the lonely hall. The girl was dressed so strangely. Jade clasps fit her wrists, and the dress formed so well over her body, it seemed to be part of her skin. Dagny had never seen anything like it.

"Where are we?" Dagny asked.

"You are on the other side of Dretgaol," Lieta said, moving quickly, and speaking softly. "The Prince's territory is a dreadful place."

"Right."

"You are fortunate the Prince is feeling sorrowful."

"It didn't feel fortunate," Dagny responded.

"Believe me, it was. When melancholy overtakes the Prince, he's less likely to care if someone slips away. He can be quite horrible otherwise. You *are* one of the uninvited. I can sense it."

"Uninvited? Yeah, I suppose so."

"It's no matter to me. I know not everyone from the outside intends to harm this place, but the Prince fails to see any distinction."

"Who... or *what* is he?"

"A protector. Somewhat." The hallway began to curve, as if they were skirting the wall of an enormous tower. In a certain way, it reminded Dagny of the Oracle Tower on the lagoon.

"I heard he takes people's eyes and ears," Dagny said.

"Yes. I know the same stories," Lieta said. Her voice was soft and pleasant. "These days, there are other things to worry about."

"Is it true, though? About the eyes?"

Lieta toyed with her emerald hair as they walked. "Different versions are told of the same event." Dagny thought that was an odd response. Hadn't Melwes said something similar? "The Prince is very old," Lieta continued. "When so much time passes, memories become distorted."

"How old is he, really?" Dagny asked.

"It's hard to say. There's no one around who can confirm it." Lieta looked back and raised her eyebrows. "But he's older than the city itself."

"That's hard to believe."

Lieta stopped, appeared to listen for any other sounds, then continued, speaking even quieter than before. "All the same, it is true."

The hallway sloped gently upward. There were other mirrored windows here, just like the one she passed through. They peered into more metal rooms on the other side.

"Where are we headed? Is this the way out?" Dagny asked, looking through the glass. She saw a pair of the faceless knights standing guard, seemingly oblivious to her presence.

Lieta turned and considered something for a moment. There was a look of pity on her face. "This is *Dretgaol*," she said. "I'm sorry, but there is no easy way out."

8

"Wait," Dagny said. "Where are you taking me?"

Lieta smiled, trying to set her at ease. "Away from the Prince, of course. He's certain to know that you've escaped, but don't be afraid. You'll be fine so long as—"

"I need to find a way out," Dagny said, her anxiousness once again welling up. "I can't stay here."

Lieta looked down the hall. "We shouldn't linger so close to the border. Something could hear us and pull you back." She reached out and took Dagny's hand. "Come along now. Quickly."

The hallway continued to funnel them upward, and the distance between false mirrors—portals back into the Prince's domain—became wider and wider until Dagny stopped seeing them altogether.

"Does the Prince know about *you*?" Dagny whispered after some time.

"He did once. Though, he's probably forgotten all about me," Lieta said. "I rarely wander over here."

"Well, I appreciate your help," Dagny said. "I really do. But... I need to find someone. A friend. He's in danger."

Lieta shook her head sympathetically. "*You're* the one in danger now, and if you try to leave before its safe, you'll be trapped forever. I hope I've made that clear without frightening you."

"Forever?" she asked, to which Lieta responded by nodding.

With an audible gulp, Dagny continued, "Maybe if you could just—"

"Only the Prince can grant you permission to leave," Lieta said softly. "Perhaps you can persuade him. Although none have before."

Dagny sighed, deciding to let it go for the time being. Her legs were burning from the steep walk. "Where are we? Is this still a part of the Keep?"

"In a way. This is one of the towers. The forgotten Moon Needle," Lieta said. "It used to be quite beautiful. Not to worry, we're getting close."

The girl didn't slow down. In fact, she didn't even seem tired. Dagny tried to keep pace and was about to tell Lieta that she needed to stop, when the ascending hall finally evened out and opened into a cream-colored great room. Several other hallways branched out from this area, leading deeper into the tower. Opulent furniture, covered in dust and touched by decay, lay about the room, and a set of glass doors opened to an outside balcony.

"You can stay here and gather yourself," Lieta said. "I haven't been rude, have I? It's been some time since I've met anyone new..."

"No. You've actually been very nice."

"Can I ask your name?" the girl said, twirling a strand of emerald hair around her finger.

"Dag... Dagny Losh."

"Kustav is around here somewhere," Lieta said. "She'll know you're a guest of mine."

"Who's that?"

"She keeps order in the Needle. The Prince has likely forgotten about her as well. She'll make sure you're cared for. There's an old bedchamber through that hall, just past the dining room, that you can rest in. Feel free to explore, but you must not go back the way we came, or leave the gardens. It isn't safe."

"The gardens?" Dagny asked.

Lieta pointed to the glass doors. A blanket of mold had overtaken much of the interior walls nearby, staining them green and purple. "I need to be clear, do not leave the gardens," she repeated.

Dagny stepped to the doors and gazed outside. A stone staircase led down to a wild area where old tree roots overtook crumbling walls, and in the distance, Dagny could see another building atop a small hill. It was dark and formidable, with a flat roof, sitting somewhere beyond the gardens. Dagny wanted to ask about the building, but instead replied, "Okay. I won't."

When she turned around, Lieta was gone. Dagny scanned the hall and then rushed over to an adjacent doorway, quietly calling out for the girl. She passed through the dining room, and entered a hallway that traced the contour of the tower. Gorgeous brass-framed windows looked down on a yard thick with flowers and dotted with the occasional fountain or statue. Lieta was nowhere to be found.

That's disappointing, Dagny thought. At least she was safe for the moment. Just like everyone Dagny had met from Jud, the green-haired girl left her with more questions than answers.

On the other side of the hallway, Dagny poked her head into a small bath chamber, hopeful that she might finally be able to wash off. But the porcelain sink and tub were stained red and cracked with age. There hadn't been water here for quite some time. Maybe this *Kustav* could help with that.

She did find one room of interest. A little way down, tucked next to a sitting area, was a small library. Cozy and charming, it looked like it had belonged to a young girl. A velvety soft sofa sat underneath a window; and someone had painted a colorful mural of animals having a picnic by a river. They were dressed like people: an otter wearing boots and a nightshirt lounged next to pigeons in hats, and they all listened to a giant toad who donned a cape and sword, frozen in mid-speech.

The books appeared to be children's stories. From what Dagny could tell, some were written in Ostrothian; some were from her own language of the Vahnland; and others were in a tongue completely unrecognizable to her. The books were also diverse in their age. A few were so old they looked ready to crumble, while others seemed relatively new. Dagny suddenly thought of Max and examined the shelves, hoping to find a book about the goose who flew to the moon, but didn't see it.

Hopefully, Lieta would appear again and explain how to get out of the Keep. Dagny couldn't wait much longer. Melwes could still be trapped in that castle, hiding from the cat, and Grete had been in danger for months while Dagny sat around in the underground. Enough time had been wasted already.

Perhaps it was the isolation of the Moon Needle, but for the first time in a long while, Dagny felt a sudden emptiness wash over her. The same sense of loneliness she used to feel in the City. She wondered what Max would be doing now. Would he be missing her? Or would he have moved on with his life? She knew she couldn't be upset if he had, leaving the way she did. He easily could've found another person to spend his time with. Max deserved to be happy. Dagny thought about what it'd be like to hug him again and feel the warmth of his body; to reach up and touch his face.

She pushed her nose against the glass of the small window. Through a break in the distant trees, Dagny could see a faint gray sketch of buildings with scattered chimneys and peaked roofs. *Jud.* It was so peaceful and serene here in the library. How could a place like this exist so close to the Prince's compound of hard metal? The Moon Needle and the yard outside seemed enormous; how in the world could the Thorned Prince just forget it all?

The velvet sofa was the most comfortable thing Dagny had sat on in months; so plush and soft that she could've stayed there for hours. She pulled her knees into her chest and continued to gaze out the window. Regardless of what happened here, no matter what Lieta told her, Dagny needed a plan. There was obviously something unusual about the girl, and she hoped Lieta really was kind. If Dagny had to guess, Lieta appeared to be no more than seventeen years old, but something about her felt much older.

Seventeen... it was the same age Dagny had been when she fell into the Oracle's Tower and crossed through Limer's Town. So much had happened in such a short amount of time. Falling into that tower had changed her life, entirely. In many ways, Dagny felt like a completely different person now.

Eventually, the feeling of emptiness subsided, and the afternoon passed by with Dagny thumbing through the library's books. She read about a girl who lived under a swamp and about mouse knights riding giant bees. As the day turned to twilight, she watched the yard outside, anxiously waiting for the shift. But if something happened, she barely noticed. Dagny heard no sounds but thought the distant skyline might have changed *slightly*. It was much, much different from the last time she'd witnessed the shift; caught in the wall of the secret castle.

It was dark by the time Dagny stepped into the hallway, driven to find food by an aching hunger in her belly. She wandered back to the dining room and to her delight, a magnificent feast was displayed across the table. There was a glazed bird with apples coated in thick syrup, onion soup, and boiled potatoes. Two dozen candles lit the space, and a fine silk cloth ran the length of the table, upon which fragile glassware was filled with sweet wine. This must've been the work of Kustav. Dagny still hadn't caught sight of the woman yet.

As hungry as she was, Dagny still ate slowly, trying to be respectful. She was conscious of her rough appearance in this regal-looking place and wanted to at least act with some amount of etiquette, even though she was alone. Lieta had rescued her, after all, and this was her home.

When she finished, Dagny wandered back to the small bath, wondering if accommodations had been made there as well. Sure enough, the tub had been filled with warm water, complete with soap and a brush. Between this and the meal, it was truly amazing how well Kustav and Lieta were treating her. She wished she could thank them, but a quick look back into the hall revealed no one. Dagny kicked off her boots and threw her clothes to the floor, keeping on Grete's bracelet. It felt like it had been years since she had a proper bath. She didn't know that she could miss a simple thing so much.

Pinching her nose shut, Dagny ducked under the water and held her breath for as long as she could. She pictured the flakes of rust and the grime of the underworld slowly peeling from her body. Months of dirt and muck. The water was warm, but she wished it was *hot*. So hot it could burn away what didn't wash off.

She emerged and opened her eyes to the grayest face she'd ever seen. Like a witch from a horrible child-eating fairytale, the nose was crooked and long, and the chin, slightly off-center, seemed to be crusted with dark scales.

Dagny gasped, too terrified to scream. The woman was watching her as she sat naked in the bath. Cracked lips peeled apart, revealing a mouth of swollen gums framing dark teeth. Suddenly, the woman's hand reached toward Dagny's head.

"No!" Dagny cried, jolting away. Only then did she notice that the woman's gnarled fist held the washing brush.

"Be still," was all the woman croaked out. Her free hand grabbed Dagny's bare shoulder while the brush worked its way through her wet hair, pulling through knots.

"*Ow*," Dagny cried out. It was all so shocking that Dagny didn't know how to respond. Her brain slogged through what was happening: the woman's appearance; the rough hand on her skin. Dagny finally muttered, "You don't need to do that. It hurts."

The old woman held her firmly in place, ignoring her complaints, and after a while, the knots began to free. Once Dagny's hair was combed, the woman pushed her forward and started scrubbing her back, muttering, "Filthy, filthy thing."

Dagny almost laughed at the absurdity of her situation. Lieta had no doubt sent Kustav to care for her, and in the process, almost frightened Dagny to death.

The woman spun her around, intent to wash her front, when Dagny covered herself and shouted, "No! That's enough. I'll do it!"

"Fine, then." Kustav dropped the soap into the tub and stepped back. Crossing her arms, the woman looked offended.

"I'm sorry about how I reacted," Dagny said. "You surprised me."

Kustav leaned down toward Dagny's face. "'Cause of *this*?" she asked, pointing to her gray nose.

Dagny sucked in air. "No."

Kustav gave her a suspicious look. "Beauty wrinkles," she whispered, pointing now to her crusty lips. "It erodes and cracks and withers. Everything crumbles. Preservation occurs only in the amber. In the blood of Lazim."

"Alright..." Dagny said, trying to stay polite. "Thank you for your assistance. I'd like to be alone now."

Kustav huffed, gave Dagny's body one last look, then turned around and left.

As soon as she was certain that Kustav was gone, Dagny leapt out of the tub and closed the door. That was one of the weirder things to happen, even in a city of faceless knights, giant cats, and an eye-stealing prince. Dagny glanced at the wet floor. Kustav had taken her shirt and pants, leaving only her boots. She considered chasing after the old woman, but the experience had left her rattled, and the last thing Dagny wanted was a confrontation in the nude.

The boots smelled awful, but Dagny pulled them on anyway, then sat for a while on the edge of the tub. Lieta had mentioned a bedroom, and Dagny thought she'd seen one nearby. Perhaps there was an outfit there that Dagny could borrow until she retrieved her clothes from Kustav. Lieta seemed like she would be a similar fit, after all.

When enough time had passed, Dagny peeked into the hallway, then clumsily tiptoed down the passage. Sure enough, the room she had thought was a bedchamber contained an enormous mattress large enough to fit four people. She grabbed a blanket from the floor and covered herself before wandering over to a massive wardrobe against the opposite wall. Everything inside was nicer than what Dagny would've chosen to wear. She took out a delicate dress the color of midnight and pulled it down over her head. The hem stopped just below her knees, but Dagny was glad about the length. The outfit wouldn't restrict her, and she could easily move... or run if she had to.

Dagny walked to a silver-framed mirror by the fireplace and looked herself over. A long scratch marked the top of her lip, and her cheeks were pale and gaunt from months of eating mushrooms and worms in the dark, but the shape of the dress hugged her form surprisingly well. *If this tailor ever moved to the City, they'd sell enough to buy a palace,* Dagny thought. She stepped back and ran her hand over the silky fabric. In an odd way, she looked almost... *seductive.* Dagny shook her head at the stupidity of it.

It seemed like she had aged years since last seeing her reflection. What would men think of her now, dressed like this? None of them had paid her much attention before, other than Max. It was amazing what power women could possess if they were beautiful. Women like Cate Benzara, or Telga. Even her sister. Dagny wondered if she would ever appear pretty enough to experience that.

Lieta's jewelry chest stood near the wardrobe, and Dagny tried on a pair of earrings and a silver necklace. What was it that truly drove a person's desire? She knew the simple answer, of course. But was it *really* just beauty and the promise of sex? It seemed so ridiculous. There had to be something else. Did love factor into it at all? Dagny stood at the mirror for a long time, studying her face and the bottom row of her crooked teeth, wondering how much she even cared.

9

The next morning, Dagny snuck out of the library as dawn was breaking and quietly made her way into the great hall. She wished she had a better outfit for trekking through the gardens, but the thin black dress would have to make do.

This whole place was strange beyond anything Dagny could've imagined, and there was something else, too, gnawing in the back of her mind. Maybe it was nerves over Melwes and Grete. Her pulse quickened every time she thought about them. She needed to escape the Needle and find the boy, and she needed to find her sister. Dagny had done her best to shut Grete out of her mind during those months in the underground—when all she could do was wait—and now that she was so close, it felt as though her chest might explode.

When she was certain that Kustav wasn't around, Dagny crossed the hall to the garden balcony and rushed down the stone steps into the yard. Yesterday had been a whirlwind of emotions. Actually, ever since she entered the wall with Melwes, it had been one stressful encounter after another. She had hoped last night would've given her a chance to collect her thoughts, but that was proving to be impossible.

Dagny reached the canopy of crooked trees shortly before the sun lit up the field. Almost immediately, the path became wild and rambling, branching off in all directions like tentacles. It had looked all too easy from the library's window. However, down here in the gardens, Dagny couldn't figure out which way to go.

She sighed and picked a pathway to her right. If she couldn't find her way to the building today, she would try again tomorrow or in the days after. Even though Lieta warned her about leaving the grounds, this had to be the way through. Dagny only needed to make sure not to get lost, and to make it back before twilight.

An idea came to her. She could leave her own trail markers. Dagny rubbed her fingers over the dress, considering the thinness of the material, then she pulled the dress over her head, placed the hem in her mouth, and bit at it until she could tear off a few sections.

She started down the trail, tying the strips to tree limbs whenever the path split. Hopefully, Lieta wouldn't be too upset at the ruined garment if she saw her again. The girl seemed to have plenty of outfits to spare.

The torn skirt was well above her knees when Dagny stumbled into the clearing of statues. The sun was bright here, and the ground was made up entirely of wildflowers. Vines had overtaken many of the statues themselves, but Dagny still caught glimpses of the carved men and animals in the foliage, their faces worn away by time.

Dagny surveyed the bushes surrounding the clearing, making sure nothing was watching her from the shadows before entering. It felt peaceful in the open space. The wind rustled the trees nearby, and the sun warmed her body, making for a pleasant change.

As she moved forward, Dagny spotted even more statues further away, blending into the far end of the clearing. One of them, a large and hulking giant, towered over all the others. At first Dagny thought it to be just an odd-shaped earthen mound, but it was a statue alright—a massive lump of weeds and dirt-covered stone... and easily climbable.

A minute later, Dagny found herself halfway up the statue's back. When she reached the shoulders, she stopped to gather herself and gazed over the clearing. The area below looked like some kind of royal court cluttered with other crown-wearing figures, and one who appeared to be a knight, although its sword was broken. They all looked as though they were coming to pay the giant tribute.

Crunching her way over bits of crumbled rock, Dagny stepped onto the giant's broad head, took a deep breath, and turned her attention to the tree line. She found the dark building almost immediately: fifty or so yards away, on top of a small hill; it was windowless and rectangular, with jagged battlements framing its roof. The building jutted out from an enormous wall like a gatehouse, and from what Dagny could tell, the wall looked as though it surrounded the entire gardens.

Taking her time, and studying the scene further, Dagny was almost certain that the key to getting out of the gardens ran straight through that building. She committed the route to memory, and once she was sure of the approach, Dagny carefully climbed back to the ground and left the clearing behind.

Making her way through the wild brush, Dagny skirted an outcrop breaking above the bushes and stepped across a shallow creek. Its cold water seeped into her boots and froze her toes. But she kept pushing forward, until finally, she broke out of the trees and found herself standing at the edge of a winding path leading up to the wall.

The building was made of old, rough stone; the kind that could snag your clothes and never let go, and the entry doors were made of wood.

Heavy and black, they soaked up every ray of sunlight and buckled outward from the weight of the stones above.

The most unusual thing was the crystalized face resting on the surface of the doors. The face appeared feminine, but Dagny couldn't tell if it was meant to be a man or woman. Weird lettering, also made of crystals, lay under the chin. Dagny didn't *think* it was another language—the lettering was disjointed and inconsistent—it was more nonsensical than anything else. She walked up to the doors and pushed, and just as she expected, they didn't budge.

Still, Dagny hadn't come all this way for nothing. There had to be some kind of trick here. She rubbed her finger over the crystals, and to her surprise, they moved. Like pieces on a game board, the letters were attached to the door but could slide around. That had to be the way inside. Just rearranging the letters in a certain order to open the doors. It seemed simple enough, but Dagny had no idea where to start and was hesitant about fiddling with the thing too much. Lieta had warned her that leaving the gardens was dangerous. The last thing Dagny wanted to do was set off some sort of trap.

When the sun began to pass its peak in the sky, Dagny reluctantly turned away from the building and headed back to the Needle, following the black ribbons. She left them hanging in the tree branches so she could find the path again, optimistic that no one else would stumble upon them in the meantime.

❧

Dagny was hoping to see Lieta upon her return to the Needle, but once again, the girl was nowhere to be found. She did catch a glimpse of

Kustav shambling down the hall, and quickly dodged into the library to avoid an encounter with the woman.

After quietly closing the door, Dagny settled onto the sofa and ended up falling asleep while reading a book about some artist from Ostrotha whose paintings created doorways into magical worlds. When she finally awoke, it was pitch dark. Dagny stumbled into the hallway, rubbing the sleep from her eyes, feeling like she'd consumed a barrel of wine. A faint light flickered from the direction of the dining chamber, and Dagny wandered toward it, wondering if another feast awaited her.

When she entered the room, however, there was only that single flickering candle. Dagny found the kitchen nearby, coated in cobwebs. The stove was rusty, and the entire space looked like it hadn't been used in decades.

"Am I losing my senses?" Dagny mumbled aloud. *Caught in a dream?* She took the candle from the table and walked the floor, moving into the great hall near the gardens. It was there that she discovered a circular staircase hidden behind a decorative screen. With nothing else to do, and curious as to where it led, Dagny traveled up the steps, passing small landings and doors that opened into an assortment of rooms: an artist's studio with easels and a table covered in splotches of paint; another with a narrow bed, its mattress stained black, like someone had spilled ink, or something else, there.

Further and further she climbed until she could hear wind rustling and caught the scent of fresh air. She emerged onto the rooftop: a flat space, open to the sky. It was dark, but Dagny could make out Lieta sitting alone at a small table, her hair catching the dim light from Dagny's candle.

"I thought you left me," Lieta said with a hint of sadness in her voice.

"Left you? Where would I go? I fell asleep in the library."

Lieta turned toward her. "I looked for you there."

"That's weird," Dagny said. "I don't know what to say. I *was* there, though. I wouldn't lie to you."

"You wouldn't?" Lieta asked, rising.

"No..." Dagny stepped back, nervously. The cool wind cut through her thin dress, and she grasped the lamp tightly to stop her hands from shaking.

"You promise?" Lieta asked. "You *promise* you wouldn't lie to me?" Her hair looked wild and alive.

"Of course."

Lieta moved close, into the light. "It's unfortunate you can't see the stars tonight," she said. "The fog drifts up from the weeds and covers the sky. You can never go into the fog—"

"Alright—"

"I wouldn't want you to get lost."

Dagny chewed her lip before speaking. "Umm, look, I really need to find a way out of here. Too much time has passed—"

"The solstice."

"What?"

"The solstice," Lieta repeated. "That's when the Prince leaves for a day and a night."

"How long until—"

"Two weeks."

The words hit Dagny like a gust of frigid air. "No. I can't..."

"That's longer than you were hoping for, I know," Lieta said. "If there was any other way, I'd show you, but I'm concerned for your safety."

"How come you care so much?" Dagny asked. "You don't even know me."

Lieta's eyes widened. "But I *want* to. I want to know you. That's why I wished to speak with you tonight. So you could tell me."

Dagny wasn't sure what Lieta wanted to know exactly. "Well, I'm from a neighborhood called Rork, by the lagoon."

"The lagoon..." Lieta echoed. "And what do you do there?" She appeared to be genuinely interested.

"I don't know. Try to learn new things? Explore? Listen to music." It sounded embarrassingly childish.

"That's nice," Lieta said, leaning even closer.

"Where did you go before?" Dagny asked suddenly. "You just vanished."

"I had places where I was needed." Lieta pointed at Dagny's body and grinned. "I'm glad you found a dress you like. Your other clothes were a bit messy. I don't mind that it's torn."

Dagny felt awkward having the girl examine her. "Yeah, sorry about that. It's been a while since I had a fresh outfit. I hope it's okay that I borrowed it."

Lieta nodded. "You can keep it. You can have anything here you like."

"Really? Why?" Dagny asked.

"I'll never wear most of those things," Lieta said with a shrug. "I'm glad to share."

Dagny gave her a polite smile. "Kustav took my old clothes, so I didn't have much of a choice."

"Did you have a pleasant time with her?"

"Kustav?" Dagny watched Lieta's expression, trying to figure out if she was joking. "It was... fine." She took a deep breath of the night air, fragrant with the sweet rot of wet earth. "How does this tower exist in the same place as the Silent Keep?" she asked. "It seems too big to be forgotten about."

"Be that as it may, the Prince has forgotten it all the same."

"Who is he, really?"

"The Prince came from the stars at the beginning of one of the creation cycles. In the early years, he created many towers trying to bridge the gap in the sky. The Silent Keep is what remains from his first tower. It was here before Jud and before the world changed."

Dagny reflected on the stories she'd heard. "I don't know much... I thought Odestinas built the city."

"Jud, yes. But there have always been things that came before. There's never been a true beginning—to anything, really. It's all a cycle, and the Prince's tower marks the end of the last one. He's lived an entire age; however, he may well pass before the peak of this next one." Lieta gazed up at the fog. "I feel like a child whenever I'm under the night sky, even when it's clouded... is that strange? It's as though I can feel myself getting younger. Rebirthed in a way."

Dagny wasn't ready to shift topics, so she continued with her questions about the Prince. "So what's his connection to Jud? Why is he still here?"

"He'd been looking for a way back to the stars but never found it. I'm afraid he's completely abandoned the idea of ever returning. I can't fault him for giving up. He's been searching since before the floods, after all."

"Are you talking about the flood myth?" Dagny asked. "When the world drowned?"

Lieta lowered her face and closed her eyes. When she spoke again, it was as if recalling a distant memory. "When the waters receded, the forest emerged from the mists and took root in the fertile ground of the vanishing sea. That's what brought Odestinas here. She's from the forest and appeared when it did. She met the Prince in his hallowed hall and spent a thousand years dwelling with him. He made this palace for her, joining it with his tower."

"The Moon Needle? The Needle is the palace where Odestinas first lived?"

"It's a part of it."

"And at some point, she decided to build Jud?" Dagny asked.

"Create is a better word. She wanted to give life to dreams of the time before. That's what Jud is: a memory."

"From before the floods..." Dagny said.

"Yes."

"What happened to her?"

"Odestinas watched over Jud for a long time. But it wasn't *all* she did. She would vanish on occasion... for years or decades, returning to Lazim or—as some would say—ruling over a very different court in the deep underground. The Prince would sulk and withdraw into his tower when she left, and *others* would try to rule the city."

"Others? You mean like the Kings of Amber?" Dagny asked.

Lieta glanced at her. "Yes."

"I heard they hid Jud from the outside world."

"They thought Jud was theirs," Lieta said. "But Jud didn't belong to them. They had no right to rule it."

"And Odestinas... she would return from time to time?"

Lieta nodded. "Until the Imposter came."

"I've heard about him, too," Dagny said. "Who was he exactly? What happened?"

"The Imposter was a warlord and Emperor of Man. He drenched the world in metal and ushered in the new era. He promised the Prince a way to reach the stars and was granted an invitation to Jud. But he was a liar and only sought to plunder Jud of its dreams. He imprisoned Odestinas under the Cauldron."

"Wasn't she exiled?" Dagny said. "I thought she wandered the land until she died."

Lieta frowned at Dagny. "Odestinas was sealed away in the deep. Underneath an impenetrable slab of black iron, the *Sepulcha Hungus*, along with her most loyal companions."

Companions... A horrible realization overtook Dagny. "You mean the animals? The great bear guardian—"

"She had raised the animal as a cub with the Prince. The Imposter buried it, too."

"That's terrible," Dagny said.

"No one knew what happened to Odestinas, and the city's daughters and knights searched all over for her. Then one night during the lunar celebration, the Imposter invited Jud's princesses to his great ironworks, built at the forest's edge, where he promised to reveal the Queen's whereabouts. Instead, he turned all the daughters to metal, where they spent their remaining years watching the world pass. The Prince hunted for the Imposter, looking for vengeance, but the Emperor of Man had already vanished. Now the Prince sits silently in his tower, having lost both Odestinas and his way back home."

Dagny took a moment before responding. "I think that's the saddest story I've ever heard."

"Not many people know what really happened to the Queen. Even to this day, there are so many different tales. People believe what they want."

"I've heard about the princesses before..."

"Some of them used to live here. I came much later, of course."

"Are *you* a princess? Was Odestinas your mother?" Dagny asked, suddenly realizing the foolishness of her question. The Queen would've been thousands of years old, possibly, and Lieta was a teenager.

"In a way, she is the mother of every child who comes to Jud."

"What's that mean?"

"The children of Jud were scattered across the land during the rupturing. Their spirits spread like dandy-flower seeds blown by the wind. For those who belong here, traces of old Jud remain deep inside. Such children need only to follow the path set by Odestinas and return." Lieta turned her attention back to Dagny. "Would you like it, if I were a princess?"

"I don't know," Dagny said, shrugging. "It wouldn't matter."

Lieta smiled.

Dagny wasn't sure how much of these stories she should believe. Lieta was talking about Jud emerging from a dream. Melwes had said something similar, and then, of course, there were the dreams that Grete had. But that was only after Grete left the Rakesmount and joined up with Sliver. Even then, Grete seemed convinced the dreams were somehow connected to the puzzle box; Dagny didn't remember her sister having such intense dreams as a little girl. It all made her head spin.

Lieta took Dagny's hand and sat her down on a stone bench close to the edge. "Can I say something?" she asked.

"Sure," Dagny answered.

"I know you're just being nice to me because I helped you, and you have nowhere to go right now."

The comment surprised her. Dagny was about to respond when Lieta cut her off. "Don't lie to me, please."

Dagny chewed her lip again and nodded. "Right. Fine... This whole place, it's very strange. I feel vulnerable here. What am I supposed to say? You make me nervous."

"But why?" Lieta looked hurt.

"You just do. I'm not from here. I don't understand it. I don't understand you."

Lieta rocked back and forth on the bench, staring at the floor. "Is that all?"

"...You asked me to be honest."

"That's fine. You can go. We've talked long enough."

"I didn't mean to make you upset," Dagny said, immediately regretting the harshness of her words. "This is difficult for me."

"I'm sorry if I'm *strange*. I'm sorry I make you uncomfortable." Lieta seemed on the verge of crying.

"It's alright," Dagny said. "Really. I'm strange, too. Everyone thought so back home."

"It's so lonely here." Lieta put her face in her hands. "I'm so alone. You wouldn't understand."

Dagny let out a nervous chuckle.

"You're laughing at me?"

"No. I can relate, that's all. Loneliness is something I understand." Dagny tried her best to be gentle. "I take back what I said before. You caught me when I was tired and not thinking clearly. Can you forgive me?"

Lieta lifted her head and eyed Dagny suspiciously. "You don't mean that. You're just trying to be nice again."

Dagny smiled. "What's wrong with being nice? And I *do* mean it. I told you I wouldn't lie."

Lieta took in a slow, deep breath. "I feel so foolish. It's been a while since I felt anything. Even sadness. Something about your presence here has made me want to feel again." Lieta gazed out into the night. "When it's not cloudy, you can see every star that's ever existed. I wish I could've shown you that."

"It sounds beautiful." Dagny looked out now, too. "Even though it's foggy, it's still beautiful."

"Sometimes I come here, shut my eyes and imagine I'm floating away." Without warning, Lieta leapt up and stepped toward the edge of the tower.

Dagny felt anxious. There was no fence or wall around the platform, just a straight drop-off to the ground below. "What are you doing?" she asked, trying not to sound too alarmed.

Lieta ignored her question, spun around, and continued to slide backward until her heels were hanging over the edge. Then she closed her eyes and spread her arms wide.

"*Lieta,*" Dagny whispered. "Come back. You're scaring me."

"Sometimes I think about stepping off, but I never do. Maybe tonight I finally will."

"Wait, what?" Dagny said, rising. "Please, just come back here. Let's talk more."

Lieta didn't answer.

Dagny was hesitant about moving too close. The last thing she wanted was for Lieta to fall and pull her along. But she was also concerned about the girl, and despite her better judgment, Dagny carefully reached toward her. Just then, Lieta tilted backward. Was she really going to do it? Without another thought, Dagny sprung forward, grabbed the top of Lieta's green dress, and yanked her away from the edge. They both fell to the stone floor, with Lieta tumbling on top of her.

"What is wrong with you?!" Dagny shouted. The night's chill had evaporated in an instant. Sweat streamed down her neck and slicked the undersides of her arms.

Lieta opened her eyes and smiled wildly. "You've never thought about jumping into the unknown?" she asked. "If only to see what would happen?"

"No!" Dagny replied, panting hard. "And it's not an unknown. You'd smash onto the ground and die."

"I wouldn't really jump," Lieta said, still smiling. "I told you I'm strange."

That was an understatement. "Don't do that again," Dagny said, trying to squirm out from under her. "Can you get off of me, please?"

Suddenly, Lieta leaned down and kissed her.

The move surprised Dagny. She turned her face away and tried to swallow, but her mouth was dry. "What was that for?"

"Caring whether I fall." The full weight of Lieta's body was on top of her now. It felt like the girl was deliberately trying to make herself heavier.

Before any more words could be said, Lieta gently pressed her forehead into Dagny's. For a moment, Dagny thought she might kiss her again, but instead, Lieta whispered, "Can I tell you something else?"

"Okay..." Dagny replied, nervous over what Lieta was about to say.

"Sometimes I think I'm already dead."

10

Dagny asked no more questions on the roof of the tower. She just wanted to get somewhere safe, where she didn't have to worry about Lieta leaping off into the darkness.

They wandered down to the dining room, where there was now a large bowl of fruit on the table. Lieta plucked at it, acting like nothing had happened.

"It's late," she said. "You'll forgive Kustav if this is all she allows us tonight."

"Sure," Dagny said, still feeling anxious. "I don't need much. Where is she, anyway?"

"Oh, probably watching us."

"That's creepy," Dagny said, scanning the walls for hidden holes.

"Yes. I suppose it is," Lieta said, then grabbed several large berries, ate one, and placed another in Dagny's mouth. Her fingers were warm and salty, not the hands of a corpse. As ridiculous as it seemed, Dagny had considered the possibility that Lieta really was a ghost, stalking the Moon Needle for the last thousand years.

"Who is she?" Dagny asked, squishing the berry in her mouth and wiping the juice from her chin. "Kustav?"

"The steward of the Needle. This will sound odd, but I don't know much about her, even after all these years—where she's from, how old she is—it's all a mystery to me. There used to be others. She's the only one left now."

Dagny nodded. "And where did you come from?"

"Somewhere else." Her statement was followed by a long silence.

"We don't have to talk about it," Dagny said, sensing her discomfort.

Lieta put her head on the table and gazed up at Dagny, an innocent expression on her face. "Can you tell me more of what your life is like? Would that be alright?"

"Sure. That would be fine."

Lieta closed her eyes. "Tell me something nice."

The girl seemed like a child now, lying down for the evening, listening to a bedtime story. Dagny told her about the Viddry Park Zoo, and playing Talvarind at Sorn Rue. She felt sad for Lieta, stuck in this tower. It reminded her of finding Grete in the old palace gardens. Her sister was desperate for a peaceful life, just an opportunity to live like a normal person with friends and family, doing normal things that anyone should be allowed to do.

Dagny thought of Lucas and Abrielle. She told Lieta of the children and playing games like *Hunters and the Hunted*, and about how she hoped they would understand why she had to leave without saying goodbye. When Dagny paused, waiting for Lieta to respond, she realized the girl was asleep.

Dagny reached over and moved a strand of emerald hair away from Lieta's mouth. She seemed so serene and delicate in the quiet stillness of the dining hall, her head resting on the polished table. The loneliness of the Moon Needle was too much. Why would anyone choose to live here for so many years? Lieta was certainly old enough to be making her own way. It was obvious that she *wanted* more. The only thing Dagny could think of was that something must've traumatized Lieta into staying at the tower with Kustav. And that just felt wrong. Didn't Lieta deserve a fulfilling life like the rest of them?

Dagny took a quiet breath. She was glad Lieta was sleeping. This whole night had been too much already. She needed to get her head straight. Dagny left Lieta in the dining hall, taking one last look at her before quietly slipping away.

❧

In the darkness of the bedroom, Dagny recounted her journey into the Oracle Tower almost a year ago. She remembered that the boy, Jorgie, had also been driven there because of a dream. Dagny wished she had asked him more about it—she'd been so focused on getting out of the tower alive that she let the details of it slip past her. Seanmare mentioned the Oracle, too, during their celebration in the Marsh. What was it she had said? Something about the Oracles coming from the Eternal Forest; that they existed in a separate reality from everyone else. Dagny felt like she was caught inside of a puzzle, certain that the pieces fit together, but unsure of where and how.

The towers... when she first saw the Oracle Tower with Rodolph and Max, Dagny thought it was nothing more than some abandoned structure in the lagoon. She quickly discovered there was much more to it than that. That tower had attracted the crow and the Oracle, and was built to study the sky. Maybe it had even marked an entrance to the Under Road before sinking into the swamp. Then there was the

Nedgling Tower, where Dagny almost lost her life to Jago and his men. Marfisi said it was the tallest tower ever built, but had since crumbled into ruin. Now, lying in the Moon Needle, Dagny couldn't help wondering if the Thorned Prince had some role in building all of the old towers from here to the lagoon.

The Needle was different from those others, of course. Although lonely, it wasn't crumbling. It still held some of the mysterious romance from when it housed Odestinas' princesses and was the center of Jud. The place was seductive, in a ghoulish sort of way. Dagny could almost feel the weight of the sadness here, like a solid, tangible thing. There was a loss within these walls. The loss of youth; the denial of passion and life. It seemed to make her ache to be loved and touched.

The feeling came on suddenly. Dagny sighed and rolled onto her back. Although she hadn't felt this way for a long time, she wished that someone was lying next to her. Someone who could hold her; put their hand on her stomach and pull her body into theirs. It didn't matter if it was Max or someone else. Anyone with lips and fingers, who could caress her bare hip, and the inside of her thigh and...

Something sharp pinched her leg. A nail plucking the skin just below her groin. Dagny kicked and threw the covers off, pushing herself back against the far wall. She was blind in the darkness. The bedchamber might as well have been a tomb far underground. Swinging her arms out, Dagny felt for a shape, but there was nothing.

"Who's there?" she shouted.

When no one answered, Dagny pulled her leg into her chest, then thrust it out furiously, hoping to connect with whatever hovered over the bed. Her foot found only air.

Something *had* been here, though, only moments before. She could feel the twinge of pain on her thigh and rubbed the sore spot.

"Who's *there*?" she cried. Just then, a thought came to her: *Kustav.* Dagny didn't know why she thought of the old woman, but imagined her all the same; her gray nails pinching and twisting her skin.

Dagny rolled across the giant bed and fell onto the floor. She crawled over to the door, found the handle, and lunged into the hallway. A single lamp and a tiny orb of light hung in the distance. Dagny rushed forward. If the woman thought she was going to sneak away after that, she was mistaken.

Dagny was beyond angry. Steward or not, how dare Kustav slip into her room and touch her like that? The bathtub was one thing. That encounter had shocked her, and she let it go, as uncomfortable as it had been. But this? This was different.

Clinching her teeth, Dagny broke into a sprint, readying herself for a confrontation. When she reached the light, however, she found only a small candle encased in glass and resting alone on a stone ledge. The old woman was nowhere to be seen.

Had she imagined the whole thing? Dagny pulled up her dress and examined her thigh in the faint light. Sure enough, a bloody welt marked her skin. Maybe something else had caused it... a bug, perhaps? But no, that didn't feel right. Dagny had been bitten by plenty of bugs before, and she knew the difference between that and a pinch. A memory sprung up in her mind. Of a time when four of her cousins had chased her into a corner of their tenement building and scratched and pinched her arms until she fell to the floor crying. Those cousins were probably dead now, too. Buried beneath mud and rotten wood.

Dagny took the candle off the wall, walked back to the bedroom and stopped. There was no way she'd be able to sleep in there again. She thought for a moment. *The library.* Yes, she could make that work. Dagny pushed open the bedroom door, grabbed her boots, and hurried down the hall.

Almost immediately, she felt comforted in the presence of Lieta's books. There was no lock on the door, so Dagny did her best to barricade it with one of the cushioned chairs. At the very least, she'd be able to hear it drag across the floor if someone decided to push their way in. When that was finished, Dagny curled up on the sofa and tried her best to relax.

Two weeks. Two weeks until the summer solstice. Then Dagny could leave and find Grete. It already felt like she'd been at the Needle for a month. In the back of her mind, Dagny wondered if she'd really be able to leave at the solstice, or if Lieta was misleading her.

Dagny pressed her face to the window. The sky was still cloudy, blocking out every star, but somehow she could see the ground below; something was illuminating it. Dagny scanned the grounds until she found the source: a lamp, hovering near one of the headless statues. This one rocked slowly, and its light caught a hunched figure, bathing it in amber.

Dagny was smushing her nose so hard against the glass that the entire window pane fogged over, and she had to quickly wipe it off and adjust her position before looking back down.

By the time she did, the lamp had made its way further down the path and into the garden proper. It took a minute for Dagny to spot the figure again, and this time she was certain of who it was. There were only two other people in the Needle, and Dagny recognized the shuffling gait of Kustav. But what was she doing out there?

Instinctively, Dagny reached down and touched her leg, rubbing the welt. She considered rushing out of the tower and chasing after the woman, but Lieta's warning about staying clear of the fog echoed in her mind, and the old woman also frightened her. If Kustav really was the type of person to sneak into a bedroom and tear at someone's skin, did Dagny really want to catch her outside in the dark?

She continued to watch Kustav shuffle and weave between trees and hedges. On several occasions, Dagny lost sight of her completely and thought the woman simply vanished into the night, only to see her reappear some distance away.

The glow of Kustav's lamp became so faint, it was almost impossible to see. Just a tiny pinprick of light on the far horizon. It stopped for a while, hovering in the air, until Dagny's vision blurred. And then the light went out. Dagny strained her eyes, searching for it, but couldn't see anything except the reflection of her own candle in the glass. It was alright, though. She knew where Kustav had gone. That much was clear to her. The old woman was heading to the crystal face and the dark building on the hill.

11

The mystery of the building on the hill consumed Dagny. She couldn't get the crystalized face out of her mind but didn't want to return until she had some idea of how to unlock it. She spent the next morning and afternoon skimming through every book in the small library for clues, checking the hallway often for Lieta.

By nightfall, the girl still hadn't appeared.

Dagny tried to focus during her time alone, reminding herself of why she'd come to Jud in the first place. This wasn't her city. And although she never felt like she belonged in Rork, she certainly didn't belong in the Moon Needle.

When it came to Lieta, it was hard to figure out the right decision. Dagny was planning to leave at the first opportunity and wondered if she should try to convince Lieta to come with. She could tell the girl desired to leave this place. Could it be that Kustav was keeping her against her will? A prisoner instead of a ward.

It was a lot to manage. Melwes, Grete... now Lieta. During brief moments of selfishness, Dagny fantasized about leaving everyone behind and making her way across the Vahnland, playing Talvarind in river towns along the Morca, listening to music with strangers who meant nothing to her. She wouldn't do that, of course. It was just a fantasy. Although such thoughts helped to ease the pressure.

There was also the fact that none of those people had actually *asked* for Dagny's help. Melwes could very well be back on the Under Road, and Grete's decision to leave was her own. But Dagny couldn't shake the feeling that something bad was coming for her sister.

Or was it? Maybe that was all in her head. Maybe Dagny *needed* a reason to chase after Grete. It would be easier to deal with than the alternative—that Grete was perfectly fine leaving her. That *everyone* had actually been fine leaving her. Just as Dagny's father had left... and Morgan... Maybe she wasn't all that important to anyone.

Morgan died. He didn't leave you on purpose, she told herself.

He left all the same. And he risked his life knowing you and Grete would be left alone in the Mount. He did leave you, just in the worst kind of way.

Dagny grabbed the library's small bronze lamp and slipped into the hallway, keenly aware of her thoughts beginning to spiral. Maybe the only people who stayed in her life were the ones who wanted to use her for something. Was Lieta using her to feel alive and connected to someone? How could the girl actually care about her?

Her breathing turned heavy. Dagny was suddenly enraged at her family's failure, at everyone who *should've* cared for her, but instead, tossed her to the side with no guidance whatsoever. She didn't know how to navigate any of this. Other people seemed to have an internal sense of how things worked, or at least how they were *supposed* to work. Something inside that pointed them toward right and wrong. Dagny never had that. In fact, so much of her life she spent clueless. How much had she actually grown over the years? She still felt like a child. Anything that Dagny had ever figured out, she had to figure out on her own, and only after struggling way too much. It made her feel vulnerable and dumb. And she *hated* those feelings.

Walking further along the lonely hall, Dagny tried to calm down and let her mind drift. A memory, locked inside the farthest reaches of her brain, began to squirm its way out, starting out fuzzy and vague, then slowly sharpening enough until an image took hold. She was somewhere dark, like a pit, staring up at sunlight breaking across grated metal bars. A putrid smell hung in the air like vomit, and although she could taste it in her mouth, it wasn't her own. She saw the nails on her fingers: filthy, with streams of blackness running down to her knuckles, dripping onto wet stone. And then, just as quickly as it had come on, the memory slipped off and Dagny lost it, but not before appreciating what the memory had trapped: the vents of the rendering pit. She'd been there. Finkle and her mother had *actually* sent her to the vents. But... she had no other recollection. Had she escaped and gone back to the Mount? Dagny struggled in the darkness, trying to will herself to recall more details, but it was too late. The memory was gone.

The muscles in her chest constricted, and her hands trembled. Dagny had to find a way out of here. Racing down the hall, her lamplight flickering against ancient stone, she caught a sudden glimpse of emerald green turning the corner ahead.

Lieta?

Dagny increased her pace, sprinting harder than before. She lost sight of the image, and in her hurry, almost ran straight past a narrow side passage blending into the wall.

Is that where the girl had gone?

Squeezing through the stone, Dagny had only taken a few steps when her light revealed a staircase descending deep into the darkness. "Lieta?

Are you there?" Dagny whispered. She thought she heard a reply, but couldn't make out the words.

The stairs curved around the right side wall, and on her left was an enormous drop-off into a pit of black with no guardrails to block someone from falling. Far below, something dripped, echoing through the chamber.

A way out? Dagny thought. *Maybe an entrance into the Great Below?* It made her think of the Under Road and Melwes and their time together. She steadied her breathing. The last thing she wanted to do was become emotional here.

A short while later, the stairs skirted close to a large flat landing that jutted out from the opposite wall. Dagny saw another flash of green appear in the gloomy darkness there, only to vanish again.

Dagny leapt onto the landing and examined her surroundings. Tall bookshelves stretched high against the wall and a rickety old ladder rested between them. *Another library?*

"Lieta? Where are you?" she asked. "Why won't you come out?"

As Dagny wandered closer to the back wall, a stone fireplace came into view, and then she finally heard a voice echoing from the shadows. "This way," it whispered. "This is where I hide it." The voice sounded like the girl, but faint and haunting, like a murmur from a ghost.

Dagny squeezed into the fireplace. "What exactly am I supposed to be looking for?" she asked. Was this another hidden passage?

"I had a dream about this place. That's how I found it," Lieta's ghost voice said.

"Stop hiding from me. What's in here?" Dagny asked nervously. She rubbed the stone, searching for latches or handles, and when she found none, planted her feet and leaned hard into the wall. As if on a swivel, the stone swung open, revealing a dark chamber.

Lieta whispered again, "The hand I had to find on my own. I thought this was the best place to hide it."

"The hand?" Dagny asked, and when there was no answer, she repeated, "Lieta? The *hand*?"

Reluctantly, Dagny stepped into the circular chamber as sweat dripped down her forehead. Arched windows stared out into the blackness of the underground, and a cool breeze blew into the space, sending a shiver across her body. She was hoping to find Lieta, but the only thing inside was a simple wooden chest, resting in the center of the room.

"It's not the warmest place in the Needle," Lieta said. Dagny could now tell where the voice was coming from—just beyond the windows, echoing up from below.

Dagny shuddered. *The chest... open the chest.* It was as if the thought wasn't even her own.

Carefully, she approached and lifted the lid. In the dimness of the lamplight, Dagny could make out what appeared to be an iron hand and forearm resting on a bed of velvet. The edge of the arm looked corroded, like it had broken apart below the elbow.

"Is this what I think it is?" Dagny asked. *But it couldn't be... could it? The hand of a princess?*

She leaned closer. The hand had knuckles and fingernails and small fortune lines on the palm. There was even a pair of veins at the wrist.

Lieta's voice drifted on the breeze, soft as a breath. "You must take it away... you must free her from this place...."

Dagny nodded, although there was no one to watch her. "Who's hand is this? What is the princess's name?" But there was no response.

☙

She ran back down the main hallway, past the library and the bedchamber where Kustav had pinched her, through the dining room and into the great hall, clutching the metal hand close to her breast.

She needed to escape. Lieta had hidden the piece, quite purposefully from Kustav, and now it was Dagny's responsibility. Who knew what the old woman would do if she caught Dagny holding onto it now?

The garden walls would be too tall and smooth to climb, and she still hadn't figured out the crystal face, but one way or the other Dagny was getting out of here, tonight. Reaching toward the balcony's glass door, she was just about to push it open when someone whispered, "Girl, over here."

Dagny turned and scanned the shadows. "Who's there?" she said. "Show yourself."

As if springing from nowhere, Pren appeared at her side; his raccoon eyes were a mask of night in the darkened room.

"*You,*" she gasped. "How did—"

Pren pressed a finger to his lips and listened. Once he was satisfied that no one else was around, he whispered in her ear. "I've been searching for you for days. We need to go. Something else is in the Keep."

"I'm aware."

"I'm not talking about the Prince and his knights. Something *else...* something worse. We can't go back the way I came. Have you explored this place? There's got to be an exit." Pren glanced through the glass doors. "What about out there?"

"There's a building across the gardens. It's sealed by a crystal face. I think it leads through the garden wall, but I don't know how to open it."

Pren nodded his head. "A sigil of ancient Jud. Was it a man's or woman's face?"

"I couldn't tell."

Pren replied with another quick nod.

"How did you find me?"

"There's only so many places to hide in the Keep," he said. "I had no idea you would've made it to the Moon Needle, though. This place has been abandoned for centuries. I'm impressed that you escaped the Prince and found it."

Dagny put her hand on the glass door again and thought of Lieta. She wished the girl was here so they could say their goodbyes. She didn't feel good about running off without a word. "I didn't really find the Needle. I was brought here. It's not totally abandoned."

Pren grabbed her shoulder and whispered again, "Who else is here?"

"Lieta and Kustav."

"Who are they?" The sudden intensity in his eyes was terrifying.

"A young girl who saved me, and an old woman," Dagny muttered. "She's the keeper of the Needle."

His hand trembled on her shoulder. "Where is she now?"

"I don't know. Why?" Dagny tried to give the appearance of calm, but inside, her heart was hammering.

Glancing over Pren's shoulder, Dagny spotted movement from the direction of the dining hall. And a shape, brooding and twisted. Even though the passage beyond was dark, the shape was darker still, with arms and legs and a long, gray face.

Dagny froze, suddenly aware of no other sound but her own shallow breathing. She could feel a faint rumble in the floor, and when she looked down, she realized she was clenching the metal hand so hard that her knuckles had turned white.

The shape spoke with a throaty voice, wheezing out a single word that sounded like, "*Greeegoul...*"

Something in her mind snapped, and Dagny stumbled backward, almost falling. Pren reached for her, but Dagny regained herself and leapt past him, her boots catching traction on the old stone as she hurtled into the balcony doors, throwing them open.

Pren was behind her, shouting, "Go! Get away from the tower!"

They leapt down the stairs and ran through the yard. Dagny pointed to the trees in the distance. "That way!"

As soon as they reached the woods, Dagny almost collapsed on the ground, struggling for air. Pren keeled over as well, panting heavily. "Do you see her?" he huffed.

Peeking over a gnarled stump, Dagny studied the field. It didn't look like Kustav had left the Needle.

"Why did she stop?" Dagny asked.

"Who cares," Pren replied. "Just be glad she did."

"What *is* she?"

"That *Kustav,* as you called her, is a sliver from another age, broken off and escaped from the prison of time. She is probably the most dangerous thing in Jud, besides the Prince... or at least she was."

"What's that mean?"

"Like I said, something else has come to Jud and the Keep. I felt its presence stalking the halls. That's how I was able to get through—even the knights had fled from it. I could feel this weird energy there, like the world had changed." Pren looked into the darkened woods, then pulled out a small lamp from his satchel. "We have to get out. Which way?"

"To where?" Dagny asked. "The sigil?"

"Yes. You said it will lead us out of the garden."

"I think it will. I *think* it goes through the wall," Dagny said. "And I don't know how to open it, remember?"

"Take me there." Pren raised the lamp and put a hand on his hip, looking like a human teakettle. "I'm fairly good with locks."

"Fine. Look for black threads." Dagny gestured at her ruined skirt. "They look like this. I tied them on tree limbs."

Pren smiled. "You're inventive. What's that?" he asked, pointing to the metal hand.

"Something I found that I need to take with me."

"Fair enough."

"Why did you come for me?" Dagny asked, as Pren started examining branches.

"I don't believe anyone should have their eyes gouged out by an ancient prince," he said.

"Well, I appreciate that. Do you know anything about Lieta?" Dagny asked. "The girl who lives in the Needle?"

"You sure they're not one and the same?" Pren ran over to a tree limb. "Found one!"

"Huh? Wait! One and the same?"

"Yes," Pren said, grabbing onto the knotted black ribbon. "You certain they're not the same person?"

Dagny's voice caught in her throat. A moment later, she suddenly felt very queasy. No, that wasn't possible. Lieta and Kustav couldn't be the same person. She'd seen them both together... hadn't she?

"Let's go," Pren said. "This could take a while."

Dagny's mind swirled as Pren led the way, inspecting the tree branches. Why would Pren suggest such a thing? She tried to remember if she'd actually seen Lieta and Kustav together, then decided it didn't matter. There was absolutely no way that was true. Dagny felt the panic start to fade. As horrible as this had all been, she couldn't bear the thought that Lieta was really somehow Kustav in disguise, transformed by some bizarre magic.

"They're not the same person," Dagny said confidently.

"Alright," Pren replied without looking back. "Over here," he said, pointing down a split in the path.

Dagny rushed after him. "Lieta was very nice to me. She saved me from the Prince. I wish there was something I could do to help her."

"Where is she now?" Pren asked.

"I'm not sure."

"Hmm, that solves that, don't you think?"

"I guess," Dagny said. "I just hate leaving like this. I know that sounds stupid."

"It does. When Kustav is looking to trap your soul inside the Moon Needle, you leave. She's a greedy one."

Into the clearing they strode, past the giant dirt-covered statue, and toward the opposite end.

"How much do you know about the princesses of Jud?" Dagny asked, cradling the hand.

"Is that what you think you've got there?" Pren replied.

"I don't know."

"Well, best to keep it hidden. Don't want anyone getting the wrong idea in their head 'bout thieving it." Pren opened the satchel strung across his chest and ruffled inside until he found a canvas pouch. "Here, put it in this."

"Thanks."

"The princesses come from the Sillweed, supposedly," he replied. "But it's all rumors."

The Sillweed... Melwes had mentioned that in one of his stories. "That's not the first time I've heard about it," Dagny said. "How do you get there?"

"Oh, the weeds are not a *real* place... you understand what I'm trying to say? They exist, but they're not real. Not like this," Pren said, patting one of the crowned statues by the tree line. "There's no way to *get there.*"

Dagny didn't say any more about it as they pushed through the woods and crossed the shallow stream on their way to the dark building. Then, they climbed the winding path in silence until finally reaching the black doors and the crystalized face.

"Ah... one of *these* sigils," Pren said. "Yeah. I don't know how to open this."

"Are you serious?" Dagny asked. She could've screamed at him. "What do we do now?"

Pren placed his hand on the crystal letters. "Well, look at that, these crystals move."

Dagny huffed disapprovingly and glanced down the path, trying to make sure nothing else was coming up behind them.

"There's the beginning of a word here," Pren muttered, unscrambling some of the letters. "Yes, there we go. It's the old word for the forest..I can't make out the rest. *Something* of Lazim."

Dagny moved next to him. "Is that the key?" she asked.

"I'm certain it is. But I'm lost as to the rest of the phrase."

"You don't have any idea?"

"No. Not yet."

Dagny tried to think. "I saw Kustav come this way one night... Try *queen* of Lazim."

Pren rearranged the letters on the door. "No. That doesn't work. You're close, though. Looks like it's got five letters."

Dagny started chewing on her nails. She only had one interaction with Kustav, when the old woman almost frightened her to death in the tub. What had Kustav said? Something about... "Try *amber.*"

Pren slid more crystals around, then slapped his hand on the door. "Ugh. Not amber. We could be here all night, and it's entirely possible the correct word is something from the old tongue you've never heard of."

Dagny bit her thumbnail so hard it tore at the edge and began to bleed, forcing a hiss from her lips.

"What'd you do?" Pren asked with more irritation than concern.

"Nothing." Dagny stared down the dark path as the wind rustled around them. Did someone just move in the bushes?

Pren was counting on his fingers and then sliding the crystals on the door. "Five letters... *Woods*... No... *Thorns*... Nah."

"Are you worried about it being a trap?" Dagny asked. "Like, if we get too many wrong, something terrible will happen?"

The door looked even blacker and more foreboding than before. Pren slowly withdrew his hand and took a step back. "I am now."

A warm, wet sensation trickled down Dagny's hand. Instinctively, she licked at it, tasting the iron in her own blood. Stupid habit. She'd hurt herself worse than she realized, but it brought about a sudden moment of clarity.

"Pren," she whispered. "I've got it. Try blood... *The blood of Lazim.*"

Without another word, his hands were back on the crystals, sliding them into place, and spelling out the phrase she suggested. Just before connecting the final letter, Pren took a deep breath and said, "Here it goes." There was a brief pause, and then something clicked. The door opened and the chamber beyond twinkled in gorgeous orange light. "Nicely done," Pren said, staring ahead.

Dagny listened carefully. There didn't seem to be any sound coming from inside. "So, what now?" she asked.

"You're the riddle master," he replied. "Lead the way."

The floor was the first thing that caught Dagny's attention: sticky like syrup; it sucked at her boots and threatened to send her reeling forward if she moved too fast.

"Be careful," Pren said. "You don't want to fall onto this... whatever it is."

Dagny had no intention of falling. She'd take it as slow as she needed to, one step at a time.

The next things that she saw were the massive columns, covered in the same goopy substance, supporting the flat ceiling overhead. The entire chamber was cast in tones of orange, yellow and brown.

"Let's move quick," Pren said from over her shoulder. "Keep going, but be careful."

"Careful *and* quick, huh?"

"Exactly."

Just past the first set of columns, the chamber opened up, revealing other shapes coated in the goop—awkward blobs of varying sizes plopped down at random places on the floor like enormous drips from a ceiling of honey. The entire area smelled both earthy and sweet.

"I don't like this," Dagny said. "I really don't." She had the feeling that something was watching them move.

Pren passed her and pointed across the room. "I think there's a door up there. See it?"

More shapes littered the chamber ahead, lots of them. Some appeared to have hardened into stone... or...

"*Pren...*" Dagny called out. "Just stop. I think this is resin. I think that's amber in front of us."

Pren did stop, then held up his lamp. Dagny realized there was another light here, dimly illuminating the space, but she couldn't tell where it was located.

"There's something inside," Pren said, pointing at one of the blocks.

Dagny saw it, too. Within the goopy piles, as well as the hardened stone, there were *things* trapped inside. Some blocks were so murky that Dagny could only glimpse the vague outline of a form, but others she saw clearly. They contained human shapes in various poses, frozen in time; appearing as statues, like the weed-covered ones in the clearing. Of course Dagny knew they weren't.

It had been hard to appreciate the sheer number of blocky shapes until now. She stood with Pren in the middle of dozens, if not hundreds, of bodies engulfed in resin. Panic erupted inside her. Dagny turned to escape and stared straight into the eyes of a human head, floating in orange.

Catching herself before she screamed, Dagny spun away and clenched her eyes shut. "Pren... we need... to go."

"Open your eyes," Pren said. "Keep moving. They can't hurt you, but we need to get out before..."

"Before what?" Dagny opened her eyes and saw Pren standing in front of an orange block.

"I know this one," he said.

Dagny peeled her boots off the floor and approached. "What? Who is it?"

"A wanderer who came through the outskirts a while back. It's not important anymore."

Trapped within the sticky block was a man, his hands stretched out as if trying to push his way through the goopy prison, his face twisted into a grotesque expression of fear. The resin appeared soft. It would probably be years before it hardened into stone. And the man seemed, somehow, vaguely familiar, but the surface was so cloudy it was hard to get a good look at his features.

"Let's go," Pren said. Dagny ignored him and moved around the shape, hoping to get a better angle on the man. "I said it wasn't important," Pren continued.

"Shh..." Dagny replied. The light hit a corner of the block that had begun to crystalize, allowing for a view inside. She recognized the man now, his handsome face, and sleepy gray eyes. *Maris.*

This time, Dagny yelped and threw a hand over her mouth. She reached for the body, but Pren grabbed her before she touched the resin.

"I know him..." she gasped. "He's dead, isn't he?" She glanced at Pren, who just stood there awkwardly.

Another voice spoke now, from somewhere across the room. "You shouldn't have come here. I *told* you not to come here."

Dagny spun around. Standing by the entrance was Lieta, her emerald hair wild in the orange light.

"You?!" Dagny shouted. "You did this?!"

"*Me?*" Lieta replied. "How could you think that?"

Dagny tried to step toward her, but Pren held her back. "What is going on here?" she shouted. "He was a friend of mine!"

"I'm sorry," Lieta said, shaking her head. "There's nothing I can do."

A wave of emotion washed over Dagny, and tears were suddenly streaming down her cheeks. "Did you know about this?" And when Lieta didn't answer, Dagny screamed, "Did you know?"

"I'm sorry!" Lieta shouted back.

"How?" Dagny gestured at the chamber. "How could all of this happen?"

"It was Kustav."

Dagny sucked in air and tried to steady herself.

"Dagny..." Pren whispered. "The door... we need to go."

Lieta stretched her hand out, but she didn't move into the chamber. "Please don't leave me. Please, come back."

"This is so horrible," Dagny said, shaking her head violently, as if she could somehow throw off the cruelty surrounding her. She turned and pointed to the door. "Is that the way out, Lieta? Has it been there this entire time?"

The girl just stared at her.

"Is it?" Dagny asked.

"Please..." Lieta begged. "Please don't."

Dagny took another breath. Reminding herself that Lieta was a victim as well. Imprisoned by that awful Kustav. "I took the hand like you asked me to. I can tell... you want to escape. Lieta," Dagny said, her voice steady. "You need to come with us."

But the girl backed away. "No. I can't."

"It's Kustav, isn't it?" Dagny said. "She's keeping you here."

"Just come back," Lieta said. "I can keep you safe... Stay until we can leave together."

"And when will that be? The solstice? Longer?"

"Soon. I promise."

"Dagny..." Pren whispered from behind. "We need to leave *now*."

In that moment, Dagny didn't know what to do. She couldn't return with Lieta. She could only gaze at the girl with uncertainty.

"Are you really going to leave me?" Lieta asked. "Are you really abandoning me?"

Dagny glanced at the ground.

"Just run away then," Lieta said. "If you don't care about me, then just go."

In an instant, Dagny was in the air with Pren's arm wrapped around her waist. He was marching her toward the exit, his boots squishing and popping across the sticky ground. Dagny could've fought back and slipped from Pren's arms, but she didn't.

Lieta continued to watch from her place near the entrance, staring straight into Dagny's eyes, until Pren carried her from the building and slammed the door closed. Leaving Kustav and Lieta and the Moon Needle behind.

PART

2

12

A simple door: iron with peeling red paint, framed by brown bricks at the end of an alley. It was the only thing that marked the way back to the Needle and Dretgaol. Dagny stared at the door for a long time, trying to make sense of what had just happened—the loss of days; the body of Maris imprisoned in amber; Lieta; the Thorned Prince... all of it.

The alley looked like any other from back home. There were even balconies, complete with metal railings, curtained windows, old stools and clay pots. She wondered if anyone was living here.

For a brief moment, Dagny thought she might very well be in Viddry or City Centre; that something in her brain really had snapped, and that this experience was all a delusion. But then Pren spoke, breaking her from the spell.

"I'm going to look around," he said. "I'm not *exactly* sure where we're at, but it won't take long to find out." With that he was gone, turning the corner ahead without looking back.

Dagny let him go. As strange as it was, the only thing she could think of now was how comfortable her boots felt, and how glad she was that she hadn't left them at the Needle. Then her mind went to the hand. Dagny considered whether she should keep the thing or fling it into the gutter.

Lieta had wanted her to take it so badly, but after that awful amber room, Dagny didn't know if she could trust anything the girl had said.

Reaching into the pouch, Dagny pulled out the object and held it into the moonlight. It seemed so real, so delicate. Years had taken a toll on the metal, almost to the point where Dagny thought it could shatter if dropped on the stoney road. *Could this really be the hand of a young girl?* she thought. As sick as she was over everything, Dagny also didn't want to abandon it just yet. Things were simply too confusing right now to make a clear decision.

The sky was bright with stars, and Dagny was able to navigate the alley until reaching the crossroads. She didn't see any other doors, which was odd, and the only smell in the air was that of dust and dirt and possibly smoke from somewhere far away. If there had been people here, if she *had been* in Viddry or Rork, there'd be the smell of the City: food and waste; ginger and spice.

Lieta... Even though she was still in shock, Dagny was keenly aware that once she regained herself—in the days, weeks, or months ahead—that this one would hurt. She had begun to trust the girl. Now she just felt betrayed.

Pren stood in the middle of a narrow street, barely wide enough for a single carriage. How much could she trust him?

Glancing over, Pren opened his mouth to talk, but Dagny cut him off before he could speak.

"What was stalking the Keep?" she asked.

"I told you, I didn't—"

"Have you heard of the Drowned Twins of Gort?"

Pren watched her, side-eyed. "I've heard of them..."

"I think they're here. In the city," Dagny said.

Pren looked skeptical. "Why would you say that?"

"Because they're after my sister. I saw them once, you know, in the underground, far from here. Maybe it was them in the Keep."

Pren twisted his mouth, then spoke. "So, it's a hunch you got."

"What do you mean?"

"About the twins. You're only guessing they're here."

"It's more than that," Dagny said.

"Explain it to me, then. How can you be sure they're in the city? 'Cause you saw them once, somewhere else?"

"I just know they are. It's a strong feeling."

"I doubt it was the twins you saw before," Pren said, shaking his head. "If you really had run into 'em, you wouldn't be here right now. I'm not saying you're lying. You may well have *thought* you saw them."

"I *did* see them," Dagny said.

Pren almost laughed. "Oh, did you? Do you know what the girl one is called?"

"Galwed," Dagny replied. "The Collector."

"That's right... she *collects* people. The Drowned Twins of Gort don't let people get away."

"I'm not interested in arguing about it, Pren," Dagny said. "I'm also not interested in keeping secrets anymore. I want to find my sister and be done with this."

"Your sister..." Pren mumbled.

"If she doesn't want to come with me... if she wants to stay here, that's fine," Dagny said, staring down at the cobblestone road. "I need to find her one more time, just to make sure she doesn't need me. I owe her that much."

Pren nodded and softened his tone. "I didn't mean to argue with you. Look, if you want my help, I'll help. We're getting close to the Inner City, anyway. I recognize this road. Up ahead is Dog's Den. We can rest there for the night." Pren patted his satchel. "I've got some stuff to trade for the both of us. You can repay me, if you want. If not, that's fine, too."

"Do people actually live in this city? Or is it just filled with dead and rusted things?"

Pren narrowed his eyes. "What do you mean, rusted things?"

"You know, rusted towers, rusted princesses... *Rusted things.*"

"Are the princesses well known outside of Jud?" Pren asked.

"Somewhat," Dagny replied. Although she had never heard of them until Tash.

"Hmm. Well, to answer your question, it's not *filled* with those things. We're nearing the border of Jud proper. You'll see."

"Hold on," Dagny said. "Before we go any further. Just tell me who you are. I don't want to find out that you're some horrible ghost, wandering Jud like Kustav wanders the Needle. I don't want to find out later you're wicked. If there's something going on with you, tell me."

Pren shrugged. "I'm not a ghost and I'm not wicked."

"So you have a family, then? Here in the city?"

"You could say that."

Dagny sighed. "What's that mean? See, you're being cryptic again. Just tell me."

"I don't speak with my family. My father disappeared into the depths years ago. I have two brothers. Do you need to know more?"

"Yes."

"I've left Jud before and explored the world outside. I've visited towns in the wild plains and listened to conversations along the river. I'm familiar with where you come from. I spend my time searching for lost relics hidden throughout Jud, revealed by the shift... Is that enough?"

Dagny watched him closely for any sign that he was lying, then muttered, "Sure."

The once-dense buildings spread further and further apart until they were finally replaced by fenced yards and dotted with the occasional sign post. Dagny heard a dull bell, and when she glanced over, a spotted goat stuck its head between two wooden slats and wiggled its tongue at her.

"I think that's the first animal I've seen since I've been here, other than birds," Dagny said.

"Oh, right," Pren said. "There's nothing but birds in the 'skirts. Anything else that might wander in, the Grouchers gobble up."

"Do people eat goats here?"

"I don't," Pren said, incredulously. "Once you slaughter something, that's it. It's gone forever." Pren looked at her. "Do you eat goats?"

"No."

Pren seemed relieved, then pointed forward. In the distance, Dagny could see a tall, broad building set against the black sky. Several windows on the first floor glowed orange from a fire within. "Dog's Den," Pren said. "Come on. I'm getting tired."

⁑

There were people inside. Actual people. Dagny could hear them chatting and laughing well before they reached the front door. Off to the side of the building stood a mill, slowly churning in the wind. "Dog makes some of the best bread in all of Jud," Pren said. "Can you smell it?"

She could. Faint over the scent of burning wood. It smelled hearty and delicious. "I'm surprised they're baking bread now," Dagny said. "It must be well past midnight."

"People keep all sorts of hours here. As long as there are mouths to feed, Dog keeps busy."

"So, Dog's his name then?" Dagny asked, as Pren pushed open the door.

She never got an answer to her question. Almost immediately after stepping inside, a burly, red-headed man came running over and slapped Pren across the chest. The boy stumbled backward, then wheezed as the man grabbed him around the torso and raised him into the air.

"Jimbert saw you enter Dretgaol. I thought I'd be making an empty casket for your brothers to bury," the man said.

"No... I'm still here," Pren hissed. "Put... me... down."

"And who's this?" the man asked, nodding to Dagny.

"A girl I found," Pren responded. "From the outside."

"Welcome, *girl*," the man said, extending a hand. "Roger Red. That's me." The man appeared to be in his forties but had the energy and demeanor of someone *much* younger.

Dagny shook his hand, which felt softer than she was expecting. "I'm Dag."

Roger's eyes beamed. "Welcome to Dag's Den Dog... er, Dog's Dag Den." He made a fluttering gesture with his fingers. "The words... they twist the mouth."

"That's alright," Dagny said, then turned to Pren. "Can I get some of that bread?"

Pren reached into his satchel and produced a metal whistle and clay mug. "Here, give him these. And get enough for the both of us."

The ground level of Dog's Den was one enormous room. A haphazard assortment of tables, chairs, and cushions were strewn across the floor, and the far wall contained the fireplace with an open kitchen. Also, the place was packed. Dagny skirted three younger girls sitting on a gray-stained mattress who giggled as she passed. Others sat engaged in private conversation in nooks carved into the sidewalls. Up until now, Dagny could count the number of people she'd seen in Jud on her hands. There was probably triple that amount in here.

"Dog" was presumably the man standing behind the makeshift bar in the back corner. He had long hair, and when Dagny approached, she noticed a patchy beard and rough skin. She squeezed between two bodies and gave Dog a friendly wave.

"Ah, a new face," Dog said, wiping down the counter with a wet rag. "Where you coming from, dear?"

"Originally or earlier?" Dagny asked.

"Let's start with earlier."

"Umm. The Moon Needle?"

Dog chuckled. "Alright... Do you know how things work here? Need to trade if you want something." The man pointed at the tin bracelet on her wrist. "That'll do."

Dagny hid her arm behind her back. "No. Not that," she said, then placed Pren's clay mug and whistle on the counter. "This. We'd like lots of bread and something to drink."

"And a space for the night?" Dog asked, collecting the trade.

Dagny glanced back at Pren, who was still talking with Roger Red. "Sure."

Just then, Dagny caught a scent of something peppery and sweet. "Is that cinnamon?"

"Yep. There's a grove of cinnamon trees in Rosinda's Field, a short walk from here, but my family's the only one allowed to harvest it. Royal decree."

"I haven't smelled it for a long time," Dagny said, trying to catch another whiff of the fragrance.

"You want some? Maybe for your tea?" Dog asked with a half-smile, and when Dagny nodded, he pointed to the arm still hidden behind her back. "Bracelet," he said. "Gimme."

"No. Never mind," Dagny said. "I'll just wait for the bread."

"Special to you, is it?"

"Yes," she said with a laugh. "Obviously."

Turning her attention back to the room, Dagny watched the various groups, each formed into their own self-contained little worlds. There was no consistency in the way anyone looked. Long robes and short pants; handmade caps; soft shoes, heavy boots, bare feet. A boy with frizzy hair waved to his friend at the bar, who wore a white jacket and fingerless gloves. Someone sitting in front of the fire played a flute, badly.

"All set, friend," Dog said from behind. Dagny turned around to find two goblets of tea, a loaf of bread, and a pouch of cinnamon. She started to say thank you, but Dog had already wandered to the kitchen.

"When did you speak to Jimbert?" Pren asked Roger, as Dagny approached.

"Yesterday morning," Roger replied. "He came and found me at Eyster's. He was worried about you and figured no one else but me would care."

"Who's Jimbert?" Dagny asked, handing Pren a mug.

"The Sanctuary's resident ghost," Roger joked.

Pren clicked his tongue disapprovingly. "This girl doesn't like ghosts."

Roger placed a hand on her shoulder. "Oh, he's not *really* a ghost, Dagny. He just sees things no one else sees, and seems to be everywhere all at once, in a very ghost-like kind of way."

"You haven't seen my brothers, have you?" Pren asked him.

"Not yet, but I'm sure they'll know you're back soon enough."

Pren sipped his tea and seemed to eye the room more carefully now.

"Is there something I should be aware of?" Dagny asked.

"No, it's fine," Pren replied.

"Yeah," Roger said, then laughed. "His brothers like to play surprises, you could say."

They took a seat inside of an empty nook, and Roger squeezed next to Dagny, unaware that he was squishing her into the wall. Still, there were worse places to be, and even though she could feel sweat through the man's shirt, Dagny didn't mind too much. She felt a sense of protection next to the beefy Roger Red. If Kustav or the twins barged in here, they'd have to get through him first. And there was a lot of him to get through. As long as Dagny could move her hands and tear into the bread, she'd be fine.

Pren and Roger spoke of places and things she'd never heard of: Besides Eyster's, there was Old Veil and New Veil; scroungers of the waste yards; witches gathering bones; and who might want to trade for a junk-wrench.

"I also need to find another compass," Pren said. "The Grouchers got mine."

"Good luck with that," Roger said. "Not many of those lying around anymore."

"I know. There's only one left at Barentok, but my brothers would never let me have it." Pren reached for the bread, and finding only crumbs, glanced up at Dagny.

"Sorry," she muttered. "I was hungrier than I thought."

"You gotta be quick with this one," Roger said, gesturing at Dagny.

Pren nodded. "I see that."

"So, what's special about the compass?" Dagny asked, trying to change the subject.

"It's an ancient Night Orbiter," Roger answered. "It shows you how the stars looked when Jud was first created."

Maris... Dagny thought. That must've been what he'd found all those months ago: the Star Compass. It's what brought him to Alex, and in another way, what brought Dagny to Max and the Naverung. The last time she'd seen it was on the floor by the old palace kitchens, near the wall where Galwed had been trapped.

"And why is seeing the stars important?" Dagny asked.

Roger cleared his throat, which morphed into a violent cough, turning his face red and shaking the table and bench. Other people in the Den stopped their conversations and glanced over, but Pren just sat back, arms crossed, completely unconcerned. After finally catching his breath, Roger spoke as if nothing had happened. "Well... Jud's creation was based on those ancient stars. If you can determine where a constellation is located at any given time, you can find certain places throughout the city."

"Are you confused?" Pren asked.

Dagny shook her head. "I think I understand. Keep going."

Roger gave her a friendly wink. "Take the Twin Fire Hunters. If you find them on your Night Orbiter, it will always lead you toward the Low

Gate. The Hydra will point toward Sanctuary itself. The Doomed Satyr to the castle... get it?"

"The castle? The one with Yunis?"

The friendliness left Roger's face, replaced by one of concern. "Yes." He glanced at Pren. "How'd she know about that?"

Pren scratched his head. "I'm learning more about her every second. She's oblivious about some stuff, but will surprise you on other things."

The oblivious remark irritated her. "You can talk *to* me, you know," Dagny said. "If you have a question, ask me directly."

"Alright, little one," Roger said, then continued on with Pren. "There's a rumor going around that some of the witches are close to finding the *Sepulcha*—"

"The tomb?" Dagny said, interrupting.

Pren shushed her. It made her feel like a child. "You said you weren't looking for Odestinas," he said.

"I'm not," Dagny replied, "but I've still heard things." She lowered her voice. "Did I do something to upset you?"

Pren had a puzzled look on his face. "No. Why?"

"Because you're acting like I'm annoying you."

Roger laughed. "Learn some manners, Pren."

"I didn't mean anything by it," Pren said. "You're taking it the wrong way."

"Am I?" Dagny asked, then rubbed her face. "I'm very tired, and the last few days have completely blurred my head. I just need someone to be nice to me right now, okay?"

Pren nodded. "I can appreciate that."

"I'll make sure he acts nicer," Roger said, then nudged Dagny. "Go on. You were going to say something?"

"Oh." Dagny gathered her thoughts. "I was wondering... is it true? That the Imposter imprisoned Odestinas under a slab of iron?"

Pren shrugged. "Maybe."

"And there's something else," Roger said to Pren. "Since you've been gone, a special outsider has come to the Inner City, drawing a lot of attention. They're holed up at Spirit's place."

"An outsider?" Pren looked at Dagny. "Sounds like something you'd be interested in."

"Why?" she asked.

"You said your sister was with Marfisi, right?"

"Yeah."

Pren licked his fingers and rubbed them over the bread crumbs. "Well, that's Marfisi. They call her *Spirit* here. I'll guess the outsider is your sister. What's her name?"

"Grete..." Dagny whispered. A surge of excitement swept through her, but she tried to appear calm. "How far is Spirit's place?"

"Not too far. We'll get there in the morning," Pren said.

"We can't leave now?"

Pren sighed. "I'd like to rest. You think *you're* tired? It's been a rough few days trying to find you."

"Is there anything dangerous between here and there?" Dagny asked. "Traps or Grouchers or silver-faced knights? Anything?"

Pren shook his head. "No. It's actually fairly pleasant this side of the Keep."

"Yeah," Roger chuckled. "Real boring."

Dagny relaxed into the wall, allowing Roger's body to squish her a bit more. As close as she was, she still didn't want to go wandering off into the night by herself. Even though these two *said* the route was safe, the last time she walked off, she ended up trapped in the Moon Needle for several days, and likely would've been there much longer if Kustav had her way. Tomorrow morning would have to do.

∞

She slept on the bottom bunk in a room the size of a closet. Or at least she *tried* to sleep. Pren passed out on the mattress above her almost instantly, and soon enough, the room was filled with the jerky cadence of his snoring.

It was going to be a long night. Dagny rolled onto her side and stared at the moon through the room's only window. *Hours.* Only hours were separating her from Grete. It didn't seem real. Her heart still pounded and her stomach twisted in knots. She couldn't tell if that was excitement she felt or anxiety. What would Dagny even say to her sister after all of this? *Hi, I know you left me at Tash's house, but surprise, here I am. How are you? Oh, and by the way, I think the drowned twins are looking to kill you for some reason. Maybe it's got something to do with that heart you ate in your dream. Don't worry though. I'll protect you.*

Dagny slapped her hand over her eyes. It was so incredibly foolish. During all those months in the underground, she only imagined how excited Grete would be to see her again, but now—with the clarity of being so close—Dagny had to prepare for the very real possibility that Grete might not want to see her at all. And it could happen as soon as tomorrow morning. Maybe Grete was going to be absolutely livid at her for coming. *Well, that's not your decision to make,* Dagny thought. *I'm your older sister. I had to do this.* She had to care. What kind of person would Dagny be if she didn't?

But Grete was a stranger, bound only in blood. A Limer's Town orphan. Maybe their lives had been too different to connect now, to have any kind of meaningful relationship. Dagny realized how important those in-between years were, when children grow into themselves. She'd been sheltered in Rork, and Grete was thrown into a snake pit. How could they *ever* relate to each other after all of this? What a cruel trick played by the universe—to join them together, only to keep tearing them apart.

If she could *save* Grete, though. Somehow. Save her from misery and sadness; from the twins; from whatever was going on with Marfisi and Odestinas. If Dagny could bring about the life Grete truly wanted, maybe that would be enough. Maybe Dagny could live with that.

The floor creaked in the hallway. Dagny perked up, listening closely. She heard two men talking in a hushed tone, and quickly poked Pren through the thin mattress above her. His snoring stopped, but the boy said nothing. Perhaps he was listening, too.

Just then, the door flew open and heavy boots came thundering inside, rushing over to Dagny and the bunks. She was eye-level with dark pants banded with metal strips. But the men didn't reach for her. Pren flopped wildly and tried to shout. One of the men must've been covering his mouth.

Shock and fear froze Dagny on the mattress. She couldn't be captured again. She couldn't go back to the Keep or wherever these men were planning to take Pren. The boy kicked, and one man stumbled and crashed into the wall. The other man grunted, struggling to yank Pren out of the bunk. They were making so much noise. Where was everybody? Shouldn't someone be coming to help? Where was Dog or Roger Red? Or any of the other dozens of people in the Den?

She had to do *something*. Dagny took a deep breath, then rolled onto the floor. Before either of the men could react, Dagny latched onto a leg, found the soft spot between metal bands, and bit down. Hard.

"What the—*aargh!*" the man cried. "Arnon! Arnon! Get this *thing off of me!*" He tried to shake her off, but Dagny's grip held.

The other man rushed over and lifted Dagny off the ground by her legs like a wheelbarrow. "Get off!" he shouted.

"It hurts!" the first man screamed. "Crack its skull! Crack it!"

The threat caused Dagny to drop her bite and fall to the floor. "No, don't please! I'm off," she cried. "I'm off."

"*Why?*" the first man said, grabbing his leg and hobbling away from her. "You bit clean through the meat."

The second man, Arnon, lifted Dagny upside down by the ankles. "Keep those teeth away from me or I'll kick you!" he warned.

"What are you doing here?" Dagny cried; the room spinning as blood rushed to her head. "Why are you attacking my friend?"

"Your friend, huh?" the first man said through a clenched jaw. "That's a first. You know you have a friend, Puddle?"

Puddle?

A moment later, Pren hopped off the bed. "She was just trying to help me," he said. "Put her down."

Arnon scoffed. "This biter? No, I don't think so."

Pren stepped over and slapped the man's arm, causing him to release her. Dagny tumbled awkwardly onto her back, then found herself staring up at the group as she struggled for air.

"Sorry about that," Pren said, meeting her gaze. "Dagny... this is Arnon and Boulder. These are my brothers."

13

The men looked like knights. Not the sleek, silent knights of Dretgaol with perfect posture and cold hands, but knights of the waste yards. They wore open-faced helmets and dented cuirasses, and one of them—the brother called Boulder—carried a scary-looking hammer on his back. Their shirts were dirty and patched in several places. Both men were huge.

"We're so glad to see you, Puddle," Arnon said, clutching Pren's collar. "Don't bother trying to run."

Pren tried to shake off his brother's grasp. "I'm not running. You could've just knocked and done away with all of this. It's ridiculous."

Boulder huffed, still grimacing from his wounded leg. He was definitely the sulkier of the two. "You're the ridiculous one, thinking we'd let you slip off again. Let's go. Get your stuff."

Pren moved to the wall where his satchel hung. Arnon followed, holding Pren's collar the entire time. "Who's the girl?" he asked.

"Someone I met," Pren replied.

"Obviously." Arnon kept his eyes fixed on her, delivering a silent warning not to stand. "Where'd she come from? Why is she with you?"

"I'm from the lagoon," Dagny said, content to remain lying on the ground. "Pren helped me a couple times."

"I doubt that," Boulder said. "More like your pleasure toy for the night, huh, Pud?"

"Don't be crude," Pren replied. "You're just mad 'cause she almost took you down. The mighty Bear Knight."

"Yeah. I am mighty." Boulder pointed his finger in Pren's face. "You better remember that. And you'll be glad for my mightiness when the Cauldron opens up and vomits devils from the abyss. Now *move!*"

Arnon pushed Pren into the hall, and Dagny scurried to her feet to follow them.

"No. Not you," Boulder said, poking her in the forehead.

"Where are you taking him?" she demanded. Pren was her best chance at finding Spirit's place and Grete, and these men were dragging him off.

"They're taking me to Barentok," Pren said. "I'm afraid I can't help you anymore." Arnon pushed him forward, but Pren had just enough time to reach into his pocket and toss her a key. "Give it to Dog. Ask him about Spirit."

Dagny quickly grabbed her pouch with the metal hand and followed the group down the stairs, keeping her distance from Boulder. "What's Barentok?" she called out.

"Our home," Pren shouted. "It'll be a while before I can leave again."

"You'll *never* leave again," Arnon said. "Not until you follow through with the oath."

"It's not my oath," Pren said.

A small crowd had gathered near the front door of the common room, and in the middle of them was Roger Red. For a moment, Dagny thought the burly man would attempt a rescue, but something was off. She noticed Roger avoiding Pren's eyes, and looking timidly at the ground.

"You mutton-headed traitor!" Pren yelled at him. "You fetched them, didn't you?"

"They were worried about you," Roger replied. "We all were."

"You're dead to me!" Pren screamed, as Arnon opened the door and shoved him outside. "You hear me?! Dead! Don't ever—"

The door slammed closed and the common room fell into a murmur. Roger glanced at Dagny and started to shuffle away.

"Wait!" Dagny ran over and tugged his shirt.

"Leave me alone," Roger said. "I already feel bad enough."

"What was that about?" Dagny asked.

"Pren's been gone for a long time, and events have been set in motion. His family needs him."

"Why?"

Roger looked straight into her eyes now. "What do you know about Pren?" he asked. For the first time, Dagny noticed a curved knife on the man's belt.

"Apparently nothing at all," she replied. "I thought he was a scavenger."

Roger smiled. "He does scavenge, that one. And I do love him, you know, like a little brother of my own. But Pren is not my family. His family leads the Knights Eternal—Light of the Deep. They're not a group you can dissuade or go against."

"What are they going to do with him?"

"Search the Deep," Roger said, matter-of-factly. "His father, Tarn Orben, disappeared years ago—leading an excursion down below. Presumably, he got lost somewhere along the Endless Staircase and didn't make it back before the Cauldron closed. They've been trying to find him ever since. The pit will open again soon, and into it they shall go."

Dagny gasped at the man. "Into a pit that can close and trap you underground?"

"Possibly. But these are the Knights Eternal. They know what they're doing."

"Roger..." Dagny said, quietly, "did you send Pren to his death?"

The man's red face turned redder. "What? How *dare you* accuse me of such things? How *dare* you! This discussion is over."

Roger stormed off to the back door, and Dagny watched him leave. She had no interest in chasing after him or associating with betrayers. Turning the key over in her hand, she thought about what Pren had said—find Dog.

The sky outside was beginning to break. One of the younger patrons of the Den, a girl wearing a crown of white flowers, directed Dagny to the old mill. She found Dog there, drinking a mug of tea and staring off into the horizon.

"Hey, remember me?" she asked. "You gave me that cinnamon."

"Oh. Hello," Dog said, his voice subdued.

"That was nice of you. It reminded me of home."

Dog scratched at his patchy beard. "I'm glad. And where is home, exactly?"

"Oh, far from here." Dagny sat on the ground next to him and watched the dawning sun with the windmill paddles slowly creaking behind her. "Did you know those knights took Pren?"

"Mm-hmm. There's not much I could do about it, though. Can't get involved in those sorts of things."

His response disappointed her, but Dagny didn't say anything. She held the key into the light, examining the shape. It was tinted green, and the bow looked like an eye. "What's this supposed to unlock?" she asked.

Dog glanced over, clapped his hands together, and laughed. "Damn," he said. "How long have you been hiding from me? Time to come home."

"Hold on," Dagny said, pulling the key away as Dog reached for it. "I'm not going to just *give* it to you."

"But... that's mine. I only lost it."

"I need something first. I need to find the way to Spirit's place."

"Spirit, huh? That witch girl?"

Witch? Dagny thought, then quickly nodded. "Yeah. That's the one."

"Ah, well, it's easy enough," Dog said. "You head down Raggle Street, cut through Pratchett, cross the Bridges, and then you're almost there."

It was Dagny who laughed this time. "No. You need to show me. I'm not trying to follow those directions."

"Show you? I got the Den to run. I can't go wandering off."

"Alright, then. No key." Dagny stood and dusted off the back of her ruined skirt.

"Hold on. *Hold. On*," Dog said, rising. "Weren't you with Roger Red? I saw him around here a bit ago. He'd know the way."

"I'm not wasting my time on that one," Dagny said. "I need *you* to show me." She twisted the key in her hand.

Dog narrowed his eyes and studied her for a long while. "Tell you what. I'll take you most of the way there. That's the best I can do."

Dagny rubbed her neck, considering it. "No. I can't do that. I need you to take me all the way. Come on... Don't you want your key?"

"Look. It's not that I don't want to. But Spirit lives near the Bridges, and... well... let's say people like me aren't allowed through there."

"What's that mean?" Dagny asked. "What did you do?"

"Got old, I guess. So anyway, that's the offer."

Dagny thought for a moment. She was all out of options, and it was better than nothing. "Okay. We have an agreement."

"Great," Dog said, grabbing her hand and shaking it. "If you're ready, let's go. I need to be back before the midday meal."

Upon realizing Dagny had no other possessions, Dog fetched a pack, a lime-green shirt, and a pair of loose-fitting, multicolored pants from the Den. "This is all stuff that's been left behind by guests," he said. "Not worth much to me." The outfit looked like it had been dipped in a rainbow, but Dagny was glad to have a change of clothes again.

"Thanks," she said.

"There's some goat cheese and bread in the pack for you, too, and hopefully I'm taking you to friends, so you won't be starving."

"You are. I think."

"Good. Can I have that key now?" he asked.

Dagny reached into her pocket and clutched it. "No. Not yet. Once we get to the Bridges, then it's all yours. But... I need to get there first."

"That's fair."

With Dog's Den fading away in the distance, the city grew dense once again. There was no main road that Dagny could make sense of, just a series of narrow streets and alleys breaking apart the wall of tall buildings. But Dog knew exactly where he was going, weaving through seemingly random passageways.

"Some days are trickier than others," Dog said. "Pratchett seems particularly thick today."

"Cause of the shift?" Dagny asked. She kept an eye out for other people, but saw no one.

"Of course. You've never been to the Inner City?" Dog made a soft clicking sound on the roof of his mouth, like he was tasting something in the air.

"No."

"You're in for a surprise, then. There's nothing like the place."

Nothing like the place, huh? Dagny thought. Ever since leaving Rork, her journey had been a constant series of unusual places. Everything here seemed impossible. "What makes the Inner City so special?" she asked.

"It's the heart of Jud. The city's birthplace. The border between creation and oblivion. It's the hub... the center of the wheel." Dog stopped in the middle of the alley and pushed open a door that blended into their surroundings so well as to render it nearly invisible. "Am I making sense?"

"Yep. Perfect sense," Dagny replied. "And what about this Cauldron I've been hearing about?"

"Oh, that? Most days, it remains closed. An enormous hunk of metal in the ground outside of Sanctuary. But now and then, the shift causes it to open and reveal its true self: a passage straight into the depths."

"And then it closes again?"

"That's right. It only stays open for a day, and if you don't make it out before the next shift..." Dog drew a line across his throat. "Sometimes it can take years before the Cauldron opens back up. It's all random, even if some people think they can predict the timing."

They stepped through the hidden door and entered a courtyard. Rusted benches rested under shaded trees and brown grass mixed with pebbled stone.

"Sanctuary..." Dog muttered. "Now *that's* a beautiful place. I should get back there. It's been some time since I visited."

"How come?" Dagny asked, paying more attention to the courtyard than to Dog.

"Like I said, I've got the Den to run. Can't go running off, unless there's good reason." Dog walked to the opposite wall and made the strange clicking sound again. "There's another door here, somewhere. Help me find it."

Dagny wandered over and examined the area, not quite sure what she should be looking for.

"Know why they call me Dog?" he asked, running his hand over the stone wall. "Because I'm loyal and I can sniff out deceit. But I'm also prideful. I'll make an honest trade, and as you know, I'm keen to help someone who's struggling. I don't appreciate thieves, though, and I *don't* appreciate tricks."

"Tricks?" Dagny asked, not sure what Dog was getting at.

"Just a warning. I'm not sure how you got that key."

"I-I didn't steal it. I'm just trying to find my sister," Dagny said, suddenly feeling very nervous. "I'm not trying to trick you."

Dog didn't answer, and Dagny was all too aware of how alone they were in the courtyard.

She tried to steady her voice. "Pren gave me that key as he was being dragged out. He said you could help... Dog?"

"What?" he said, his gaze rooted on the wall in front of them.

"You're not going to... do something bad, are you?"

Dog chuckled. "That's a complicated question."

Suddenly, Dagny heard a crunch on the pebbled stones behind them, but she didn't dare turn to look. Something had followed them here—one of Dog's companions, perhaps? Was he planning to betray her, like Roger? Her mind raced. As much as Dagny wanted to turn around, she feared things would escalate so quickly that she'd lose all control of the situation.

"You can have the key," Dagny said calmly, pulling it from her pocket and holding it out. Maybe if she just handed it over, Dog would back off from whatever he was planning. "I knew I'd get lost if it wasn't for you. I don't have any family except for Grete. That's all I was trying to do... get back to my sister."

Dog gave her a confused look, then smiled and took the key. "Uh. Thanks." A moment later, he was back at the wall, running his finger along the mortar line.

The thing behind her moved again, its enormous shadow spreading over the ground and onto the wall. Whatever it was, it wasn't human. Dagny started to tremble with fear. "*Dog...*" she whispered. "*Please. Don't...*"

"What are you getting at? Don't what?"

Something heavy pressed into her thigh, almost knocking her off balance. Dagny leapt forward, and before the beast had a chance to grab her, she sprinted along the edge of the courtyard, trying to circle back toward the entrance.

"Damnit," she heard Dog mutter. "Girl! Come back here!"

The courtyard was a rectangular block, framed by tall buildings. Dagny rushed over to the opposite wall, looking for the door they had entered from, but it had disappeared. She was trapped.

Frantically, Dagny rubbed her hands over the stone, searching for a hidden switch or latch or *something*. Her heart pounded. Any second now they would descend upon her... and for what? Holding onto a key?

She stepped back and quickly scanned the buildings. A couple of them had windows, but they were shuttered and too far up to reach.

She yelled, "Hello?! Anyone?! Help me!"

Nothing.

Dagny slammed her hands on the wall, pushing hard on the solid stone, shouting, "*Help me!*" Her voice echoed briefly around the courtyard, and then silence.

"Girl!" Dog called out. "What's gotten into you?"

Wiping sweat from her eyes, Dagny glanced over and saw Dog holding his palms up defensively. But behind him stood the beast she feared: a massive, four-legged creature the color of night. It was the shape of a wolf and the size of a small horse. It cocked its head, calmly watching her.

"Be easy," Dog said.

"W-what is that?" Dagny panted. "What are you going to do? I gave you the key!"

"I'm not going to do anything. Just take you to the Bridges, like I said." Dog gestured to the giant wolf. "Eidfur is a friend. You got nothing to worry about, alright? Calm down." He stretched his hand out.

Dagny didn't take it. Instead, she rubbed her face and tried to relax. "I'm fine... I thought... never mind."

"Thought what? That I would hurt you?" Dog asked. He gently reached forward to touch her shoulder, but decided against it.

"Why is that wolf here?" Dagny asked, still fearful, but faking composure.

"Eidfur can escort you the rest of the way to Spirit's—if you're polite to him. I told you, I'd make sure you got there."

"You should've warned me."

"I wasn't certain Eidfur would respond. I didn't want to make a false promise." The wolf stepped next to Dog, then sat on its hind legs. "But what about you? All that screaming. I was afraid your heart was going to stop."

"I told you, I'm fine," Dagny snapped. Only she didn't feel fine. It felt like her mind had shattered.

Dog lowered his head. "Maybe you should come back to the Den with me," he said. "I can help you get back home, and we'll take care of you until then."

"No."

"I've seen this before. Your reaction was... severe. I'm not sure exactly what you've experienced, but I know trauma when I see it. You need to take your time. You need to be somewhere safe right now."

Dagny laughed at him. "Somewhere safe? Really? And you're going to provide it? Isn't that nice. Just take me where I need to go, okay? Just honor our agreement, please."

Dog took a step back and frowned. His eyes were sad.

Dagny laughed even harder. A mean, mocking laugh. It sounded foreign to her. "You're *pitying* me?"

"No. Not pity."

"Good." Dagny marched past him to the opposite wall, keeping her distance from the wolf. "Let's find this door."

14

It took longer than it should have to open the wall. After pushing and prodding every inch of mortar and stone, Dog finally remembered that this was one of those *responding* walls, and all he had to do was ask nicely and the door would appear.

As soon as the word "please" left his mouth, the stone spread apart and revealed another alleyway. Eidfur went first, sniffing the air and stepping off to the left. The beast was old, no doubt, walking with a slight limp, and Dagny noticed small patches of fur missing from its back. But despite its age, the creature stood as tall as her, and when it glanced over with its solid gray eyes, her blood went cold—a reminder, perhaps, of her flight from the last great beast she encountered, inside of a different wall.

Every part of the city felt old, but this alley felt *old* old. Black and yellow lichen covered the narrow walls, which stretched so high they blocked out the sun, and puddles of water collected on the cobblestone path even though Dagny hadn't seen it rain once since she'd been in Jud.

The alley was a straight tunnel. Dagny followed Dog, and Dog followed the wolf. "Eidfur knows his way around these parts better than anything," Dog said. "You won't get lost with him around. How? You might ask? When the shift causes things to change daily? Well, Eidfur has seen it all, every iteration of Jud that's ever been. He's got them all memorized."

A cool breeze swept down the tunnel, causing Dagny's arms to break out in goosebumps. Dog's tone was light and friendly now. Any hint of pity he'd felt for her had left as quickly as it had come on. That was probably for the best. Dagny couldn't make sense of what was going on inside of her, and there wasn't any time for reflection. *Just get to Grete. You're so close. If you can do that, then everything will be fine.*

"How far away are the Bridges?" Dagny asked.

"Oh, we're here," Dog said. "We just need to reach them." He pointed up to a series of platforms and rickety planks criss-crossing the alley. They seemed to run between dark holes in the walls high above.

"*Those* are the Bridges?" Dagny said, trying to take it all in. "Do people actually use them? Does anyone live here?"

"Yep."

"Who?"

Instead of answering her question, Dog asked, "How old are you?"

"Eighteen."

The man frowned and twisted his mouth, then quickly smiled. "Anyone ever tell you that you look younger?"

"Yeah. I've heard that."

"Eighteen," he repeated. "Well, you should be fine. And you got Eidfur."

That response didn't make Dagny feel good. "What lives here?"

"The young clans, mostly. They're a bit full of themselves, and it's just easier for people like me to avoid them. It can be a challenge when they're in their obnoxious little packs."

"People like you?"

"Yeah. Grown men."

"Wait. You're talking about children here?" Dagny asked.

"Call 'em what you want. Every now and then, a couple will venture over to the Den, trying to blend in with the others. I still serve them, even though I shouldn't."

Packs of children terrorizing intruders? Dagny stopped. "I don't know about this..."

"It'll be fine." Dog turned, scratched his chin, and looked her up and down, as if seeing her for the first time. "They're not gonna bother you. They'll probably love you." Then he laughed. "You'll probably fit right in."

"Why do they live here?"

"I don't know. So they can live by their own rules? Most newcomers to the Inner City head straight for Sanctuary, but some are too wild for that place, and they end up in the Bridges."

"Why are they all children? I mean, eventually people age."

"True," Dog said. "But haven't you noticed there aren't too many old men like me around?"

"You're not that old," Dagny replied. "And yes, I've noticed."

"That's because people here have sworn to restore Jud, and as they age, they need to fulfill that oath. Bridge-dweller or not. Whether it's a pilgrimage into the Great Below, or undertaking other quests in the world beyond. If you benefit from Jud, you've got a part to play. You need to give back in the end."

"Like Pren."

"What's that?" Dog asked.

"Pren's brothers took him away, saying he needed to fulfill his oath. Roger Red claims they're going to force him into the underground."

"I see," Dog said. "I like that boy, but… we all have our roles."

"He helped me out quite a bit. I wish I could repay him."

"Those are family matters. You shouldn't get involved."

Dagny scoffed. "Why? Just because it's your family doesn't mean you should be tortured by them, or be forced into the depths with them to die."

"That's one opinion," Dog said, not looking to argue.

"And what quest are you on?" Dagny asked.

"Oh. My family is one of the few that's integral to Jud's existence. We're better off staying put." Dog pointed ahead to a split in the alley. "Getting close. Our time together is almost at its end."

Dagny followed behind, stepping through the puddles. Eidfur sniffed the air again, then yawned.

"You hear that?" Dog asked with a smile.

The sound was so faint it was almost nonexistent, but Dagny did hear something. Actually, she could feel it. A dim, steady beating in the back of her head. At first, she thought it was the pulse of blood rushing from her own heart; an echo of the panic she'd felt in the courtyard. "Are those drums?" she asked.

"I think you're in luck," Dog said. "Sounds like the bridge-dwellers are having one of their little gatherings. You should be able to make it across rather quickly, *and* you'll be able to tell where they're at. Just avoid the drumming."

They reached the split in the path. To the right, the alley narrowed even more to allow for a set of stairs that worked their way up the wall. Dog kneeled down beside Eidfur and whispered in his ear. Dagny backed off and studied her surroundings. The stairs seemed to stretch almost to the rooftops. Across from her, etched in big, clear letters, was the phrase: *Murk Dour*. And it looked like someone had scratched a deep line through it.

When Dog finished speaking with the beast, he walked over and put his hand on Dagny's shoulder. "I enjoyed meeting you. Eidfur will take over from here."

"What's *Murk Dour* mean?" Dagny asked, pointing to the phrase on the wall, not ready to say goodbye just yet.

"It basically means a knight of Jud, but it's an insult. Don't call 'em that unless you're looking to get clobbered."

"Did one of the knights try to scratch it out?"

"Nah. The scratch means to get rid of them. So, the phrase here means, *Death to Knights.*"

Dagny couldn't blame someone for writing that; she had yet to meet a single knight she liked. "Do you really need to leave?" she asked with sudden vulnerability. The thought of being alone again brought another rise of anxiousness.

"You'd be in more trouble *with* me." Dog gestured at the giant wolf. "He's a better companion going forward. Don't worry."

"Are the bridge-dwellers afraid of Eidfur?"

"Something like that. Take care of yourself, alright? Whatever you're dealing with, don't bury it so far inside that it becomes impossible to root out."

"Okay," Dagny said, not quite sure what he was getting at. "I'm sorry for snapping at you earlier. Thanks for bringing me here."

Dog smiled and gave her a quick nod. "Spirit's place is just on the other side. In the shade of the Alypso tree. It's impossible to miss."

The man stood back and watched them ascend. Once again, Eidfur led the way, slowly plodding along as the stairs creaked and groaned under their weight. Dagny focused on the wolf, almost expecting it to stumble off the side, but the creature was nimble when it needed to be, deftly turning corners whenever the stairs zigzagged the wall. As frightening as Eidfur appeared, Dagny was glad she wasn't alone right now, and a wolf wouldn't lie to you. If it was going to do you harm, you'd know it.

The stairs ended at an open doorway near the roof. Dagny glanced down, hoping to give Dog one final wave, but he was already gone.

The path ahead was dark, but not pitch black. Sunlight broke in through gaps in the ceiling, illuminating the space: a weathered hallway, musty and barren. She'd have to watch her step here. There were plenty of gaps in the floor, too.

There were no rooms along this route. Just the singular hall, funneling them into the heart of whatever building this was. Foreign scribblings adorned the peeling plaster walls, similar to the *Murk Dour* etching below, but Dagny couldn't make sense of the writing. Maybe it was all nonsensical slang of the bridge-dwellers: *Klep touters Crash; Meegwaah; Simples Plimptolls.*

Meegwaah. Dagny thought that was a funny word, and she imagined a gang of ten-year-olds shouting it at old men, chasing them from the territory.

The drumming was still faint, but Dagny could hear it more clearly now. An *aye-ie* carried out over the beating, followed by a breathy group chant. Yep, there were definitely people around. She couldn't make out the next word they shouted, but it sounded like "hunt."

"Let's try our best to avoid them," Dagny whispered. "What do you say, Eidfur?"

If the beast heard her, it didn't show.

When they finally reached the end of the hallway, the ground below gave out, and the path continued along a narrow metal beam that connected to a platform far away on the other side. It was an enormous interior chasm they would be crossing. Dagny could see other beams and planks connecting other passages in the distance, and below lay the wreckage of past "bridges," smashed across the gray stone ground. There were lamps or fires down there, too, and although Dagny thought she might've seen shapes hiding in shadows, she couldn't be certain.

Eidfur nudged her forward. "Oh, now you want me to go first?" Dagny whispered. "How brave of you." The wolf lowered his head and silently stared at her. He seemed impatient. "Okay, fine," Dagny said, carefully stepping onto the beam.

Heights never made her nervous. Still, she wasn't stupid. There'd be no surviving a fall if the crossing wasn't secure. Fortunately, the beam was thick and solid and made of iron, welded together like some sort of rail track. How it got up here was anyone's guess. As soon as she got her bearings, Dagny stretched her arms out for balance, took a breath, and scuttled across. Hopefully, Eidfur could make his way over without issue. Dagny could only worry about so much.

The sun broke through the ceiling here as well. Translucent, crooked fingers of light simultaneously revealing and covering the dangers of the beam: hidden rivets and snags in the metal that sprung out of the darkness; pools of corrosion; sharp bits... and traps. Yeah, someone had placed a trap here. Dagny saw it well in advance—a crude trip wire strung across the beam. She glanced back at Eidfur and pointed to it. The wolf stared at her with those brooding eyes. Dagny thought she saw him nod.

The chamber was so wide, it felt like she was crossing an abyss. Like she was back in the underground with Melwes and the spirit lights, traversing the legendary Fire Gorge. She'd never been inside of a building this large before. She didn't even know buildings like this could exist. It was a world unto itself. The drums continued to pound, vibrating flakes of rust along the beam, growing louder and louder. The sound offered Dagny a clue as to where the Bridge-dwellers were gathering now: somewhere below and ahead.

When she was halfway across the beam, the metal started to fall apart. A chunk of iron broke free next to her foot with a shuddering groan, and then silently fell. Dagny's stomach sank as she watched the metal tumble toward the ground, but before her mind could process what was actually happening, something yanked her into the air.

She landed on the next section of beam just before the iron crashed onto the floor below. It was followed a moment later with a blast so loud it sounded like the world had ended. The next thing Dagny knew, she was in the air again, then landing, then flying, until finally, she came to rest on the opposite ledge. Only then did Dagny realize her pack was clinched between Eidfur's powerful jaws.

The wolf carefully released her and sat down, as if nothing had happened.

Dagny looked back at the beam, now a pier of jagged broken metal. An entire section had collapsed behind her, sending shockwaves throughout the Bridges. And Eidfur had saved her life.

She reached out and touched the wolf, unsure of what else to do. There was incense in the air: earthy and fragrant. Perhaps a part of whatever ceremony the Bridge-dwellers were having.

The drumming... it had stopped, and the silence brought about another wave of alarm. Anyone from here to Dog's Den had probably heard the crash. The Bridge-dwellers were certain to come investigate.

They needed to move, quickly. Dagny glanced over the space. There was a series of passages ahead, branching off from the main one.

As if he'd heard her thoughts, Eidfur trotted forward and cut down a hallway to their left.

"Wait," Dagny hissed, charging after him. Thick yellow candles, dripping wax onto the floorboards, illuminated the next passage. The wolf continued to race forward, darting and weaving through a series of interconnected rooms. Dagny had to sprint to keep up, catching only brief glimpses of the creature as it rounded corners and zipped from one room to the next.

It had been a long time since the building's original inhabitants had lived here (whoever they were). Now it was a playground for the newcomers. Rubbish lay strewn across the area: pots and toys, metal poles and polished rocks. Hopping over a piece of broken furniture, Dagny almost barreled straight into Eidfur. The wolf had stopped at a staircase leading down into a pit of blackness.

"Here?" Dagny whispered. It was oddly quiet. She expected to hear the rage of a thousand little shouts by now, accompanied by the thundering of two thousand little feet. *What were the Bridge-dwellers doing?* Why were they waiting?

"I'm ready whenever you are," Dagny said. The wolf nuzzled her hand, then flung it onto his head. Even though the fur appeared sleek and slick as oil, it was prickly and rough. Dagny rested her hand on Eidfur's back and allowed herself to be guided into the darkness.

They moved slowly. After the first few steps, Dagny was totally blind, and she wondered how much the great wolf could see in here. She side-stepped down the stairs, pressing herself into the wolf's body. The beast smelled musky, a touch metallic, and there was a hint of something else there. A slight rotting scent like death. She could feel the creature breathing against her, and its massive heart pulsating under thick muscle.

Deeper and deeper they descended. It was hard to tell how far they had gone, given their pace in the dark. Dagny was glad to be done with bridges for the moment and hoped the stairs would lead them out of the territory. They had to be getting close to Marfisi's house. Dagny started to picture Grete and thought about how she should act. *Don't be too emotional. Don't make Grete feel uncomfortable. Don't act strange.*

A single drum began to pound. Dagny instinctively gripped Eidfur tighter and buried her face into his fur, but they kept moving. This drum sounded louder... closer, like they were heading straight for it.

They're only children. Trust Dog. Eidfur will keep you safe. If anything, the mere sight of the giant wolf would probably send the Bridge-dwellers fleeing in terror.

Two drums pounded now. Dagny could feel it in her chest; could hear it amplify throughout the staircase. By the time the other drums joined in, the sound was all-consuming.

Eidfur never wavered, though. His pulse never quickened and his breath never strained. The beast just kept stepping methodically down the stairs.

So long as the Bridge-dwellers stayed in their chamber, pounding away, they might never know Dagny was here. She was slight and sneaky, and Eidfur was surprisingly quiet, given his size.

All of a sudden, the stairs and stone wall surrounding them became brighter, etched out in dark gray, the color of charcoal. And the further they descended, the lighter the stone became. Something was brightening their path, but whatever it was, it didn't sway or flicker; it wasn't a flame.

Dagny tried to stop. She wanted to understand what they were walking into, but Eidfur refused to slow down and started to slip through her arms. Dagny quickly matched his pace. She couldn't risk losing the wolf. She felt protected near him: touching his fur; inhaling the scent of musky death; drawing the same breath.

Just then, she saw a reflection of pale light moving fast against the gray wall, sliding along the contours of the staircase. Her heart quickened. She thought of the drowned twins, with their pale candles, chasing her from the old palace kitchens; stretching toward Tash with black nails; glaring at her with their sunken, fish-scale eyes. Could the great wolf protect her against such horrible things?

Before Dagny could react, before she could warn Eidfur or turn and run up the stairwell, the light barreled out of the darkness. A single, floating orb.

Dagny sucked in air, as if she had just emerged from the bottom of a deep lake, and the fear immediately washed from her body. *A spirit light.* Was this really happening? Was this one of the same lights from the Under Road? Was Melwes close by? Did this orb escape from Yunis?

"Do I know you?" Dagny whispered, grinning so wide her face hurt.

The orb spun around her head, swirled through the air, and then rested on her nose, glowing so brightly, Dagny had to shut her eyes. She *did* know this one. "Are you... Mia?" Dagny asked.

The orb shot up to the ceiling and spun itself into a frenzy, zipping faster than Dagny thought an orb could zip. Eidfur cocked his head and watched. "It's okay, this is a friend," Dagny told the wolf.

The orb began to pulsate, beating with the drums. Then it slowly retreated down the stairs, as if trying to draw her along.

Dagny gently patted the great beast's prickly fur. "Come on, Eidfur. You can follow me now."

15

The stairs ended, and they found themselves at the bottom of the enormous chamber. Dagny could barely see the remains of the beam, jutting out from the wall high above like the twisted plank of some strange pirate ship.

"Mia, wait," she called out. "What about Melwes? Is he with you?"

The orb didn't react. It just continued to glide further into the chamber. Dagny shrugged and followed, while Eidfur slinked along behind her. So quiet was the great wolf that Dagny had to glance back every few steps to make sure he was still there.

She hoped with all of her heart that Mia was taking them to Melwes. Dagny *needed* to see the boy again. She needed to know he was safe. If something happened to Melwes... if he was hurt or dead, Dagny knew she would never recover from it.

The floor here was smooth and gray, a mix of concrete and marble. It reflected the fires that Dagny had seen earlier while crossing the beam, casting a shadowy, orange glow over the area. The fires themselves were unattended at the moment, and they seemed to be fed by all manner of rubbish; from scraps of wood to ruined furniture and melted objects that Dagny couldn't identify. She mostly kept her eyes on the other "bridges," though. The last thing she wanted was to be smashed by another falling beam.

The drums continued to beat. It sounded like there were hundreds of them. As if every dweller of this self-contained world was hammering on buckets, barrels and skin. The vibrations rattled the beams above, sending rust and dirt to drift over the chamber like snow in a ruined wasteland. Eidfur seemed unfazed, but Dagny had to walk with her hands over her ears.

Mia guided them along the edge of the wall. They passed a table where flies buzzed around moldy bread and half-finished bowls of stew; they passed a crude sculpture of a giant wolf made from colored fabric and clay. It looked like Eidfur, if Eidfur were yellow and purple with a lumpy head too big for his body.

Finally, Mia stopped at an enormous set of double doors, engraved with geometric symbols, that shook from the sound within. This was it. This was the entrance to the chamber of drums. The gathering hall.

Mia hovered near the brass push plates.

"You want us to go in there?" Dagny asked. "Right into the thick of it?" She looked over at Eidfur, who yawned and flapped his ears. He might as well have been getting ready to settle down for a nap.

Mia darted in front of Dagny's face, then circled her wrist.

"Fine," Dagny said. If no one else was concerned, why should she be? And if things went wrong, she could at least count on Eidfur and that friendly smile of his.

Dagny placed her hands on the brass plate. Mia buzzed with an eagerness. "I'm going, I'm going," Dagny whispered to the orb. Then she took a deep breath and pushed.

She had seen a painting once of an assembly room at the Palace of Stars. Gilded and elegant. With vaulted ceilings where some old emperor was being anointed, surrounded by adoring retainers and stern-faced guardsmen. The chamber in front of her now was like a distorted, dream version of that event. It stretched far longer though, and instead of noble retainers and armor-clad guardsmen, hundreds of sooty-faced children glared at her ferociously from the sides of the room.

The drumming stopped as soon as she stepped inside, as if all the children had been staring at the door, waiting for her to enter.

The smoky fog of incense was so thick it burned her eyes. Dagny drew in air, readying herself to greet the chamber, but choked out a cough instead. None of the children moved. They only watched, brimming with feral tension.

And then Eidfur entered. His giant wolf face appearing from out of the blackness. In an instant, the energy of the great hall shifted into chaos. The children shrieked and scattered into shaded corners. Some of them tripped, and others trampled over their fallen companions, desperate to get away from the creature. The panicked crying came next, followed by the pleading.

"Is there something you need to tell me?" Dagny asked the wolf, quietly. "Did you do something bad here?"

Eidfur bared his teeth, took a step forward, and the entire hall screamed in unison. Or, *almost* the entire hall. One figure stood alone, lit by candlelight. It didn't carry any weapons but stood bravely, hands on hips, wearing a crown.

Dagny cleared her throat and yelled out over the children. "Hello there, I am Dagny Losh... umm... friend of the lights!" She had lost track of Mia during the initial confusion, but saw the orb now, fluttering by the figure in the distance. Silhouetted by the spirit light, the figure stepped toward her, slowly at first, then breaking into a run.

Dagny's heart leapt. She felt like both crying and laughing. The other children became a blur. Eidfur vanished in the shadows. All at once, it was only Dagny and the boy. She met him halfway, unaware that she'd even been running, and embraced Melwes so hard, the boy let out a loud wheeze. She lifted him into the air, spinning around in circles.

He didn't protest, and even though Dagny couldn't see his face, she knew he was smiling, too. Melwes. The boy who'd refused every hug she'd tried to give in the underground now clung to her tightly. She felt his body quiver and heave as he cried into her chest.

They didn't say anything. But they didn't really need to. The boy was alive; he was safe. That's all Dagny needed to know. Another light came fluttering over from across the room and circled Mia. Dagny could see Melwes' face clearly in the soft blue glow. There was so much sooty dirt on his forehead and around his eyes, it was hard to get a good sense of his condition.

"We need to get out of here," Dagny said. "Do you know where the exit is?" The boy answered by nodding slowly and pointing toward the back of the chamber.

Dagny wasted no more time. She took the boy's hand and marched through the horde of frightened children. Some had painted faces and carried sharpened poles; some wore tusks fashioned from bone or wood; and others simply held their hands over their eyes, muttering quietly; but none accosted her.

Melwes directed her to a side tunnel, another short flight of stairs, and finally to a rusted door that creaked something horrid when she pushed it open. Sunlight flooded the staircase, and Dagny stepped out into a field of grass that abutted the enormous building behind her. Glancing back, the structure looked even larger than she expected it would, appearing to scratch the sky itself.

Eidfur pushed past her and sniffed the fresh air, while the lights fluttered just above Melwes' head.

Dagny leaned down and met his eyes. "I was so worried about you. I'm *so sorry* I lost you. I'm so sorry…"

Melwes stuck his bottom lip out. Tears continued to drip down his face.

"You're not hurt or anything? Have you had enough to eat?" Dagny asked. She suddenly remembered the food in her pack and opened it, handing Melwes the cheese and tearing off a heel of bread.

"I'm not hurt," he said, quietly.

"Thank goodness." She wanted to ask how he got away from Yunis but stopped herself, not wanting to trigger any distress. "How long were you in there for?"

"I don't know," Melwes said. "Ever since you left."

Dagny nodded, then licked her thumb and tried to wipe some of the dirt from the boy's forehead.

Melwes let her clean him off, then bit into the wheel of cheese, slobbering over himself as he chewed. "I fell into the dark and landed on a forgotten stretch of the Under Road. It took me there," he said, pointing to the building behind them.

"And those Bridge-dwellers, they were nice to you?"

"Yes. They were strange, though."

Dagny laughed. "Yeah. I suppose so." She glanced over at the pair of spirit lights hovering nearby. "I see Mia has a friend. That *is* Mia, right?"

"Mm-hmm. And Fig. They're the only ones left."

Dagny's heart sunk. "The *only* ones?"

Melwes took the crown off his head and stared at her, a serious expression on his face. "The others got eaten by Yunis. You saw it."

"I know... I guess I was hoping more got away."

"Maybe..." Melwes said, a far-off look in his eyes. "Maybe they did... But... maybe they didn't."

"Who's Fig?" Dagny asked, trying to direct the boy's attention away from his thoughts.

"Oh," Melwes said, snapping back to the present. "Fig is a new guardian. He's from the forest and the mist that breathes life into the world. He was young. Like me."

"Hello, Fig," Dagny said to the orb.

"We don't talk about how he died," Melwes whispered. "He gets upset."

Fig started to vibrate and floated high over their heads.

"I don't blame him," Dagny whispered back to the boy. "Who'd wanna talk about that?"

"Yeah."

"Do you recognize any of this?" Dagny said, gazing out over the field. A short distance away, the city started up again, turning into a jumbled facade of staggered buildings, painted in bright tones of yellow and orange. "Know where we are?"

Melwes looked sad. "No."

"That's okay."

The boy closed his eyes tightly and shook. He seemed to be struggling with something.

"Melwes," Dagny whispered. "What's wrong?" When he didn't answer, she placed her hands on his shoulders and said, "It's alright. Just let it go."

After a series of deep breaths, Melwes opened his eyes, once again in control of himself. "It's hard to remember anything from before," he said.

"What do you mean?"

"From before the lights found me. I can't remember it."

"You mean from years ago... You can't remember anything?" Dagny asked softly.

Melwes shook his head. He seemed so young and innocent in the sunlight. Just a boy, lost without his spirit lights. "No. Not really. I just get images of things."

"Maybe it will come back to you someday. Sometimes that happens. A lot of my own memories are stuck deep inside my head. Just the other day, I remembered one from when I was a child. A big one that I had forgotten all about."

"Really?" Melwes asked. "What was it?"

Dagny thought about the memory of being trapped in the rendering pit. "It wasn't pleasant," she said. "But that doesn't mean yours won't be. Maybe I can help you."

"How?"

"Well, we could talk about it more. If you're okay with that." Dagny smiled. "It might take a while, though. You might have to talk to me more than you like."

Melwes looked at the ground. "How long are you staying this time?"

"Oh, I don't know," Dagny said. "Forever? How does that sound?"

The boy twisted his mouth and frowned.

"I mean it," Dagny said. "You and me... we're friends forever now. I'm not leaving you again, alright? Melwes?" She swept the greasy hair from his eyes. "Alright?"

After a long pause, Melwes nodded, then whispered back, "Alright."

"Good. Now that's settled. I need to find my sister. She's supposed to be close by. Under an Alypso tree." Dagny studied the buildings in the distance. "Think there are any Alypso trees over there?"

"What's an Alypso tree?" Melwes asked.

"Well..." Dagny began. "I was hoping you might know."

In the time they'd spent talking, Eidfur had wandered off and now stood atop a pile of bricks in the field.

"See something?" Dagny called out to the wolf, as she began to walk over.

Suddenly, Eidfur let out a guttural howl so loud Dagny felt it in her chest. It was a primal, ancient call. Not the sound of a normal wolf seeking its pack, but the sound of something extinct, from a bygone time, when Man huddled around primitive fires and smartly feared what hunted them when the sun went down.

Before Dagny could regain herself, Eidfur leapt off the bricks and darted toward a set of buildings on the horizon.

Without a second thought, Dagny reached back and grabbed Melwes' hand. "Hurry!" she yelled, running off after the wolf even though she had no hope of catching him. She was tired of losing new friends; sick of everyone disappearing.

But that's exactly what *she* had done, wasn't it? Run off and disappeared from all the people in her life.

Dagny reached the pile of bricks as Eidfur neared the buildings. She was going to lose him any moment now; just a few more strides and the wolf would be gone. Melwes pulled his hand away and sprinted next to her without saying a word, followed by Mia and Fig.

She kept running, even after the wolf had vanished into the brightly painted facade. She kept running until she and the boy were both out of breath, panting heavily in the shadows of the old buildings.

"Why'd he leave?" Melwes wheezed.

Dagny shrugged and did her best to keep moving. Like every other part of Jud, the district in front of her was strange in its own unique way. Up close, the yellow and orange buildings were even more brilliant than when she'd viewed them from the field. The paint looked fresh—not dull and faded like everything before it—and the buildings sparkled as if dusted with powdered glass.

"Should we call after him?" Dagny whispered to Melwes, hesitant about stepping into the district.

"No," the boy replied. "He wouldn't come back. He wanted to leave us. Where'd you find him?"

"In the alleys of Pratchett. You could say he's a new friend of a new friend."

"The other children didn't like him very much."

Dagny stifled a laugh and focused on the buildings. "No, they didn't. Think it's safe to go forward?"

"There's not many of them around anymore," Melwes said, ignoring her question. "The ancient creatures."

"Right. The ancient creatures..." Dagny repeated. "Do you think Eidfur is as old as Yunis?" *Or the crow*, she thought.

"Hard to know how old any of them are. Jorm and the Grondel."

"What's that?" Dagny asked.

"Those were the first two. All the other great ones are descended from either Jorm or the Grondel. The kinder creatures—and the protectors—would be Jorm. And the *other* ones are from the Grondel."

"Like Yunis, then? She'd be a Grondel."

Melwes shook his head. "No. Yunis lost her sense. That's why she's like that. She'd been trapped in that castle for so long, it confused her. I'm sad about what she did, but I don't hate her." Melwes scratched at his head, like he was digging for insects. "The Grondel are worse."

"So you think Yunis was kind at one time?"

"I like to think that," Melwes said. "Don't you?"

"It's a nice thought, but... it's all pretty horrible," Dagny said. "Someone putting Yunis in that castle for such a long time—the fact that she could've been kind and friendly when it happened—makes it all that much worse."

Melwes tightened his face and nodded. "Yeah."

"Well, I guess we should go forward," Dagny said, gesturing at the mass of buildings. "Can't stand out here forever."

There was no obvious sign of people in the brightly colored district. There were windows and doors, but everything was tightly shuttered, and Dagny didn't think she should start knocking.

They walked along the first block of buildings and reached a crossroads on the other side. Dagny caught a whiff of something metallic and sour in the air. *Eidfur.*

"Do you smell that?" she asked Melwes.

The boy held his nose. "Uh-huh."

"Any idea where it's coming from?"

Suddenly, someone appeared on a nearby rooftop. "You looking for that wolf? It went that way," the person said, pointing off to the left.

"Oh, okay. Thank you," Dagny called back. The figure was shaded by the sun, but Dagny could see various plants and vines growing around them. A rooftop garden. "Excuse me, do you know if there's an Alypso tree around here?" she asked.

"Alypso tree? You looking for that witch girl, eh?"

"Yeah. I suppose so."

"You and everyone else these days." The person shielded their eyes and appeared to study Dagny and Melwes before continuing. "The tree is that way, too. Maybe your wolf meant to beat you to it."

"Oh, great! Thanks again," Dagny said, and before hurrying off down the path, shouted back, "Why is everyone else looking for her?"

"I'm not one to gossip... but I'm thinking it's got something to do with her new companion. She's been *seeing* things."

Grete.

Dagny pulled Melwes down the path. The figure muttered something else, but Dagny couldn't make out the words.

The road continued on for a time before sloping downward and circling the base of a small mound. Growing up from the middle of the mound was an enormous bone-white tree with no leaves. And next to it stood a three-story, wood-framed tower. This was it. Marfisi's home. *Spirit's place.*

A sickening wave of anticipation rushed over her, causing Dagny to bend down and grip her thighs. It felt like her legs were about to buckle and send her tumbling down the path.

"What's wrong with you?" Melwes asked.

Dagny shook her head. "I don't feel well. Give me a moment."

The boy sighed and shifted his weight around impatiently. "That's probably the tree, you know. The *Alypso.*"

"Yeah. I do know."

Melwes spoke slowly, as if Dagny wasn't understanding him. "Your sister's probably in there... The one you've been looking for."

"Yeah..."

"You want me to go get her for you?"

"No. I'm coming..." Dagny took a deep breath and stood. "Ease up. Don't rush me."

"You're trying to figure out what to say?"

Dagny nodded. "Something like that."

"Just say..." Melwes scratched his head. "I missed you, and I wanted to see you again."

That made her smile. Those words were as good as any.

They were halfway down the hill when the shouting started.

"Keep that beast away from me!" a man demanded, his shrill voice cutting through the air.

Dagny gave Melwes a look, and they both started running.

The road flattened, and immediately after rounding the bend, the scene spread out in front of them. Eidfur had three large men cornered against a garden wall. Behind the wolf was a skinny girl dressed in a blocky canvas shirt that came down to her knees, exposing pale legs that looked like twigs sticking out of boots several sizes too large. She looked familiar. *Feruda?* Dagny thought. One of Marfisi's musicians, and Sarna's crush for a time.

"I told you to leave! You have no right here!" the girl shouted.

"We have all the rights we need," the man replied, trying to sound brave but failing. He had long black hair and was dressed like one of the Knights Eternal. *Knights of the waste yards.* In fact, all three of the men wore dented, tarnished metal and carried clubs. But the weapons did little to dissuade Eidfur. The hulking wolf stared the men down, his back prickled like a porcupine.

"Hand over the stranger, and we'll be on our way," the man continued.

Feruda picked a small stone from the ground and chucked it at the man's head, narrowly missing him. "You'll leave *now*!" she shouted. "Go! There's no strangers here, only the Invited!"

"Fetch the witch!" a different, taller man said, stepping forward. "We demand it!"

Just then, Eidfur snarled and leapt forward, cutting the distance to the men in half. The Knights scattered and stumbled over themselves, running straight past Dagny and Melwes, as they fled the courtyard.

"Go! Get! Never come back!" Feruda screamed, chasing after the men for several strides.

Once the knights had disappeared around the hill, Feruda swept the hair from her eyes and picked up a boot that had fallen off during the pursuit. She drew deep, hard breaths, looking fiery and furious.

The girl glared at Dagny, opened her mouth to say something, then quickly closed it. A realization spread across her face. "You..." she whispered. "It's... *you*. You're here..."

"Hello, Feruda," Dagny said, offering a shy wave. She wasn't sure how Feruda was going to react, but suddenly the girl embraced her.

"The sister..." Feruda whispered to herself. "How did you get here?"

"It's a long story," Dagny replied, then introduced Melwes and the lights. "And I see you already met Eidfur."

"He's with you?" Feruda asked.

Dagny answered with a quick nod. "I thought he was done with us, but it looks like he sensed trouble ahead."

"I'm very thankful for his help," Feruda replied, leading them into the courtyard surrounding the tower and tree. "I don't know how long I could've managed without him. This is the first time that three of the knights have come. Marfisi is gone for the day and, well, it's just me and..." it sounded like Feruda was about to say a different name, then caught herself, "Gretchen."

"Were those men talking about Grete?" Dagny asked. "Is that who they wanted to take?"

"Yes. They've been relentless lately." Feruda glanced at Eidfur and smiled. "Although they'll probably think better of harassing us now."

The wolf circled the courtyard, found a spot in the shade of the tower, and rested with a sigh.

"Is she inside?" Dagny asked.

Feruda nodded. "At the top. Do you want me to tell her you're here?"

"No. That's okay," Dagny replied. "I'll just go up." She took a moment, trying to relax, before heading to the door.

"Dagny," Feruda said from behind. "It's good that you're here."

The first floor was crowded with all manner of eclectic furnishings and random items. Plants hung in pots overhead; various musical instruments lay strewn about the room; colored blankets covered wooden chairs and benches; and a small kitchen sat off to the side, dominated by a large, black stove and stacks of dishes and mugs. A tight, spiraling staircase sprouted from the middle of the room, connecting the upper levels.

Dagny had taken only a few steps when a voice called out from above.

"Are those men gone?"

It almost made her heart stop. *Grete.* It was actually happening. Months of waiting in Old Rork. Months more in the underground...

Yunis and the castle; the Silent Keep; Lieta and Kustav; shifting roads and Grouchers and Bridge-dwellers... all leading to this. Dagny wasn't sure what to do. She didn't want to have this conversation from the room below. So, instead, she took another step up the creaking staircase.

"Feruda? Who's there?"

This time, Dagny didn't have a chance to respond. Grete's smooth, dark face peered over the railing and gasped.

"Hi," Dagny said, smiling awkwardly. It was all she could think of to say.

"Dag..." A faint smile formed on Grete's face, only to disappear just as quickly. "Why are you here?" she asked, her voice suddenly cool and unwelcoming.

Dagny's heart thundered. She paused, gripping the wooden handrails with sweaty hands. "I missed you."

"You *missed* me?" Grete asked, sounding incredulous, on the verge of anger.

"Yeah. I wanted to see you again. I thought—"

"You shouldn't have come."

"Why not? I thought you'd be happy to see your adoring sister," Dagny said nervously, trying desperately to lighten the mood.

"You shouldn't have come after me," Grete said, then moved away from the staircase, disappearing back into the room.

Dagny was starting to feel angry herself. And embarrassed. She wiped her palms on her shirt while her mind raced. What was she supposed to do now? After a moment, she asked, "Do you want me to leave?" Then repeated it when Grete didn't answer.

Really? You're not even going to respond? Dagny thought, shaking her head.

Marching up the stairs, Dagny readied herself for a confrontation, but the room she climbed into sucked all the energy from her body. Windowless, black and barren; Grete sat cross-legged with her head in her hands, in front of a single candle and surrounded by what appeared to be animal bones.

"What is this?" Dagny whispered.

"You couldn't understand," Grete replied without looking up. "I left the City to save you... and now you're here."

Dagny cursed under her breath, her concern for Gretchen overshadowing all other emotions. "What are you talking about, Grete? What is going on? Are these *bones?*"

"Things are moving so quickly now." Gretchen looked up, her eyes cold and unwavering, but her voice was sad. "You've ruined everything, sister. Do you hear me? You've *ruined* everything."

16

"I'm not quite sure how to explain it," Feruda said, sitting next to Dagny on a stone bench in the courtyard. "How much do you know?"

"Nothing," Dagny replied. "Grete just left in the middle of the night. I had a feeling she ran off with you and Marfisi because of what happened that day in the woods."

Feruda nodded, her eyebrows connected into a single, wispy line above her pale eyes. "I thought you would be upset with us for taking her."

"Oh, I am," Dagny said, then raised and lowered a shoulder. "But what good does any of that do now? I'm here... We should get along."

"We should've handled it better," Feruda admitted. "Gretchen didn't want you getting involved."

"It was already too late for that." Dagny thought of Jago and the others from Limer's Town. "There were men who tried to kill me in those woods."

Feruda narrowed her eyes slightly. "Kill?"

"Never mind. I shouldn't have said anything. I don't want to make things worse." It was a bad memory, and Dagny didn't want to dwell on it.

The girl seemed willing to let the comment go. "She cares about you," Feruda said, gesturing at the building behind them. "Even if Gretchen doesn't say so. She does."

Her sister sure hadn't acted like it. "Does she even talk about me? In all the months that she's been here, does my name even come up?"

Feruda hesitated. "There's... been a lot going on."

"I see." Dagny stood and twisted her hands together. "I've been thinking about Grete constantly. Every single day since she left. But she's been... focused on other things, apparently. I don't know. I guess I was hoping..."

"Hoping? For what?"

"That it wasn't too late. That I could still salvage something between us. That she hadn't changed so much in the time we lost. That I could still have a sister."

"She's still your sister," Feruda said. "Even if things are not how you wanted them to be."

"I know." Dagny sighed and stared up at Grete's room. "Maybe I should just leave. Go back to Rork."

"Okay," Feruda said. "If that's all it took, then maybe you should."

Dagny faced her. "Really?"

"If that's all it takes for you to dismiss her. Then yes, maybe you're not meant to be here." Feruda stood up. "This isn't about you, Dagny. None of it is. Gretchen didn't want you to get hurt, that's all. Don't be so selfish."

Dagny realized she was gawking at Feruda, then quickly closed her mouth and swallowed. "That's painfully honest."

Feruda kept her voice calm and easy. "I don't mean to attack you. But, really. Either be here and support Gretchen, or don't."

Dagny closed her eyes, feeling horribly embarrassed. "What's going on with her? Why is she so important to this place?"

"Gretchen knows things about the Long Ago—things no one else does. Not even the Weavers in Sanctuary."

"What kinds of things?"

"Gaps in the histories, names of the Scarred Children, the full body of melodies... Everyone was skeptical at first. But then, Gretchen led us to the First Step. Sealed and hidden away for thousands of years."

"Can you explain that, please?"

"The First Step is an ancient gathering place. Buried out in Old Veil. It was marked by a single latch in a wall of stone. It's where Odestinas anointed the original protectors. It's the *first step* to finding the Queen, and since then, people have all sorts of ideas about Gretchen."

"Like what?"

"Some think she's a witch or an Oracle; others believe she's the Queen herself, reincarnated."

Dagny gazed over at Melwes, curled up in the shadow of Eidfur, while Fig and Mia hovered and twinkled over their heads. "The Queen, huh?" Dagny couldn't say she was surprised that people would believe such things. Although Dagny couldn't explain how her sister knew so much about Jud, it didn't mean that Grete was Odestinas reincarnated. That was just, well, ridiculous. Sometimes, when people wanted things so badly, they jumped at believing the impossible.

"I know how all of this sounds," Feruda replied.

"And what do *you* think she is?"

"Me?" Feruda lowered her voice. "I think your sister is someone special. I *know* it, actually."

"Why do you keep her in that black room with the bones?" Dagny asked. "It's not good, you know. It's disturbing."

"It was Gretchen's idea. She's been trying to focus. Trying to expand her vision. We only want to support her."

"Gretchen's idea…You sure it wasn't Marfisi's?" Dagny asked, a touch of bitterness in her voice.

Feruda shook her head slowly. "No. You have the wrong impression. Marfisi doesn't control things here, and neither do I."

"Who does?"

Feruda scrunched her thin eyebrow into a frown. "Well, when it comes to Gretchen… Gretchen does."

"You're telling me she wants to be in that room?"

"Yes."

Dagny squeezed her eyes closed again. *What happened to you?* she thought. What happened to her beautiful sister? "…She told me I was ruining everything."

"Gretchen's been temperamental lately," Feruda said. "I don't fault her, it's a lot to deal with… I should've warned you."

"And what am I supposed to be *ruining*, exactly?"

"I don't know," Feruda said. "It's in her head."

Dagny bit at her fingernail. "Did she tell you about the heart?"

"No."

"It was inside of an ancient puzzle box. Discovered near Limer's Town by a man named Sliver Farn. Grete believes she solved the puzzle, and then ate the heart inside. What do you think about that?"

Feruda looked nervous. "I'm not really the right person to ask. I'm not a Weaver. I'm just trying to do the right thing. Although, it's becoming harder and harder to know what that is."

Dagny paced around the bench. "I know the feeling."

"She just doesn't want to be distracted," Feruda said. "Gretchen thinks she's so close now."

"Close to what?"

"Discovering what so many have been searching for. The tomb."

"That's why the knights want her," Dagny said. "So that she'll lead them into the dark. To the tomb."

"It's not just the knights. *Everyone* wants to find it."

Not everyone, Dagny thought. Pren sure didn't seem to care much. She wondered if he was okay now, confined in his family's stronghold. "Do you know where Barentok is?" Dagny asked.

Feruda gave her an odd look. "That's a weird turn of topics."

"Do you know?"

"Yes. It's not too far."

Dagny sighed. She felt totally unmoored, unable to focus on anything. Her mind spinning in circles. "I don't know what to do with myself."

"Maybe you don't need to do anything at the moment," Feruda said. "Give Gretchen some time. Try to relax here. Appreciate the calmness around you. You never know when that might change."

Calmness? It sure didn't feel calm. Dagny sat and put her head in her lap, feeling more exhausted than anything. "This was the only thing that kept me going for so long... finding Grete. I just wanted my sister back. I wanted her to be okay after everything. Now she's... I don't even know what."

Feruda rested a hand on Dagny's back. "Like I said, she's still your sister."

"Yeah."

A short while later, Marfisi returned, lugging a sack over her shoulder that rattled with every step she took. She was taller than Dagny remembered, wearing a faded white dress; her hair braided into three long cords. Marfisi carried herself with such relaxed, quiet dignity—a person who was always in control, always aware of her own importance. It reminded Dagny of the first time she saw the singer, standing on stage at the Ironhead, commanding the entire room with her beautiful songs.

"How were the waste yards?" Feruda asked with a smile.

"Eventful, as always." Marfisi glanced at Dagny and nodded. It was such an unconcerned, indifferent greeting, Dagny wasn't sure if the girl recognized her.

"Hello," Dagny began. "I'm—"

"You're the sister. Welcome," Marfisi said, then looked back at Feruda. "How is she?"

"The same," Feruda replied. "We had some visitors earlier. Our friends from Barentok."

"Oh?"

Feruda scoffed. "Three of them this time. And they were very demanding. But Dagny showed up with friends of her own."

"You're acquainted with Eidfur," Marfisi said, acknowledging the wolf resting in the shade. "That's a rare fellowship to hold. It's been some time since I've seen him."

"What's in the sack?" Dagny asked. "More bones?"

Marfisi tried to give a polite smile, but to Dagny, it came across as haughty and condescending. "This is not something you would understand."

"I'm a bit tired of everyone telling me that," Dagny said. "I understand more than you think. I made it here on my own." That wasn't completely true. She had Melwes and Pren and Eidfur, but Dagny didn't feel like that was necessary to mention.

"You're upset," Marfisi replied calmly. "No doubt it's been a long trip, and you need your rest. You may stay here for as long as you'd like." Marfisi then gestured at Melwes and the wolf. "All are welcome."

Whether or not Marfisi was attempting to disarm her, Dagny only felt more frustrated. Before Dagny could respond, however, Marfisi stepped into the tower and out of sight.

"The bones help with focusing," Feruda whispered. "Gretchen had visions that Odestinas was surrounded by dead animals, trapped in a dark place—the tomb most likely—and the more Gretchen can put herself in the same state of mind as the Queen, the clearer she can see."

"Dead animals, trapped in dark tombs..." Dagny shook her head. "Everything here is so sad. It's wearing on me."

"No. Not everything," Feruda said. "The outskirts beyond the Inner City are haunting and bleak. This part of the city is different."

"Whoever built this place did a great job," Dagny said sarcastically.

"Marfisi was right. You should rest. Would you like me to prepare a bath?"

Dagny sighed and glanced at the windowless room at the top of the tower. "No. Not really."

∞

It took some persuading to get Melwes into the water, but once he was in, the boy seemed content to just sit there and be scrubbed. The tub turned black almost immediately, and Dagny picked off so many bugs with her fingers that she could have started a collection. By the time they had finished, the water was a frothy stew of muck.

Dagny washed both of her outfits—the one from Dog and the black dress from the Needle—in the well out back, and then spent the rest of the day napping under thin covers on a cot next to the kitchen. No one bothered her, and when she awoke, the sun had set and her clothes had dried.

It was a muggy evening, and Dagny decided to wear the black dress with her boots. She had tried her best to put Lieta out of her mind since escaping Dretgaol, but found herself thinking about her now—wondering if Lieta was sitting alone in her library, or getting ready to watch the stars from the observatory up top. Dagny didn't know how she was supposed to feel. The things she'd seen in that amber chamber were just so terrible... Maris... the others. How many people had Kustav sealed away in resin? And Lieta *knew*. But Dagny also felt bad for her. She kept envisioning Lieta's sad eyes and the way her voice sounded as she pleaded for Dagny to stay. It broke her heart, even now. Lieta seemed to be a prisoner, just like everyone else who wandered into the Keep, and if that was truly the case, she didn't have a choice in what went on there. Suddenly, Dagny had a horrible thought: what if Lieta was so distraught at Dagny leaving that she'd flung herself off the tower like she'd imagined doing so many times before?

"What's wrong?" Feruda asked, joining Dagny on the bench outside.

"Oh, I was... thinking about someone," Dagny said, trying to shake off her sadness. "I'm trying my best to figure out this place."

"It *can be* very confusing," Feruda said.

"I'm glad you appreciate that. No one else does."

"I've only been here a few years myself," Feruda said. "I'm from the Vahnland."

"Really?"

"That's where I met Marfisi. I was wandering the river towns, playing music."

"And then what? You decided to live here?"

"There wasn't much else for me. This is where I belong. And it's not like we don't leave... You know that much."

"Sure," Dagny said, nodding. "When I saw you last, there were two other musicians with your group."

"Oh, Vega and Vex. Yeah, they join us from time to time. Especially, when we venture into the bigger cities. They love those places."

"You were quite good."

"Thanks." Feruda smiled awkwardly. It was clear she felt uncomfortable with praise.

"Do you ever think of her?" Dagny asked.

"Sarna, you mean?"

"Yeah."

"I visited her last winter," Feruda said. "I was only able to stay for one night. And I had to tell her it was our last night together. It wasn't fair to her... to fall for someone like me."

"I'm sure that was very hard for her," Dagny said. "Sarna's such a passionate person. She feels things deeply."

"Do *you* miss her?" Feruda asked. "I know you were friends."

"Yes, I do," Dagny said. "I don't know what happened between us. I don't know why our friendship ended. I acted terribly, but... there was a lot going on, and I didn't understand how to deal with it." Dagny shook her head. "I wish I could take it all back."

"Tell her that," Feruda said. "Go see her. She'll forgive you."

"Sure."

"Hold on," Feruda said with sudden enthusiasm. "I know what will make this night better." Then she ran into the building, emerging a few minutes later with a bucket.

"What's that?" Dagny asked.

"Oh, something delicious." As Feruda sat back down, a purplish liquid sloshed out from the bucket onto the stone floor.

"It is nice to relax for a moment," Dagny said. "I've been running from one thing to the next, and I've just grown more and more confused about Jud... about everything."

"Well..." Feruda began, taking a giant chug from the bucket, then wiping her mouth. "What do you want to know?"

"Umm, how about a ruler? Does Jud have one?"

"A *ruler*? Oh, no. Jud's history is one long tragedy of people who tried to rule, and it didn't work out. Everyone here is very distrustful of rulers. There are various groups, and they all sorta do their own thing."

"I've encountered a few of them. The Grouchers, the Bridge-dwellers, the Knights... people at Dog's Den."

"Yeah. Basically, there are *scavengers* like the Grouchers and those children at the Bridges, then there are *providers* and *seekers* and *protectors*... those aren't official titles or anything. Just a simpler way to explain it."

Feruda burped and passed the bucket to Dagny, who took a gulp of her own. It tasted like some kind of sweet juice but was probably a crude wine.

"The providers help out with food," Feruda continued. "Harvesting from the wild gardens and field pockets throughout Jud, and distributing it to those who need it. The seekers are those of us who seek to understand the world. And the protectors—"

"The Thorned Prince and Yunis?" Dagny said.

"Yes," Feruda said, somewhat surprised at her answer. "Even the knights and your friend Eidfur. But the most important protector, the one almost everyone forgets, is the Giant."

"I've heard mention of a giant before. What is that?"

"The Giant goes unseen. It's said he is unfathomably large and encompasses all of Jud. Supporting the city from his place in the underground. The Giant watches everything... the streets... the gates. If the city had an unspoken ruler, it would be him—the final arbiter on who is allowed and who shall be denied. As you made it here, the Giant has decided even your fate, Dagny. Although you wouldn't know it."

"That's both comforting and frightening," Dagny said.

"I agree."

"I'm surprised there's not *more* of a difference here," Dagny said. "Between the people of Jud and people on the outside."

"Sure, but people speak the same language and have a similar culture throughout all of the Vahnland—from the lagoon to Ostrotha, all the way to the Ilvar even. It used to be a single country." Feruda took a sip of wine and gazed at the city buildings above them. "We're not that far removed here in Jud. Of course, there are many things that are distinctly Jud. It's a blend."

"I have a hard time imagining those knights as protectors," Dagny said. "I don't see them caring a whole lot about protecting people."

"Me neither. But they sure like the attention."

"I ran into a few of them at Dog's Den. Do you know a boy named Pren?"

"Pren Orben? Tarn's son?"

"Yeah, I guess."

"I know him. Why?"

"He helped me to get here. A couple of his brothers ambushed us at the Den and took him away. It wasn't pleasant."

Feruda spit a purplish glob onto the ground. "Pfft, *knights.*"

"Is he a good person, though?"

"His reputation is fine."

"That's good. It's hard to know who to trust." Dagny leaned back, feeling the relaxed numbness from the wine take root in her head. "Barentok," she whispered. "I'd like to see the place. See if Pren's alright."

Feruda laughed. "Wouldn't that be something? Us showing up to their home for a change. Demanding to speak with Pren Orben, *Sieour* Tarn's youngest son. They wouldn't expect that."

"Hey, knights!" Dagny said, imitating a challenge. "Feruda and Dag here... Ever have your teeth knocked out by a witch?"

Feruda stared at her. Dagny couldn't tell if she offended the girl, but lowered her voice anyway. "Sorry. Was that too much?"

"No," Feruda said, her intense stare turning into a broad grin. "I like it."

Dagny smiled and watched the spirit lights across the courtyard drift down and rest on Eidfur's hulking shoulders. She was enjoying Feruda's company much more than she would've thought. Maybe she *could* try to relax here. She found Grete after all, and her sister seemed to be safe and secure, around decent people, even if she was dealing with something Dagny couldn't understand.

Feruda stood and walked over to the entrance of the courtyard, carrying the bucket of purple wine. "Well?" the girl asked. "You coming?"

"Coming?" Dagny replied.

"Yeah. I thought you wanted to see the knights."

17

The so-called knights, with their dented and ill-fitting armor, may have reminded Dagny of brutes assembled from the waste yards, but the sturdy fortress of Barentok was nothing short of magnificent. Capped by an ebony dome, the building towered over the plaza leading up to it, and two enormous statues framed the entryway. To the left, a bronze chimera stared coldly ahead, its tail ending in the open mouth of a serpent; to the right, a massive elephant, dignified and formidable, wore a silver sash that read *Tok Eternal.*

"No guards?" Dagny whispered.

"Oh, they're here," Feruda replied, as she took a swig of bucket wine. "Watching from the shadows." The skinny girl turned her attention to the darkened cloister surrounding the plaza and yelled, "You're here, aren't you?"

The streets had been mostly quiet during their walk through the Inner City, but unlike other parts of Jud, Dagny felt life in these districts. Voices murmured from behind closed doors, and the occasional laugh or cough slipped through the window shutters. Cats prowled the alleys, and the scent of a dozen dinners drifted on the smoky breeze. Dagny hadn't realized how much she missed those things, but sure enough, they triggered something in her brain, bringing her back to Rork and warm summer nights spent walking with Lucas and Abrielle.

The Knights Eternal made their presence known well before the stronghold of Barentok. A teenage boy with a bowl-shaped haircut had accosted them at the border of the territory. With a smug grin, the boy held his hand up defiantly as they approached, but before he could challenge them, Feruda smacked it away hard, telling the boy to scatter—which he did, almost tripping over his feet.

Weathered banners decorated the walls of tunnel-like streets on the approach. It wasn't the most creative heraldry Dagny had seen—a simple "K.E." on a blue field—it got the point across, though. This was *Murk Dour* territory indeed.

Eventually the maze of narrow passages gave way, spilling them out into the broad, open-air plaza they found themselves in now.

"What do we do? Knock?" Dagny asked Feruda, as she continued to scan the area.

Just then, almost as if he'd heard her, a man with a bearded, brown face appeared from a second-floor balcony. "You've a lot of guts coming here," he said.

"You know me?" Feruda called back.

"You're one of the Alypso witches. I'm familiar."

"We've come for... uhm..." Feruda scratched her head.

"Pren..." Dagny reminded her.

"Oh, of course." Feruda sucked in air and screamed, "Pren!"

The sound was so jarring, the man above flinched, and Dagny had to cover her mouth to stifle a laugh.

"That's enough!" the man shouted back, his own voice booming and angry.

"Look, is he in there or not?" Dagny asked. Her head was foggy, but she was still aware of the slight slur in her voice. The wine had given her a boost of courage, making her care little for how these knights might react.

The bearded man turned away and spoke with another person who Dagny couldn't see. "I don't know... some girl and a witch," he said, then disappeared. Dagny heard a door close.

"Hey!" Feruda yelled. "Come back here." She started scanning the ground, searching for something.

"What are you looking for?" Dagny asked.

"Ah, here we go," she said, picking up a stone. A moment later, Feruda heaved it through the air and over the balcony, shouting, "I said, come back!"

The stone thudded against wood. Dagny's heart pounded with nervous energy as she took one more gulp from Feruda's bucket, then searched for a rock of her own.

"That's the attitude," Feruda said, cheering her on. "Make 'em eat it."

Before Dagny could chuck the stone, however, the front entry door creaked open and out walked two men, both of them quite recognizable.

Roger Red wore a crimson suit, too tight for his body, and behind him stood Boulder. One of Pren's brother's. The man she had bitten.

Boulder scowled and pushed past Roger. "*You.*"

"We've come for Pren—" Feruda began.

The knight pointed at Dagny. "I know this weasel," he said to Roger. "She's one of Puddle's mutts. Caught them in the Den together mixing fluids."

Roger eyed her cautiously but said nothing.

"You're an ass," Dagny mumbled. Despite the alcohol coursing through her body, she felt a twinge of fear facing down the two men. Who knew what they were capable of?

"We want Pren," Feruda said.

"Oh, yeah?" Boulder said, rushing forward. "You gonna make a demand of me?" He jerked his arm back, readying a slap, but Feruda didn't flinch.

"We just want to know that he's okay," Dagny said.

"No," Feruda said sharply, glancing at her with a look that commanded, *Be quiet.* "We want him released."

There was a long pause. Boulder seemed confused about how to handle the situation. It was apparent that for all his efforts to intimidate, he was concerned about actually beating two young girls in the plaza of Barentok.

Finally, Roger Red let out a nervous laugh. "Pren's fine. He's simply meditating on his transgressions." Then Roger pointed a finger at them. "You should leave. Before things get bad. Boulder is within his rights to imprison you both for a trespass here."

Boulder nodded his head. "That's right. A trespass."

"And what's the punishment for betraying a friend?" Dagny asked. "You should be disgusted with yourself, Roger. Really."

Roger Red turned furious. "How dare you? You should not say such things!"

Dagny laughed at him. "You really are a pair of *Murk Dours.*"

Everyone went silent and the air turned heavy. Even Feruda looked nervous.

"...What did you call us?" Boulder growled.

Dagny swallowed hard. Perhaps she really had crossed a line.

Suddenly, Feruda flung the wine bucket at the burly man and screamed, "*Murk Dour!*" Before the bucket had a chance to land, Feruda grabbed Dagny's wrist and pulled her away.

The girls raced out of the plaza into the narrow, winding streets of the district beyond. Boulder chased them briefly, then gave up, shouting one final curse as Feruda led Dagny around a curve in the road. They were both laughing so hard by then that Dagny had to lean against a wall to keep from falling.

"You're... something else," Feruda said, struggling for breath. "I've never seen them so mad."

"It's a good thing they're slow," Dagny replied. Glancing down, she realized she was still clenching the stone and let it fall to the ground. "What do you think they'd have done? If they caught us?"

Feruda shrugged, grabbed one of the "K.E." banners adorning the wall, and tried to yank it off. Dagny wasn't sure they should pour more salt in the wound. She'd known prideful men like that, and those types usually weren't willing to let things go.

"Let's head back," Dagny said. "It's late enough."

"Hold on." Feruda grunted as she hoisted herself up by the banner and pressed her feet into the wall. "I... almost got it."

With a loud rip, the fabric gave out, and both Feruda and the blanket of blue canvas collapsed onto the street. She sprung up quickly, gathered the banner into a huge bundle, and shouted, "*Go!*"

It wasn't long before they were hurrying out of Barentok territory with Dagny holding the end of the banner like it was the tail of some ceremonial gown. The teenage boy was back at the border, and although he didn't interfere this time, he was certainly paying close attention. So much for secrecy.

Dagny felt like she might vomit by the time they reached the slope leading down to Marfisi's house. Too much wine and adrenaline, and *too much* jostling.

"Where do you wanna keep it?" Feruda asked. While Dagny had to keep her eyes focused on the road to stop her head from spinning, Feruda seemed even more refreshed than before.

"Keep it?" Dagny huffed.

"Yeah. Your memento. I don't want this thing."

Was she kidding? "Well, I don't want it, either," Dagny said. "What am I going to do with a dumb knight banner?"

"We could hang it from the house," Feruda said. "Start a new tradition. Trophies from our enemies, defeated in glorious combat."

"Heh, we didn't really defeat them."

"Close enough."

The girls struggled to get down the hill, and Dagny dropped the tail as soon as they reached the courtyard. "That was more eventful than I thought it'd be," Dagny said. "Hope Pren's alright."

"Oh, they wouldn't hurt him or anything. He's his father's favorite cub." Feruda glanced at her sideways. "What was that about you and him mixing fluids?" she asked.

"Some lie. We're just friends. Not even that. We were just companions for a moment."

"And Roger Red... you met him before, too?"

"Yeah," Dagny said with a chuckle. "Don't you know by now? I've been all over the place."

"He's hard to figure out. I've never trusted him, but he's always been friendly. Until tonight. Come to think of it, they all seemed real tense."

"Well, we did just march up to their home and start screaming."

"I know, but... there was something else," Feruda said. "Forget it. I'm drunk."

Dagny peeked inside the house and after seeing Melwes asleep in the kitchen, she stepped away and collapsed on the ground near the Alypso tree. Its leafless, stark white frame seemed to glow against the dark blue sky.

"Boulder called you an Alypso witch," Dagny said to Feruda, who had taken her boots off nearby and was rubbing her feet. "What's special about this tree?"

"The Alypso is the most sacred and magical thing in Jud. Its roots spread down to that hidden grotto where the first black waters of creation still flow and quench the tree's thirst. For those of us who are blessed with the sensation to walk in dreams, the tree allows us to do so much more freely. It's connected to those other worlds—the ones that could've been, in the beginning, when all things were infinite and possible."

"Can you walk in dreams?" Dagny asked, not entirely sure what that meant, but gathered it had something to do with what Grete was experiencing.

"No. Not me. Just Marfisi... and your sister, of course."

Dagny stretched her arms wide and stared at the stars. The spinning in her head was much more intense now, lying on her back, but she didn't care. The stars swirled above, blurring themselves into a vortex of light and dark, as if they meant to sweep her up into the universe and pry her apart. "I met a girl in the Moon Needle," Dagny said, speaking into the darkness. "Her name is Lieta, and she has hair the color of emeralds."

"The Moon Needle?" Feruda asked. "In Dretgaol? I thought that place vanished hundreds of years ago."

"What do you mean, vanished?" Dagny asked, still focused on the sky.

"Sucked into the shift, never to return... or torn apart by the Prince during one of his furies. The stories vary." Feruda paused, perhaps waiting for a response, then asked, "How did you get there?"

"Lieta."

Feruda may have asked another question, but Dagny could no longer contain the brewing sickness in her head. She rolled onto her side and spewed hot, purple vomit across the ground.

Feruda rushed over and pulled Dagny's hair from her face. "There, it's alright, take a deep—"

Dagny almost managed to mutter "sorry" before another wave of puke erupted from her stomach like a geyser. She tried unsuccessfully to cover her mouth, but it just caused more of a mess, with bile-mixed bucket wine squirting through her fingers and onto her dress.

Dagny braced herself. She knew she looked ridiculous, propped up like a dog on the ground, but there was nothing to be done about it. The fluid burned her nostrils, and she wiped her chin, apologizing profusely between bouts of heaving.

"That's alright," Feruda said calmly, patting Dagny's back. "Get it out." Then she chuckled, "I thought you'd be able to handle it better."

"Me too," Dagny croaked.

In the darkness of night, everything was a blur. The only light was that from the stars and the spirit lights. One buzzed around Dagny's head, and the other floated close to Melwes, who stood just out of range, holding his nose.

Dagny tried to wave him away before retching again. She was embarrassed enough with just Feruda as a witness. The last thing she wanted was an audience, but when she glanced back up, Marfisi was standing next to the boy with her arms crossed.

When Dagny awoke on the kitchen floor, birds were chirping outside, and sunlight had lit up the room, shimmering against copper pots and glass goblets on the counter above. She had no memory of making it inside.

Her head was in a lap, and as soon as she stirred, a gentle hand brushed her hair back. It was so caring and kind, Dagny immediately felt comforted, as if she was waking from an awful dream and emerging into the life she was always meant to have.

"Easy," Grete said. "Take your time and breathe."

Dagny inhaled. A fresh scent of lavender and sage wafted up through her nose, drifted behind her eyes, and swept into her brain. "That's nice," she mumbled.

"My sweet sister," Grete said, still petting her head. "I missed you."

It was an unexplained but welcomed change from the way Gretchen had acted yesterday, but that interaction no longer mattered to Dagny. She closed her eyes, took another breath, and released it slowly.

"You're the only person I care about," Grete continued. "I only wanted to protect you."

"I know. It's okay. Are you glad I'm here?"

"Yes." Grete's body seemed to soften. "What did you get into last night?" she asked, her tone noticeably lighter.

"Bucket wine."

Grete chuckled quietly. "Feruda is a wild one. She won't tell anyone what her recipe is, but it's more than alcohol."

"Oh." Dagny paused, trying to focus before whispering, "Thanks. For coming back around. My heart felt crushed when I thought you were mad at me."

"I'm sorry. I forget who I am sometimes. There's... *a lot* going on, but now that you're here, you might as well know."

Dagny rolled over, staring up at Grete's face. "Tell me."

"Soon. I promise."

"No. Tell me now." Dagny rubbed her fingers over a strand of Grete's ink-black hair. "Please. What's going on?"

Grete nodded, then lowered her voice to a quiet whisper. "Yes. Alright. I'm close to being rid of all of this."

"Rid of what?"

"The heart. *Her* heart. It's in me."

"You mean the Queen?" Dagny asked. She was studying her sister's face intently, looking for any sign of delusion.

"Yes. Odestinas. Before she was imprisoned, her heart was removed."

"By the Imposter?"

"That's one of his names. But there are others. The Emperor of Man will also be known someday as the Basilisk. He's been around in various forms since the beginning of time."

Dagny sat up abruptly, causing her head to swim. "What do you mean *someday*? The Basilisk is an old fairytale."

"No. It's a prophecy. Told to the world by the Oracles of Lazim," Grete said. She spoke with such confidence, Dagny simply nodded in agreement.

"How do you know all this?" Dagny asked.

"I can feel the Queen's thoughts as they come to her. She's still thinking, reflecting on things in the underground. Before I came here, I could see her memories randomly, in my dreams. But now, beneath the Alypso tree, they come to me much more frequently. I can almost control them."

"The heart from the puzzle box? You really think you ate it?"

"I know I did."

"Why was it removed?"

"To separate Odestinas from her power. She's everlasting in a way—so connected to the mists of creation that she can never truly be extinguished."

Grete seemed *off*. It had taken Dagny some time to figure out why, but it was coming to her now—the way Grete was speaking was... well... different. She didn't sound like the sister who came up in the Rakesmount and Limer's Town. She sounded more like one of the mysterious woman of Jud, like Marfisi or Lieta.

"So that's why you spend so much time in that black room with the bones," Dagny said.

"It helps me focus if I envision that I'm inside of her prison."

"And what now?" Dagny asked. "What are you trying to do?"

"I'm trying to find her." Grete leaned forward. "And I'm close. I can feel it. Just on the other side... but I'm stuck."

"Stuck? Where?"

"There's a chamber deep in the underground that surrounds the tomb. It was built by the Imposter's engineers to serve as both a warning and a reflection of the Imposter's power. I don't know where it's located, but I can see the tomb, like I'm looking with Odestinas' vision, peering through a hole."

"What do you see?"

"Giant statues reaching to the sky. Rulers of the Night Kingdom, like your Talvarind sets, and among them is the Imposter, his face obscured by a peaked hood." Grete took a breath. "And a lizard."

"A lizard?"

"It's always there, skittering across the floor, disappearing through holes in the wall. I don't know what it all means, but I need to figure it out soon. That's why I've been so focused. I got upset when you appeared because it took me away from the Queen in my mind." Grete tapped her head. "The Cauldron is going to open in three days, and I *have* to be ready."

Dagny tensed. "You're planning to go down there?"

"I have to."

"Why? What's so important about finding this tomb? Why is it so important to everyone?"

Grete shook her head. "I don't care about the tomb. I care about the heart. I don't want it. And I plan to give it back."

18

Sometimes, when Dagny was a child, she would leave the Rakesmount with Morgan and wander into City Centre. It was a special time, just for the two of them. They'd watch performers near the Azure Fountain, pick through the rubbish for barely touched sweet bread, and then stroll past the cafes and shops lining the street by Viddry Park. Dagny didn't remember Grete ever coming along, but it wasn't surprising. Her sister always seemed so much younger back then.

"You're her protector," Morgan would say. "When I'm gone, there's no one else to trust in the Mount. I mean it, not mother and not those *cousins*, and definitely not the Ogre."

Protector. That was the word he used.

Later, after the flood, Dagny had a recurring nightmare that haunted her for years. She would be alone, inside of the Benzara house, and it would be raining (it was always raining in the dream). And she would know that something stood just outside, on her bedroom balcony, watching her. She didn't want to approach the glass doors to check; she wanted to run and get Alex, but she could never stop herself. And as she got close to the glass, a face would slowly come into view. It was dead and rotting with brown, hairy skin clinging to ruined meat. And then another face would appear, and another. They were the faces of her family. In the dream, her mother always wore a wet gown (even though she hadn't owned a single dress in the Mount) and the Ogre was always naked—his blubbery, waterlogged belly dripping down to his knees.

Dagny would panic and try to flee, but whenever she reached the stairs, her feet would stop, like they were sucked into the floorboards. She'd try to force herself free, as her drowned cousins broke through the glass doors, entered her bedroom, and plodded into the hallway. They were angry at her for leaving them; hateful and furious at her for not dying in the flood. Their thoughts came pouring into her head. How dare she think that she was better than them? That *she* should be the one to live? The ratty runt of the Rakesmount. *How dare she?* If anyone should've died in that awful dark place, it should have been her.

And then, just as the Ogre came lumbering over to grab her, Dagny would hear the front door open, and standing in the entryway would be Gretchen—smiling and full of life. She would gesture at Dagny to leave the house and come with her, but as soon as Dagny started to move again, as soon as she found herself racing down the stairs, she would wake up.

The nightmare came back to her so often that Dagny would be terrified to sleep in her room, and she'd beg Alex and Cate to allow her to sleep in theirs, even if just on the floor. They'd refuse, of course, and Alex tried his best to explain how dreams were illusions and couldn't hurt you. But he was uncomfortable at trying to be comforting, and his words didn't really matter. If anything, they seemed to make it worse. Again and again and again, the nightmare would come, until finally, one day Dagny had grown so frustrated and so *angry* at the demons in her head that she started sleeping outside, on her balcony, with a knife. Ready to confront her dead cousins as soon as they appeared. And once she started doing that, they stopped coming.

The cowards.

Dagny didn't understand why certain memories came back to you when they did. It was probably all of this talk about dreams and visions by Grete and Feruda that had her reflecting on such dreams of her own.

And something else had been on her mind today. Something much more recent. *Lieta.* Dagny hunched over on the courtyard bench and turned the metal hand over, studying it intently. Lieta had seemed to know so much about old Jud: the weeds, the Queen, the true history of the Prince... she'd known more about the tomb, the *Sepulcha Hungus,* than anyone else Dagny had met. If anyone had clues about its location, wouldn't it be her?

But Lieta was so far away, and Dagny couldn't risk going back to the Needle.

Grete was planning to enter the Cauldron, to find Odestinas, and somehow rid herself of the heart without even knowing where the tomb was hidden. Dagny had to figure out a way to help. Otherwise her sister could become trapped like Pren's poor father, doomed to decay in the underground.

On the other side of the courtyard, Melwes was playing with several balls of glass that Feruda had given him; rolling them across the ground, then giving chase.

Eidfur loomed nearby, watching the boy. Dagny wondered why the wolf was still around. He'd done more than she could've asked for, and she certainly didn't mind his company. She just found it peculiar.

Dagny rubbed her head and wandered over to the house. Maybe she should talk to Feruda about her concerns.

Do you ever think about jumping? Just to see what would happen?

The voice sounded so close. A whisper at her ear. Dagny spun around. There was only Melwes, playfully chasing his glass spheres.

"Lieta?" Dagny said into the air. "Are you here?" She stretched her hand out, hoping to feel something.

Perhaps it was a coincidence, but just then, Eidfur cocked his head and sniffed the wind.

"Did you say something?" Feruda asked from the doorway. She wore a nightshirt, and her hair was clumped in messy knots.

"No... sorry," Dagny said. "Thought I heard something."

Feruda smiled and invited her inside to sit at the dining table. "I'm putting together another batch," she said, gesturing at a bucket on the kitchen counter. "Don't worry, you'll get used to it."

Just the sight of the bucket made Dagny want to retch. "I don't know if you're joking or not, but I never want to drink that again. Seriously."

"You're no fun," Feruda said casually, as she focused on something in the sink. "I'm glad you're feeling better."

Dagny put her forehead down on the table. "It's relative."

"Gretchen told you about the Cauldron opening soon, didn't she?"

"Yes," Dagny said into the wood. "Are you planning to go, too?"

"No. Not me."

"Are you afraid?"

Feruda shrugged. "I mean... a little, but Gretchen has the vision. She knows what to do."

Does she? Dagny thought. She wondered how much Grete told the witch girl about the tomb and the chamber of Night Princes, and how she had no idea where it was located.

"What's that?" Feruda asked.

Dagny had forgotten she was still holding the metal hand. Before she could respond, however, Feruda gasped, "Is that what I think…"

"The hand of a princess? I'm not sure. It could be." Dagny lifted the object into sunlight streaming through the window. "I found it in the Moon Needle. Do you know anything about them?"

"A bit… I've never seen one, though. Most of the statues have rotted away and are nothing but dust now. Some of the other princesses were rescued and preserved in secret chambers, in case their curses could be reversed, although those locations have been lost to time."

"Were there many of them? The princesses?"

"Twenty-nine, supposedly. It's said you can peer into the weeds if you've befriended one."

"How do you befriend one?"

Feruda bit her lip, then quickly shook her head. "These aren't things you should be playing with. Even Marfisi—"

"I'm not looking to *play* with it," Dagny said, cutting her off. "Did Grete tell you about the tomb? How she doesn't know where it is?"

"What do you mean?"

"It's blocked to her. I think she's planning to go down there, regardless."

"I'm confused," Feruda said, sitting at the table. "What does this have to do with that hand?"

Dagny sighed. "I don't know… I don't know anything, anymore."

Fortunately, Marfisi did.

She'd been listening from the top of the stairs. And as Feruda filled two cups with black tea, Marfisi came gliding into the room, announcing herself with a deep sigh of her own.

"The weeds are not a place for living beings," she said. "Like reentering the mother's womb after birth, they are hospitable for creation, but suffocating for the awakened. Still, there is true knowledge inside."

Feruda scrunched her face and nodded.

"How do you know?" Dagny asked. "If you've never been there?"

"What?"

"How do you know?" Dagny repeated slowly.

Marfisi frowned and softened her tone. "Why are you so upset with me? I'm only trying to help. I've been nothing but welcoming, haven't I?"

"It's not personal," Dagny said. Although it was, sort of. "I'm just trying to figure all this out. If you've never been to the Sillweed, then how do you know what it's like?"

Marfisi cleared her throat. "I know, because I know. The mist of the *Rhyming Sea* seeps from that earlier world into our own. The Sillweed of which it forms, covers Jud and hides the city, deceiving the stranger."

"Okay," Dagny said, feeling overwhelmed.

"You're intelligent and your skepticism is welcome," Marfisi continued. Her voice was so gentle and smooth, it was hard to resist being swept away in it. "Forgive me if I made you think we're enemies, when I mean to be friends."

The comment relaxed her. "I don't want to be enemies, either." Dagny tapped her fingers on the table, trying to figure out what to say in the awkward silence that followed. "I've been upset with you for taking my sister away. She just wanted a normal life after everything she'd been through."

"I know," Marfisi said. "But what's done is done. Gretchen was on this path before she met us."

"Right. I realize that now," Dagny said. She knew Marfisi had nothing to do with Grete meeting Sliver, or finding his puzzle box, or eating that heart. "I'll try to do better. I'd like to be friends, too."

"Good," Marfisi said. "It's an unusual journey you've taken to get here. There aren't many who've taken the path through the Silent Keep, and even less who've managed to see the Moon Needle. I wasn't sure it existed anymore."

"That's what Feruda said: that the Needle vanished centuries ago," Dagny replied. "It's not true, of course. I was there."

Marfisi smiled politely. "Of course. There was another, though? With you in the Needle?"

"Yes. Lieta. She's the one who helped me... and the Steward, Kustav."

"I'm familiar enough," Marfisi said, solemnly. "Although I don't profess to know where such beings come from, only that they are powerful creations of Lazim."

"There are others, like Kustav?" Dagny asked.

"Not many, but yes. They inhabit the old places of the world, anything that is connected to a deeper time. It's no wonder she was attracted to the Moon Needle."

The old places of the world. The phrase struck Dagny as familiar. "Like the Oracles," she said. "They inhabited old places. Towers."

"Yes. I suppose people of the Vahnland have called them Oracles." Marfisi leaned forward. "But such beings are not so easily categorized."

"So... wait a second," Dagny said, raising her hands. "Kustav is the same as... I mean... is she an *Oracle*?"

"To the people of the Vahnland, she would be. Again, it's a title they've created. There are many variations among the spirits of the forest."

Dagny felt like she was on the verge of discovering something important.

"We shouldn't lose any more time," Marfisi said, looking at Feruda. "There are still plenty of preparations to make."

"Wait," Dagny said. "Can you talk with me for a bit longer? Why would Kustav hold Lieta in the Needle?"

"I've heard that it's in the visions and dreams of certain children that the *Oracles* scour the world outside of Lazim," she replied.

Dagny bit her lip. "Lieta's hardly a child. She's my own age. Is there a way to help her? She saved me, after all."

"The Cauldron is opening soon. How many do you intend to help?" Marfisi asked.

Dagny didn't have an answer for her.

"Sometimes, there is nothing you can do."

Marfisi walked back up the stairs, and Feruda placed her hand on Dagny's shoulder, whispering, "Would you like to try?"

Dagny cocked her head. "Huh? Try what?"

"To gaze into the weeds. The Alypso is the most connected place in all of Jud. Follow me."

Feruda led her outside and around the tower, to a small mound near the back of the Alypso where the tree's roots weaved into the ground, buckling and splitting the earth.

"I wouldn't suggest this if not for what you told me about Gretchen's uncertainty. Do you know which princess that hand belongs to?" Feruda asked.

"No," Dagny said. She was more focused on where the girl was taking her than questions about princesses.

"They weren't all good."

"What?"

"They weren't all martyrs," Feruda said. "I know that's unpopular to say, but it's true. Some of the daughters came from dark places. I looked into it once—the depths beneath Jud, and one of them saw me." Feruda was trying to be brave, but Dagny could tell the memory was haunting her.

"Are you okay?" Dagny asked.

Feruda laughed nervously. "It was terrifying, actually. It was the Gaunt Lady I saw, and she's come back to me ever since... in my dreams."

"Who's that?" The words alone sent shivers down Dagny's spine.

"Shade of the Black Sun. In my nightmares, the Gaunt Lady is a horrible, crooked monster who stalks me through a twisted labyrinth of night. She wants to devour me. I can feel it, and she won't let me go..."

Dagny gulped. "Is she real?"

"She's real to me. When I first saw her, I was so frightened I couldn't speak for days. But enough about that. I shouldn't have said anything. Sorry."

The ground near the roots was cracked, exposing a series of narrow tunnels burrowing deep into the soil. Feruda kneeled down next to one particularly enormous root and said, "This will lead us to a chamber directly underneath the Alypso."

With Feruda's story about the Gaunt Lady fresh in her mind, Dagny asked, "Is it safe?"

"Yes. This is the Alypso tree." Feruda's tone made Dagny feel foolish.

"I don't like tight spaces." Dagny glanced into the tunnel.

"It's a straight path. Don't worry, I'll go first and I'll go slow. Once we get into the chamber, there's some light that breaks through. It's dim, but you can still see." With that, Feruda lay down on her belly and slithered her way into the tunnel.

"Why does everything have to be underground?" Dagny muttered.

"What's that?" Feruda called back, her boots sticking out of the dirt like those of a corpse someone had tired of burying.

"Nothing," Dagny replied, then gently prodded Feruda with her own boot. Once the girl's body disappeared, she squeezed into the tunnel and crawled along after her.

Dagny's clothes were filthy by the time she entered the chamber. It had a dome shape and resembled what Dagny imagined a beaver's home to look like. There was barely room enough to stand, but the space was plenty wide.

"Alright, this is it. The closest we can get," Feruda said, squatting near the center. "Pretend you're alone."

"What should I do?" Dagny asked, wiping dirt from her face.

"Try setting the hand down and focus on it. Relax your mind. Open yourself up."

"Okay," Dagny said, feeling both frustrated and naive. "...And how do I do that?"

"Concentrate on your breathing. Nothing else. You're not a person. You're an empty vessel. Nothing exists but you and the hand."

"Right." Dagny kneeled down and examined the metal fingers. They seemed so delicate in the faint light. "You said that some princesses weren't good?"

"Don't worry about that now," Feruda whispered.

"...What if this hand belonged to one of them?"

Feruda just shrugged.

Dagny tried to shake off the thought and inhaled slowly, filling her lungs with earthy air until they felt like they would burst. She concentrated on the fortune marks lining the metal palm, and imagined them connecting to the roots of the Alypso. And the moment she felt like another thought was coming on, she pushed it out of her mind with another slow breath.

Then came a thought that she couldn't escape.

Dagny was back in the Moon Needle, sitting on the floor with Lieta.

Can I trust you? Lieta asked. Her voice sounded far away, like it was drifting on the wind. *I feel like I can trust you...*

"Yes," Dagny whispered into the air. "You can trust me."

There's a place called the Sillweed. It exists all around us, even though you can't see it. It's where Jud's daughters were birthed and where they are promised to return...

Dagny felt a slight tremor in the ground. She was shaking and had to grasp the metal hand to keep it from slipping.

Close your eyes now, Lieta said, and Dagny obeyed.

It's coming. It comes quickly when called, but don't be afraid.

The air grew cold and dense, and no longer smelled earthy.

"Are you here in the mist? How do I find you?" Dagny asked.

Don't you worry about that, Lieta said. *Now that you've arrived, I will find you.*

19

When Dagny opened her eyes, dense fog had filled the chamber. She called for Feruda, but there was no reply.

The fog—or mist, whatever it was—seemed to be funneling into the space from the same tunnel they had crawled down to get here. And since there was no other route available, Dagny made her way back outside, slithering up and through the passage.

She felt much lighter in this gray world. When she emerged into the courtyard, Dagny seemed to float momentarily before settling back onto the ground.

The entire area was blanketed by the opaque mist, as if clouds had descended on Jud, transforming the city into something even more surreal. Maybe this is what Marfisi was referring to when she spoke of Jud being hidden by the weeds.

Dagny would have lost all sense of direction had it not been for the Alypso. The tree was the only thing that broke free from the gray landscape. The starkness of its trunk and branches glowed a brilliant white, almost pulsating like a beacon in the fog.

She didn't know how to feel about finding Lieta. It's what she wanted, though, wasn't it? Dagny needed to help Grete. She needed to learn all she could about the underground and the hidden tomb. But could Lieta really help?

The mist was disorienting. She needed to get some perspective on what was happening. Glancing back at the Alypso, gleaming bright and stretching high, Dagny decided to climb it.

Bounding up the roots and latching onto the low, thicker branches, she easily made her way toward the outer limbs. Once again, Dagny was weightless here, gliding higher and higher until she was above the mist itself and looking across the cityscape of Jud.

There were other buildings that broke free from the clouds beneath her. She saw the spires of Dretgaol, and in the opposite direction the battlements of an enormous wall, along with several smaller towers. She wondered if that was the wall she had entered so many days ago with Melwes. Dagny tried to pick out other landmarks, but the foggy mist ebbed and flowed like smoke in the wind. Just as soon as a new rooftop appeared, the gray clouds would shift, hiding the building once again.

How long would it take Lieta to find her? The Needle seemed so far away. Dagny recounted the journey in her mind: the amber room with Maris, the walk to Dog's Den and through Pratchett. The Bridges. Jud was beyond fascinating, with all of its wonders and horrors; metal princesses and peculiar lords. How could a place like this really exist in the same world that she was from? The City of Water and Glass; old Rork and the Rakesmount; Southend and Stardust; Sorn Rue and the lagoon. That was a different life; an awakened one. This was a dream.

She wondered how much Alex or Morgan had known of Jud. They'd certainly never been here, Dagny knew that much. *This* would have been an impossible secret to keep. She felt somewhat proud of herself now, perched on the limb of the Alypso tree, gazing out over the fog of the Sillweed, having escaped from Yunis and the Thorned Prince and Kustav. Alex and Morgan had their own memories of places bizarre, but they had never seen this.

It wasn't long before Lieta's emerald head crested the cloud-line, and the pale girl was scurrying across the branches toward her.

"How is this possible?" Dagny asked. "Are you a ghost?"

"A ghost?" Lieta replied. "Hardly."

"I thought you couldn't leave the Needle."

"The weeds are different. We can only slip into them for a moment."

"How did you find me so quickly?" Dagny asked.

"I know the city like I know my person," Lieta responded, crawling slowly now, the tips of her long hair brushing against the tree limb. There was a sadness in her eyes that she couldn't hide. "You hurt me, you realize."

"I'm sorry," Dagny replied. "But you frightened me, and that room—"

"I know. There was nothing I could do about such things."

"You could've told me," Dagny said. "You could've done that much."

Lieta inched closer to her. "And then what? You would've panicked. Kustav would have *known* that you knew, and then…"

"What? She would've trapped me in amber, too?" Dagny asked.

Lieta's lip quivered. "I'm sorry. I don't know what I'm supposed to do. I didn't want to be alone anymore."

Dagny shook her head. She didn't know how much time she had. "Look, I need your help, if you're able to give it."

"Your sister," Lieta said.

"Yes—"

"She's the one. The one that everybody has been talking about. The girl with the Queen's vision."

How did everyone know about Grete? Even Lieta, sealed away in the Moon Needle, knew. "Yeah, that's her," Dagny said, adjusting her position.

"The city is desperate for your sister to find Odestinas."

"And what about you?" Dagny asked. "Would you like the Queen to be found?"

"I'm not sure. It's bound to change things, but no one knows how."

Dagny sighed. "I want this all to be over with, and for that to happen, I need help finding the tomb. Grete says there is a secret chamber, filled with images of the Night Princes."

"Mm-hmm," Lieta mumbled, chewing her lip. "Did you miss me?"

Dagny thought for a moment. Had she? It was hard to know.

"Well?" Lieta asked.

"It's hard for me."

"What is?" Lieta asked.

"Feeling things. It's like I'm numb so much of the time." Dagny gestured out across the mist-covered city. "Even here. In Jud. I feel like I'm just passing through it. Disconnected from the world around me. Does that make sense?"

"Yes." Lieta stood on the branch and balanced herself awkwardly, like she was crossing a tightrope. "Come, take my hand."

The change in conversation left Dagny confused. "Why?"

Lieta grinned. "*Trust me...*"

Dagny eyed her skeptically. "I also don't want to die."

Lieta laughed. "*Die?* I don't want you to die, either. What do you think I'm planning to do?"

"Jump off this tree?"

Lieta's grin turned into a smirk.

"That's it," Dagny said. "Isn't it?"

Lieta reached toward her. "Take my hand."

Dagny stared at it. The girl had not fully regained her trust. "No. I'm fine."

"Do as you want," Lieta said with a shrug, then pointed to the north. "The mist is darker there, do you see?"

Slowly, carefully, Dagny stood and craned her neck over the web of outer branches. "I can't tell. It looks like it could be."

"It is," Lieta said. "That's where the Cauldron is located, within the walls of Sanctuary."

"You know where the tomb is, don't you?" Dagny asked, then chuckled. "I bet you're the only one here who knows."

"Odestinas is sealed within the Giant's mind." Lieta tapped her forehead and made a scooping motion with her finger. "The Imposter burrowed into it, trapped the Queen, and capped the Giant's skull with his slab of iron."

"Every story here is horrible, you know that?"

"It's not a story," Lieta said with an intensity that was almost frightening. "What do you think happened to the Giant after that?"

"I don't know—"

"His mind was ruined, and his ruin consumed Jud and caused the shift. It's blurred the lines between histories. There are things here that shouldn't exist anymore—their time has ended—and yet, exist they do. Odestinas became the city's dreams, and the Giant controls the external."

"What's all this mean?"

"It doesn't mean anything," Lieta said. "It's just what it is."

Dagny watched Lieta's hair swirl around in the misty wind. It was wavy and wild and brilliant, while Lieta herself was pale and delicate. The girl looked so much a part of this world. "How does Grete find it?" Dagny asked. "The tomb?"

"It's burrowed in the Giant's head," Lieta repeated.

"You said that..."

"The Giant had a companion. The pitiful Yalow Lizard—"

"The Lizard! Grete had visions of a lizard."

"It would visit the Giant in the Underground and whisper into his thoughts. You need to follow the path of the Lizard. It'll take you into the mind."

"How?" Dagny asked, but Lieta just twisted her mouth. After a long pause, Dagny said, "You're not gonna tell me anything else?"

"You're going to leave again as soon as I do."

"This isn't about me or you," Dagny said. "I'm trying to save my sister. I'm trying to get her life back."

Lieta gazed out over the clouds.

"Why do you even care?" Dagny asked.

"Why don't you? Why doesn't anyone? They've all left me there, in the Needle to rot."

The comment caught Dagny off guard. "I didn't say I don't care," she muttered. "I'm trying my best to do the right thing. I wanted you to come with us. Even after that awful room. Even after Maris. I want you to be safe. I wanted you to escape the Needle."

"I know." Lieta hung her head. "But I couldn't... Kustav—"

"She's an Oracle, and a bad one," Dagny said. "Do you know what that is?"

Lieta's face softened. In a way, she looked like a young child. "No."

"Really?" Dagny asked. "How do you know so much, but don't know that?"

"I only know what I know. From books or wandering the mists."

Dagny reached out and took Lieta's hand. "I won't leave you forever, alright? I'll help you, too. I just don't know how to do that yet, and time is running out for Grete."

Lieta nodded. "The Lizard's path is set in the stars. You'll need to figure that part out."

"In the stars?"

Voices drifted up from somewhere nearby. But they were only murmurs.

"Okay," Dagny continued. "Assuming I can find it, you're sure it will lead to Odestinas?"

"Yes. It is the path."

Dagny scratched her chin nervously. "It makes sense," she said. But did it? Did any of this *make sense*?

Lieta leaned close, and Dagny could feel her breath, cold and dense like the mist. "Could I kiss you again before you leave? Just once?" she asked.

There was a muffled shout from below. It was high-pitched, like a girl's voice.

"Did you hear that?" Dagny asked, turning her face toward the sound.

Lieta took her chin and pulled it back. "Just once," she whispered and placed her lips on Dagny's own. It felt like kissing a block of ice; Lieta's lips were so frigid, they sent a chill down Dagny's back.

"We're all like this in the weeds," Lieta said, sensing Dagny's surprise. "We're not really here." Lieta stared into her eyes. "I hope you'll find me someday, when you've done what you need to." And with that, she pushed Dagny off the branch and into the fog.

When Dagny opened her eyes again, she was back in the chamber beneath the Alypso tree. Feruda was shaking her, gentle but firm. "We need to go," she said. "The knights are here."

Dagny sucked in air and tried to stand, but her wobbly legs threatened to send her straight back down.

Don't forget me.

The words echoed in her mind.

"Hold on, let me help you," Feruda said, taking Dagny around the waist and leading her to the tunnel. "Did you do it? Did you enter the weeds?"

"Yes... What happened?" Dagny asked.

"I don't know. The whole area filled with fog and I lost sight of you. I told you the tree was powerful," Feruda replied, her face beaming.

The girls quickly squirmed their way through the tunnel and into the sunlit courtyard.

The knights had come, alright. And by the look of it, Pren's brothers had brought the entirety of Barentok with them. There were maybe fifty men; all adorned in dull armor, surrounding the tree and the tower-house.

As soon as Dagny popped out from the roots, several men rushed toward her and someone shouted, "Over here, we got a couple more!"

Dagny tried to run away, but a man's hand was around her shirt and a moment later he grasped her neck. She heard Feruda scream and the skidding of boots on stone. Someone had muffled the girl's mouth, but she was still putting up quite a fight. Dagny thought it better to conserve energy. No sense in wasting it now. She gripped the metal hand tightly, but otherwise allowed her body to go limp.

The men took her to the front of the tower, where Boulder and Arnon stood with twenty others. Eidfur and Melwes were nowhere to be seen, and Dagny secretly hoped the wolf had taken the boy to safety. Melwes wouldn't do well confined in the knight's prison; and he shouldn't be punished for the girls' actions last night.

"That's them!" Boulder shouted, nudging his brother and pointing sharply at Dagny and Feruda.

Marfisi stood near the entryway. "Release them both," she demanded. "This is a serious offense, Arnon. You are committing a breach of our civility."

Boulder scoffed. "You want to talk about breach of civility?" He ran over and took the torn banner from one of his men. "You have stolen from us and disgraced our home—"

"You are also offering shelter to an uninvited," Arnon said. A steel visor covered his face, muffling his voice and causing his cold, calm tone to hum across the courtyard.

Uninvited. The word resonated in Dagny's mind. He was clearly talking about her.

"Even so. This is not the proper way to handle any such accusations," Marfisi replied. "You need to seek relief with the Weavers—"

"Things have changed," Arnon replied. "The Weavers have failed all of us. All decisions affecting the sanctity and restoration of Jud will now be decided by its protectors."

"And who gave you such authority?" Marfisi asked, likely knowing full well what the knight's response would be.

"We did," Arnon said. "The Knights Eternal." With that, all the men began stomping on the earth and thumping their breastplates.

Dagny scanned the crowd, hoping to see Pren, but he was probably still sealed in his room at Barentok.

The man holding Dagny carried her forward and dropped her on the ground in front of the brother knights. A group encircled her, preventing any chance of escape.

Arnon cocked his steel face. "I remember you. Puddle's mutt. The biter."

Dagny just continued to sit there quietly.

"Back off, let her be!" Marfisi shouted. Dagny heard a commotion and assumed Marfisi was attempting to push toward her, to no avail.

"Not so much arrogance in you now," Boulder said to Dagny, leaning down to stare at her. "Beg for our mercy. I want to hear it. Speak."

She could see it in the man's eyes. He hated her. Truly hated her. Dagny had seen that look in others, and she knew what it could bring. There was an excitement in him. He wanted to do her harm. She could *feel* it radiating from his thick body.

A second later, Boulder's eyes moved to her lap, where she was covering the metal hand.

"What's that?" he asked, then gestured to his brother. "She's got something there."

"Open up, girl," Arnon said, but Dagny only clenched her hands tighter and turned away.

"I said, *open up!*"

Marfisi shouted again, her voice turning into a scream. Arnon grabbed Dagny's wrist and twisted it, sending a jolt of pain through her arm, and causing the hand to fall to the ground.

"What the…" Boulder muttered. "Is that…"

"It's iron," Arnon said, still clenching Dagny's wrist. "This is important to you, huh?" The hum of the man's voice seemed to rattle in the back of her mouth. "Think this is *important*, Boulder?"

"Oh yeah. It's definitely important," he replied.

"Good," Arnon said, and stomped down, crushing the rusted hand underneath his massive boot.

Dagny didn't see it happen, but she heard the crunch and then the sick chuckle of Boulder. In an instant, it was gone, her only route into the mist; her only chance of speaking to Lieta again. This time Dagny screamed. Not in pain or sadness, but in fury.

It only made Boulder laugh harder. "I think she hates you, brother."

Dagny heard Grete's voice now. *"Leave her alone!"*

Arnon raised his masked face but continued to hold onto Dagny.

And then, something else happened.

It started slowly. In the ground. A slight change in color. Glancing down, Dagny saw the dark stone and earth lighten, turning from black into gray. The color of ash. Some of the men must've noticed it, too. She heard a murmur take hold, a buzzing of concern and awe. Boulder only realized the change once the ground began to soften, causing him to pull his boots out, one at a time, as if he was trapped in the swamp.

Dagny couldn't tell what Arnon's reaction was behind the mask, but the man finally let go of her wrist as the mist rolled in.

An image appeared between Dagny and the brother knights. A female, dressed in a long, white gown. Her yellow hair flowed down, past her feet, and spread across the yard. Then Dagny noticed the woman's limbs, ghostly and pale, almost translucent, and missing a hand.

Dagny thought Arnon said something. A word, or a name; she couldn't hear it clearly. It sounded like *Slurgle*. And as the knight turned to flee the apparition, the weave of yellow hair took hold of his ankles and sucked him into the silvery ground.

He was gone.

For a brief moment, everything went silent, as if every man in the yard was holding his breath. Boulder stood there, frozen in place, watching the dirt. A second later, chaos erupted. The mass of knights went scurrying out and away, in every direction like roaches in the lamplight, trying to escape from the ghost woman. Her yellow hair blanketed the earth now, pouring forward like a flood of water. Two more knights screamed in horror as they were ripped into the underworld. Dagny hurried to her feet and leapt toward Feruda just as the ground where she had sat turned yellow as well.

Grete and Marfisi huddled by the tower door. Their wide eyes darting across the scene.

"Go!" Dagny shouted over the shrieking knights. "Run!"

A man fell in front of her, gasping. His skin turned pasty white, bubbling like curdled milk. Dagny watched as yellow strands twisted around protruding veins in the man's neck and slipped over his eyeballs.

Her head pounded so hard she felt like she might faint. She tried to push forward on trembling legs as a great shadow spread over the stone. *Move,* Dagny told herself. *Just move!* But her feet refused to budge. Was she stuck? Had she been caught already? The dying knight grasped at her ankle. He took one last look at the sky and then vanished into a puddle of mist. Focusing with all she had, Dagny tried to run, but before she could move, she was in the wolf's mouth, gliding through the air.

Grete and Marfisi had climbed into the Alypso tree and were slowly making their way higher, away from the slaughter. All around the plaza, knights were being sucked into the earth by the dozen; their screams punctuated by soft, slurping sounds of ground giving way. Their bodies replaced by a puff of fog, like steam rising from a kettle.

Feruda. Dangling helplessly in the wolf's mouth, Dagny scanned the courtyard for the girl and panicked. Did she get away? Had Feruda been caught by the ghost princess? Dagny twisted around to look for her by the tower, opened her mouth to shout, then noticed a skinny leg and foot draped around the wolf's neck. In the confusion, Feruda had somehow hopped onto Eidfur's back, mounting him like a steed.

The giant wolf only touched ground twice more, before making it out of the courtyard and coming to rest on a nearby rooftop overlooking the carnage.

Dagny embraced Feruda without saying a word. She could see Grete and Marfisi from here, clinging to the Alypso's upper branches, but they were safe. The mist seemed only to blanket the ground, and there was the woman—the ancient Jud princess—floating across the yard; her wispy, corn-colored hair stretching across the entire space, a sea of withered gold in the gloom.

A few knights remained. Some rushed around the courtyard, looking for a place of refuge, while others huddled on top of benches and the garden wall, but none of them could get high enough to escape. It wasn't long before those knights were pulled down as well. Dagny shut her eyes and pressed her fists over her ears, trying to block out the sound of men screaming. Even brutal men like this; she hated hearing their cries. It took her back to the Nedgling Tower, when Jago tried to kill her, and the crow butchered him and the others. Those screams had stayed with her for months.

Finally, when there was no one left in the yard below, Feruda squeezed her hand and whispered, *"It's over."* Only then did Dagny open her eyes and watch as the ghost princess took another pass around the Alypso tree before sinking into the ground herself, taking the mist with her.

Dagny thought about what Feruda said earlier, how not all the princesses were good. Arnon must've known, just as he was sucked into oblivion, that he had unleashed something horrible on his people by crushing the hand. In an instant, the Knights Eternal were no more. She wondered if *any* of the men had been able to flee. There were, of course, two that she hadn't seen: Pren and Roger Red.

Feruda pointed to the girls in the Alypso. Grete was waving, and Marfisi appeared to be hunched over, staring intently at the ground. Neither of them seemed to be in a hurry to climb back down. In fact, it wasn't until the twilight hour, when the rest of the city was shifting and changing, that Marfisi finally set foot on the courtyard. She wandered around, slowly for a bit, making sure it was safe, then called for Grete to come down, too.

Eidfur retrieved Dagny and Feruda from the rooftop, and then led everyone to a small bridge, under which Melwes was huddled with Mia and Fig.

"Does anyone know who that was? The ghost?" Dagny asked, but everyone just shook their heads. "Arnon said something before he vanished. I think he knew."

Marfisi cleared her throat. "The Knights have a long history. There are certain things they've studied that no one else knows. They've been questing for generations. Anything that's ever been a threat to Jud is likely to be recorded in their archives at Barentok."

"We should check on Pren," Dagny said. "I'm sure his brothers locked him up before they left. He'll need help."

Grete knelt down next to her and spoke softly, "You're always thinking about others. Even after all of this. You're a good person, Dagny."

"I don't know about that," she said. "He helped me before, and I need to do the same. He should know what happened to those men."

Grete smiled. "Okay. I'll go with you. Let the others rest here."

It was Marfisi who stood and spoke next. Her voice was firm and direct. "No. We'll all go this time. No more splitting up until this is over. We need to see it through now."

PART

3

*I dreamt of a nameless sea,
birthed at the beginning of time.
I dreamt of a shifting city, lost in
the weeds. I dreamt it, but could
never find my way.*

20

The plaza at Barentok was empty. Dagny led the way with Grete, while Eidfur took up the rear.

"Think anyone is here, other than Pren?" Feruda asked.

"Only one way to find out," Dagny replied. She rushed up the stairs and tried pushing the front doors open, but they were barred from the inside.

Feruda gazed at the upper windows and shouted, "Hey! Open up, this is important! All your knights are dead!"

Marfisi shushed her rather harshly.

"What?" Feruda shot back. "It's true."

Dagny wondered how Pren would handle it. His brothers had been bullies, but they were still his family.

The doors sprang open so forcefully that they almost sent Dagny tumbling down the steps. She regained her balance at the last minute, just as Grete grabbed her arm and held her steady. Standing in the dimly lit entryway was the burly, ruddy-faced Roger Red.

"Look who it is," he spit out with a deep scowl. He opened his mouth to say something else when Feruda interjected.

"Your friends are all dead," she said, then gestured at Marfisi. "Some of us are sorry about it."

Roger's snarl faded away, and his eyes narrowed. "You're lying."

Marfisi reached out to touch his hand, but he yanked it away. "I'm afraid not, Roger. I'm deeply sorry."

"You're trying to trick me into releasing the boy. It won't work. He's needed here." Roger chuckled nervously, perhaps to reassure himself. "If I were you, I'd be more worried about what's happening at your own home."

"Let them in," a voice boomed from the plaza behind. "...What's it matter anymore?"

Dagny spun around to see Boulder marching toward them. He was wearing a threadbare undershirt, having tossed off his armor at some point during the escape.

Roger raced down the stairs to greet him, steering clear of Eidfur. "What happened?" he asked. "Where's Arnon and the others?"

Boulder only shook his head and continued trudging forward, into the stronghold and out of sight.

Roger glanced back at the group, his face a mix of despair and fear. "It's true, then? You... *killed* them all?"

"What?" Feruda said. "Us? Are you stupid? Arnon brought it on. He summoned the princess with his violence."

"Princess?" Roger whispered. He ran his hand over his sweaty head, then sat on the stone stairs, almost collapsing on his way down. Dagny felt sad for Roger. She wanted to say something, but didn't have the words.

"Let's go," Grete said, tugging Dagny's dress. "Let's find your friend."

The interior of Barentok was simply massive. Stepping inside, Dagny could *feel* the weight of it. At first, the only light came from a set of candles framing the front doors, but as soon as Melwes entered with Mia and Fig, their glow illuminated a cavernous entry hall with multiple levels overhead.

Feruda put her hands on her hips and gazed down the various passageways branching off from the main room. There were suits of armor and old tapestries; portraits of old men; strange trophies—like the wooden statue of a water nymph that looked more appropriate on the bow of a ship than in the stronghold of knights. Everything was cast in the blue-ish glow of the two spirit lights.

Feruda sighed. "It could take us days to find him in here." She rushed back outside and shouted at Roger, "Any help would be appreciated—where's Pren?"

The man responded without turning around. "Third floor. His bedchamber."

"We don't know where that is," Feruda hissed. "This place is enormous."

When Roger didn't answer, Feruda marched over and grabbed his shirt. "Lead us to him, or I'm gonna have our wolf devour you."

"Fine," Roger muttered in defeat. Dagny could see a single tear streaming down his face when he stepped into the entryway. "It's over here," he said, gesturing at a darkened stairwell.

Feruda took a candle from the wall and walked behind him. "Alright Roger Red, move." She nodded at Eidfur, who raised his lip in return, exposing a long, gray tooth.

There were *at least* three other people in the stronghold—Roger, Pren, and Boulder—but the place could've easily held hundreds. Dagny wondered who else might be lurking nearby, studying them from the shadows.

Roger led the way, and they followed him up the stairs, single file.

"Who is this Pren person, anyway?" Grete asked from behind.

"I met him in the outskirts," Dagny replied. "Shortly after I entered Jud. Apparently, he's the youngest son of Tarn, who used to be leader of the Knights Eternal."

"Another knight, huh?"

"No. He's just related. I don't think he cares too much for them, either. He doesn't act like the others."

Grete nudged her gently as they walked. "Hey, I'm glad you're here. I really am. You caught me at a bad time before—"

"I'm glad I'm here, too," Dagny said. "You don't need to apologize again. We're fine."

"In my mind, I always imagined us together, but the world got in the way." Grete's voice was barely a whisper now, as if she was conscious of the others overhearing. "Morgan was important to me, too, you know?"

"I know he was."

"I was also sad he died."

Dagny kept her eyes on the steps ahead, wondering why Grete was mentioning this now. They followed Roger onto the third floor landing and down a high-arched hallway. There were alcoves and doorways on one side and the other side looked down into some kind of workshop on the floor below.

"I just couldn't risk you getting hurt because of me," Grete whispered. "I had to leave the City last year. I *had* to take care of this."

"You can come back home when this is over. You have nothing to worry about anymore. Sliver's men are dead." Dagny peeked over the gilded railing into the workshop, scanning it for any sign of movement.

"Huh? What are you talking about?" Grete asked.

"Jago tried to kill me, but he's the one who died." Dagny was surprised by the coolness of her own voice.

"We're getting close," Roger said. "Just a bit further."

"*Dag*," Grete said, taking hold of her arm. "What happened?"

"Jago. You remember?"

Grete shook her head in confusion. "Of course. That's not what I'm asking—"

"He tried to kill me. On top of that tower in the woods," Dagny said. "But the crow gutted him. There's nothing else to say about it. Then Alex sent the Authority into Limer's Town, and they gutted the rest. So you can come home now."

Grete looked down and frowned. "I'm sorry. I'm sorry you were hurt because of me. I left because I didn't want that to happen."

"I'm not hurt," Dagny replied, then smiled.

"There were other things, too, though," Grete said. "Those twins—"

"I was so mad at Tash for telling you that," Dagny said.

"He needed to tell me. Do you have any idea what they are?"

"Yes..." Dagny was about to say more, then she noticed Melwes staring at them with a blank look on his face, and Dagny lowered her voice. "We don't need to talk about it."

"Dag... I can feel them coming. They're after me," Grete said, tapping her chest. "They're after the heart."

"The heart? From your dream? Why?"

"Like I told you, it's the Queen's heart. It contains all of her memories from the world before." Grete let out an exhausted sigh. "I don't know why they want it. Maybe they're chasing some dream or memory of their own. Something from their place beneath the sea. It doesn't matter. I just want to be rid of all this."

Roger stopped at a door on their left and fumbled inside his pockets, presumably for a key. Feruda stood next to him. "This is it, then?" she asked.

"Who's there?" a voice responded from the other side.

"You got visitors," Roger said, pulling a key from his jacket. "Step back."

Dagny thought that was a strange response from Roger. Hadn't they made it clear they were here to get Pren released? The man was still acting like a jailor.

Roger gestured at Feruda to bring the candle closer. "I need some light, girl. My eyes can't see *that* well." He placed the key into the lock and clicked it clockwise.

No sooner had Roger done so than the door flung open and Pren came barreling out, slamming into the man's chest.

Roger stumbled backward and smacked into the railing. For a moment, Dagny thought he might go toppling over the edge, but instead, the man slid to the floor, clutching his back.

In the dim light, Dagny could barely make out Pren's face. He moved in a panicked, shaky motion and rushed straight past her and the others.

"Pren," Dagny called out. "Calm down! Stop!"

The boy did stop, although not because of her. He ran straight into Eidfur, screamed and fell.

Dagny raced to him. "Are you okay? I told you to stop."

Pren pointed at the wolf, sucking down air.

"Eidfur's a friend of ours," she said. "You don't have to be afraid."

Pren stared up at Dagny, as if seeing her for the first time. "You?" he asked. "How did you get in here? You're with Roger?"

"One thing at a time," Dagny replied, holding out her hand to help Pren up.

"...Sorry for running," Pren said, struggling to get to his feet. "I've been stuck here for a few days and..." His eyes shot between the whole group: Dagny, Grete, Melwes, Feruda and Marfisi. "What's going on?"

After a brief introduction to the others, Dagny told him, as delicately as possible, about Arnon and the knights.

"I don't understand," Pren said when she had finished. "What happened to them all?"

"The princess. She *did* something... dragged them all into the mist."

"Is my brother dead?" Pren asked.

Dagny chewed her bottom lip. "Yeah. I think so."

"Huh," Pren said, slowly nodding. "Well, thanks for getting me out. I could've died, myself, in there."

Roger walked over just then, approaching apprehensively. "I wouldn't've let that happen."

Pren shook his head. "Don't talk to me. I don't ever want to see you again," he said, sending Roger sulking back into the shadows.

Dagny studied Pren's face for a time, letting him take everything in, before finally asking if he was alright; although she couldn't see how he would be.

"I'm not sure," Pren responded. "It's a lot to hear."

"I know—"

"It's interesting, though," Pren continued. "If I would've just stayed away and left you in the Silent Keep, none of this would've happened and Arnon and all those knights would still be alive."

Dagny froze, unsure of what to say.

"I'm not blaming you," Pren said. "I know you weren't responsible, but you did bring that cursed hand with you."

"W-why are you saying this?" Dagny stuttered. "I didn't—Arnon is the one who destroyed the hand. He's the one who brought the princess from the weeds."

"I'm only making an observation. That's all." Pren stepped across the hallway and pressed his belly against the railing. "I can't remember a time when there wasn't someone down there working," he said, peering over the edge. "It's so quiet now."

Grete prodded Dagny on the shoulder. "Come on. You did what you came to do. Let's leave."

Dagny shook her off. "Pren, we're going into the underground soon. The Cauldron is opening. You said your father disappeared down there several years ago, looking for Odestinas."

"Yes. That's true," he replied, still staring into the void. "It's a death sentence searching for the Queen. And if you ask me, the whole legend is a lie. The Queen... the tomb... the only thing under the Cauldron is death."

Dagny softened her voice. "Did your father have some thoughts about where the Queen could be?"

"I'm sure he did... obviously, he's not around to tell us what they were."

"Did he ever mention—"

Pren shook his head. "No. He didn't discuss any of that with me, and I didn't want to hear it." He cleared his throat loudly, then spit over the railing. "The Queen's been rumored to be hidden in all sorts of places: in the Mist Hills... under the Shallow Sea... in Giant's Tear mountain. My father is one of the few who believed she was hidden under Sanctuary. Everyone is so obsessed about the quest, but they also know how dangerous it is. Honestly, if it wasn't for your princess taking Arnon like she did, he'd probably have suffocated down there, anyway."

Dagny huffed in frustration. "Can you stop saying that, please? It wasn't *my* princess."

"Alright. Anyway, I wish I could help you, but I can't."

Dagny stepped next to him. "Did he ever mention anything about the Yalow Lizard?"

Pren glanced at her side-eyed. "The constellation?"

"The Lizard is an actual constellation?" Dagny asked.

"It's small and easy to miss. But yes, it sits atop the horn of the Satyr."

Dagny mumbled to herself, "So, how do I find..." Then a thought sprang into her mind so clearly, so obvious, that it caused her to shake. "The Star Compass. The Night-Orbiter..."

"What about it?" Pren replied. "I lost mine, remember?"

"I know. Are there any more around? Didn't you mention there was another one here in Barentok?"

"There is. *One* more," Pren said. "But it's in the vault. And you'll need to ask Boulder to get it out."

༄

They gathered out in the courtyard, watching as the sky turned from soft blue to gold and violet. Pren did not want to spend another second within the fortress.

Boulder. The Bear Knight. Could Dagny really convince him to turn over the Orbiter? The man had hated her *before* the princess extinguished

Arnon and most of *Tok Eternal*. And like Pren said, she was responsible for bringing the hand here.

"My brother is the only one with a key. I don't care to speak with him ever again," Pren said, then he pointed a sharp finger at Roger who lurked in the shadows of the cloister. "You don't think I can see you?!" he shouted.

"I'm not trying to hide," Roger shouted back. "Someone needs to make sure you don't damage any more Barentok property. It's not like any of you can be trusted."

Pren scoffed, then turned to Dagny. "The Night Orbiter is a complicated thing. You set the dial to the path you wish to travel, and then as you move, the stars will shift—hopefully pointing you in the right direction."

"Hopefully?" Dagny asked.

"Yes. *Hopefully.* The instruments were created a long time ago, and just like everything, the mechanisms can break down. Orbiters were delicate things to begin with. Who knows the last time ours was maintained?"

Dagny pondered what he was saying. "How do I get Boulder to give it to us?"

"Who knows?" Pren shrugged. "Start by asking."

Dagny wished she hadn't left Maris' compass on the floor of the old palace kitchens. She'd just had so many things on her mind, like not getting lost in the darkness, and avoiding the drowned twins.

She looked over at Grete, who fidgeted with her hands. The stronghold loomed behind her ominously against the darkening sky.

"We can't waste any more time," Dagny said. "Is anyone else inside?"

"You're asking me?" Pren said. "I've been stuck pissing in my room for days."

Feruda stood and marched over to Roger. Dagny couldn't hear what they were saying, but when Feruda gestured at Eidfur and rubbed her belly, Roger nodded solemnly and shook his head.

"He says *there's no one left inside*," Feruda shouted, as she walked back to the group. "I think we split up and search the place as quick as possible, then meet back here."

Barentok seemed huge from what Dagny had already seen, but it was still impossible to gauge how vast the place truly was. For one thing, the structure was surrounded by the sprawling labyrinth of the Inner City—making it extremely difficult to identify its boundaries.

"Any idea where Boulder would've gone?" Dagny asked.

"No," Pren replied. "And I'm not going back inside. I'm done with this place."

Dagny was hoping he'd be more helpful, but she couldn't blame him for hating Barentok and wanting to leave. A sudden intensity welled up behind Pren's eyes, and his entire body seemed to bristle.

"I'm leaving," he said, rising from the stone ground. "Maybe I'll see you another time... then again, if you really are going down the Cauldron, maybe I won't."

21

Marfisi stayed in the courtyard with Melwes and the wolf, just in case Boulder slipped out—or anyone else thought about slipping in.

The other three split up after reentering the stronghold, each taking a candle to light the way. Dagny would explore the first floor, while Feruda and Grete would take the floors above. After each level, they agreed to reconvene at the entryway to make sure everyone was safe before moving on.

The first floor was likely to be the largest, and Dagny decided on marching straight ahead, down the main hallway. A worn-out, purple carpet ran the length of the passage, and brass lamps hung from the wall every twenty feet or so. Dagny lit each one she passed, pressing her candle flame onto the oily wicks, and soon the area was glowing bright enough for her to see the loose threads on her dress. The bottom of the garment was unraveling at such a rapid pace that she would need to replace it soon, but she dreaded the idea of taking it off. She knew that once she did, the dress would be gone, and then her memory of Lieta and the Needle would eventually fade into the foggy recesses of her mind.

It's not like Dagny cared about the Needle or the Silent Keep. The whole experience had been quite horrible. She just hated the idea of forgetting; and in particular, forgetting Lieta. It felt as though she couldn't hold onto any important memories. Everything kept slipping away.

But *objects...* the things that were connected to people, like Grete's bracelet on her wrist; Morgan's coat, before it was lost in Limer's Town; the dress she wore now. She felt something there; when she ran her finger over grooves in the tin, or glided her hand across smooth silk... it was a feeling that couldn't be taken away so easily by the forgetfulness of time.

Dagny wondered if other people had such a hard time remembering. If their minds held dark fissures that sucked away important people. Sometimes, she felt like a ghost wandering among the living.

The hallway led straight into the workshop Dagny had seen earlier from the floor above. She gazed up there and saw a light, probably from Grete or Feruda's candle, floating in the air. She thought about calling out, but decided not to draw attention to herself, just in case.

Walking further into the area, Dagny passed long tables and benches covered by maps and diagrams, gears and mechanical objects, pieces of armor and tools. She picked up a small brass pocket watch and clicked it open. The hands were frozen in time but started to tick once she gave it a quick windup. The knights were much more skilled than she'd given them credit for. It couldn't be easy maintaining such intricate gears.

A rich orange glow washed over the walls of a tunnel to her left; no doubt firelight coming from somewhere beyond. Dagny stuck the brass watch in her boot and told herself that any new outfit needed to have pockets. Then she hurried toward the firelight and entered a small stone chamber. It reminded her of a shrine to a forgotten saint. A host of candles surrounded a painting of a bearded man in armor, and against the far wall was the fireplace. Sitting in between was Boulder, drinking from a metal tankard. A huge hammer was slung across his back, just below his massive, bulging neck.

"There was no body to bury," the man said, as Dagny stepped forward. "So this is where we honor him. My father."

Dagny took a deep breath. "I'm sorry about your brother and the others. I didn't want any of that to happen." She noticed his hands for the first time, raw and scarred, like he'd been burnt by fire.

Boulder rubbed his face. He may have been wiping away tears, but Dagny couldn't see. "It was our own reckless pride and arrogance," he said, speaking slowly, like someone on the verge of exhaustion. "The stewards warned us about such vices."

"Do you know who she was? The princess? I thought I heard Arnon call her Slurgle or something."

"*Salarel*. We all know of her," Boulder said. "She was a princess of the Alustra."

"What's the Alustra?" Dagny asked.

"A place far from here. It's been called many different names. Odestinas summoned her as one of the first. If Arnon had known that was Salarel's hand..." Boulder sighed. "You should've warned him."

"Warned him? How?" Dagny replied. "And when was I supposed to do that? After I was tossed to the ground and your men were getting ready to beat me?"

"You're overreacting—"

"I didn't know whose hand that was," Dagny said calmly. "And I'm not overreacting. You came to the Alypso to punish us for embarrassing you."

Boulder groaned and gazed back into the fire. "What do you want?"

"I need to get into the vault. I need the Night Orbiter."

"Why?"

Dagny took a step closer. "The Cauldron is opening tomorrow, and we're going down it. To find the Queen."

Her statement was met by a long silence. So long, in fact, that Dagny almost walked up to Boulder to make sure he hadn't passed out, when the man finally spoke. "You couldn't possibly know where she is."

"Really? The Knights Eternal have been *very* interested in my sister, for a long time, I think. And why is that? Because she can see the Queen's dreams."

Boulder faced Dagny once again, watching her closely.

"Don't you want to see how this turns out?" Dagny leaned forward. "Help us reach Odestinas."

"Hmph," Boulder croaked. Then he rose slowly and wandered to the shrine. "My father thought he knew where Odestinas was buried, too, but he never made it back out. I wonder sometimes if he found her."

"Get me the Orbiter," Dagny said. "And then... maybe... we can find out what happened to Tarn."

"You think you found a secret path, huh?"

"I know we did." Dagny smiled. "I thought you were the fighter here, but you seem to know more than a scholar."

"Oh. I'm the fighter." Boulder laughed. "You know, I still have a mark from the bite you gave me. My leg is likely to scar."

Dagny shrugged. "Sorry, I guess, but what did you expect me to do? I didn't know you were Pren's brother."

"You got some teeth, girl. You're like a rabid, little beast," Boulder said, imitating a wild creature while holding his hands out, fingers spread. Dagny didn't appreciate the comparison.

"So anyway," she said. "About the vault—"

Boulder shook his head and said under hushed breath, "The Knights Eternal... brought to ruin by a nipping twig-girl and her magic hand. Don't worry, I'll take you to the vault."

"Alright. Thanks," Dagny said. "I appreciate—"

"Under one condition," he said.

"And what's that?"

Boulder stretched, cracking his back. "I'm going down the Cauldron with you."

∾

Dagny and Boulder met Grete back at the entryway, but Feruda hadn't returned yet.

"She went to inspect the third floor," Grete said.

"Think she got lost?" Dagny asked, gazing up the darkened staircase.

Boulder responded, "It'd be tough to get lost on the third level. It's a circle. Eventually, you'll come back to the stairs." He shifted his weight around impatiently. "Hey, you want the Orbiter? Let's get this over with."

Dagny glanced outside and saw Marfisi sitting with Eidfur and Melwes on the ground, all of them illuminated by the spirit lights.

"You go," Grete told her. "I'll look for Feruda. She's probably searching through every room."

"Okay," Dagny said, nodding her head. "As soon as you find her, go outside with Marfisi. This place is eerie." Roger Red had mentioned that no one else was inside, but Dagny couldn't really trust him.

Grete agreed, gave Dagny a hug, and walked off into the darkness with her candle.

"She doesn't seem like a witch," Boulder said. "Then again, it can be hard to tell."

"She's not a witch. She just sees things differently."

"And dreams of a dead queen." Boulder snorted. "That sounds like a witch to me."

Dagny followed the knight through a series of corridors toward the rear of Barentok. They passed galleries; trophy rooms and studies; and a particularly large gymnasium with old mats on the floor. Dagny watched the hammer slap against Boulder's back as he led the way. She wondered if he'd actually used it before in a fight, but didn't want to ask. Instead, she said, "This place is enormous. Who built it?"

"The Amber Kings. It was their stronghold before the ruin and the rupturing. After they were driven out, Barentok sat empty for a while, until the Knights took over."

"How do you know all this?" Dagny said, as she peered into a dusty storage room on her right.

"What do you mean?" Boulder replied.

"Whenever someone tells me about Jud, it's never the whole story," Dagny said. "It's always just a hint of something bigger. Is the city's history written down anywhere?"

"No. The histories of Jud are kept in stories and songs. The weavers of Sanctuary hold on to 'em."

"Oh." Dagny twisted her lips and thought for a second. "So, how do you know they're true, then?"

"Huh?" Boulder replied. Dagny saw a lime-green door appear at the edge of their light.

"How do you know the stories are true?" Dagny repeated. "If it only depends on someone singing you a song or telling you a story? What if the storyteller made it all up, or changed a detail? You'd never know. Especially if they've been told for hundreds of years."

Boulder huffed. "No. That's not how it works."

"I didn't mean to make you upset," Dagny said, as Boulder stepped to the door and pushed it open.

"Don't worry, twig," he said. "You'd know if you made me upset."

Another long hallway greeted them, with cobwebs covering the ceiling and walls. Obviously, it hadn't been maintained for years. "Is the vault nearby?" Dagny asked, staring down the dark tunnel.

"Yes. No one comes here much. The vault is just filled with old relics, not anything useful. The only other thing of any importance is the old chapel at the end of this hall. It's where the Amber Kings held court." Boulder swatted webs out of his face as he walked. "I don't even know if that Orbiter will work, so don't get your hopes up."

"It better work," Dagny replied. "I don't have any other options."

"Which star path are you trying to find?" Boulder asked, and she almost responded before catching herself. This man could become a lot more dangerous if he knew the route to Odestinas without her. What would stop him from bashing her head against the wall after that, then finding the tomb himself?

Dagny shrugged. "The *witches* haven't told me," she said jokingly, trying to keep the mood light. "All I know is, we need the Orbiter."

"Mm-hmm," Boulder said, a doubtful tone to his voice. "The vault and everything in it belong to the heirs of Tarn. So that means it belongs to me now. You're lucky I feel like lending it to you."

"What about Pren? Isn't he an heir of Tarn, too?"

"*Pren?*" Boulder said. "He doesn't have any rights here anymore. He gave 'em up when he gave up on the oath."

Dagny was about to ask more questions when Boulder glanced over his shoulder, down the passage they came from. "Did you hear something?"

Dagny shook her head. She hadn't. "What did it sound like?"

"Like someone quietly running."

A slight panic rose in her chest. "No one else is here, though, right? That's what everyone has been telling me... Barentok is empty."

"Let's be quick," Boulder said. "Part of the reason no one came to this wing is because there's ghosts here. Brought by the artifacts kept below."

Ghosts? A year ago, Dagny wouldn't have believed him, but she'd seen so many unusual things during that time. She only hoped the ghosts of Barentok weren't as dangerous as Princess Salarel.

The vault was past an iron gate and down a flight of stairs. They must've been far below the city streets when Boulder finally stopped and unsealed the heavy block of metal that guarded the strongroom.

"It may take some searching. I can't remember where everything is kept," Boulder said, holding his lantern forward. Dagny expected the vault to resemble a fancy treasure horde, complete with golden statues and jeweled artifacts, but it looked more like a converted prison: a series of cells branching off from a long tunnel. The place was dense with objects glinting in the light.

"You know what to look for?" Boulder asked.

"Yeah. I've seen one before," Dagny replied.

Boulder raised an eyebrow. "Really?"

"Yep," Dagny said. She stepped past a stack of shiny, black cubes, not having the slightest idea what they were used for. "I'll take the left."

The first cell contained an enormous pile of weathered books. "Those are journals," Boulder said from behind her. "A record of every knight who ever set foot in the Great Below, or wandered far into Lazim."

Her mind turned to the Gaunt Lady who had haunted Feruda's dreams. "Anything useful in there?" Dagny asked, although it didn't really matter. She certainly didn't have time to start reading through the journals.

"Useful? Of course."

"Anything on the Black Sun?"

Boulder stopped. "Where did you hear about that?"

"From a friend... is it true? Does the Gaunt Lady really exist?"

"She may have. She was a shade, and the shades were birthed by a memory called Nyne, also known as the Black Sun. Nyne was another queen of sorts, but one who ruled the underground as Odestinas ruled the land above. Where Odestinas was light, Nyne was dark."

"So, what happened to Nyne and the shades?"

"I've told you all I know," Boulder replied, somewhat sharply. "Just look for the Orbiter."

The Orbiter wasn't in cells two or three, either. Those chambers contained long brass tubes large enough to hold a person, like a coffin. Dagny would've asked what those were used for as well, but didn't want to set the man off. It was apparent Boulder wanted to get out of here as soon as possible.

She found it in the fourth one. An exact copy of the "compass" Maris had brought to Alex in the summer of last year. A small heap of dark metal. It sat next to a circular glass helmet on the floor, and as Dagny's candlelight caught the shape, a colorful assortment of spots representing the night sky spread over the cell.

She approached cautiously, as if the sound of her steps might scare the spots away, or the air from her breath might shatter the relic into a thousand pieces.

"You find it?" Boulder asked from the tunnel outside. Dagny just nodded her head and knelt down next to the Orbiter. There was a delicate chain attached to the top of it by a small hook. Dagny lifted it slowly, placing the chain around her neck.

Boulder stepped into the cell and whistled softly. "That thing is remarkable when the light catches it. You know how to use it?"

"Not exactly. I was hoping to figure it out," she replied.

Boulder pursed his lips. "Puddle may know. He was always more interested in this stuff than we were. Anyway, you can hold onto it for now. One less object for me to carry," he said, patting his hammer. "But don't go forgetting that the Orbiter belongs to me."

"Of course," Dagny said. "We're all after the same thing."

They were almost back at the lime-green door when Dagny saw Grete and Feruda approach. Or whom she thought were Grete and Feruda. Two candles glowed against the dark at the edge of her vision, but they didn't move; they just hovered there, flickering.

Dagny called out her sister's name. And when she didn't answer, Dagny felt her skin go cold. Boulder kept walking, then stopped so suddenly, he slipped and had to hold the wall for balance.

She knew at that very moment who was standing at the end of the hallway, waiting. Their faces slowly appeared now in the shadowy candlelight, like a boat emerging from the wet fog. Two drowned things. Pale and scarred. The boy's mouth gaped open, ready to speak or scream.

Boulder leapt forward and slammed the green door closed, pressing his weight against it. "Quick," he told her. His voice was so calm it was unsettling. "Hide in the chapel at the back."

Dagny was about to protest—to warn him about what was coming—but then Boulder turned his head and shouted, "*Now!*"

Into the darkness she ran, covering her candle flame with one hand. Her heart pounding in her throat. She passed the stairs leading to the vault and rushed headlong into a mess of cobwebs, sucking in a mouthful of soft threads.

Why were the twins here in Barentok? Had they tracked her somehow? Dagny hadn't seen them since the old palace kitchens, where Galwed watched her and Tash from the slit in the wall. In the back recesses of Dagny's mind, she'd foolishly hoped the twins were far away. That her meeting them before was only accidental, and that her fear of the twins hunting Grete had been a mistake.

Dagny saw a rainbow of light at the end of the hallway, and a short time later, stumbled into the chapel, wiping cobwebs from her face. The opposite wall framed a large stained-glass window of three angelic creatures looking over a land on fire. In front of the window was an altar and throne.

The angels set in glass were so bewilderingly beautiful, Dagny almost lost her sense of urgency. Even at the Palace of Stars and Sorn Rue back home, there were no windows like this. The details were so intricate, and the forms so lifelike, it was nothing short of amazing. She wondered who could've crafted such a thing, in a city as old as civilization itself.

here was no time to ponder it further. Scouring the room, Dagny confirmed what she had feared: there were no other doors or passages.

The chapel was a dead end. *Grete, Melwes, Feruda...* how could she possibly warn them now?

She'd taken only a few steps toward the altar when she heard a tremendous boom erupt from the passage behind her. The twins had shattered the door. In a panic, Dagny looked for a place to hide, but there were few options. Other than the altar and throne itself, the chamber contained nothing but a set of pews and shallow alcoves in the wall. She was trapped.

From somewhere far away, Dagny thought she heard a wolf howl.

22

Dagny's lips trembled. She stared down the pitch-black passageway, straining for a glimpse of those horrible white faces that she knew were marching toward her now. Maybe Boulder had slowed the twins, but she doubted it. He certainly couldn't have stopped them. Dagny wondered if anything could.

Move. Get away. The thought came on sharply, causing a nervous twitch to jolt her shoulders. But it was only a frightened, primal instinct that hadn't connected with the logic of her brain. There was nowhere to go.

Still, Dagny whirled around, her eyes darting rapidly across the room. The three angels in glass gazed down, each with a look of dismissive apathy that seemed to say her fate was already decided and not worthy of interference. Vague, distant images of a sinking world passed through Dagny's mind. It was the same vision she'd had in the old palace kitchens, when the twins had chased her and Tash into the wall.

Dagny crossed the chamber toward the altar, then stopped indecisively. Pressing her tongue hard against the roof of her mouth, she considered her options. She could curl up under a pew or crouch behind the throne and wait for the twins to grab her, or she could run back to the vault... there still might be enough time to reach it, then she could close the heavy door and seal herself inside. But as she glanced down the hall, Dagny knew she couldn't charge into the darkness. Her heart wouldn't allow it.

She noticed two iron candelabras resting on either side of the altar, their candles long since melted away. Dagny picked one up and held it like a spear, knowing full well that there was no way she could fight the twins off.

Her back stiffened. The long, heavy candleholder shook in her nervous hands. Colorful sunlight glinted across its metallic surface and reflected back over the room, casting rainbow shimmers onto the walls and floor.

Sunlight.

She stared at the angels and the stained-glass world they hovered over. The glass must've been a thousand years old, perhaps older, placed by the Amber Kings to serve as the focal point of their chapel. Maybe the angels were worshipped here at one time, but their names had faded from history long ago. Dagny thought they looked smug and undeserving of the gorgeous world that melted in flame beneath them. She hesitated only for a moment before pulling the candleholder across her shoulder and sending it through the air.

The iron base crashed into an angel's eye, and Dagny ducked, covering her head, as the window exploded outward, shattering into a thousand brilliant shards. If the twins weren't running before, they were sure to be running now.

Hopping on one leg, Dagny peeled her boot off and stuck her fist inside, ready to knock as much glass from the frame as possible before leaping over. Outside was a small courtyard, and at the opposite end, a spiked fence. Silent buildings bordered the pathway beyond. If Dagny could reach them, then maybe she could lose the twins in the maze of streets that surrounded Barentok.

Dagny smashed her booted fist through a jagged row of stained-glass teeth and took a quick look over her shoulder before making her move. The hallway leading into the chapel was still dark and empty, and there was a considerable gap between there and the window. She pulled her boot back on and carefully placed her shaking hands on the ledge. Small bits of glass remained, tucked into the stone fold, and they bit into her palms. She felt the sting, but barely flinched, and swung her leg around, mindful of keeping her bare thigh raised as high as possible.

It wasn't too far of a drop. At one time, there had been plants below, probably something beautiful like roses or lilies, and although they were long gone, a patch of black earth was ready to greet her after the fall. Dagny teetered on the border, ready to tip her weight and tumble onto the ground.

Her body swayed, and her heart leapt with anxious excitement. For a brief moment, gravity took over, pulling her down toward the earth. She felt the rush of hot summertime wind, and the glare of sunshine on her face. And a sharp pain tear across her scalp.

Dagny was no longer falling. She was being wrenched backward, watching helplessly as the courtyard and sun pulled away from her, and the shattered gaze of glass angels came back into view. Her leg dragged over the window's broken threshold, splitting open on the row of jagged teeth.

It was *them*. They had her hair. Nails dug into her skull and yanked her to the chapel's cold stone floor. Then Tewdred appeared, stepping into Dagny's line of sight. The drowned boy tilted his ghostly face and watched Dagny squirm from behind murky gray eyes.

Dagny's brain struggled to keep up. She could see both of Tewdred's hands, which meant that the sister was gripping her hair. *Galwed*. The Collector.

She dragged Dagny across the floor toward the hallway, then quickly pivoted and straddled her chest. The girl's knees pressed painfully into Dagny's forearms, trapping her to the ground.

Black hair, wet and long, dripped down over a scarred face. Dagny could see an eye between the strands, glaring at her neck, then the girl's gaze moved down to her chest. The only noise Dagny heard was the wheezing of her own raspy breath, nothing else. Neither of the twins made a sound.

But then, something else sounded. The crashing of water on stone. Dagny shrieked and flailed, trying her best to push Galwed off, but nothing could move the drowned girl. Terror swept through Dagny, closing her throat. She glanced up and over at Tewdred, who just stood there watching. The gray, sagging skin around his mouth twitched, as if the boy was trying to speak.

Dagny sucked air in through her nostrils. The scent of the chapel had turned musty and putrid. She tried to wish Eidfur into the room to save her, like the crow had done at the Nedgling Tower, ready to ravage her attackers. Then her mind turned to something worse. What if the twins had already found Eidfur, Grete and the others? What if there was no one left to save her?

Dagny's body tensed, stiff as a corpse. She risked another look at Galwed. The drowned girl held a single finger to the sky. A dark nail grew from the tip, jagged and long. It reminded Dagny of Kustav's nails. The ones that pinched and plucked at her thigh all those nights ago.

But Galwed wasn't interested in pinching her. The girl twisted her cruel finger in the sunlight, where the blackness swelling at the nail bed seemed to suck all of the brightness from the room. Galwed gazed at the finger, as if contemplating something profound, or dreaming wistfully of somewhere else entirely. And when she'd finished, she glanced back at Dagny. With no more hesitation, Galwed bent her wrist sharply, pointing her finger straight down, and plunged the nail deep into Dagny's chest.

There was the twist of agony, and the cold shock of horror. Dagny clenched her jaw and fists, and felt her leg kick out reflexively. The sunlight turned red—or was that her imagination? The color of blood and rust washed over the throne where Amber Kings had sat. She heard the rush of waves again and smelled salt in the air. Galwed continued to straddle her, her eyes shut tightly now, pressing that dark finger into the soft skin of Dagny's breast. Over her heart. *Her heart?* Dagny's breathing turned rapid. Was the girl actually inside of her heart?

She heard water hit the floor, rushing into the chapel from the broken window. A moment later, Dagny felt it sweep over her legs and arms, and pool against her shoulders, then wet her neck and the back of her head. It was as if the entire room was sinking into the sea.

The water rose quickly. Small waves lapping against her body. It crested over her stomach and chest. Dagny tried to lift her head but struggled to move—such was the hold that Galwed had over her. She was frozen on the floor. Paralyzed. The waves entered her mouth and washed into her nose. Dagny choked and gasped for air, staring into the drowned girl's milky face. Pleading desperately with her eyes.

Suddenly, Galwed's own eye sprung open. Dagny could see light in it and the dim reflection of crumbling buildings; ramparts of an old city...

A moment later, Galwed snapped her finger forward, breaking the nail off in her breast, and Dagny's world went blue.

She was underwater, sinking quickly. Tewdred and Galwed floated above her, drifting away as she fell. She watched the chapel rise—like the floor had dropped out beneath her and she was falling into a deep sea. The walls and pews and broken, stain-glassed angels all vanished into that red sun. Dagny couldn't tell if she was breathing anymore and glanced at her hands. They looked so strange, almost green in the dying light. Enormous, dark shapes swam past her, just at the edge of her vision. There was a mountain in the distance. *An actual mountain of sunken night.* Its crest jagged and distorted, like the tip of Galwed's nail.

Still she fell, and the mountain drifted away, washing into the inky black. Dagny knew that she was no longer breathing. She had drowned. Blind and numb, but not completely devoid of all senses. She could taste the cold salt of her new world; she could hear a deep, deep rumbling from somewhere beneath her. An unrelenting, quaking groan like the world devouring itself in a mad hunger.

Something brushed against her arm. She should've panicked. Her heart *should've* stopped right then (maybe it already had), yet she was strangely content, slipping further and further down into the abyss.

At the beginning of time, at the shaping of the world, there was only dark water. An endless ocean, stretching between the moon and sun; blanketing the mass that would become the nameless first realm. Ages later, dark water would rise again, washing away the creations of the world. The land would wither and burn, cycling through ages of devastation. History, or at least that which was known, seemed to be a never-ending struggle between destroyer and creator. Dreams and death.

Dagny had known none of these things until beginning her new life in Rork. At the Rakesmount, her life was survival. She'd forgotten who taught her the early histories—probably some tutor, whose name escaped her now at the bottom of the sea, but it didn't matter. Nothing mattered anymore. In the eternal darkness, life and dreams blended together. And at the time of death, memories, no matter how important, faded into oblivion. If there was no one left to remember a thing, did it ever truly exist?

Her body came to rest on the seabed. Or what she thought was the seabed. There was flat stone here. She felt slimy pavers underneath—a road, perhaps? She lay there for a minute or a year, her body quivering in rhythm to that deep rumbling. In the darkness, she imagined her mother, sitting in a bare room, staring into a fireplace; rubbing together her brown-spotted hands. A woman incapable of affection. But she'd given birth to Morgan and Grete and her, and all of *them* had loved each other. Dagny knew that much about herself. She knew she had loved at one time, if nothing else.

On quiet, hot, summer days, they would wander to an inlet by River's End, where the canal boats docked. The water was so clear there. Morgan would climb to a balcony that overlooked the embankment and dive in, and Dagny would watch him glide across. He was so sleek and athletic. The sharpest person she'd ever known. He could've done anything.

He was smiling at her now, a shimmering image in the otherwise black void. With a sweep of his hand, Morgan pushed his blue hair away from his face, exposing a deep pit where his left eye should've been. Dagny stretched her hand toward it, intending to cover up the wound and return Morgan to normal. But just before she did, Dagny noticed something there, glittering in the dark. Small, silver, and twinkling. A star in the night.

Slowly, it grew in size until it engulfed Morgan's entire head, then his body, stopping short of engulfing her. It illuminated the seabed for miles. Dagny turned and gazed upon an entire city, broken and deformed, sprawled out in every direction. Grotesque, multi-tiered towers, covered in gray seaweed, looked down on the doomed buildings and boulevards. All seemed to shrivel under the weight of the star.

She stared back into the light. Morgan had vanished, consumed by star fire, and Dagny felt the heat now as well. It scorched her hands and melted her fingers down to blood and bone, morphing her skin into pink wax. She glanced at her chest. Galwed's jagged nail stuck out of her exposed breast and vibrated, sending rippling waves across her torso. She watched her nipple—a blistering red button—turn into black ash, and the bones of her ribcage wither and crack, as the pale white flames licked her body until there was nothing left except her heart.

Still, that heart beat there in the water—hovering over the ancient, sunken city at the bottom of the sea—it beat, and beat, *and beat...*

Dagny sprung up, gasping for air. She was alive. Her flesh was solid. It was dark in the chapel, but moonlight snuck in from the broken window, casting odd gray shadows across the stone floor. She slapped her hand over her chest and flinched in pain as her palm found the place where Galwed's nail had been pressed inside. Her heart was thundering so rapidly she thought it might rupture.

There was no sign of the twins. The chapel was dead quiet, and the floor was bone dry, covered in dust. Dagny's eyes darted across the chamber as she simultaneously tried to pull her dress back up, but it was no use. The garment was ruined. Why was she still alive? *How* was she still breathing?

Dagny grabbed the Night Orbiter from the floor, rushed to the broken window, and leapt outside without another thought. She landed on the soft patch of dirt and raced across the courtyard to the maze of alleyways beyond. Only then did she stop and try to gather herself.

Grete... Melwes... Feruda... she needed to find them. Dagny looked back at Barentok. She couldn't go through the chapel again. The twins must've encountered Boulder first. If he was dead, lying there on the hallway floor, she didn't think her mind could handle the sight of it. There'd been too much death already. And what if the twins were still around? Or what if they were planning to come back and Dagny had simply recovered sooner than expected?

She felt like *something* had rescued her down there in the sunken city. She didn't think the twins simply meant for her to come back, after all of that. And if it *had* been a rescue, Dagny wouldn't spite it by wandering back inside. Even if her sister and friends were there, Dagny would have to find another way to reach them.

So, having made up her mind, Dagny turned away and marched down the dimly lit alley, leaving the chapel behind.

Dagny flipped the Orbiter onto her back to keep it from rubbing against her wound. She didn't know this part of the district. The streets that she had wandered before with Feruda were on the opposite side of the stronghold. Everything seemed narrower here, and on more than one occasion, her shoulders bumped and dragged along the backsides of buildings framing the alley.

Her mind was foggy, amplified by the suffocating darkness. It was like she was in a trance she couldn't break out of. Ever since entering the

Sillweed... actually, ever since entering Jud, Dagny felt outside of herself, wandering through some kind of waking dream.

There was no one else around, but Dagny still walked with one hand covering her breast, at the same time trying to pluck Galwed's nail out of her skin. It was there. She could feel it lodged inside, just beneath the surface. Dagny tried to focus on other things while her fingers went to work on the rotten nail; if she gave it too much attention, she knew she'd slip into a full-fledged panic at the grotesqueness of the thing.

Dagny hated the way this place touched her. From the Grouchers in the Outskirts to the Knights of the Silent Keep; from Kustav's nails to Galwed's nails, and everything in-between. She missed the soft way Max had touched her, and she concentrated on that. It had been thrilling and new and honest and welcomed. The opposite of the way she felt now.

The alley split, and Dagny did her best to follow the route back to Barentok. Maybe everyone was still camped in the entry plaza. They wouldn't have just left her, would they? Certainly not Grete and Melwes. But how come no one had found her? Sure, the chapel was tucked away in the back, but it wouldn't have been *that* hard to find. She must've been lying there for hours.

Dagny didn't want to think about it too much until she reached the stronghold's entrance. The road widened, allowing enough of the moonlight through for Dagny to see her own body, silvery gray in the light. Blood was trickling out of the wound in her chest, sending black streams down her pale skin. She needed to stop clawing at the thing. It was only making matters worse. Try as she might, she could not dislodge the fingernail.

The alley turned into a proper road that snaked around the border of the Barentok District. *Knights Eternal* banners began appearing on the nearby walls, and after a short walk, Dagny saw a building in the distance, recognizing it as the guardhouse where the teenage boy had accosted her and Feruda the other night. The sight of it excited her. She wanted to see someone familiar, even if her last interaction with the boy was less than friendly, but as Dagny approached, she quickly realized the place was empty. She hoped the boy hadn't been with the knights when Salarel set into them. He didn't deserve that. None of them did.

The way Salarel had ripped those men out of this world seemed frighteningly similar to the way Galwed sent Dagny to that place beneath the waves. Just like how the girl's fingernail reminded her of Kustav's, and in another way... the metal fingers of Salarel. Even though it all seemed vaguely connected somehow, Dagny doubted she would ever figure it out.

Besides, she didn't really care. She just wanted to leave this city. She wanted Galwed's nail out of her body, and she wanted Grete to return to normal. She wanted to be done with all of this. She wanted to be back in Rork.

From the guardhouse, it was easy enough to find her way back to the entry plaza. Dagny retraced her steps through the district's streets until she reached the wall where she and Feruda had torn down the Knight's banner. She stood there for a moment, reflecting on how that simple act had more or less sparked the quick, violent demise of the Eternal order. Sure, Arnon was mostly at fault. The stupid, brutal man acted recklessly, but even so...

Any clouds in the sky had cleared by the time Dagny stepped into the plaza, and the moon and stars were so bright, she could easily see to the other side.

The place was empty, gripped by an eerie silence. Dagny walked forward cautiously, careful not to make too much noise. The mighty doors of Tok Eternal remained open—in the same position they had been the last time Dagny was here—and as bright as the moon was, there were still dark shadows within the surrounding cloister. Dagny doubted anyone was hiding in there, but she kept an eye out for movement and readied herself to run at a moment's notice. She didn't plan to go exploring Barentok again. She only needed to look inside, just in case Grete or any of the others were nearby.

When she was about halfway across, a light breeze blew down and rustled Dagny's ruined dress. The garment had been so beautiful when she'd found it inside Lieta's wardrobe; now the thing was hardly more than a rag. A onetime delicate outfit, weaved by an expert hand, it wasn't meant for the outside world. The outside world had destroyed it.

Dagny sniffed the breeze, hoping to catch a whiff of the great wolf, for some clue as to where her companions had gone, but the air was clean and crisp. She reached the stone elephant and lion statues framing the staircase and hesitated. Tewdred and Galwed were fresh in her mind, and the twins were so fast and quiet. If they were still here, Dagny knew she wouldn't be able to escape them again. Maybe Grete and the others had gone back to the Alypso tree. Maybe they'd tried to look for her but came across Boulder's body and ran away. If so, the sight must've been so horrible that Dagny couldn't fault them for leaving. Maybe they were mourning her right now.

She was about to turn and leave when a figure walked past the stronghold doors. It stepped from the shadows into the moonlight, revealing the slight, pale frame of Feruda. "There you are!" she shouted to Dagny. "I've been looking all over for you."

23

Dagny rushed up the steps and embraced Feruda so tightly, they almost fell to the ground.

"Where have you been?" Feruda exclaimed. "What happened to you?"

Dagny turned her body away, once again conscious of the ruined dress and how much it exposed. The two of them could not have looked more different. Feruda: comical in her oversized boots, skirt and shirt; and Dagny: blood-streaked and filthy, dressed in torn, black rags; covering her wounded breast.

"Are you *really* here?" Dagny asked. "Or..."

"Yes, I'm here," Feruda replied. "What happened? You look..."

"I'm hurt," Dagny said, lowering her hand enough to show Feruda where Galwed had pierced her skin. "But I need to find Grete. Where is she?"

"Grete and the others had to leave. I stayed behind to find you."

"Was it because of the twins? Is that why they fled?"

Feruda raised her eyebrow in confusion. "The twins?"

Dagny did her best to explain the events in the chapel and how Galwed broke her twisted nail off into her breast. "I... passed out. How long has it been?"

Feruda's eyes were so large, Dagny thought they might pop out of her head. "We need to get that nail out immediately. We're going back to the Alypso."

"What about the ghost princess?"

"There's a dark thing inside of you, and the Alypso is the only power I know of that might help. We have to risk it."

Dagny nodded and whispered, "Okay." After everything, she was more than happy for someone else to take control and lead for a change.

They left the plaza, walking side by side toward Marfisi's house, and didn't speak until reaching the border.

"I tried to get it out, myself," Dagny said. "But I couldn't reach the nail, and I think I just made it worse with all my digging."

Feruda touched her shoulder. "I'm sorry that happened to you."

"Why would she do that to me? The drowned girl. What was the purpose of it?" Dagny asked.

Feruda bit her lip.

She knew something more, didn't she? Something about the source of this wicked magic. After a moment of silence, waiting, Dagny blurted out, "Just tell me."

"There's an old way about creatures like that. From a time when the fingers could see more than the eyes or mind. The power found in their ancient nails developed when such beings wandered the darkness of the Great Below, clawing and feeling their way through the abyss." Feruda studied Dagny's face before continuing. "They're likely jealous of your beauty and life, and through disfigurement they can subjugate and control, overtaking your spirit, melding it with their own, so you become nothing more than an extension of them. Losing every part of yourself in the process. The piece inside of you needs to be purged."

Dread swelled up from her stomach. Feruda was talking about a form of possession, a type one might never recover from. Dagny stared down at the small gash in her skin. She no longer cared about covering herself, only getting the nail out. "How do I do that? How do I *purge* it?" she asked.

"The Alypso tree..." Feruda whispered. "We have tools there, and ways to tap into it."

"Are you going to cut it out?"

"We need to."

Dagny took a deep breath. "I want it gone. I don't care how deep you need to cut." Before Feruda could respond, Dagny quickened her pace, almost breaking into a sprint.

The courtyard was silent, and Marfisi's tower-house was dark. There was no sign of Salarel or anything else for that matter. A thin layer of opaque mist covered the ground, causing Dagny to hesitate before continuing on.

"How are you feeling now?" Feruda asked.

"Nervous."

"Do you feel *different* at all?"

Dagny scoffed. "Do I feel like a drowned twin is taking control of my body?"

Feruda replied with a shrug and a terse, "Well?"

"I don't know." Dagny took a breath and gazed over the mist-filled yard. "Think Salarel is here?"

"Maybe, but that princess was upset because of what those men did. *We* haven't done anything."

Dagny reflected on what she'd heard about the metal princesses crumbling into oblivion. "That's why Salarel appeared like she did. Arnon destroyed the last piece of her body when he crushed the hand."

"Likely, yes."

"I thought princesses would be more pleasant."

"You can't fault her, can you?" Feruda asked. "After what they were subjected to."

"No. Not really," Dagny replied. "It's terrible. Girls and young women imprisoned like that."

"They were denied their own existence. It's no wonder they're angry now." Feruda turned and studied Dagny's body, softening her voice. "How's your chest?"

"I'm hurting."

Feruda took Dagny's hand and squeezed it before leading her toward the tower. Dagny kept a careful watch on the ground, expecting Salarel's ghost hair to sweep over her legs at any moment, but the only thing to happen was when Feruda tripped over the empty helmet of a lost knight.

They entered the house and Feruda rushed over to the kitchen shutters, pushing them open. The moon and stars barely penetrated the room, but it was better than nothing.

The space appeared the same as when Dagny last saw it. Dirty plates rested on the kitchen table, and a bucket of Feruda's wine sat on the floor nearby.

"We'll need the flame," Feruda said, motioning at the hearth. "Work on a fire."

Dagny nodded, gathering tinder and flint, while Feruda searched through the kitchen for various supplies. "I've treated plenty of wounds before, but this one is different," the girl said. "We'll need the Ritual of Assistance."

A short time later, Dagny had a small fire going, and Feruda brought over a pot of water to boil. "Can't lose sight of the basics; first thing is a clean blade."

Dagny let out a nervous laugh. "That nail under my skin is probably the dirtiest thing imaginable."

"Well, we don't want to add any more dirt, do we?" Feruda said. She positioned Dagny near the firelight and laid her instruments on a soft cloth. They consisted of two small knives, a pair of tongs, and a sowing needle from Feruda's kit. Dagny gulped and looked away.

The heat from the flames was sweltering, and Dagny's mind drifted to the pale sun beneath the sea that had burnt her flesh and consumed her brother. "I had a vision when the twins attacked me," she whispered. "Of a sunken place. I think it was Gort."

Feruda dropped the knives and needle into the boiling water, then etched a circle onto the floor with a dripping twig. "Branch of the Alypso. Its sap will keep foul energies away while we work."

When she had finished, Feruda gently pulled down what remained of Dagny's dress, slowly rolling it to her waist. Dagny's skin looked ghostly white by the fire, and she half-expected it to blister and blacken.

Feruda leaned close and whispered, "Think of something else." But that was easier said than done. Dagny glanced down at her naked chest and watched the skin over her heart throb.

"I don't know what to think about."

"Take a deep breath and relax," Feruda said. "You need to stop sweating. I don't want the blade to slip."

The comment only made Dagny more nervous. "It's not something I can control. And besides, this heat doesn't help."

Feruda took the soft cloth and blotted Dagny's neck and chest. "It won't take long. I know you're frightened. Tell me about why you came here."

"To save Grete. You know that."

"What does she need to be saved from?" Feruda asked. She took the tongs and carefully removed the knives and needle from the pot.

"Visions," Dagny said.

Feruda crouched next to her, and gently covered Dagny's breast with her free hand, pulling the skin around her wound taut. "She loves you, you know."

Dagny gulped again, even though her mouth was dry. Sweat streamed down her head and into her eyes. "I know."

Dagny looked away as Feruda set the knife against her skin. "Please be careful. I'm scared..." she whispered.

"What are your favorite memories of back home?" Feruda's voice was steady and calm, and Dagny could only hope that her hand was the same.

"Playing games with the children. Reading books in the study."

Feruda sliced the skin, sending a sharp pain across Dagny's body. "Easy now. Don't move," she said.

Dagny tried her best to comply, clenching her fists and teeth, and staring straight into the fire.

"I like playing music," Feruda continued, as she cut and dug. "It fills me with joy."

Dagny wheezed. Her stomach felt slick, but she couldn't tell if it was sweat or blood. "I can't do this... Please, Feruda. Stop—"

Suddenly, the girl yelped with excitement. "Ooh, I can see something!"

Dagny dared to glance down. Feruda had the needle point pressed into a bloody gash inches away from the center of Dagny's breast, and she was pushing out something black and hard. No, not *something*... Dagny knew exactly what it was. She wanted to look back into the fire, but she couldn't take her eyes off the thing. The gross horror of it transfixed her completely.

Slowly, it emerged: a jagged, black talon. Longer than Dagny had expected it to be. Seeping out like some vile little slug. Feruda kept pushing the needle deeper into her skin, and was gripping Dagny so hard that her knuckles had turned bone white. Then, just when Dagny thought the fingernail might finally pop out, it was sucked back inside.

Dagny screamed. She shoved Feruda away and scrambled toward the door. She couldn't take this anymore.

"Come back to the fire!" Feruda shouted. "We need to try again."

Dagny shook her head, sobbing heavily, feeling as though she would vomit. "No. I can't. It's too much... Why won't it come out?"

"We have to try again," Feruda repeated.

"I can't do it," Dagny said, gingerly touching the gash on her chest. The shock and pain were unbearable. There was no way she could bring herself to sit back down.

Feruda wiped sweat from her own brow. "We have to be quick. Now that the nail knows what we're doing, it will try to work its way deeper inside."

"What?!" Dagny screamed. "Where's my sister? I need her!"

Feruda approached Dagny slowly, gently leading her back into the circle. "Stay calm. Close your eyes and don't move."

Dagny obeyed. This was the most vulnerable she'd ever felt. Half-naked and terrified; in the same plaza where Salarel had slaughtered a hundred men; sitting across from a girl she barely knew.

Dagny's head pounded, and her neck ached from stress. She was clenching her jaw so hard she thought it might break. She pictured herself back on the lagoon, watching the stars with Max. The wind blowing the sail of Rodolph's boat, funneling them across the water.

In the back of her mind, she kept waiting for Feruda to speak, readying herself for the surge of sharp pain that was about to bite her skin.

Will you travel to Vahnes with me? Max asked. *We can journey up the Morca on my father's river boat and watch musicians play the towns along the way.*

"Yes," Dagny whispered. "I'll come with you. There's just something I need to do first..."

She heard a log pop in the fireplace, and smelled the smoky ash. She heard a relaxed sigh and felt sweat drip down her nose. But then Dagny noticed something else—she no longer felt the *pain.*

She wanted to touch the wound; to press down on the mark and see if she could still feel Galwed's nail lodged inside, but she was afraid and kept her hands clinched at her side.

The air became noticeably lighter, and a hand touched her arm. "It's over now," Feruda said. "You can look again."

Dagny took a deep breath and slowly opened her eyes. If the fingernail was there, after all of this, her mind was going to break. She just knew it.

There was still a gash, and blood still pooled where Feruda had cut her, but when Dagny placed her hand over the area and pressed, she could no longer feel anything beneath the skin.

A wave of relief swept over her, and Dagny continued to pat her chest lightly, making sure the nail was really gone.

Feruda stepped back and cross her arms.

"How did that happen?" Dagny asked. "Did you see anything? Did the nail come out?"

"I tossed it in the fire."

"Are you sure?"

Feruda's mouth dropped and she burst into a nervous laugh. "Of course, I'm sure. Why are you so doubtful?"

"It's just how I was made. How did you do it?"

"Lots of focus. And besides, I am a witch."

Feruda took a piece of cloth, turned to the hearth, and soaked it in the pot of hot water.

The whole experience had left Dagny unusually cold. She sat with her back near the fire, watching Feruda. "You were so brave just now," Dagny said. "I was terrified."

"You had good reason to be. And I was only acting brave. I was quite scared, too. But it wouldn't have been good to tell you that." Feruda went to work on Dagny's thigh, slathering ointment into her wound from the chapel.

"I really appreciate what you did," Dagny said. "Actually, everything you've done... ever since we met. Thanks."

When Feruda had finished, she returned to the pot and retrieved the cloth. "I feel like we're similar in a lot of ways, and I like your sister. We make a good group." With a light touch, she gently washed the bloody marks from Dagny's breast and leg as she talked.

"But there's something you need to know now," Feruda continued. Her soft smile turning into a frown.

"What?" Dagny asked, feeling nervous once again.

"...You were missing for quite a while."

"What do you mean? For how long?"

"An entire day and night. The Cauldron opened at twilight. And Grete went down it."

24

Dagny's mouth went dry, and she gnawed at her thumb, trying to make sense of what she was hearing. "How can that be?" Could she really have been under the sea for so long?

"We searched all over for you," Feruda said. "Grete swore me to keep looking, but that wasn't a hard thing to promise. I wasn't going to stop."

"Did you search the chapel?"

"Yes. Was it you that broke the windows in there—"

"Did you find Boulder?"

Feruda's eyes narrowed. "No. We didn't. What happened to him?"

"I'm not sure," Dagny said.

"Grete *had* to go down the Cauldron, you understand. She couldn't wait any longer. Please forgive her."

Dagny swallowed hard. "Did she go alone?"

"No. Everyone else left with her," Feruda said. "I stayed behind at Barentok."

Everyone? "Even Melwes?"

Feruda nodded. "They all left."

"I have to go after them."

"I was afraid you would say that," Feruda said with a frown. "I didn't want to tell you, but felt you needed to know."

"Of course I needed to know," Dagny replied. She pulled off what was left of her dress and tossed it on the floor. "Where are the clothes?"

"Second floor," Feruda said, pointing at the stairs.

As Dagny rushed up the steps and crossed a small bedchamber to a wardrobe, she suddenly had a horrible image of Grete trying to climb out of the underground just as the Cauldron closed above her. And the twins... they were still out there, too. Dagny wondered if Galwed was planning to sink her wicked nail into Grete's heart, sending her sister to the city beneath the waves.

A messy pile of clothing spilled onto the floor as soon as Dagny opened the wardrobe. Most of the items smelled musty or ripe, but that was okay with her. She had smelled worse.

Less than a minute later, Dagny pulled a baggy brown shirt from the pile, tossed it over her head, and rolled the sleeves up to her elbows. Then she slipped on a pair of loose-fitting pants that she cinched with a broad belt.

She stepped in front of the mirror and studied herself. In an odd way, the outfit excited her. There was life in these clothes; she could smell Feruda in them. It made her feel like an adventurer and—for the first time in a long while—like her brother's sister.

Feruda stood in the kitchen, hastily shoving provisions into a sack.

"Are you coming with me?" Dagny asked.

"You really shouldn't go," the girl replied. "They've probably been down there for hours. You wouldn't even know how to find them. You should trust Grete."

"I don't have a choice. I have to go."

Feruda stopped for a moment and glanced at her. "I know."

They finished packing whatever supplies they could muster, making sure the sack wouldn't be too heavy for the journey. Dagny draped the Night Orbiter over her neck, then the two of them made their way outside and gazed across the yard.

"Is the Cauldron nearby?" Dagny asked.

"Somewhat," Feruda replied. "It's in the plaza of Sanctuary."

Dagny took a breath. "Will you go down there with me?" Before Feruda could respond, however, Dagny continued, "I don't know why I said that. I can't ask you—"

"Let me think about it, okay?"

The girls crossed the courtyard and crested the hill, onto the winding streets of Inner Jud. It could've been early morning, just before dawn, but it was hard to tell, exactly. So much had happened over the course of last night. Dagny wondered what she was about to get herself into.

In many ways, her existence had been one of desperation; failures and stumbles, chasing after an elusive *something* that could offer her life meaning in the face of so much emptiness. Even from a young age, she was acutely aware of this, gripped by a dread that such meaning might not exist. She had wrapped herself up in her brother's stories of adventure and travels across fascinating lands, convincing herself that it was the life she, too, had wanted to live. But the world was a dangerous place, and now she was marching toward a tomb and quite possibly a horrible death. Was this truly the *meaning* she had been searching for?

"What are you thinking about?" Feruda asked.

"Nothing," Dagny replied. "It's not important."

Feruda nodded slowly, considering something. "I hope I've done right by you. I hope I haven't made things worse, somehow."

"Don't say that. You've done everything right."

The street connected to a broad roadway. "We're close," Feruda said. "Straight ahead is the last gate and Sanctuary. It can be overwhelming if you've never seen it before."

"I'm sure I'd be overwhelmed if my brain ever had a chance to catch up," Dagny said. "It's like I'm in a dream, and I keep thinking I'll wake up in Rork."

"What if it was a dream?" Feruda asked. "Would it be better if this never happened? If you never came here?"

Dagny raised her shoulders. "It has happened. I've spent a lot of time wishing for certain things to be different in my life. I don't want to think like that anymore."

"Give me an example," Feruda said, glancing over at her as they walked. "What did you wish would've been different?"

"Things I couldn't control. My brother's death. Losing Grete. My mind was stuck for so long. Maybe some part of me didn't think I deserved to have my own life. I want to move past it, but—"

"You don't know how..." Feruda said.

"No, I don't. Or I didn't, anyway." Dagny gazed up and down the roadway, making sure they were still alone. "And what about you? Do you intend to stay in Jud?"

Feruda pushed her hair back. "There was a book I read a long time ago. A poetic book of *Long Water*, where the author writes about a never-ending journey across the never-ending sea, and how they passed over all of these places from the world before. It's an allegory on life. How one moment follows the next, and a purpose is discovered, not decided. So, to answer your question, I don't know what I'll do. But I'll *intend* to discover it."

The gate into the Sanctuary plaza was a giant set of dented bronze doors that towered over their heads. It was cracked open, wide enough for a cart to squeeze through.

Someone whistled from a side street nearby. Dagny turned her head and saw the burly shape of Roger Red approaching. He carried a lantern that turned his normally red face and hair into a strange burnished orange. "I come peacefully," he said with a laugh. The comment made Dagny's blood boil.

"What are you doing here?" she demanded.

"Calm down," Roger snapped. "I've had all I'm going to take from you. I understand you were upset about Pren and everything, but get over it."

Dagny stuttered, caught off guard by Roger's response and sudden change in demeanor. "Who do you think you are, talking to us like that?"

Roger dipped his head as if introducing himself for the first time. "Why I am Sieour Red, the Liege of *Fall Dagger Falls*, and a sworn Friend of Jud."

Dagny turned to Feruda. "Friend of Jud? What's that?"

"There's only a few of us, dear," Roger said. "It means you should respect me more than you do. We're tasked with a great amount of responsibility. Don't judge what has already occurred so harshly; there are patterns in the weave that you cannot comprehend."

Dagny shrugged. "Okay. What do you want, Friend of Jud? We're in a hurry."

Roger huffed, causing his breasts and belly to jiggle. "You're going down the Cauldron after them, aren't you?"

"Maybe," Dagny said.

"I was thinking about going down myself," Roger said. "But, I can't bring myself to do it, no matter how much I care for Pren's life. Maybe I am pigeon-hearted. Who knows how much time they have left, but it isn't long."

"There's enough time," Dagny said. "The Cauldron will close at twilight, during the shift. We at least have until then, right?"

"No. Not everything changes with the shift," he replied. "Some things are on their own pattern. Although the Cauldron *opened* at twilight, the Giant will make his own decision about when to close it."

"What are you saying? It could close *now*? In an hour? When?" Dagny asked.

Roger just stared at her.

"Is this true?" Dagny asked Feruda, but the girl's hesitancy in responding sent a surge of anxiety through her.

Dagny bolted away from Roger and Feruda, twisted around the bronze doors, and sprinted into the plaza.

It was a quiet place. A sprawling rectangle of pavement that gradually sloped down toward the center. She was surrounded by high walls and arched windows, reminiscent of an enormous, fortified monastery.

Sanctuary.

Dawn was almost here. The emerging sun had begun to wash out the black sky, but Dagny was still dependent on the moon and stars to see, which provided just enough illumination to define the hole in the center of the plaza. A massive, black pit that seemed to absorb what little light there was.

She slowed and approached the edge cautiously. Nothing about the pit resembled a cauldron. If anything, it reminded Dagny of those sinkholes that would sometimes appear in the land outside the city, ruining farms or anything else unlucky enough to exist where they sprang.

Peering over, Dagny saw the way down. There weren't stairs, exactly. More like a series of overlapping ledges. Places where the metal and stone had splintered out from the walls like gnarled teeth.

"Wait," Roger called from behind. He was jogging toward her with Feruda in tow. "Just wait a moment."

Dagny spun around. "I don't have a moment. You said yourself there's no knowing when it will close."

"All the more reason... to think about... what you're planning to do," Roger said, huffing for air.

"I'm surprised you even care what I do."

"I don't, truth be told," he replied. "Still, I wouldn't feel good about anyone dying in that hole."

"Melwes. Did he go down there, too?" Dagny asked, peering over the edge once again.

"The child, you mean? No. He's been waiting on the other side of the plaza. That wolf won't let me get close enough to check on him."

Although her pulse continued to race, Dagny did feel a slight wave of relief that Melwes had stayed behind. She told Feruda she'd be right back, then wandered across the plaza to look for him.

It didn't take long. The boy was asleep, curled into the side of the great wolf, cast in the soft blue glow of Mia and Fig. Eidfur raised his head and watched her approach with his dark, brooding eyes.

Dagny hesitated about waking the boy. She was going into the underground—that much was certain—and Dagny didn't want to risk Melwes deciding to join her. He needed to stay above ground, where it was safe. He'd given her so much already, and her heart swelled watching him now.

One of the spirit lights drifted toward her. She couldn't tell which one it was, but Dagny *felt* like it was Mia. She wondered how long she'd known this particular light. Had she seen it at the Lomenthal Station? Could Mia have been one of the first orbs that floated down over the balcony and led her into the ballroom? One of the lights that guided her and Tash away from the twins, and sealed Galwed in the wall?

The orb hovered in front of the Night Orbiter hanging from her neck.

"Would you come with me?" Dagny whispered as softly as possible. "Would you help to light the way?"

Melwes stirred, rolling onto his back, and Dagny held her breath. She didn't want Melwes *or* Eidfur to come. She wanted them both to stay like this, forever in her mind. So Dagny stepped back, ever so slowly, away from the boy and the wolf, and returned to the Cauldron. With Mia following close behind.

25

"How deep does it go?" Dagny asked, gazing over the edge.

Roger cleared his throat and whispered, as if fearful his voice would echo into the pit. "I've never dared to venture down, but it goes so deep that the sun's light won't reach... or so I've heard."

"People have come back, then," Dagny said.

"Some. Although once, when I was a child, an entire expedition became trapped... The Cauldron closed so quickly that no one got out. It didn't open again until years later." Roger shook his head. "Tragic."

Dagny tried to imagine what it would be like down there. Dark, dusty and stale? Would there be rats or spiders? She supposed that would depend on how tightly the place was sealed. But just because rats or bugs could find their way in and out, didn't mean people could. There would certainly be bones and rotten things; bags and clothing from the ones who went before.

And what was this place below them? What had it been *before* the stories? What was it *really*?

"Is there a warning before it closes? Something to look out for?" Dagny asked.

"Impossible to say."

Dagny stepped back and glanced at Feruda. "I don't know if I can do this."

The girl nodded. "You're afraid. It's alright."

"Yes. I am," Dagny said. She stared across the plaza to where Melwes slept.

"Is there something else?" Feruda asked. "Something about the boy?"

"I told him I wouldn't ever leave again. And I could possibly be leaving him forever. I've turned into a liar."

"What would you have done differently?"

"Not made false promises." But there was nothing she could do about it now. Dagny imagined her sister, Pren, and Marfisi lost in the darkness. She turned to Roger. "You're sure they went down? You saw them?"

"I did. I tried to speak to the lad before they went. He wouldn't even look at me."

Dagny shifted her pack from one shoulder to the other. What if Roger was lying? But Melwes and Eidfur were here. Dagny's head ached with tension.

"If you're going to do this, we should go," Feruda said, softly. "Time is moving quickly."

"I shouldn't have asked you to go down there with me."

"Stop it. I'm coming."

Dagny did not argue the point. She really did not want to do this alone.

She stepped to the edge and stared at the first stone plank jutting out from an unseen wall. Suddenly, Mia spun through the air, circled her legs, and then drifted into the Cauldron, illuminating the way down.

Roger assisted her onto that first ledge. "I'll be here. And if something happens, I'll make sure the child is taken care of. You have my word."

Dagny nodded. What good would it do to stay angry at Roger now? She said nothing else to the red-haired man, and instead focused her attention on descending the overlapping planks that vanished into the gloom beneath her. They were flat and sturdy. And each time Dagny landed on the one below, a large puff of dust enveloped her legs, thickening the air. Feruda followed behind and Mia lit the way forward, washing the underground with tones of gentle blue. It brought back memories of exploring the Under Road with Melwes. It calmed her, and when Dagny glanced back to check on Feruda, she could tell it was calming her as well.

On and on they went. Lying flat on their stomachs, scooting to the edge of one plank, twisting their legs over the side, and then dropping onto the next. One wrong step could've sent either one of them tumbling into the darkness.

Even still, going down was certain to be easier than climbing back out. Both of the girls were short, and Dagny knew that pulling themselves up and over each ledge was going to be exhausting. No wonder so many people failed to escape the Cauldron in time. Just then, as if the pit was predicting her thoughts, Dagny dropped onto a busted ribcage. She gasped and stumbled, crushing something under her boot. There were at least two skeletons here; both wearing tarnished helmets, both staring up toward the sun from empty eye sockets.

Feruda hopped down and quickly took Dagny's hand. "Don't look at that. There's nothing to be done. Just keep moving."

Three more planks and then the mist appeared. It was faint, like the early morning fog of a dewy field, and hung in the air, unwavering.

"We're at the border of the weeds now," Feruda said. "Take comfort in it. These are old worlds."

The mist seemed to amplify Mia's light, softening their stark surroundings, turning them into something almost enchanting.

They landed in dirt. Inside of an enormous chamber undefined by borders, like a field in the night. There were remnants of prior expeditions here. Fire pits and trappings; decayed bodies huddled next to each other in the darkness with hands and faces turned to brown leather.

"This must've been a staging area," Dagny said to Feruda. "A base camp for the explorers." She gazed into the blackness beyond the blue. "I'm not sure where to go. I can't even see the walls. This place *feels* huge."

"The Yalow Lizard, right?" Feruda whispered. "We need to follow its path."

Dagny took the Night Orbiter from her neck and gently pried it open, just like she had seen Maris do almost a year ago in Alex's study. Without any hesitation, Mia flew inside. Her glow brightened and countless tiny lights appeared, creating a dome of false stars that glittered and twinkled.

"A replica of the night sky," Dagny muttered. "I don't know where to start. There must be a hundred constellations here."

Feruda leaned close to the Orbiter and whispered, "The trail of the Yalow Lizard. Do you know it little light?"

Suddenly, the false stars swirled around them; some faded while others brightened even more. The dome turned abruptly, like a dial clicking into place, making Dagny queasy, and when it came to a stop, one constellation shimmered brighter than the rest.

"This is it," Feruda said. "This is the path. We follow the trail now." She pointed in the direction of the nearest star. "Thank you, little light."

Dagny started forward, then stopped. "Wait. No. We have to find Grete first." But how was she going to do that?

Feruda gestured into the darkness. "Trust that Grete had some idea of where to go. She must've known where to start at least."

Dagny drew in a deep breath, struggling to see through the mist and past the Orbiter's heaven of stars.

Feruda tugged Dagny's sleeve. "I don't want to be caught down here, either. We have to decide. We have to move. The Lizard Trail is the only thing we know about."

"Okay," Dagny said reluctantly, overwhelmed by their situation. "Go ahead, I'll follow."

"Me?" Feruda shook her head. "No. You have the Orbiter. You have to do it. That spirit light is attuned to you. It's your guide. *Trust it.*"

Dagny looked into the Orbiter and caught sight of Mia's brilliant core. *Protector of the Under Road.*

This wasn't the Under Road, though. This was something cut off from that other world. A splinter of the Great Below, perhaps, but one that was separate and dead. A silent tomb of earth and stone.

Dagny stepped toward the first star of the Lizard Trail, and as she moved, the star seemed to keep its distance, always staying just out of reach. She grasped Feruda's hand, concerned about losing the girl in the cavern. If they somehow became separated, they might never find one another again.

She became vaguely aware of passing under an enormous archway, and the floor flattening out into an even sprawl. There was no longer thick dirt under her boots, only dust.

Next, walls appeared, framing the way ahead. They were milky white and glossy, like polished marble. She saw ancient markings scrawled along the surface: strange lines and symbols in colors of faded red and apple green. She saw human-like faces, ghostly apparitions worn by time, intricately carved on those same walls. They contained various expressions of terror—an open mouth conveying a scream with hollow eyes; another with its face split by a jagged line.

Feruda squeezed her hand. "Look," she whispered. The star they were following began to dim, and another one, off to its left, began to brighten. "It's working," she said, gleefully. "We're actually on the trail."

Other passageways appeared at the edge of their light. And they passed stairs—real, man-made stairs—leading further down into the earth. They ignored them all, staying focused, continuing to follow the star path.

Dagny wondered if she should call out to Grete. What if her sister's group had mistakenly traveled down one of these other passages? What if their light had gone out, and they were blindly clawing their way through the darkness? Dagny opened her mouth, took in air, and prepared to holler when she heard a strange, alien groaning. She glanced at Feruda, who simply shook her head in confusion.

It sounded like some kind of instrument; not strings. More like reeds, if the reeds were metal and being slowly bent as the wind blew across.

Feruda pointed sharply at the star, motioning for Dagny to keep moving.

She'd been concerned about rats or spiders, but the further they walked, the more convinced she was that nothing else lived in this place. Nothing *natural* anyway. The corpses they had seen were eroded by the passing of years, not chewed up by beasts. Still, Dagny couldn't help but feel a presence. And that *groaning*... it seemed to rattle her insides: her ribs and her teeth. She could feel it in her stomach, creating the very uncomfortable sensation of having to urinate.

The tunnel brought them to another vast chamber where a great bridge passed over an abyss of seemingly impenetrable blackness. Dagny debated lighting a candle and dropping it into the chasm, then decided against it. If there *was* something that existed down here, the last thing she wanted to do was disturb it.

The star trail was leading them across the bridge, and as Dagny prepared to step onto the surface, she glanced back, hoping with all of her heart that she wasn't leaving Grete behind, trapped in some darkened passage.

"The Giant's Tongue," Feruda suddenly whispered. Dagny had become so engrossed by the groaning sound that the girl's voice startled her, causing Dagny's shoulders to jerk.

"What?" Dagny asked.

"Ancient knights wrote of crossing the Giant's Tongue. A fabled bridge under the Cauldron. This must be it."

Dagny set her foot down on the bridge. It was wide and solid, with a metallic surface that reflected the light of the Orbiter. And there was something else, too. A slight vibration that crept into Dagny's feet and shook her legs.

"I don't like this," Dagny said. "Let's cross as quick as we can." Without waiting for a reply, Dagny started off, doing her best to stay in the center of the bridge while concentrating on her footing.

She could hear Feruda behind her, shuffling along. "That groaning sound is coming from beneath us," Feruda said. "I don't think it's the bridge. It's something else."

They left the landing far behind. Dagny knew it had vanished in the dark without needing to look back. She was more concerned about what they would be approaching, and the suffocating blackness that surrounded them. But as far as they had walked, the opposite end of the bridge was still nowhere to be seen.

And that *sound*. It was intensifying; consuming her thoughts; growling louder. The bridge shook as well. The Night Orbiter trembled in her hands. The false stars wobbled and blurred.

Dagny tucked her chin down and kept marching. She was so focused on getting across that she hadn't noticed the changes in the mist until now. It had grown thicker on the bridge—no longer the dewy mist of early morning, now it was like heavy fog rolling in from the sea, blanketing ship decks and obscuring buildings. Playing tricks on her mind.

She could feel it. Soft and wet on her neck. She could taste the moisture on her tongue, along with something sweet and rotten.

Dagny stopped. Was she still in the center of the bridge? The fog swept over her ankles and she was suddenly terrified of falling off into the abyss. Feruda stepped into her just then, and Dagny stumbled, falling to her knees.

"Are you alright?" Feruda asked, grabbing Dagny's arm.

"I can't see," Dagny huffed. "Can you see *anything?*"

"We're in a swirl," Feruda replied. "I've never seen it so thick before. It's not the weeds, though. This is something different."

"Like what?"

"I don't know. There are other things that breathe in the Deep."

"What's that mean? What's happening?" Dagny's teeth rattled from the shuddering bridge.

"We need to go," Feruda said. While her words were urgent, her voice was calm. "Stand up, carefully."

Dagny obeyed, struggling with her movements. The bridge felt like it could shake her off at any moment. When she finally made it back to her feet, Dagny hunched forward and studied the area ahead. There was something there. Something in the mist. Black forms, like shadows, on the other side of the opaque gray.

"What... is that?" Dagny whispered, squinting hard. "Feruda?" Dagny turned around to face the girl, but Feruda was frozen in place; her typically relaxed expression morphed into one of sheer terror.

Dagny grabbed Feruda's head with both hands. "What is it?!" she screamed over the groaning. "Feruda, look at me!" The girl tried to speak then, but the only sound to escape her quivering jaw was a soft whimper.

There was a clunk on the bridge behind them. Something had stepped—or fallen—onto it. For once, Dagny appreciated her ignorance. If she had any clue what was terrifying Feruda so badly, she might have leapt off into the darkness herself. Dagny grabbed Feruda's wrist and pulled her forward, staring straight at the bright star emblazoned on the mist wall. She could only hope that Mia's path would keep her on the bridge and out of the abyss.

More forms appeared at the edge of her vision. They were vaguely human, but with lanky arms that hung unnaturally long. Dagny quickened her pace. Feruda was dragging; slowing her down. *Come on*, Dagny told herself. *Move. Faster.*

One of those lanky arms stretched out of the mist, reaching toward her face. Dagny ducked away, and it seized her pack instead.

Her hand slipped from Feruda's. Dagny turned around, ready to grab it once again, when she saw the shape on the bridge. It moved in a jerky and shambling motion. Its form crooked and bent.

Feruda screamed. "*No! No! Pleeease!*" The girl fell to the ground and covered her head; her wild hair splayed across her body and the bridge like a net.

The shape stepped closer. "Did you think you'd get away from me?" it croaked.

"Please!" Feruda cried. "Let me go!"

Dagny suddenly realized this shape must be the same creature who had haunted Feruda's dreams. The Gaunt Lady. Shade of the Black Sun. The Lady was almost triple the height of the two girls, and flicked its tongue like a serpent. Feruda was shaking, clawing at her head, screaming into the floor.

"Stop," Dagny called out. Her voice was only a shallow gasp, drowned out by the surrounding screams and the groaning.

The Gaunt Lady moved next to the trembling mound of hair and leaned awkwardly over Feruda.

Dagny tried to step forward, but fear had rooted her legs in place. "*Stop!*" she yelled, louder this time. "Leave her alone."

The Gaunt Lady's eyes remained fixated on Feruda, and the way she smiled now was one of the most horrible things Dagny had ever seen. A cruel, gaping smile exposed a mouth of pinkish gray with teeth that became longer and longer as the Lady's mouth grew wider and wider. Then Dagny realized she wasn't actually *smiling* at all.

The mouth elongated, and the jaw dislodged, similar to what Dagny imagined a giant snake might do before consuming its prey.

Feruda had stopped screaming. Instead, she was sucking down huge gasps of air while her body convulsed.

In a single, sweeping motion, the Lady swooped Feruda with her giant spoon of a hand, and funneled the girl into her mouth. Dagny watched, horrified, as the Lady's throat and stomach expanded, and the muscles in her neck strained to gobble down the body.

It wasn't until Feruda fell into the Lady's gut that Dagny screamed.

Dagny was running now. Barreling toward the Lady, hands stretched wide, intent on ripping her open.

But the Lady was fast and strong. In an instant, she swatted Dagny to the ground, sending her skidding across the bridge. Dagny tried to dig her fingers into metal, screeching to a stop mere inches from the edge. Only then did she appreciate how bright it had become.

There were no more shadows. The surrounding fog sizzled, evaporating like steam in the sun, and the surface of the bridge blazed so brilliantly that Dagny had to cover her eyes.

Mia.

The orb had come loose from the Orbiter and pulsated overhead, sending ripples of light across the Tongue and into the abyss.

Dagny scurried to her feet, desperate to reach Feruda.

The Lady was no longer smiling, but that's not what caught her eye. It was the bloated belly—a murky pouch that sagged over the Lady's groin—and inside, Dagny could see a swirling storm of dark hair.

Dagny clenched her jaw and rushed forward once again.

The Gaunt Lady stretched her lanky arm, reaching for Dagny's head in an effort to twist it off, but that didn't frighten her. If anything, Dagny was surprised by how *slowly* the Lady was moving. Actually, how slowly *everything* was moving. She saw the other phantom shades melt in the light. She saw Mia—the size of a small sun, blazing with fire—grow brighter and brighter and brighter...

And she saw the Gaunt Lady's mouth turn to a gasp, as Mia's flame washed her dark body pale. Then, like an early morning shadow caught by the day, the shade stretched apart and vanished in the light, dropping Feruda onto the bridge.

Dagny fell to her knees and embraced the girl. Feruda's eyes were glazed, and she was struggling to breathe, but she was alive.

"Are you okay?" Dagny screamed. "Can you hear me?"

Feruda nodded. "*The Lady*..."

"She's gone. Mia destroyed her. She can't hurt you anymore."

"Mia?"

The orb zipped over and spun rapidly around Feruda's head. The light had dimmed and shrunk back to its normal size, but continued to pulsate, like a heartbeat.

"How?" Feruda muttered.

"I don't know." Dagny glanced over the edge into the abyss, making sure there were no more shades hiding in the darkness, then pushed herself up.

As difficult as this had been, they needed to keep moving. They *had* to. The Cauldron would still be closing. Time was still running against them.

26

Mia twinkled, then drifted over. Dagny opened the latch of the Night Orbiter, and once again, the false stars appeared, guiding the pair across the bridge.

Dagny supported Feruda as they walked, and it wasn't long before the opposite side came into view. The starlight illuminated the craggy surface of the cavern wall, and the end of the bridge—the Tongue—disappeared into an oblong tunnel. *You must be the mouth*, Dagny thought. *And the mind then... must be up there.* She tilted her head back and gazed over the surface—the Giant's face, perhaps, although she couldn't make out any features. It seemed to stretch on forever.

A dozen steps later, they were inside the cave.

Huge, thorned spikes extended from floor to ceiling. They looked man-made, not the stalagmites of somewhere natural. These were barbed cones of iron, planted in defined rows. Horrible teeth eager to maim and devour.

Maybe it was her imagination, but the floor seemed soft, almost squishy. It narrowed into a tunnel ahead and dipped down into blackness. Into the throat.

Dagny studied the area before moving across. This whole place felt wrong. She looked closer at the floor, scanning it for bones or other trappings, any sign that someone had tried to cross through *unsuccessfully*.

The brightest star of the Lizard Trail glittered against the blackness of the tunnel, beckoning her onward. Despite the frightening nature of the cave, Dagny started to relax. The chamber was certainly ominous, but it seemed to be intentionally made that way. As if someone had *designed* it to scare off intruders.

But why? Why would people go through so much effort to build this place just to seal it off from the world, carefully placing elaborate warnings throughout? So no one would search for a fabled queen? Dagny shook her head. It didn't make sense to her. Whatever the Cauldron's original purpose had been, so much time must've passed that any memory of *why* had likely washed away from the consciousness of humankind ages ago.

"What do you think?" Dagny asked.

"Don't stop now," Feruda replied. "If Mia wants us to go this way, then we should follow."

They were deep inside the cavern when the floor buckled. Dagny gripped the Orbiter as tight as she could, terrified of dropping the object here, and at the same time, desperately tried to steady her footing. But she stumbled as the ground spasmed, then lurched forward and collapsed onto her stomach.

The cave was trying to consume them. The thorned spikes no longer looked like a warning but a very real threat. Dagny reached for one, intent on climbing out of this place as quickly as she could, when suddenly the floor dropped out. Feruda slid past her, grasping at air, and a moment later, Dagny was tumbling down as well, into the darkness.

It wasn't a straight drop, but it was close. Dagny tried to steady her body, scraping her hands and arms as she fell. It took everything she had not to topple end over end. One wrong twist and her neck could snap.

The tunnel spit her onto something hard and rough. Surprisingly, the Night Orbiter was still intact, lying close by, and Mia's glow illuminated the scene in front of her. There were bones here. Hundreds of them; brittle and stone gray. Her right hand rested near a broken skull, and Dagny began to push herself up as Feruda came over to help. Although Dagny's heart raced from the fall, she was otherwise stunned by how calm she felt. Despite the bones, there was no stink of death in the air, only the scent of dust and time.

Carefully, they stepped over the skeletal remains, making their way to a flattened part of the chamber. Mia hovered nearby, but when Dagny opened the Night Orbiter to usher the orb inside, Mia drifted off and sparkled brightly.

"What are you doing?" Dagny said. "We need to get out of here." She reached for the spirit light, which only caused it to float further away. "Stop," Dagny said. "I need your help." But just then, Mia darted forward, out of sight, leaving the girls alone in the darkness.

There was no stopping the panic this time. It didn't slowly build; it erupted like the sea in a storm.

In the black chamber, Dagny's mind went back to the bones. Why were there so many here? Would so many people have fallen down the tunnel and perished? Or had something brought them to this place? An awful hoarding of death?

She readied herself to scream after Mia, but in that moment when her breath peaked, catching on her vocal cords, she heard a muttering from somewhere nearby. Feruda heard it too, suddenly slapping a hand over Dagny's mouth.

There was a muted grumbling; the pattering of feet. Something shuffled. Then, what sounded like muffled speech.

Dagny leaned forward, struggling to make out words. Were those human voices? She had an image of ghost princesses; raspy voices from the Sillweed.

She caught a word: *Careful.*

They were closer now. In the same chamber as her. "We don't know what came down," a voice whispered.

Another replied, "It's her. I know it is." A rush of excitement washed over Dagny as she recognized the voice this time. Grete.

Dagny stood and called out for her sister. The pattering of feet turned into a run. A split second later, lantern light swept into the room. She caught sight of Pren and Marfisi, each of them holding lamps, and behind them strode Gretchen. Mia came blazing overhead and darted to Dagny, drenching her in blue light.

Dagny's heart leapt. She was lost in a sea of bones, but the long dead seemed so serene and peaceful now. And there was Grete; her beautiful sister grinning wide. The horror of only moments before, transformed so quickly into hope and joy, deep in the bowels of the Giant.

Pren was the first one to reach her. A moment later, Grete was at her side, touching her face. "Dag... I don't believe it. You're here. We looked for you. We searched every inch of that stronghold, but you were gone."

Grete kissed Dagny on the head and pulled Feruda into a tight embrace.

"I'm so glad they didn't get you," Dagny said.

"Who?" Grete asked.

"The twins—"

A frightened expression overtook her sister. "You saw them?"

"Hey, you're bleeding," Pren said, pointing at Dagny's chest and the circular blot of red seeping through her shirt.

She glanced down and patted the wound. "I'm okay, though. Just needs time to heal."

"It kind of smells," Marfisi said, leaning into her wound and sniffing deeply. "Strange... it smells like the sea. In a bad way. I think it's infected."

"One thing at a time," Dagny replied. She could tell Feruda was watching her but avoided the girl's stare. "There's nothing I can do about it now, anyway." She smiled, trying to reassure the group that she was fine.

Grete wasn't convinced. She reached out, grabbing both of Dagny's shoulders. "What happened to you? What about the twins? How do you know—"

"They found me, but like I said, I'm okay."

Grete was squeezing her. "What *happened?*"

"It's hard to describe. It's not pleasant," Dagny said.

Pren gave a hard cough. "Can we talk about this on the outside?"

"Yes. Pren's right," Marfisi said, stepping closer. "Time is against us."

Grete ignored them and pressed the question. "Tell me."

"They caught me in the chapel. Galwed and that brother of hers. She sunk her fingernail into my skin, breaking it off," Dagny said, pointing at her breast. "And then I was lost in a sort of dream. The floor fell away, and I was surrounded by water, plummeting deep into a dark ocean. I didn't stop until I came to rest in a drowned city on the seafloor."

Grete was staring at her intensely, then whispered one word. "Gort."

Marfisi nodded in agreement. "They were collecting you. Or trying to, anyway."

"You know about them?" Dagny asked.

"A little," Marfisi replied. "I know you're incredibly fortunate to get away. I doubt anyone else has. Ever."

"How did you do it?" Grete asked. "How *did* you get away?"

"I-I'm not sure. I saw Morgan. He appeared to me like a vision. And then there was this star... a sun. It melted everything away, and I woke back up in the chapel and everyone was gone."

"Boulder... my brother," Pren said. Although he was trying to hide it, there was a look of worry in his eyes. "Did you see him?"

Dagny wondered what to tell him, and in that brief moment of hesitation, Pren nodded and looked away.

Marfisi leaned close to her chest again. "What about the fingernail? Is it still in there?"

"No. We got it out. Well, Feruda did." Dagny wanted to change the subject. She was still in shock over what had happened in the chapel, and all this chatting about Galwed's nail wasn't helping things. "How did you cross the Tongue? Did you see the shades?"

Pren replied loudly, "Grete spoke to them—"

"You what?" Dagny asked. "How did you know what to say?"

"The words.... came to me. I can't explain it."

Marfisi was studying Feruda now. "Something's wrong... What is it?"

"The Lady..." Feruda whispered. Her voice sounded scratchy and hoarse, then she bent over and grabbed her knees.

Dagny leaned down and embraced her.

"I'll be alright," Feruda said. "I'm just overwhelmed."

There was a murmur from Pren. Someone put their hand on Dagny's back.

A moment later, Feruda inhaled deeply, as if nothing had happened, and stood tall. "What's going on now? Did you find a way through?"

"Not really," Pren mumbled. "This way..."

The girls followed him across the chamber of bones. "We've hit a wall of sorts," he said. "I'm glad you brought that Orbiter."

"How long have you been stuck here?" Dagny asked. Mia continued to circle through the air, illuminating the group and path ahead.

"I don't know," Pren replied. "Hours?"

"Roger Red seemed to think that the Cauldron could close at any moment," Dagny said.

"You saw him, too, huh?" Pren asked.

"Yeah. He was pretty distraught."

Pren smirked. "Glad to hear it. He should be. Hey, about earlier... at Barentok. I shouldn't have been so harsh to you."

"I understand," Dagny said. "You've been through a lot, too. Everyone has. Let's all agree that everyone is forgiven for whatever came before."

"Agreed," Pren said with a smile.

"And thanks for coming."

Pren sighed. "I always knew I would make the journey. My father's down here, somewhere. It felt like my destiny to join him."

Grete shook her head and handed Dagny a canteen. "Don't say it like that. I plan on getting out... and don't listen to anything Roger Red says about when the Cauldron is supposed to close."

"I didn't mean I plan on dying," Pren replied. "But if we want to avoid such things, we need to figure out this room..."

As he led them into the next chamber, the ceiling disappeared, replaced by a gaping chimney-like hole—a massive, distorted cavity.

"There's probably thirty or so passages here," Pren said, gesturing across the space. "We've explored four of them."

Grete pulled out a piece of chalk and scratched a line onto the floor. "I didn't have time to mark this off when your spirit guide found us."

"Lucky for you," Pren said, then pointed at a dark staircase. "We were about to take this passage when the light came darting over. We need to go up. Into the Giant's head. Think your *friend* can help us? Does it have a name?"

"Mia." Dagny looked over the area and the group. Each of them watched her with hopeful eyes.

"I saw the path to the Giant clearly in my mind," Grete said. "Only now... I've lost it."

Dagny tried to rub the stress from her neck. "Mia, can you guide us once again, please? Help us find the Yalow Lizard Trail." The orb drifted over to her hand and twinkled.

"...That's incredible," Pren whispered.

Yes. It is incredible, Dagny thought. Even amongst so much gloom and death, the beauty of the spirit light... of her sister... of so much hope and courage... none of it was lost on her. Dagny smiled, pried open the Orbiter, and gazed upon the stars.

27

"Any idea what's at the bottom?" Dagny asked, as they wandered along the secret passage, leaving the main chamber behind.

They hadn't seen the entrance until one of the Orbiter's stars flashed over it: a small rectangular hole, about halfway up the wall. The oddness of the hidden opening reminded Dagny of the first door into Jud. The one she had taken with Melwes on their way to the castle.

"The bottom of the Giant?" Pren replied. He walked behind Dagny and kept his own lantern lit.

"Yeah."

"No," Pren said. "No one knows."

"Some people believe the abyss underneath us is endless," Feruda said. "I heard a Weaver say that once."

"Well, it's gotta end somewhere, don't it? Just because no one's been down there, doesn't make it endless," he said. "Those Weavers don't know as much as everyone thinks they do."

"They know enough to be dangerous," Marfisi said. She seemed happy to contribute to the discussion. "If you believe what they claim to know about the Giant, you'd perish like so many others. Take this passage, for instance. There's no way we would've found it without Mia and the Orbiter."

"Trust the witches," Pren said. "That's what I've always believed. You can ask anyone that knows me."

Feruda laughed. "Easy. You don't need to stretch the truth so much. You're already in our good graces."

It was nice to hear her laugh again. Dagny hoped the recent trauma on the bridge hadn't ingrained itself too deeply in her friend.

"My father predicted the route to Odestinas would be hidden and winding," Pren said, "not the straight, obvious passage. And as the *true* roads of Jud are twisted... I'd say we found it."

This tunnel certainly fit those characteristics. It felt more natural, like water had slowly eroded it over the course of millennia. It rose and dipped, and weaved itself through the Giant, generally keeping an upward slope, snaking to the right like a spiraling ramp.

Dagny glanced over, catching Pren's eye. "I'm sorry about your brothers. I want you to know that. I truly am."

"It's a strange thing," he replied. "I never liked them. Still... it's a strange thing."

"Yeah."

"Do you think Boulder is trapped in that sunken city like you were?"

Dagny shook her head. "I don't know what happened."

"Does it really exist?" he asked. "Or is it something else? Like a dream?"

Dagny shrugged.

Pren replied with a smile and said, "I know you don't have an answer, I'm only asking. I'm glad you escaped."

"That's yet to be determined," Marfisi said from behind. "Who knows if any of us will escape?"

"I meant from the twins. From the sunken city," Pren said. "Not from the Cauldron."

"I know," Marfisi answered. "So did I."

"What's that mean?" Pren asked.

Marfisi raised an eyebrow. "You think they just came here for your *brother*?"

The passage ended abruptly, and they had to climb up the rugged knots of the cave wall, then squeeze through a narrow hole in the ceiling. When they emerged, they stood inside an enormous grotto where stalactites dripped out of the darkness above and crystalized fields of quartz reflected their light in dazzling displays of azure blue. The space was so large that Dagny could easily imagine it housing giants themselves, instead of being housed inside of one.

"Can you steady the Orbiter?" Pren asked. "The stars keep bouncing around these damned crystals."

Dagny grasped it with both hands and tried to comply, but it was useless. She sighed with frustration, saying, "It's got nothing to do with the Orbiter itself. The light keeps reflecting."

"Well, we know the general direction," Pren said, putting his head down and trudging forward. "Don't get charmed by this place. It's probably meant to mesmerize you."

Dagny's mind drifted as they walked across the crystal field. Everything up to this point had been a blur. Her time in Jud; the emotions she'd felt over the course of the last few weeks. It seemed as though she'd spent an entire lifetime here, while another part of her felt like she'd only just arrived. It was hard to unravel her feelings, but what Dagny *did* know; what she *felt* whole-heartedly was that Grete was important to her, and if there was any way to save her, she was determined to find it.

Pren opened his own lamp now, and raised it high, staring in awe at a high archway and columns etched with ancient inscriptions. A set of stairs climbed into the blackness.

"This has to be the way," he said. "I bet the tomb is just beyond. I bet this path leads straight into the Giant's mind."

Pren's excitement was met with silence. Marfisi scratched her chin and examined the columns, while Grete only glared at the staircase.

"What are you thinking?" Dagny whispered to her sister.

"I don't know... I don't recognize this."

Pren stepped inside the archway. "What's everyone waiting for? This is it."

"It looks a bit *straight and obvious*, doesn't it?" Dagny said.

"Huh?" Pren spun around to face her. "I suppose... but... what else would it be?"

"Maybe we should keep looking," Feruda said. "It's impossible to know for sure without the Orbiter working here."

Pren huffed in frustration. "And how long do you want to do that for? How long until the Cauldron closes, you think? We still have to get back, remember? And climbing out of the Giant's mouth won't be easy."

Dagny turned to Marfisi. "What do you think? Any idea what those inscriptions say?"

"No. I don't even recognize the language," she said.

"Alright, hear me out," Pren began. "You stay here and I'll look ahead. I won't go far."

"And what if it's a trap?" Dagny asked. "We might not be able to get you out."

"*None* of us will be able to get out if we wait any longer," he stressed. "I'm going. In the meantime, go explore the cave if you want and see if there are any other paths." With that, Pren charged forward and bounded up the stairs.

The others began to gaze over the crystal grotto and wander off, intent on searching for other passages. Dagny remained at the archway, focused on the staircase. The *last* thing she thought they should do was split up. But what could she do? Pren had reacted so swiftly, and Dagny's head was still in a fog. All of her actions seemed to be happening in slow motion.

"Dag," Grete called out. "Bring that Orbiter over here and help us look."

Instead, Dagny shot her a quick glance and raised a finger, signaling to Grete to hold still. She stepped under the archway, away from the crystals, and held the Orbiter high. Once again, its light held steady and the false stars spread across the walls and ceiling. It took her a moment, but once Dagny found the Lizard Trail, her heart sank into her gut. The Trail led back into the crystal chamber. This staircase was most certainly *not* the way forward.

She leapt up several steps and shouted, "Pren! Pren, come back!"

Nothing.

Grete was at the archway before Dagny could turn around. "What is it?" she asked.

"This is wrong," Dagny said. "I have to get him."

Dagny didn't allow her sister an opportunity to reply. She sprinted up the staircase, leaping over steps two at a time. The Orbiter swung wildly at her side, casting dizzying streaks of light over the blackness. Dagny tried to listen for sounds as she went but could hear nothing over her own heavy panting.

She reached the top of the stairs and stumbled into a long hallway with a smooth, black floor. Pren stood in the distance with his back to her and his head down. He held something in his hand and was surrounded by what appeared to be glistening, white mounds that boiled up from the ground.

"*Pren*," Dagny hissed. "This isn't the way. Get over here." But the boy refused to move or face her.

Cautiously, Dagny stepped forward. The flooring was so polished that she thought it might be wet. Or sticky. Similar to the amber room she'd crossed with Pren after fleeing the Moon Needle. After *he* had come to rescue *her*.

Something slimy dripped from the ceiling above and landed on Dagny's neck. She quickly swatted it to the floor and shrieked, jumping further into the hall while flailing in a frantic attempt to shake loose anything else that may have attached itself to her.

That seemed to break whatever spell had overcome Pren. He came running over and slapped his free hand over her shoulders and back. "Hold still for a second," he said in vain. "Let me see."

"We need to get out of here, Pren!" Dagny screamed at him, continuing to flail. "What are you *doing*?!"

The boy glanced down and held up the object in his hand. It looked to be a large bowl with a spike on the end.

"This was my father's," he said. Turning the bowl over, Dagny recognized it as an old-fashioned helmet. He pointed to the bulbous, white mounds down the hall.

Dagny strained her eyes. It was impossible to make out any details from here. "What are they?"

"Bones... and armor. Leftovers from the Knights... my father's party, I'm sure of it. They're all melted together. A heap of corpse metal."

Dagny smacked Pren across the chest. "Get out! Now!" Then she ran. *Something* had done that. Something had morphed the bodies together in those awful mounds. Probably the same thing that had dripped ooze onto her back. This hall was looking to devour anyone who entered.

The black floor shimmered in a rainbow hue, like oil on water. Dagny sprinted across—there was no other option—and she braced herself for the inevitable slide, but the ground was just as dry as it had been when she entered. Then she realized: the floor was a reflection; whatever was causing those colors to shimmer across its surface was coming from *above*.

She didn't want to look. She *had* to look. The ceiling was one boundless, monstrous face... or faces... sprawling into infinity. It was as if she was gazing at the heavens. It seemed cosmic. Limitless. And all the while, the face shifted and morphed from one unexplainable monstrosity into the next. Dagny didn't know if she was running or standing still. But she couldn't take her eyes off the thing. When the faces gaped open, clear ooze dripped down in long strands onto the ground, and then were sucked back into the ceiling.

Pren caught her arm, yanked her forward, and leapt out of the hall onto the staircase. They tried to catch the first step, missed and tumbled down until finally skidding to a stop.

Pren grunted. "Don't look back," he muttered through gritted teeth. Dagny obeyed. If she was hurt, she didn't feel it. So much adrenaline was pumping through her body, she could've shattered her kneecaps and still would've been charging down the stairs.

Grete met them halfway. She was about to say something, but seeing the panic on their faces, decided against it and raced back into the grotto with them.

"This way!" Grete shouted, pointing to Feruda and Marfisi, who stood near a wall of crystals.

"Another passage?" Dagny asked as they ran.

"Another hole. But there's something beyond."

Dagny glanced at Pren. "Did you see those faces? What the—"

"No. I didn't dare look up. You froze as soon as you did."

She couldn't get the image out of her head, or the sense of dread that had tickled her spine.

They reached the other girls. Feruda was kneeling down, staring through a hole in the wall. "This has got to be it, right?" she asked.

Dagny pushed her way past and held the Orbiter into the hole. She didn't want to spend any more time in the grotto. Who knew if that *face* was sending its oozing tentacles toward the group, aching to pluck them back into the hall and morph them into their own single heap of flesh and bone?

There was a short passage beyond, and as Mia triggered her light, Dagny saw it. A single star twinkling in the center of the tunnel.

"Yep. This is the way," Dagny said without looking back, then plunged into the hole and skittered across the ground. "Hurry."

When she emerged, she was standing in a massive chamber with a giant black dome rising up from the center. There appeared to be etchings carved into its surface, but the room was too dark, and the dome too black to make them out clearly. Dagny heard the others crawling through the passage behind her, and when Grete emerged, she gasped.

Dagny knew what that gasp meant. This was the place. The chamber her sister had seen in those dreams of hers. The hidden crypt that so many had quested after for so long. The dome must be the tomb, and beyond, the Queen.

Sepulcha Hungus. That's what Lieta had called it. An impenetrable slab of dark iron, where the Imposter had buried Odestinas and her animal companions.

Impenetrable.

For a moment, no one dared to speak. Pren stepped next to Dagny, still carrying his father's helmet, and nodded slowly; an indication that he knew exactly what she was thinking. Grete gently took the Orbiter from Dagny's hand and walked toward the dome, casting light over its shell.

The Trail of the Yalow Lizard had faded and merged with the other false stars. Up until now, Dagny hadn't been fully convinced that the Lizard Trail would lead them here, but Lieta had been right about that, too. Dagny wondered if this must be the Giant's head. Or a part of it, anyway. And perhaps what she'd witnessed in the hall above, with the corpse heaps, was some aspect of the Giant's mind, gone insane like Yunis in her castle.

Marfisi whispered in Feruda's ear and pointed at the ceiling. Even in the faint light, Dagny could tell that it was the darkest thing in here. Blacker than ink, it made the dome appear almost gray. Marfisi gestured at the crease where the ceiling met the wall. It all appeared to be one and the same, like the chamber had been hollowed out from a single piece of stone. Or a slab of iron.

The light of the Orbiter faded, and Dagny jerked her head around to see Grete walking further along the edge of the dome. Pren quickly brightened his lamp and asked if they should follow her.

"I'll do it," Dagny said. "Just wait here for now. Give her some space to think."

The floor sloped down to the dome wall, and as Dagny closed the distance, the details on the etchings began to sharpen. There was something familiar about them, but Dagny couldn't quite comprehend what, until she reached her sister.

"The Sixth Satyr," Grete said, staring intensely at a block of wall. The carvings here resembled exactly that: a pictogram of a half-man with curved horns and hoofed feet. "The doomed Satyr who tried to cross the eternal plains and fell from the edge of the world."

"Star lines," Dagny muttered. She looked back at Pren and the girls. The amber light from his lamp illuminated not only their bodies, but other etchings on the wall behind. The entire chamber was covered in detailed carvings of various astral creatures.

"What's this mean?" Dagny asked.

"I don't know." Grete moved away from the Satyr, slowly tracing the edge of the dome and mumbling under her breath.

Dagny followed behind in silence, watching as Mia's light washed over the outlines, pulling them from the darkness. Some she recognized, while others were completely foreign to her. There was the Errant Miner, and the Chime Maidens, who signaled the passing of each year; Ory the Shepard, symbolized here as a boy and his dog. Some of the pictograms were enormous, stretching out high above and disappearing with the curvature of the dome, while others were no larger than Dagny herself;

some even smaller still. She had no idea what they should be looking for but hoped something might trigger Grete.

On and on they walked... Grete stopped periodically, placed her hand on the wall and ran her fingers along the etched lines. Dagny tried not to think about how much time they were spending here—she didn't want to rush her sister, but in their silent plodding, she couldn't help but imagine the Cauldron closing above them, shutting out the sunlight for another decade.

Finally, when they had circled the entire dome, Grete leaned against the wall without saying a word, slid to the floor, and placed her head in her hands.

"What is it?" Dagny asked, kneeling down. Although she already knew. Grete had hit a wall of her own.

Impenetrable. The word echoed again in Dagny's mind.

"I'm sorry..." Grete whispered. "I-I thought I could solve it... if I could just get here."

Solve it? Dagny placed her hand on Grete's shoulder. She could feel the tension within her sister. "Just take some time. It's okay."

"It's not okay." Grete gulped hard and slapped her chest. "I need to get it out. It's... too much."

The light from Pren's lamp swept over them as the others made their way down, and a moment later, Feruda and Marfisi knelt next to Grete, joining her on the floor.

"Close your eyes," Marfisi said to Grete. "Breathe. Recall your visions. This is the black place... When you're ready, tell us what you see."

Dagny watched as Grete obeyed and tried to steady her breathing. From the corner of her eye, she noticed Pren studying the etchings closely.

"I can't," Grete said. "I'm shut out."

Marfisi's voice was a whisper, melodic and gentle. "You can. Easy now. Find the rhythm. Find the place where you fit."

Pren walked out of sight, while Marfisi continued to guide Grete. The singer seemed serene and in control, radiating a calmness that made Dagny relax as well. But when Dagny looked at Feruda, the girl's face was tense and anxious. Feruda was all too familiar with Marfisi's skills, and the horror of their situation could not be so easily dismissed by her.

Dagny quickly looked away and concentrated on Marfisi's voice, focusing once again on the singer's words. The last thing Dagny wanted was to spiral into a state of dread. In a place like this, once that took hold, it might be impossible to break free.

She steadied her own breathing, like Marfisi had instructed Grete, and allowed her mind to drift aimlessly away. And before she knew it, Dagny was lying down, staring at the dome like it was the night sky itself. Suddenly, she was back on the lagoon, resting on Rodolph's river boat, watching the night clouds shift away to reveal a thousand shards of twinkling glass.

Max was lying next to her, pointing out lines in the sky. *Do you know the Endahl?* he asked. *What about Gylathrik? See that star next to his belt? That's the Black Star, Gylathrik's eye, after it was torn out. It's supposed to bring good luck.*

You're a lucky one, Rodolph said. *I don't know anyone who could've made it outta Limer's Town or escaped the Oracle Tower like you did.*

Max leaned close and whispered, *I love you. I think I'll love you forever.*

"Hey, is anyone curious why there are all these carvings here?" Pren asked. "This chamber is about as secret as you can get, but someone took all the time to place elaborate tracings of star figures? Where no one was ever going to find them?"

Marfisi glared at the boy, furious at his interruption.

"The Imposter did it, right?" Pren continued. "But if he was looking to seal the Queen away forever, why add all of this?"

"What's it matter?" Feruda asked.

"It tells a story, you realize," Pren said, gesturing at the dome. "We're at the end of it here, but if you walk further along, you'll come to the beginning. It's a chronicle of the last age. Isn't that strange?"

"The Satyr?" Dagny asked, looking at the wall. "This is the end?"

Pren nodded. "The goat-boy was trying to escape the ending of the world. The story doesn't say if he was successful or not."

"Can you continue this discussion somewhere else?" Marfisi asked. Grete continued to keep her eyes closed tight, while drawing in deep breaths of air.

"Where?" Pren asked.

"*Anywhere.*" Marfisi flung her arm wide. "*Just go.*"

They were about to walk off when Grete spoke. "The Imposter. He would come here. This puzzle was for him. He continued to visit *her* for years. To ask questions; to watch her suffer in loneliness..." Suddenly, Grete opened her eyes wide. "I almost had it. I could almost *see.*"

Marfisi patted her back. "It's alright. We'll try again. Take your time. Relax."

Dagny wanted to give her sister space, so she pulled Feruda away, and they followed Pren along the dome. "Why would the Imposter place a story chronicling another age?" Dagny asked. "Unless he was *purposely* leaving clues for someone else to come along later and find the Queen."

"You know, that's quite possible," Pren said. "The sense you get from the Imposter stories is of a figure that is timeless. A being who has come before and will come again. Maybe he wanted to make sure he could figure out the puzzle and entrance, if he were to come here—"

"In another form?" Dagny asked.

"Right."

Dagny was studying the etchings hard now, no longer just glancing as they walked past. She recognized the Great Bull this time around, although it had four horns instead of three. It was the Endahl *before* it was corrupted, and she found the Twin Firewalkers. The image made her shiver as she recalled another set of twins: Tewdred's milky face; Galwed collecting souls with her long fingernail.

The ones Dagny didn't recognize, she asked Pren about. There was the witch-born Anagala, first of the black, who spread the flame and firestorm; and a mute orphan named Roos, searching for a voice to warn the world of the coming doom.

They paused at a giant-sized man wearing a cloak, and though he was hooded, Dagny could see his face. Even in the darkness and framed by simple lines, the man looked dignified and regal.

"Who's this?" Dagny asked, not wanting to miss a single clue.

"That's Gylathrik," Pren replied. "Steward of Dusk. He led the meek into the sky."

Dagny stared at the figure's face again. "Gylathrik? No. That can't be right. This one is different."

Pren shrugged. "That's him, I'm telling you. I know it, sure as I know myself."

Feruda stepped close to her. "What's it mean, Dagny? What are you thinking?"

"I'm thinking... *this* one has both of his eyes."

28

The eyes looked large, even from here on the ground. Dagny examined the etching closely, observing deep grooves framing the boot and actual ridges along the belt. The design of the cloak was a criss-crossing diamond pattern that could be scaled like a ladder, and although the mouth was partially warped by the curve of the dome, she could make out what appeared to be a ledge. This figure was made to be climbed.

She tried to picture the Gylathrik constellation, thinking hard about *which* of the Night Prince's eyes had been torn out.

"The stars change, you realize," Pren said. "It takes a long time, but they change. Do you think this is what Gylathrik looked like when the Imposter built the dome? And that he knew what it would look like in the future?"

"That would have to be a long time indeed," Dagny answered.

"I'm sure," Pren said, then nudged her. "Step away. I'll climb it."

Dagny shrugged him off, dug her fingers into the groove of the boot and took a breath. "If there's an entrance up there, I'm going inside. If that happens, go get Grete, okay?"

"Be careful," he said.

"It's too late for that."

Feruda craned her neck, staring up at the dome. "It's a long way to fall."

"Don't worry about me. I can get up there."

Pren assisted Dagny with the first step. After that, she shimmied her way forward, reaching and groping the narrow cuts in the wall, hoisting herself onto the belt, giving a terrific wrench when she found the cloak, and finally heaving her body onto Gylathrik's bottom lip. From the mouth's ledge, there was an actual ladder hidden along the bridge of the nose and a walkway between the eyes.

Dagny crawled over to the left one. She'd been envisioning the constellation in her mind during the climb. The *left* eye. That had to be it. The Black Star.

The eye had seemed to sparkle from the ground, and now Dagny knew why. A plate of hardened stone, polished like silver, made up the etching's pupil. Dagny placed her hands on the surface, then shouted, "This is the way! I'm almost certain!"

"Almost?" Pren shouted back.

"Just go get Grete!"

Dagny's heart was pounding in her throat. Her hands trembled on the plate. This *had* to be the way inside. For Grete's sake. For all of theirs. Dagny muttered a quick prayer, then pushed.

The plate shifted. Dagny felt a pull, as if a vortex beyond was trying to suck her inside. Instinctively, she leaned back, her body resisting the instruction to go forward.

Is this right? she asked herself again. The plate snapped back in place, sending a vibration across the eye.

"What's going on?" Pren called from below. "Are you alright?"

The rim—the eyelid—she was standing on was better than nothing, but was still not very thick. "Get my sister, please!" Dagny shouted into the stone. "I don't want to argue right now."

Feruda said something. Hopefully, she was dragging the boy away.

Carefully, Dagny placed her hands on the plate again, but before she could even push this time, the top half of the plate swung open, and the bottom half kicked out, sending Dagny toppling over and sliding down a steep tunnel.

She landed on hard ground. It was blacker than a cave at night inside the dome, and the air was thick and odorless. Dagny felt small, bumpy ridges underneath, and the floor sloped away from her, toward the center, like the inside of a shallow egg. The wound in her chest throbbed painfully—she must've injured it again during the fall—and when Dagny touched the spot on her shirt, the cloth felt wet.

Her mouth turned incredibly dry, brought on by nerves no doubt, and Dagny was just about to check the wall behind for a way to climb out when she heard a faint wheezing coming from somewhere deeper within.

The chilling sound twisted her gut and spread down her spine. Dagny froze on the floor, with her back stiff as iron. *The Queen? Was that the Queen breathing?* Dagny asked herself. *After thousands of years, trapped in the darkness of the dome?* Could Odestinas be watching her at this very moment?

And what now? They'd never discussed it exactly; everyone had been so focused on trying to find a legend, none of them had planned for what to do *after* the Queen was found. Maybe deep inside, no one in Jud truly believed it would happen.

But they all had different reasons for searching, didn't they? The Knights, the Thorned Prince, the witches—as cryptic as those reasons were. Grete only wanted to get rid of the heart, and Dagny wanted to help her.

The wheezing stopped and was replaced by a smothering silence. It made Dagny want to hold her breath to keep from disturbing it. In the blackness, the seconds stretched like hours, and the tension in her back began to ache and spasm.

Grete should be coming soon, and she'd have Mia with her. There had to be a way back out, right? A way to climb back to the eye. If the Imposter came here to visit the Queen, like Grete said, then he must've built such a path. But if that was true, then why hadn't the Queen escaped?

Maybe she was trapped somehow; chained to a wall, or imprisoned inside of another chamber, deeper in the dome. Dagny tried to manage her fear; Odestinas was supposed to be benevolent after all. If that sound had been her wheezing; if she was somehow alive after all this time, maybe it would be fine.

Then again… what if her mind had rotted out? Like the Giant King. Like Yunis. Like a ghost princess in the weeds? Thousands of years spent imprisoned in this place? Trauma breeding trauma, fracturing the psyche of the first Queen.

Suddenly, Dagny didn't want her sister coming here. She rolled over and began to feel her way across the ground, taking hold of the ridges, trying to crawl up the curving shell. Trying to figure out where the tunnel was that had dumped her into this nightmare of a place. It was *just so dark.*

She heard a clacking, scarcely audible, echo from somewhere above. *The eye*. Grete was at the eye-plate. A moment later, the swooshing sound of a body sliding across the ground signaled Grete's arrival.

Mia followed quickly behind, illuminating the immediate area.

Dagny shielded her eyes from the glow, and caught sight of the hole and passage leading back outside. Her heart relaxed as she also noticed a row of ridges forming a sort of staircase against the shell. She could easily make *that* climb.

"*Dag…*" Grete came crawling over. "Are you okay?"

"Shh, there's something else here," Dagny whispered. "*Listen.*"

The wheezing started up again, and Mia's glow dimmed, as if she was trying to hide the two of them, but it was too late for that. Whatever lie across the dome was already aware of their presence.

Grete scrunched her nose and clicked the roof of her mouth like she was tasting something wretched. "What is that?" she asked.

"What?" Dagny replied. She couldn't taste or smell a thing.

"It's *awful.*" Grete gagged, then retched up thin streams of spittle, reminding Dagny of the ooze she had run from earlier. "Sorry…" Grete choked. "I'll be alright."

Dagny helped her sister stand, asking, "Should we…"

"Keep going? Yes."

Mia hovered above, while Dagny tried to assist Grete down the rigid shell.

"I can feel it," Grete croaked, continuing to gag as they walked. "It *wants* to come free."

"What? The *heart*?"

Grete bobbed her head, but Dagny couldn't tell if she was intentionally nodding.

The shell flattened and spread out, giving the impression that they were entering a wide-open, cavernous space. Mia's light broadened, and a simple chair appeared from the darkness. It had a metal frame and faced away, into the black.

Dagny held her tongue, thinking about the odd placement of the thing. Could this be where the Imposter sat while watching...

The Queen.

She appeared next, although it took Dagny a moment to realize it. An enormous face, dark as burnt wood and sinewy, stretched across a protrusion erupting from the opposite wall. Her arms reached across the dome, fading from the light, and the Queen's torso ended with her ribcage. Still, what remained was the size of a building, and Dagny struggled to make sense of the being, like her mind couldn't connect it with reality.

Dagny heard the wheezing, louder than before. The Queen's mouth didn't move, but that's where the noise was coming from. She was sure of it. The lips were long black lines; the eyes and nose reduced to gaping pits, flattened across a broad face.

Grete froze, her own mouth gaping. Her inky black hair framed her figure in a such way that she morphed with the darkness.

The air grew thicker. Mia darted behind Dagny, away from the Queen. The spirit light was afraid as well.

Dagny struggled with her breath, like sucking wind through a blanket, and she saw the reason why. *Fog.* The color of obsidian, seeping out of the Queen's ribcage. It spread across the floor, overtaking Dagny's boots, eclipsing her legs, stomach, chest...

Grete coughed from nearby; it sounded weak and muffled.

There are other things that breathe in the deep. The words resonated in Dagny's mind, and she wondered what shades this breath of fog might bring.

Then she heard a phrase spoken so clearly, she thought the speaker was standing next to her. But it wasn't a voice; not really. It was like the *memory* of a voice. *Time shapes differently down here,* it said. *The fleeting dreams of a broken past.*

The blackness around her started to change, from obsidian to ash, into charcoal, then steel. A milky image took hold: a person standing on the shore of a stormy sea.

"Who is that?" Dagny asked. She could smell the saltwater and feel the wind whipping harshly from over the water.

This is the beginning, the voice said, a hushed echo blowing in with the storm.

"The beginning of what?"

Of life. I am called eternal. I am the seed. I am the sun that warms the soil. The raging fire and the spark. The burnt earth that comes after. Heresy and truth.

"Are you Odestinas?" Dagny asked.

The voice roared, shaking the ground and thundering across the dome. In the murky fog, the sea swelled and smashed against the shore. *Odestinas is death!* it boomed. *There is only Nyne!*

Nyne. The thing that Boulder had mentioned. A queen of the underground—who had birthed the shades! What was she doing here? In the tomb of Odestinas? Dagny covered her ears and folded over until the trembling stopped. When she raised her head again, the sea had receded and a young forest had sprouted in its place.

I've been birthed again, Nyne said. *Re-fleshed. A fateful promise to a world un-humbled. In my being is the remembrance of time—Nyne does not forget.*

Out of the forest walked several young women; their long hair shades of green, from the color of grass to the brilliance of emerald. Taller ones came behind them; pale as the moon, with long arms and slender hands. Their nails resembled beast-like claws; otherwise the figures were angelic and radiated light like the sun.

They gathered around Dagny in a circle and began to sing, and although Dagny couldn't make out the words, the song seemed familiar.

A culling will come, the voice said over the melody. *From the simple flesh, all shall be created in the image of Nyne.*

The faces of the women turned bleak. Dagny noticed their bodies change as well. Their feet and legs hardened like clay baking in a kiln, and it spread up their torsos, reaching their necks. Knots of blistering metal formed over their skin and when it was finished, they stood like statues, staring at Dagny behind sad, pitiful eyes.

"Did *you* do this, Nyne?" Dagny asked. "Did *you* turn the daughters to metal and rust?"

I am the first and the last. All must come through me. Nyne's voice had turned whispery but penetrating.

"What became of Odestinas? The Queen of Jud?"

Once a singular purpose. Now split asunder... only Nyne remains...

Only Nyne? What was she saying? Had Odestinas and this other queen been one and the same?

A black, corrosive wind blew in from where the sea had been; from the heart of the new forest. It swept over the metal daughters, tarnishing their formerly glimmering bodies. Dagny scanned the faces, looking for one she might recognize.

And she found it. As the figures rusted and flaked away, she caught the image of Lieta standing amongst the others with green hair. Dagny reached for her, desperate to pull the girl away from the wind, and caught her hand.

But it was a memory, and Dagny was helpless to save her. Lieta crumbled away, turning from a statue into dust. Or *almost* crumbled away. A great gust of wind blew in, scattering the remains of Lieta across the forest. Everything except for a single piece of metal that remained in Dagny's grasp. A finger.

Dagny had been so fixated on Lieta that she hadn't seen the other daughters disappear. And when she finally gazed back into the fog, she was surrounded by the walls of Jud. She saw a powerful man, cradling a woman, and from his skin grew rows and rows of bloody thorns.

"The prince," Dagny whispered, shoving Lieta's finger into her pocket.

The betrayer of Nyne.

"Betrayer?"

The deceiver. The trickster. The lover of none.

"No..." Dagny muttered. "The prince had been searching for you... for Odestinas. It was the Imposter that did these things. The *Imposter* sealed Odestinas in this tomb."

All went black. From far away, Dagny heard the sound of a cat howling mournfully.

The... Immmmp-ah-sssss-tor... Nyne said, stretching the word out awkwardly, like someone learning how to speak for the first time.

A light appeared in the fog, and Dagny saw a man approach. He had a wide face and long gray hair that poured onto the ground and dragged behind him. He was surrounded by darkness, and Dagny knew that the man walked through the very dome she stood in now. He sat on the metal chair and faced her.

"You've been abandoned by those who professed you love," he said. "Left to the blackness. Your daughters play while you rot, and the one who desired your throne has succeeded, sending you here and turning your forest to ash. Only I love you. Only I..."

Only I...

Only Nyne.

The voice echoed and faded, turning once again into a faint, hissing rasp.

The man disappeared and something grabbed Dagny's arm. She screamed and spun away, ready to run, just as Mia appeared. In the blue glow, Dagny saw Grete reaching toward her. A look of pain and terror on her face.

"Grete!" Dagny screamed again, rushing back toward her sister. "What did you do to her?"

Grete's brow dripped with sweat. She opened her mouth to speak, but couldn't. Then Dagny realized, she wasn't trying to talk, she was gasping for air.

"Help her!" Dagny shouted. "Grete... no... no..." She turned to the Odestinas body stretched across the far wall. "*Please* help her!"

Gretchen flailed her arms and slapped and clawed at her throat. There was something there; lodged inside. Something *massive*. Gretchen's eyes grew so large, Dagny thought they might pop out, and a split second later, black bile poured from Grete's mouth, drenching her shirt and chest; streaming down her legs.

"No! Grete!" Dagny grabbed her sister's throat, just below the bulge, and tried to push it up into her mouth. She felt the thing move, wiggling above her hands, and *pulsate.* Dagny wanted to turn away and run, but she held firm, squeezing her eyes closed as tightly as possible. She heard more liquid spew from Grete's mouth, felt it pour over her hands, hot and thick.

Dagny kept screaming. Pushing with everything she had; so hard, she feared she would break Grete's neck. Then, just when she thought Grete was gone, that there was no way her sister could survive so long without air, the mass slid into Grete's mouth from her throat, and plopped onto the floor.

Another wave of black vomit followed. Dagny pulled Grete away, watching in horror as the thing she expelled throbbed in the puddle of liquid, continuing to pump black sludge across the ground.

The girls ran; into the darkness; away from the throbbing heart of onyx that Grete had consumed way back in Limer's Town—away from the dream prison that had trapped and consumed her for so long. Away from Nyne and the shattered mind of the first Queen. There was no saving Odestinas. There was nothing left to save. The Eternal Knights of Jud had been searching for a ghost, and they had almost found it, becoming ghosts of their own in the process. Mia flew ahead, lighting the way, blazing a path back to the eye.

The wheezing grew louder as they ran: a high-pitched whirling sound slicing through the air, rattling the very dome itself. Dagny held Grete by the wrist, pulling her along. Even with all the noise, she heard her sister hoarsely utter a single phrase, "Thank you."

As Dagny hit the curve of the wall and the row of ridges, she stretched her arms out and began to climb. So frantically did she clamber up the shell that Dagny almost missed the pair of pale lights sliding down to greet her. But then she caught a whiff of the sea and felt a twinge of pain in her breast.

29

Seventeen years ago, Gretchen Somertail was born in a mudbank shell-shack on the bank of the river Morca. *Somertail* was the surname given to the girl, due to that unusually lengthy summer at the time of her birth, and *Gretchen* was the proper name due to a gamble her mother had made with a drunken aunt who subsequently fell from a bridge and drowned. At least that was the story.

Dagny had been there at the moment of birth, although she couldn't remember it for obvious reasons. Had she been able to recall such details as a one-year-old, she would've smelled the thick tar burning in the hearth and caught images of blood-stained hay and a single-toothed maiden smiling at her mother's discomfort. Dagny's howls had been the loudest, however—she'd always been a cryer, with her older cousins even anointing her with the nickname *Sobby-fin*. *Sobby* for her tears, of course, and *fin* because her head came to a point as a baby.

There was a bond between the sisters who, along with their older brother Morgan, spent most days shuffling around the alleyways of the Rakesmount Tenements, making up stories and games to play. When Morgan grew older and began to work as a runner for the shipbuilders of River's End, Dagny and Gretchen were left to their own plots, typically involving creating costumes out of junk and weeds, and pretending they were somewhere entirely different. The younger Gretchen would gaze upon her sister with such a sense of wonder that it made Dagny feel like the most important person in the entire world. No one else in the tenement paid much mind to the two girls—that is, unless someone was feeling particularly mean and nasty.

Time worked differently back then, with the days and years stretching far longer. Eventually, Morgan connected with Alex Benzara through the renowned adventurer Magu Ogden, and the connection between brother and sisters began to weaken. Perhaps it was that loss which made Dagny focus so heavily on the memories of her brother at the sacrifice of Gretchen. Perhaps she'd taken her sister's idolization for granted; believing it would always exist. Dagny was so preoccupied with Morgan when he was away, and near the end—although she loved her sister—would grow annoyed with Gretchen's persistent presence. But Dagny was also a child herself, raised without direction, and deserving of grace.

There was so much regret over the later years, when Dagny believed she'd lost them both. It weighed her down like a wet coat she couldn't shed. She tried to put those feelings into little boxes in her mind that she could shut and lock, but every now and again, the boxes popped open and became impossible to close.

When she was growing up, Dagny would imagine becoming an adventurer herself, searching for a means to bring her brother and sister back to life. In a way, she'd found it: there on the banks of the great Marsh, south of Southend; beyond the junk heaps of the city. She'd found the promise of life amongst Corlie and the Marsh Rats. A sister Dagny'd thought she lost forever in a flood. Pulled from the waters and sent to Limer's Town. *Gretchen Somertail.*

The floods had taken so much from so many. Not just when the Morca washed the Rakesmount away. History was consumed with such stories, and whatever the actual truth behind them, the world had been irreparably traumatized. Whether contained deep within the heart of a young girl of the Rakesmount, or manifested in the shapes of the drowned twins who rushed down to greet her now. The scars were deep.

The girl appeared first; her teeth exposed by parted lips; silently striking from the darkness. Dagny didn't have a chance to scream. Galwed barreled into her, and the two went rolling down the side of the dome.

Heel over head Dagny fell, smacking her back on the cold, black shell. The glow from Mia spun rapidly as she went, blurring the distinction between light and dark. Grete shouted above the wheezing sound buzzing throughout the chamber, and from somewhere further away, Dagny heard something else.

Another scream? It was deeper, almost like a growl, and pained. Was it that cat again? Dagny couldn't make sense of it. Then she landed; thudding hard onto her back. Galwed stood over her, reminiscent of the attack in the chapel. There were nine black nails sprouting from her fingertips and a pulpy white blot marking the one that had broken off.

Dagny sucked in air just as Tewdred came skidding down the dome after them. The drowned boy was dragging Grete by the hair.

"Leave her alone," Dagny yelled, finding the voice to shout, even though every bit of strength had been sapped from her body.

Galwed cocked her head, studying Dagny. There was almost a calmness in the girl's face now. Tewdred stepped next to her, casually yanking Grete across the ground. The boy seemed relaxed as well. But their calmness didn't relax Dagny. She found their expressions even more horrific like this; lacking anger; lacking of any kind of emotion whatsoever. Although, that wasn't *exactly* true. There was an expression there, it was just so muted as to be barely noticeable. Dagny believed she saw a look of satisfaction.

Grete hissed, grasping at the fist entwined in her hair. She tried to rise, fell, and tried to rise again.

"Stop it," Dagny said. "Leave her alone."

Suddenly, Grete kicked the drowned boy. Tewdred lurched forward, but quickly recovered. Then, with a powerful swing, he tossed Grete through the air and into the blackness.

In short order, Dagny heard the thump of Grete's body on stone, the grunt, and her sister's aching cry.

Mia had swelled to twice her normal size and vibrated violently, flickering between blue, yellow and white; causing the chamber to distort in a shimmering blaze of light.

The twins lurked over Dagny, facing the darkness beyond. Dagny wanted to dart away, to find Grete and escape, but fear of the drowned pair pressed her to the ground. The twins were ignoring her for the moment, and Dagny was deathly afraid of drawing their attention. She hoped they remained focused on the darkness. Perhaps they might even wander off toward... what, precisely?

Dagny tried to orient herself. Between the fall and the strobing lights, her mind had been rattled. What *were* the twins looking at? Were they watching the Queen? Had they seen the heart pulsating and leaking black blood across the floor? Slowly, Dagny turned her head to the side and squinted into the shadows.

She saw the giant head of Odestinas, stretched across time, faintly protruding from the wall of solid night. A charcoal etching on charred-black wood. She saw the edge of the Queen's ribcage, dripping down from her torso, and although the monstrous form rested just beyond the twins, it wasn't what they stared at.

A presence dwelled on the other side of that black curtain. It had been there when she met Nyne and entered the mist; it had been there when Grete gagged and vomited out the heart. Watching and wheezing. Dagny couldn't see it, but she didn't need to anymore. She *felt* it now.

The sensation was primal—the same feeling she'd had in the Castle, right before Yunis pounced—that something tremendous and ancient was bearing down on them. A primordial storm. Fearless, and seeded with rage.

The twins seemed to sway ever so slightly. Tewdred took a step forward, and in that instant—at the moment before his foot touched ground—he was abruptly sucked into the black. Galwed dove after him; her fingers spread out like a fan of wicked knives, and the roar that followed shook the dome with such deafening ferocity that Dagny thought she might never hear again.

She flipped onto her stomach, skittered to her feet, and blindly took off, running in the direction where Grete had been tossed. Mia caught up quickly, lighting the area only a split-second before Dagny would've tripped over her sister's body.

Grete lay curled in a ball, huffing hard and squirming in pain. Dagny didn't have time to check for injuries. She grabbed Grete's arms and pulled her up as fast as she could. Immediately, Grete gasped and let out a silent scream, absorbed by the thundering dome, then collapsed to the ground.

"Come on!" Dagny shouted into the blanket of noise. "We have to go! *Please!*"

Gretchen waved her off and wept against the stone. Then Dagny saw it: her sister's leg buckled out unnaturally sharp, just below the knee. Dagny stepped back and pressed her hand over her mouth. What was she going to do? It would be hard enough for one person to climb out of the eye. How was she ever going to pull Grete out of here?

All of a sudden, Grete jerked her head around to face Dagny and screamed out a single word. "Go!"

This one Dagny heard. It seemed to cut through the deep, shattering roar. Then Gretchen squeezed her eyes closed and turned away.

Dagny gritted her teeth. She'd rather die here, in the tomb, than leave her sister again. It was never going to happen. Nyne... the twins... the beast beyond the black... they could all be buried here together, if that's how it had to be.

But Dagny also wasn't going to sit still and wait. Even if that meant hurting Grete. Forgiveness would come in time, so long as they made it out. Without another thought, Dagny knelt down and locked her arms around Grete's torso. Then she looked away, took a deep breath, and began to drag.

Mia guided their path as before. The spirit light looked even bigger now, the size of a fist, although it was hard to tell in the blinding glare. Grete trembled in Dagny's arms and clawed at the dome in an effort to escape her grasp. Dagny could feel the vibration from her sister's screams, but she wouldn't allow it to stop her from what she needed to do. One lurching, dragging step at a time.

They reached the row of ridges, where Dagny had to stop and catch a moment of rest before the climb. The muscles in her arms burned, and she doubted she had the strength to reach the eye-shaft. Where were the others? Their friends? The noise of the dome must've been heard from the outside; it probably rumbled across the entire underground. It would've been impossible to ignore. Marfisi, Pren, Feruda. Why was no one here? Had Galwed collected them as well?

Out of the shadows, another figure came running. Dagny tensed, unsure of how to respond; the image blurred against the quaking shell. She hoped it was a friend. Things were happening so fast that she struggled to keep up.

Several steps later, the figure stabilized, and Dagny caught sight of a skinny girl in boots. Feruda didn't bother trying to speak. Instead, she charged to the other side of Dagny and started to help pull Grete up the curving wall.

Using the ridges as leverage, the girls heaved, climbed, rested, and heaved again, until finally, they reached the point where the wall became too steep. Dagny glanced at Feruda, anticipating panic, but the girl seemed unexpectedly confident. She touched Dagny's shoulder to reassure her, then handed Grete over and scanned the space above.

Dagny held her sister close, a vain attempt at offering some measure of comfort. Grete's brow was drenched with sweat, and she continued to quiver and cry into the void, but at least she was no longer struggling to get away.

Feruda darted off momentarily, and when she returned, she was grasping the end of a thin cord. A surge of hope swelled in Dagny's chest. The rope disappeared into the darkness overhead, presumably leading up to the eye-shaft. Feruda moved quickly, looping the cord around Grete's torso and tying it off with a complex knot. When she'd finished, Feruda tested her work, gave the rope two hard tugs, and prepared to guide Grete up the shell.

Almost immediately, the rope went taut and Grete's body jerked away. Dagny followed behind, trying her best to support Grete's injured leg while simultaneously scaling the ridge ladder.

It was a tough climb, and the roar continued as they went, unrelenting in its fury. It had to be the bear, Dagny thought. *Calregale Untruth.* The Imposter had buried it down here with Odestinas. It should've been long dead, but Yunis had been kept alive somehow. Why not the bear? They were beings beyond Dagny's comprehension, and she was okay with that now. Some things she didn't need to understand, only that the bear guardian was here, unleashing its frenzied madness upon the twins.

As Dagny ascended the dome, she imagined the creature, ragged and limp like the Great Cat, a husk of its former greatness. It was horribly sad to think about. The bear, destined to serve its Queen, rotting away in the blackness over the course of a lost age. But there was nothing to be done about such things. Grete had given the Queen back her heart. That was all they could do.

Mia reached the shaft and spread light into the tunnel. From there, the ridge ladder ended and the walls became smooth; it also became easier to climb, like the leaning chimney of a sinking tower.

Dagny braced herself between the shaft walls and watched as Grete was pulled away by Feruda and whoever worked the rope, leaving her and Mia alone in the tunnel. She was more grateful than she'd ever been before, witnessing her sister escape the dome. Grateful for these friends who risked their own lives in order to see this matter through to the end; grateful for whatever force of destiny had guided her along. She felt it so strongly now: the thing that had taken her from the Rakesmount to Rork; from Max and the Naverung to the Under Road and Jud. She felt comforted and hopeful; even here, beneath the Cauldron, in the howling tomb of Odestinas. She felt eternal.

It was Pren at the Gylathrik eye. He had wedged himself between the eye-plate and the inner wall, and struggled to lower Grete down the outer dome. As soon as Dagny reached him, she grabbed what remained of the rope, helping to ease the load.

Marfisi was at the base. She screamed with excitement when Grete finally reached her, then shouted at the others to hurry. It was an unnecessary instruction. Feruda had almost made it to the bottom herself—scaling down the grooves of the Gylathrik etching, and Pren had already dropped the rope and was assisting Dagny onto the ledge below.

As soon as the eye-plate slammed closed, the roaring of the inner tomb ceased. Dagny didn't know if the two were related. Had the tomb been sealed so tightly that once closed again, even sound itself couldn't escape? Or had the bear somehow been subdued—by the twins or otherwise—thereby ending its howl? Maybe the twins themselves had perished, capping the final chapter in their torrid history, and with nothing left to purge, the tomb had turned quiet. Whatever the truth about what occurred inside the dome, just like the truth about Odestinas, the Giant and the underground world, Dagny doubted she would ever really know it.

By the time Dagny reached the ground, Feruda had emptied her pack and tied a makeshift bandage around Grete's leg. Marfisi was pouring a liquid down Grete's throat, telling her not to worry.

"I've got a pretty good sense of how to make it back," Pren said. "But we need to move. Who knows how much longer we have, and this will take a while."

"It was dawn when you left, correct?" Marfisi asked Dagny.

"Yeah."

She relaxed slightly. "We should still have time until twilight, then. The journey couldn't have taken that long."

Dagny, however, wasn't so sure. "Roger Red mentioned the Cauldron could close at random," she said, as the girls helped Grete onto Pren's back.

"Eh, what does he know?" Pren replied. "Besides, what good will it do worrying?" He adjusted his position and groaned. "Your sister's heavier than she looks."

"Thank you, by the way," Dagny said. "Thank you all. We couldn't have made it out if it wasn't—"

"Let's go," Pren interrupted, marching toward the crystal grotto. "Everyone can thank each other when we've seen the sky."

They exited the dome room and crossed the crystal field. Dagny was a bit apprehensive about the strands of goo that had chased her from the chamber where Pren's father died, and whether those same strands would be waiting to grab them, but the group quickly made it through without issue and back to the winding passageways leading to the Giant's gut.

It seemed like days had passed since they'd last been there. "How long were we inside the tomb?" Dagny asked.

"Not long. A few minutes, maybe?" Feruda said.

Minutes? It had felt like hours inside the mist with Nyne.

"And the twins..." Dagny continued. "I can't believe you came in after us."

"The twins?" Pren grunted from ahead. "What are you talking about?"

"Those two were in the chamber?" Feruda asked. "We didn't see anyone else go in after Gretchen."

Dagny wasn't sure how she felt about that right now.

"What we *did* see," Feruda said, "was you fall into the eye, and even though we warned Gretchen, she fell down too. Knew right then, we needed to get the rope if there was any chance of getting you back. It was an *inescapable* prison, after all."

Dagny recounted the events inside, telling the group everything that had occurred. About Odestinas becoming Nyne and what she'd seen in the mist. About Grete and the heart, the twins and the bear.

"That roaring was from the bear guardian?" Pren asked.

"I think so," Dagny replied. "But again, I couldn't see it."

Grete had stopped trembling and hung limp over Pren's back.

"Will she be alright?" Dagny said.

Marfisi smiled and gave her a nod. "Yes. She could be dealing with the injury for some time... and she may always have a limp. It could be a rough break. But the medicine I gave her will mute her pain, and I will ensure no infection sets in once we emerge."

"Speaking of infections," Feruda said, leaning in to sniff Dagny's chest. "I don't smell your wound anymore."

Marfisi nodded again. "That's good. It is not a vileness you want to linger."

"So, it really was the Queen's heart that Grete ate?" Pren asked. "I wonder what any of this means. What will happen now that it's been returned?"

"I'll get my sister back," Dagny said. "It's the only part of this I care about, and then Grete can move on with her life. Everything else can do whatever it's going to do."

Grete hummed into Pren's shoulder, then snorted and giggled like a dreaming child. It was the nicest thing Dagny had heard in a long while.

30

I t took quite some time and effort to scale the Giant's throat and work their way into its mouth, but between the four of them and the rope, they were able to guide Grete up safely.

"At least it's an easy trek from here on, until we reach the entrance, of course," Pren said. "I'm not looking forward to the climb out."

Marfisi took the lead, followed by Pren carrying Grete, and they marched straight onto the bridge—the Giant's Tongue—with no hesitation.

But Feruda hesitated. "Are the shades really gone?" she asked, glancing over the edge.

"Focus on getting across," Dagny whispered. "Nothing else. I'm here for you. Let's go see the sun."

As they walked, Dagny reached into her pocket and felt the metal finger. Her suspicions had been confirmed there in Odestinas' black tomb. Lieta was a daughter of Jud, somehow trapped by the Moon Needle Oracle.

They reached the opposite landing, joining Grete and the others. Mia's glow had steadied since leaving the tomb, calming the path. Dagny opened the Night Orbiter when they stepped from the bridge, and held it toward the orb, but Mia refused to enter.

The spirit light remembered the way from earlier, and led them along the ancient passageways, up staircases and past side tunnels, weaving through rooms great and small, until finally reaching the staging area—that enormous cavern that had marked the beginning of countless expeditions: all of them failed, until now.

How long had Odestinas truly been down here? The myths seemed to suggest a thousand years or more, although, having crossed through the underground, Dagny wouldn't have been surprised if the Queen's imprisonment had lasted much, much longer.

The world was a massive, layered place, and more had been lost than could ever be recovered. It thrilled Dagny at one time, and she wondered if it might ever do so again. She'd felt a change in herself, something irreversible, ever since that day with Maris, inside the Benzara study, when he had stumbled upon a Night Orbiter of his own. How much could a person change in a year? Dagny glanced down at her own dirty hands, bathed in blue, and then looked at Grete, straddled across Pren's back, remembering a time when they used to run together through the mud-caked streets of the Mount. How much could a person change over the course of a year, or several, or a decade? Profoundly.

"There's light up ahead!" Pren shouted with excitement. "The Cauldron must still be open!"

Dagny raised her head. In the distance, a stream of pale light filtered down from above, signaling the exit. Feruda laughed, shouldered the rope, and charged forward. "Come on, Dagny! Let's find a place to tie this off," she shouted.

Marfisi and Pren scrambled after them. "I can't believe it's still open," Pren said, happily. "I just can't believe it!"

Dagny thought of Melwes lying with Eidfur. She was glad he hadn't come down to this awful place, and grew excited at the idea of seeing the boy again. She also thought of the Benzara children, Lucas and Abrielle; and of Max and the Naverung; everything she had left behind. Those were memories she'd purposely shut out. Put on hold to protect herself, but now there was no helping it. Everything came flooding back.

They were closing in on the streams of light, and Dagny allowed herself to bask in the hope of a future life. Whatever form that might take. She deserved it. They all did.

Dagny rushed over to the staircase of planks and gazed up. The light was real, coming from somewhere beyond the layer of mist separating the underground from the Cauldron... Only... there was something *different* about it.

This wasn't light from the sun.

"What?" Feruda asked.

Dagny turned toward the girl. *Didn't she sense it, too?* "Something's wrong..."

"Wrong?" Pren asked, panting as he jogged up from behind.

"Yeah," Dagny said. "The light... I can't explain it, but—"

Suddenly, Mia blazed past them and shot up the Cauldron's shaft. Pren watched her go. "What's that about..."

"I don't really care," Feruda said, and pulled herself onto the first shelf. "Hand me Gretchen. We can figure it out later."

Dagny felt foolish for pausing, even briefly. *Just get out.* They were so close, and the Cauldron could close at a moment's notice.

They worked as quickly as possible; looping the rope around Gretchen, then climbing to the next shelf, and passing her up as they went. It was when they reached the layer of mist that Dagny realized the source of light.

She hadn't been mistaken. There was no sunlight here. *This* light was much softer and was not coming from a single source, but from many. The mist had distorted the glow, making it appear like a single stream. Dagny glanced at her companions. None of them had appreciated it yet.

She leapt onto the shelf above and grabbed the rope.

"Is it me, or is the light glittery?" Pren asked, as he prepared to lift Grete.

"Twinkling," Dagny said. "I told you it was different."

Feruda hoisted herself onto the shelf. "Twinkling? Why's the sun twinkling?"

Dagny was about to answer when a great number of spirit lights drifted down through the mist and circled her body. She heard an audible gasp from Pren.

Any fear that Dagny had before, about the Cauldron closing, evaporated in an instant. She wasn't sure how the lights were here, or how they had escaped Yunis, but she was certain Odestinas, or Nyne, must've had something to do with it.

Higher and higher they climbed until the Great Below was nothing but an afterthought. Roger Red was there to greet them, as were Melwes and a host of others whom Dagny didn't recognize. An enormous cheer erupted when she crawled out, and equal ones followed for each companion who emerged after her.

Roger Red embraced Pren and lifted him into the air, shouting, "My boy! My brother! You made it, you did!" Pren tried to maintain a scowl, but then let himself go and smiled.

It was around this time that Dagny noticed the darkening sky and stars overhead. Twilight had come and gone, and yet, the Cauldron was still open. Or was it?

The deep iron bowl that had marked the plaza of Sanctuary had been ripped apart. Huge strips of iron peeled away from the stone, curling underneath the ground like ribbons and vanishing into the mist. There would be no closing the Cauldron ever again.

"What happened here?" Marfisi asked, noticing the broken shell at the same time as Dagny.

"The stars," a man said. "They came falling from the clouds and tore open the seal."

"No, they came from the north," a woman replied, pointing to the skyline. "I saw it from my rooftop garden. They came streaming from the forest beyond the city."

"You're all wrong," another one argued.

Melwes tugged Dagny's shirt and grinned. "*The castle*," he whispered. "It was the spirit lights..."

Dagny couldn't help herself anymore. Tears came flowing down her cheeks and she pulled Melwes close, sobbing hard.

A group of Weavers, dressed in long, brown shawls, gathered around Marfisi and Gretchen. "They're here to help," Feruda told Dagny. "I wouldn't have expected them to leave Sanctuary, but I'm glad they did. It looks like those spirit lights of yours brought everyone out."

"No. Not mine," Dagny said, shaking her head.

"Listen," Feruda continued, "the Weavers will probably need to treat Grete inside of Sanctuary, and only the Invited are allowed in... I know you'll want to come. Unfortunately, there's nothing I can do about—"

"That's okay. I understand. Stay with her, alright?"

"Of course I will." Feruda grinned, and then cackled loudly. "We did it, Dagny. You and your sister have amazed me completely. They'll be telling this story for centuries. No. Longer than that!"

Dagny lost Pren and Roger in the crowd, which was just as well. There was nothing to say to them right now.

Gazing back down the pit, she saw Mia hovering at the mist's edge. Maybe it was her imagination, but somehow Mia appeared even *bigger*.

Melwes tugged Dagny's shirt again. "You're thinking something. What is it?"

The boy sure was observant. "Yeah. I'm thinking about something unfinished." As much as she wanted to rest and bask in the celebration, Dagny was beginning to feel like the moment wasn't meant for her.

"Is it a person? Do they need to be rescued?"

"Yeah."

"Then you need to go get them," Melwes said, like he was stating the obvious. "Don't you?"

"Yes." Dagny studied the boy before continuing. "I don't want you to come, though. I need you to stay here again, okay? I'm sorry. I know I promised to stay with you, but I will be back."

Melwes shrugged and gestured at the spirit lights. "You don't need me, anyway. They came from the castle for *you*. They'll guide your way... should you have to call on them."

"They're alive..." Dagny whispered, still in disbelief at the sight of so many lights. "I thought Yunis had..."

"Killed them?" the boy asked. "No. They're eternal. They're guardians of the Under Road. I told you that, remember?"

Tracing the metal finger with her thumb, Dagny knew she'd be going after Lieta. Even before she made the journey down the Cauldron, she knew she couldn't leave the girl trapped in the Needle. Dagny just needed to get her sister to safety first.

"What are you going to do?" Melwes asked. "Do you even know?"

"I have an idea."

"Whatever it is, don't be long. I don't want to come looking for you. It's exhausting."

She waited until Feruda had disappeared behind a throng of bodies, and after making sure no one else was watching, Dagny pretended she was adjusting her boots, then quietly slipped into the crowd and snuck over to the plaza gate. She didn't want any of the others to follow her. They had done enough already.

She'd been running the plan over and over in her mind. The Salarel hand had called the mist from under the Alypso tree—there was no reason why Lieta's finger wouldn't do the same.

Rushing down the main road, Dagny weaved through a wave of residents pressing toward the plaza. It seemed as though everyone in Jud wanted to get a look at the Cauldron and the spirit lights. Dagny cut across the alley she'd taken with Feruda earlier this morning, and as soon as she was covered by the shadows of the dim passage, Mia suddenly appeared. The orb twinkled briefly, then vanished again, materializing just long enough to let Dagny know she wasn't alone.

It took a while to find her way back to the district and the Alypso tree. By then, the moon was high in the sky and the clouds had all parted, allowing the true stars to shine on the mist-covered courtyard in front of Marfisi's tower-house.

Dagny stopped at the edge and removed the metal finger from her pack.

A chill swept across the yard. It was unnaturally cold, cutting through Dagny's clothes and biting into her skin, causing gooseflesh to ripple over her arms.

"Salarel?" she whispered.

A light touch tickled her leg, and a foreign phrase drifted on the wind: *Geliour Sandri oin ut... Do you remember us, or have you forgotten?* Dagny wasn't quite sure if the voice was real or in her mind.

She thought she was safe at the edge of the courtyard, away from the mist, and briefly considered running away, before realizing that she wasn't afraid. "I'm Dagny Losh. I remember you. I'm sorry for what those men did."

Why do you come?

"I need to free someone. Lieta... of the Moon Needle—"

A daughter...

"Yes, a daughter. A princess of Jud. She's imprisoned in the Needle, kept there by Kustav, an Oracle."

Dagny smelled blood in the air, and then she was touched again. It wasn't a finger—she knew that clearly now—it was braids of hair. They wrapped around her legs, anchoring her to the ground, and slid under her shirt.

...Imprisoned... the voice echoed.

"By Kustav," Dagny repeated. She surprised herself with the strength in her own voice. Despite the braids tangled around her torso, she didn't feel afraid. She felt enraged, and each phrase that she spoke grew louder and louder. "A jailor of girls and men. A creature of Lazim. The Oracle keeps them all when she has no right!"

Dagny felt warmth on her neck, and the courtyard brightened suddenly, as if dawn had come. She glanced at its source, expecting to see her guardian, blazing like it had on the Giant's Tongue, but it wasn't just Mia that had appeared. Dozens of spirit lights circled overhead.

"Do you hear me, daughters of Jud?" Dagny asked, raising the metal finger over her head. The Salarel braids quivered and loosened. "Now let me pass."

Another gust of wind whipped through the area. Dagny flung the braids from her body and walked into the courtyard.

There were whispers in the mist. More ghosts than Salarel. They giggled excitedly, sounding strangely feminine and childlike.

Dagny quickly made her way to the back of the tree and crawled under the roots. She sat in the middle of the chamber, like she had done the other day with Feruda, and held the finger in her palm, trying to remember how she'd summoned the girl before.

But there was no chance to close her eyes or clear her mind. The fog came immediately this time, seeping up from the ground. It consumed everything, so dense that it blocked out the spirit lights.

"Lieta?" Dagny called. The name felt awkward in her mouth. "Can you hear me?"

Soon, she was floating in complete darkness, vaguely aware of herself, like she was stirring from a dream. There was the weird sensation of separation; the loss of time.

Dagny felt a presence slip into the chamber and rest beside her.

A youthful voice whispered her name.

"Lieta?" Dagny asked again. "Are you here? I can't see anything."

It's alright. You will soon enough.

"I know what you are. I had a vision of the daughters in the chamber with Nyne."

She's lost herself, hasn't she? Our mother entombed.

"I'm afraid so... But I found your finger," Dagny said, holding the slender object into the fog. "I want to help you. I just don't know how."

There was a long pause before Lieta spoke again.

She tried to preserve us, hiding our essence in the fog, but time—a devourer—eventually came for us there. It's odd, looking upon it now... the only piece of me that remains.

"How do you exist in the Needle, if—"

If most of my body has crumbled away?

"...Yes."

Kustav must've trapped some part of me, a memory... Although, it's been so long I can't recall how. She has the knowledge of Lazim and sang to me curses from the Song of Leaves. She is a preserver of ruin.

Dagny stretched her hand out, in the direction of the girl's voice, and found nothing. She was beginning to doubt that any of this was real. "It's so dark. How do I know this is you? What if I'm dreaming?"

You're not. You're simply... in between...

"What do you need from me, Lieta? Tell me and I'll do it."

I've forgotten who I am. I'm so lost. I wish to see my sisters again and return to the place I had first known.

Dagny searched for the right words, trying to be gentle. "The finger is keeping you anchored here, isn't it?"

I wish for a new destiny. Unshackled from the prison of Man... released from the abductor of daughters. Yes... the finger... destroy it. Crush it into dust. The finger belongs to me, stolen away. This last act shall be mine own.

Dagny found the ground and placed the delicate finger beneath her boot, intending to crush it, like Arnon had crushed Salarel's hand. But she stopped; her heart racing with nervous energy. "What will happen then? Will you disappear? Vanish forever in the weeds?"

Why do you delay? Send me to the mist. I am ready.

"Will I be able to see you again?"

That is doubtful. The daughters will all be gone, and our connection dissolved. But know that I will still exist. And that I am thankful.

"I just..."

No more words, Dagny Losh. Be kind now. Send me home.

She took a deep breath and nodded. Without another thought, Dagny slammed her heel down, shattering the finger underneath.

31

The courtyard was quiet. The mist had all but dispersed, and there was no sign of Salarel or the other daughters. Dagny considered walking back to Sanctuary to check on Grete, but she knew her sister was being cared for, and she didn't particularly feel like speaking with anyone. So instead, Dagny took what remained of Feruda's bucket wine from inside the tower-house, and wandered into the streets of Jud.

She skirted the edge of Bright Quarter and crossed through the field that bordered the Bridges. The sky was brilliant with starlight. Dagny found a soft patch of earth and lay down, wondering if Max and Rodolph were staring up as well.

Perhaps they were with Sarna and Telga, relaxing on the roof of Stardust after a night of music. Maybe the boys were out on the river with Kimberly, plotting an excursion into Glimmer Ghost mountain, or listening to Tash talk about his latest Talvarind tournament.

And what about Alex and the Benzaras? Would she still have a home in Rork, if she decided to return? Would the children forgive her for disappearing in the night? Could she ever truly go back, even if they welcomed her?

She wondered if things had changed with her gone, or if that world simply continued on like it always had, treating her like a pebble on the roadway. Were any of the people she'd met in her life thinking about her in the same the way that she remembered them? Was it possible that she'd become a ghost in their minds? A vague memory that would fade further and further away until she was forgotten? Dagny surprised herself with a laugh. Did any of it matter?

The bucket wine tasted more sour than the first time, but it helped to warm her body in the cold night air. Dagny easily picked out the Night Princes that she knew. The Endahl sprung up from the horizon, and the Adventurer's Compass sat just off its third horn. That one shined the brightest in the sky tonight. Dagny fixed her gaze on it, recalling the first time Morgan had pointed out the star, stressing its importance to her. *The Compass will always lead you back home, should you become lost. No matter where you may find yourself.*

Even though Dagny couldn't remember how his voice sounded, it was comforting just to imagine his words.

She took a deep swig of wine and felt her fingers and toes go numb.

It wouldn't be long now. She'd already consumed more than that first night with Feruda, and as she waited for the stars to swirl, she allowed her mind to empty. When the dreams came, she expected them to come hard.

❦

She was falling into the abyss. A dim light appeared overhead, but it was still too dark to make sense of anything. Blurry shapes zipped past, streaming out ribbons of blue and yellow. She heard muffled sounds, like children playing, and the smell of the field turned to a comforting scent of boiled carrots and onion. From far away, music played.

Dag, a familiar voice said. *It's time to move on. You've stayed for too long.*

Smoke drifted up from below, but it wasn't ashy and offensive; it was sweet and fragrant. The smoke from a pipe. There was a man here, somewhere nearby. He coughed and muttered to himself. A bug fluttered onto her nose; grass tickled her ear; something damp and prickly brushed against her arm.

That last one jolted her awake.

It took a moment for Dagny to comprehend she was even alive. Her head pounded and the light was so intense it hurt her eyes. She squinted into a cloudless sky, witnessing the sun above brightening a field of pure blue. Then, the damp thing brushed her arm again, and she caught a whiff of decay.

"Easy girl," the man said. "You've been out for quite some time."

"Alex?" Dagny mumbled, still not able to see clearly. "Is that you?"

The man chuckled. "No, I'm afraid not. Though, we've met before. I'm glad to see you're getting on well enough."

Dagny placed the voice now. "Dog..."

"The same. I've been worried about you, but maybe I shouldn't've been. Looks like you've stayed in good company."

The giant, black snout of Eidfur blocked out the sunlight, and the great wolf stared down at her, cocking his head.

"What happened? Where am I?"

"You're in the fields of New Veil, at the edge of the waste yards," Dog replied. "Eidfur brought you here during the night."

Dagny sat up. Her head was a swirling mess. "My sister... the others... How far am I from Sanctuary?"

"One thing at a time. Sanctuary's not going anywhere. You've been shouting nonsense in your sleep for hours."

"What was I shouting?"

"Something about dead girls in the fog. Why don't you settle down for a moment?"

It wasn't bad advice.

Dagny tried to nod her head, and Dog continued, "Say, I'm glad our paths connected once again. I've been making good use of that key you returned."

"The key..." Dagny had a hard time remembering anything.

Dog laughed. "You definitely need your rest. I'd be derelict, and a poor steward, if I allowed you to march up the Long Walk in your current condition." He held up the green key she'd given him at the beginning of all of this. "The *key*."

"Right," she replied. "What's it for?"

"Unlocking the gates, of course." Dog smiled and twirled it in the sunlight. "My great-great-granduncle lost it in the Outskirts many, many years ago. It'd become something of a family myth. No one thought it would ever be returned."

Dagny returned his smile politely. "Then I'm glad you have it back."

"The *gates*," he stressed, leaning forward, "connect Jud to the great world. They connect all of us back to the *other* roads. Their locations are hidden, however, and I've only been able to locate one of the seven. It's nearby... in the shadow of the Forever Tower."

Dagny didn't know what to say, and simply shrugged.

"Ha," Dog blurted out. "You don't care. That's alright. I care enough for the both of us." He lowered his voice to a whisper. "Jud is a secret, you've no doubt come to appreciate, but it's not the only one. There are *many* others, hidden along forgotten *roads*."

"Like the Under Road?" Dagny asked.

"Right!" Dog said, excitedly, clapping his hands together, and sending a throbbing ache through her skull.

"Best of luck to you," Dagny said, twisting her mouth. "I think I've had enough of the Under Road for the time."

"It's understandable. The Great Campaign is not for everyone."

Eidfur snorted, then nudged her face.

"Is there anything I can do for your wolf?" Dagny asked. "He's helped me more times than I can count."

"*My* wolf? You got it wrong, dear. Eidfur serves no one. If anything, I belong to him. He's the true protector of old Jud and all things good in this place."

"Protector, huh? I'd agree with that. A lot of people think it's Odestinas or the Giant, but they're wrong, aren't they?"

"Smart girl," he said. "Odestinas was the first to emerge from the mist, and sought to blend Jud into her own image. She was never a protector." Dog scoffed and shook his head. "And the Giant was created by Man, lying defiant, but defunct, in the underground. The *truth* of the realm, is this: it belongs to a world and an age much older than all of them."

"And the Prince?"

Dog smirked. "Now that tale would take me an entire month just to explain it to you. I will tell you this—whatever story you've heard about him isn't true."

"A month?" Dagny said. "I don't have that long."

Dog studied her, not sure if she was making a joke. Then, after deciding she was, chuckled again. "Pren is in the waste yards. If you think you've got your legs steady, it's not far."

"What's he doing there?" Dagny asked, staring across the field toward a line of broken buildings and grassy mounds.

"You'd have to ask him. I don't know… scrounging for keys?"

"Does he know I'm here?"

Dog raised his shoulders. "I doubt it. Then again, that boy does have a sense about him."

Dagny thanked the man and wandered across the flower-covered field with Eidfur trudging wearily next to her. She wondered how much longer the great wolf would last. Like Yunis and the Bear, he seemed to be fading away before her eyes.

The breeze felt nice on her hot skin. She must've been sleeping for hours under the sun. Her forearms were pink and tender, and her face felt tight and sore when she scrunched it.

What a long, strange journey it had been. She had found Grete, after losing her so many years ago in the black waters of the Morca, and fulfilled a promise to herself here in Jud. Whatever path Grete took next was unknown. But Dagny felt destined to be in her sister's life, in one form or another.

The field dipped below the horizon, and Dagny found a small trail winding down into the waste yards. Huge junk heaps, reminiscent of those outside of her own city, erupted from the landscape. She spotted Pren, crouching on the closest one, picking through the rubble.

"Hey!" she called to him from the trail.

He looked up, gave her a casual wave, then continued on with his search. It wasn't exactly the welcome she was expecting, but everyone had their own way of interacting, and Pren's had always been different.

She reached the mound after a brisk walk, and proceeded to climb up to the boy. Eidfur yawned and sat at the base, preferring to rest in the sunlight.

"What you looking for?" Dagny asked, somewhat out of breath from the ascent.

"Nothing special. Just some childhood things that my brothers had tossed here. They're not worth anything in trade. I just don't want to lose the memory."

"I understand." Dagny eyed the ground, strewn with debris, then prodded a broken chest with her foot. "Anything I can help with?"

"Sure. There was a patchwork doll that my mom stitched. That's the most important thing. It's probably gone forever, though," he said with a shrug. "I was wondering what happened to you."

"Yeah. Sorry I didn't explain last night. There was... something else I had to take care of."

Pren nodded, still scanning the ground. "The girl from the Moon Needle."

"Yep."

"Did you find her? Did you do what you needed to do?"

"I think so." Dagny scratched her head, then thought some more. "Yes, I did."

"That's good. You don't want to live with regret."

"Did you see Grete after I left?" Dagny asked.

"She's still in Sanctuary with the witches and Weavers. She regained herself this morning before I left. Feruda was looking all over for you, you know." Pren sighed and stretched, content with taking as long as he needed to search the mound. "I never understood why the Knights couldn't get along with those witch girls. They're not so bad."

"No, they're not," Dagny agreed. "And Melwes?"

"He's there, too. Everyone except you and me."

Dagny relaxed and stared over the mounds toward the city. She was glad they were all together.

"What are you thinking about?" Pren asked.

"Eh, nothing I could explain."

"Some things don't need explaining," he said with a smile. "Hey, I appreciate your help, but this is going to take forever."

"That's okay," Dagny said. "There's nowhere I have to be right now."

Pren lifted a crate and checked underneath. "So, what are you going to do next? Are you staying in Jud? Heading back to your own city? Something else?"

Dagny took her time, considering an answer to his question. There were so many things she could do but none that were required anymore. She thought of Feruda's poetic book of *Long Water*. How one moment follows the next, and a purpose is discovered, not decided.

"I'm not sure what I'll do," she replied. "But for the moment, I'm going to help you find your doll. Then maybe I'll wait for twilight and watch the sunset."

"Just don't get caught in the shift," he warned jokingly.

"Oh, don't worry. I won't."

About the Author

Michael Breen is an author of speculative fiction. He has a background in theatre, used to write simple songs with good friends, and still listens to the same punk bands that he did in high school. Michael likes truthful fantasy, books that are fearless, and British TV shows. When not writing, he is usually thinking about writing or trying to figure out how a mandolin works.

Michael has won the Gold Medal for Fantasy in the Independent Publisher "IPPY" Book Awards, the Gold Medal for Young Adult Fantasy in the Readers' Favorite International Book Awards, the 1st place Outstanding Fantasy award in the Independent Author Network "IAN" Book of the Year Awards, and a Bronze Medal in the U.K.'s Wishing Shelf Book Awards, among other accolades. He is also a member of the Science Fiction & Fantasy Writers Association (SFWA).

For more content and info on new releases, please visit: MichaelBreenBooks.com

Customer reviews allow independent authors to continue sharing their stories. Please consider leaving a review on your chosen platform.